GIDEON'S
SORROW

A NOVEL

BY

MICHAEL SCOTT
HOPKINS

Black Rose Writing | Texas

ISBN: 978-1-68433-913-6
PUBLISHED BY BLACK ROSE WRITING
www.blackrosewriting.com

Printed in the United States of America
Suggested Retail Price (SRP) $21.95

Gideon's Sorrow is printed in Chaparral Pro

*As a planet-friendly publisher, Black Rose Writing does its best to eliminate unnecessary waste to reduce paper usage and energy costs, while never compromising the reading experience. As a result, the final word count vs. page count may not meet common expectations.

For all its joys, life brings terrible sorrows. Loved ones lost to life, the living lost to grief. The hardest thing in life is to lose someone you love, and the struggle to reclaim a full and vibrant life can seem insurmountable.

This is a horror novel, but it is about sorrow. It is not dedicated to any single person but to every one of us who must live and overcome the darkest despair. It is a literary expression of commiseration.

We are not alone in our sorrow, nor in the love that can see us through it.

GIDEON'S SORROW

CHAPTER 1
THE BARGAIN STRUCK

1830

Abraham Teague thought himself a damned fool, the worse fool, too, because his foolishness had gotten him killed. Presently, he lay fearful and feverish beside a trickling stream. He wanted very much not to die, but death was inevitable now. He wondered how long he had left and how badly he would suffer.

His thirst had become overpowering. Though any movement caused intense pain – from his ruined leg up into every bit of his body – he leaned over the stream and dipped his cupped hand into the water, drinking as deeply as he could. At least the stream was his. He might die next to it, but he by God owned it.

Six weeks earlier, Abraham had struck out on horseback for the eighty acres he'd purchased from the government of the United States, lying untouched in a place called Oniate County, Ohio. Not that there was anything other than a name to the area he'd come to. Forests and Indians had laid claim to the land long before Abraham Teague reckoned their time had passed and his had come. But he didn't see any Indians, and except for the animals and trees, there was likely only Abraham Teague occupying the land for any distance less than a full week's travel.

He had not been entirely sure he'd found the correct boundaries to the parcel he'd purchased. But it seemed close enough, and no one was around to tell him otherwise. So on the day he arrived, Abraham dismounted his horse and took stock of the trees that forested the land and stood between him and his. The sight dismayed him. At the beginning of his journey, he had packed his horse with all of his worldly possessions: an ax, a shovel, blanket, musket, flint, some bags of seed, a volume of Shakespeare's works, rope, his deed, and a Bible. Lots of hard work lay ahead, and likely as not he'd come ill-equipped for getting it done.

"Can't one ax and a shovel do all that needs doing," he said aloud. "But, by God, I'm Abraham Teague, and I won't be beat before I try."

Abraham was a short and slightly built man, standing just five feet tall. He had taken abuse from it over his twenty-five years, and he'd come out the other side a fighter, scrappy and determined to stand on his own two feet. No one had ever given him anything but a cruel joke, and he had long stopped hoping for more. He looked angry, even when he wasn't, a trick learned to warn against mockery. Through it all, he'd known he was more than the butt of someone's joke, a man ready to take on the whole world if need be, so long as he was willing to do it alone. But there was a fever in Abraham Teague, a deep and abiding desire to be loved and admired. Not by men, but by family. He would make his place, build it with his own hands, and someday have children who would see him as a father worthy of their respect.

The weakness in his plan, he knew, was that no woman whom he'd ever set eyes upon had set eyes on him. But with land, with the security of crops growing in the fields, he was sure some woman would find him, see what he had built, and if not love him, cleave to him for the sustenance he would bring forth from the earth. It was a hard life, he reckoned, and there were plenty of fates worse that could befall a woman than him.

He pulled his ax free from the horse and found the tree closest to him. He planted his legs firmly in the dirt, set the ax down, and spit in his hands, rubbing the saliva into his palms. He wasn't certain that a bit of spit would help the great doing that needed to be done, but it seemed a rightly ritual for a new beginning.

He picked up the ax and began his first swing at the trunk, angling in with all his might. But his right foot wasn't planted in dirt so firmly as he thought, his boot finding a bit of scat to step in. As he braced himself against his own forces on his scat-standing foot, the scat smeared, and his boot slid. He fell, mid-swing, into the dirt. The ax handle slipped loose from his spitty palms and flew into the air.

Then fate worked hard against him. The ax that had flown skyward hit the tree up high, bounced off, and fell earthward onto Abraham's leg, the sharpened bit driving through his pantleg and into the flesh of his calf.

The pain did not come right off, but the blood did, oozing up through his pantleg like eager red spring waters. The sight of it made him feel weak and nauseous, which made him angry. He fought back the tears that wanted to flow in response to another cruel joke, this one by his own clumsy hand. He was Abraham By God Teague, and he would not suffer himself to be undone by an errant ax head, which he now personalized as one alongside the living souls who had given him torment over the years.

He leaned up and grabbed the bottom of his pantleg, pulling it above the wound. The wound was deep and ugly, but not so ugly as to undo his fierce will to succeed. Yet it was ugly enough that he passed out at the first sight of it.

Consciousness returned to him moments later. He spat and cursed. Then he took hold. He dug into the dirt with his hands until he had a small pile of it lying next to him. He scooped the dirt up and slapped it angrily into the open wound. The stinging pain that came from the packing was intolerable, and he passed out once more.

He woke and saw the dirt had slowed the blood's oozing. He grabbed more dirt and drove it into the wound, pressing down hard. For a moment, consciousness wavered. He lay back down and took a deep breath. After a bit, the pain dulled. He pulled his knife from its sheath and began cutting away at the pantleg to his knee, making strips with the cloth. Then he tied the strips around his calf tightly to hold the dirt in. He lay back again and said a prayer.

An hour later, he decided he had lain uselessly in the dirt long enough. Slowly, he stood up, bearing his weight on his good leg, using the injured leg only to steady himself. The pain was intense, but for Abraham Teague, that meant it must be fought against. He picked up the ax, cursed it, and gripped the handle tightly. Then he took the swing he'd first meant to take at the tree. He nearly fell again with his bad leg trying to give in to the pain and collapse. Abraham willed it otherwise and took a second swing at the tree. As the day turned to dusk, the tree fell, and Abraham declared this would be the first of the logs from which he would build his home.

With the day's work done, he limped to his horse and took the reins. He led the horse to the shallow stream that crossed his land. Surrounding the stream was a small meadow. Abraham hobbled the horse, unpacked his gear, and removed the saddle. Then he turned the horse loose to drink and graze. He gathered fallen branches and dry leaves to start a fire. Once the fire was lit and going strong, he rolled out his blanket next to it and lay down to sleep, hungry, as he had not had time to hunt.

Abraham rose with the morning light. His calf was stiff and sore, but somewhat better than it had been the day before, the pain less intense. He carefully loaded his musket and set off for the woods. Fortune favored Abraham that day, and he saw a buck standing idly beneath a tree. Abraham shot true. The buck died, and Abraham was fed.

He left the horse in the meadow and trekked back to where he had felled the first tree. Three more fell that day, and before dusk, Abraham had stripped the trees of their branches, leaving clean logs to build with later.

There was no moon, and Abraham had not carried a lantern with him into the wilderness. Beside the stream, he gently unwrapped the strips holding the dirt packed into his wound. He could not see in the dark, but the wound felt hot to the touch. He thrust his leg into the stream and let the cool flowing waters wash away the packed in dirt. Then he cut away his good pantleg to the knee and made fresh strips of cloth to bind the wound, leaving some aside to use later. He washed the crusted strips that had previously covered the wound in the stream and laid them across a rock to dry.

Carefully, he explored the wound with his fingertips. The blood seemed to have stopped, but some stickiness still oozed forth. He brought his fingers to his nose and smelled. Whatever was coming from the wound smelled foul on his fingertips. He washed his hands and put his leg back into the water. After a while, he took his leg back out and wrapped it in the new strips.

On the third day he woke with a fever. His groin pained him, and he felt lumps on his throat. A terrible heat rose from the wound, and he saw yellow pus oozing around the bandages. It seemed to Abraham that nothing was ever going to be fair or just where he was concerned. This angered him, and he spat in disgust, rising despite his misery.

Coyotes had been at the buck's carcass, yet Abraham found there was enough left to cut some meat free. He thought to restart the fire to cook it, but decided he had no appetite. So he left the meat and carcass for the coyotes. He grabbed his ax. That day, two trees fell, and Abraham Teague fell exhausted and sick on his blanket, burning hot through the night.

The next day, he thought himself a fool and knew he was going to die. He crawled to the stream and took what he thought would be his last drink. The unfairness of it struck him bitterly. He had been an outcast all his life, so he'd cast himself out to stand strong, if alone, here in the wilderness, determined to bend a hardscrabble bit of land to his will. No one had ever given him anything, but now he was stopped by his own hand before he could finally take his due.

The fever began to take his mind from him. He hallucinated and cried out beside his stream. Once or twice, his horse looked over to see what the noise was. Then it returned to grazing on Abraham Teague's tiny meadow.

At some point, clarity and anger returned to him. He shouted out to God.

"Help me, God! Don't let me die the fool."

Then he heard a voice.

"I'm here, Abraham!"

"Oh, Jesus," Abraham thought, clearly enough to know the voice could not be real. "I'm going to die hearing things that ain't even there."

"I'm here, Abraham!" the voice repeated. "Open your eyes and behold me!"

The fever left Abraham then, instantly. He felt strong again. He opened his eyes. Sitting before him, on a rock next to the stream, was an old man, shaven, with a full head of white hair slicked back over his head. He looked wise, grandfatherly. Yet he was a large man and appeared powerful, despite his years. He was dressed in black garments and was carving a stick with a pearl-handled knife.

Insensible at the sight, Abraham asked, "Are you God?"

"I've been called that by many, and I have been given many names," the man said. He smiled mirthfully at Abraham as if there was some amusing secret to what he had said. "But I will not lie to you, Abraham. I am not the God you called out to."

Abraham sat up and wondered.

"Have you cured me?"

"Not yet, Abraham," the man said. "I might. I might not. Depends on whether we can come to an agreement."

Suddenly, Abraham feared the man had come to take what little he had.

"It's my land," Abraham said stubbornly. "I won't give it away."

The man laughed hard, an infectious, mirthful laugh.

"Oh, Abraham! I don't want to take what's yours! I come to offer more!"

Abraham sat, bewildered. How was it he was feeling fine again if this wasn't God come to work a miracle?

"What have you come for?" he asked.

"Nothing. Nothing yet. Now, Abraham, I can leave you the moment you wish it, and you'll fall back into your fever and die here." The man pointed to the buck's carcass Abraham had hauled to the meadow. "By tomorrow, you'll be as torn through by coyotes as that young buck you killed."

Despite the kindly, wizened visage of the figure before him, Abraham began to sense that he lay at the foot of evil.

"Why don't you leave?" Abraham asked then, wishing it but not wishing it. Suddenly the fever was on him again, and the heat of infection burned his body. His mind fell back into delirium. In the delirium, Abraham saw flames against a darkness that lay beyond, and the man with the white hair stood in the flames, yet he was not consumed by them.

"You have tasted what I can give you," the man said. "A moment ago, you were yourself again. Without me, *this* is where you shall go, but briefly. What comes after you die, even I cannot say other than what the coyotes will do to you."

Abraham's reason was lost to him. He felt only pain and suffering.

"What do you want of me?" he cried out, fearful he was being tested somehow by God and failing.

"I want only that you have the things *you* want, Abraham, the things you fought for until that foul ax found your flesh. You see, Abraham, I heard your cry. I see what has befallen you is unfair. It is not what you deserve."

"I don't understand," Abraham said, and because he'd forgotten asking before, he asked, "Are you God?"

"No, Abraham. God left you to this. I'll leave you to your hopes and dreams. Sons, fine strong sons to worship you; a faithful woman to bear those sons and to love you. I will make this land prosper. Do you want those things still, Abraham? Or do you want what God has left you?"

"I . . ." Abraham's mind was lost to rational thought, but it knew the man spoke of things Abraham had wanted with all his soul.

"Just say yes, Abraham. Say yes, and they will be yours."

Fearing in his fevered mind that saying yes would damn his soul, Abraham was silent.

Then his mind was back in his body beside the stream, strong. He opened his eyes and saw the man at his calf, working the blade of the pearl-handled knife into the flesh of his wound. The pain made him scream, a thing Abraham By God Teague had never done, but the intensity of the pain was beyond anything Abraham could have imagined. Tears streamed from his eyes, and he tried to pull away. But he could not move.

The man smiled at him, compassionately.

"Gotta work the rotted flesh out of you, Abraham. Gotta dig into it, down deep."

The man smiled again and went back to work. Abraham passed out.

When he awoke, the wound was healed, only a deep scar remaining.

"That's just to let you know I can do what I say I can," the man said, gesturing to the wound with the knife. "But it's only if you say yes. Say no, and the knife goes back in to put it the way you left it."

"Will I be damned?" Abraham asked.

The man seemed to consider it.

"Don't know," he finally answered. "I am what I am, and that I know. Can't speak for others."

"What do you want of me?" Abraham asked, deciding himself otherwise forsaken and thinking he might say yes. Yet, he was afraid of his God.

"You will have your sons," the man said. "They will love you. No matter the man you are, they will worship you. And you will have your wife, and this land will bring forth all that you ask of it."

"Why?" Abraham asked. "Why would you do this?"

"Because I am like you, Abraham. Just as you would strike out and lay claim to new lands, I wish to lay claim to those lands as well, to hold my own humble dominion over them. You are the rock upon which I shall build my prosperity."

"But you have a price," Abraham whispered, knowing he *would* be damned if he took anything from this man willingly.

"Of course, I do," the man said. "No man can prosper without putting a price on things. I cannot lie to you, Abraham. The bargain won't stick if I do. Say yes, and you'll have all those things. But the sons who worship you will perish before their time; the woman you love will live only as long as it takes to give those sons to you and ensure they are quickened to life. Their souls will be their own so long as they walk this earth, but in death, I shall have a claim on them."

"That's too much!" Abraham cried.

"Maybe you're right, Abraham," the man smiled. "But if I don't give those things to you, you'll never have them in the first place. The sons will never be born, and your wife will perish in bondage. Think of it! Your sons will never see the light of day, never exist at all unless you say yes. Would you deny them their own lives, Abraham, to fill the belly of a coyote?"

Abraham thought he could not bring sons into this world if they'd be damned for the bringing, damned before they'd even begun. So, in a firm voice, he said, "No!" But in his heart, he wanted all those things, and he did not want to die. It made him angry to die. Because of this, his true heart whispered yes.

The man was gone. Abraham was healed.

The next day, he felled five more trees. At dusk, Abraham lay on his blanket and wondered what he had done.

In the morning, he woke to the sounds of a woman screaming. He looked up and saw a man riding a horse slowly across the meadow. Behind him, a rope pulled another horse, packed high with heavy bags and equipment. Behind that horse, a tall, slender woman with red hair followed. Her wrists were manacled, and the manacles were tied to another rope, this one attached to the second horse.

"Got no right, mister!" the woman screamed, pulling uselessly against the rope and chain. Her wrists were bleeding from her efforts. Tears fell from her eyes.

The man riding the horse ignored her.

Abraham scarcely believed what he saw. He'd heard of such things happening to slaves who'd run away from their masters, and to white men as well, when a bounty was placed on them. But the woman he saw was not a Negro, so not a slave – and though she seemed unnaturally tall for a woman, she surely was not a man.

Abraham was confused, but roused to purpose nevertheless. He stood and demanded, "Hey, there, mister! What are you about?"

Then, repeating what the woman had said, he shouted, "You got no right!"

The man pulled on the reins and brought his train to a halt. He looked at Abraham and hollered in response, "Just passing through, young fella. No need to get angry 'bout it. I ain't staying."

"No need to get angry!?!" Abraham yelled. "You're draggin' a woman across my land against her will! I won't stand for it."

Abraham leaned down and picked up his musket. He began loading powder and ball into the barrel. The man looked at him and laughed.

"Okay, now, take'r easy," he said. "I can see why you'd be concerned, but it ain't the way you're seeing it."

The man dismounted and began walking slowly toward Abraham, holding papers high above his head.

"Take a look at these before you go off half-cocked," he said. "You'll see you're interferin' with the law."

Warily, holding both hands up to show he held no weapons, the man came closer to Abraham. Despite the man's weaponless hands, Abraham noted a pistol was tucked into his pants at the waist, and a sheath held a long knife against his thigh.

"Hold it right there," Abraham commanded, raising his musket. "Before you come any closer to me, you take that pistol and knife of yours and throw them behind you a ways."

The man smiled.

"I'll set them down and come forward, with your permission," he said, reasonably. "Can't say I want to toss a fine weapon around to get damaged."

"Fine. Do that then."

The man eased his pistol out, holding it by the barrel, and set it gently on the grass. Then he took his knife and set it beside the pistol. Once relieved, he held his hands up high again.

"See? I'm no threat to you. Can I come forward now?"

"You can."

The man moved toward Abraham and handed him the papers. "Can you read?"

Abraham took the papers. One was a wanted poster, showing a drawn likeness that seemed to resemble the woman and described her as a runaway slave named Bessie. The other was a signed affidavit, claiming ownership over a slave named Bessie.

"I read just fine," Abraham answered, handing the papers back. "These say some fella owns a runaway slaved named Bessie. But this here's a white woman, not no slave."

"That's where your confusion comes in," the man explained. "You seen the picture. It's her. I'll give it to you she's light-skinned. That's what fooled you. Not all darkies are all Negro. This one's a quadroon. A quarter Negro, so she's light-skinned. But that don't make her white. She's property."

"I know what quadroon means," Abraham said, appearing calm, but seething inside. Abraham had an abiding hatred of slavery. He'd felt the misery of slaves like he felt his own misery, living among men but derided by them, given no account upon his actual worth. He at least could walk away, even if it was into the wilderness to die. A slave didn't even have that. They were mocked with servitude over their natural beings, and because of that, Abraham hated all men who would own a slave.

"So," the man continued, "this is all legal. Soon as I find a judge, I'll get a certificate and take her back home. The law says that's the way it is."

The man added in warning, though seeming to commiserate with Abraham, "Law also makes it illegal for any man to interfere. So, are we square?"

Abraham stood silently, figuring what he was going to do. The man shrugged and walked back to his horse, retrieving his knife and pistol along the way. Then he mounted his horse and began moving the train forward again.

Abraham looked at the woman. She lurched forward with the pull of the rope, looking to Abraham now with pleading tears. Abraham was moved. She was a slave. It didn't matter to Abraham then whether she was a quadroon or as black as iron. He would not abide slavery on his land.

"Looks to me like she don't want to go with you," he finally shouted. "Why don't you set her free, and you can pass over my land after that."

The man looked back over his shoulder and laughed.

"You'd have to pay me more than I'm getting to take her back, son," he replied. "I'd suffer reputation damage, too. I don't fail to bring back what I'm paid to bring. Bad for business. You don't look like you got a dollar to your name, and I'm getting five hundred dollars to bring this one back. The light-skinned ones is extra valuable."

"All the same," Abraham shouted. "You brung her on my land, and my rules is what governs here. I say leave her be."

The man shook his head and seemed to sigh. Nevertheless, he kept moving, though Abraham noted his hand had dropped to hold the hilt of his pistol.

Abraham decided his course. He leveled his musket at the man and pulled the trigger. The powder lit. The musket fired and missed, but the man stopped.

"You ought not've done that," he said, pulling the pistol free. He stopped the horse, leaned back in his saddle, and took careful aim at Abraham. Then he fired.

Abraham felt the ball tear away part of his ear. Blood began to flow down his neck.

The man cursed for missing and jumped quickly from his horse, pulling the long-bladed knife from its sheath. He ran at Abraham, holding the knife in his fist.

Abraham didn't have time to reload, but he held his musket and his ground. Abraham Teague had lost many fights, but he'd never once backed down from one. The man kept coming at Abraham, knife held high and ready to plunge into Abraham Teague once he closed in.

Abraham dropped his musket and steadied himself on both legs, ready to move whichever way survival dictated. Then the man was over him, bringing the knife downward. Abraham easily moved out of the way and kicked the man in the gut. Abraham heard a loud "oomph!" and the man fell on his back, dropping the knife. Abraham picked it up and drove it into the man's heart.

Abraham kicked the corpse and spat. Then he rifled around the man's clothing until he found a key. He took it and walked to the woman. She was crying.

"It's all right now," Abraham said. "Ain't no man taking you without you want to go."

He unlocked the manacles. Warily, the woman backed away. Abraham noted that she was nearing six feet tall and looming above him. If she wanted to put up a fight, Abraham might find her more than a handful to tangle with.

"Don't you need to be afraid of *me*," Abraham said. "You're free. Take that man's stuff, if you want it. It's yours. Go where you will."

The woman looked uncomprehendingly at Abraham.

"You mean it? I can go?"

Abraham felt a flash of anger.

"I didn't kill no man so as I could steal a slave. You're as free in this world as any man, so long as you don't let one catch you."

The woman looked at Abraham and cried, "I can't never be free. I run off, and they come and get me. I go back home, and they whip me, and they gonna sell me or put me in the fields this time. There ain't no freedom in this world, no freedom until the good Lord takes me home."

Abraham considered. What she said was likely true.

"You can stay here then," he said, finally. "Be free here. I won't put no manacles on you, and I won't sell you back to where you come from. I'll keep you hid if hiding's what's needed. Otherwise, you're to be as free as me upon this land. You won't need to do that thing with me, neither. I put no hold over you."

The man's horses bore tools of all kinds, saws and knives and pots and pans and a large tent that Abraham made a home of until a log cabin could be built to live in. The horses bore the heavy work that Abraham could not do alone or with a single horse. It was like a gift from God, though murder had brought it forth.

Like the papers said, the woman's name was Bessie, and she stayed and fell in love with the determination and courage of the small and cantankerous Abraham Teague. Beside him, she worked and toiled upon the land, shaping logs, building the cabin they would live in, plowing the fields, and sowing and reaping. On the land with Abraham Teague, she was something she had never been before: a partner and an equal to a man who, strange and angry as he was, cherished her for who she was, not what he had determined she would be. In the heart of Abraham Teague, she found no division between woman and man, no imaginings of station or servitude. Together, they built their world, and it was nothing like the world of men each had fled.

Yet had it not been for the bargain Abraham had made with the dark-souled being by the stream, Abraham would have perished, and Bessie would have remained bound to her captor and been taken through Abraham's land to her former masters. And had it not been for the bargain made, even together, Bessie and Abraham would have perished upon their land, failing despite their devotions to one another and their work to bend the land to their will.

Instead, crops came easily from the earth; rain fell whenever needed; and animals of all kinds, hogs and fowl and even cattle, inexplicably wandered onto the land, to be kept and corralled behind fences and in sheds built by Bessie and Abraham. Winters were mild. Disease never took hold, and water came forth from stream and well, wholesome and pure.

One day, after the first year's bounty, Bessie sat beside Abraham on the porch they had built. She smiled at the man she called her husband by then and said playfully, "The God of Abraham has blessed us, sure."

Abraham found no mirth. He looked to the woman he called wife and spat in the dirt, afraid of what he had wrought.

Bessie bore five strong sons in the years that followed, each growing heartily and sure upon the land. Yet as time moved forward, the haven Bessie and Abraham built no longer stood as a refuge apart from the world of men. Other settlers had come to Oniate County during the years Bessie and Abraham brought their sons to life, farmers seeking to take their own due from the land, and the small town of Salud had sprung up not five miles from their home, sputtering along with the beginnings of business and commerce, slaves seldom seen within its boundaries but they accompanied their masters passing through from the south.

And so, as the world followed the Teagues to Oniate County, Bessie knew fear.

She remembered well what men saw in the heritage of skin. Closely, she watched her growing sons, seeking in each of them a trace of the lineage she had bequeathed to them. But she lost the fear she had secretly hidden from Abraham, seeing in each of her boys skin so close to white that none would ever find himself bound to servitude on account of it.

"No man will put shackles on my sons!" she proclaimed to Abraham. "They will stand among them and be proud!"

"There'd be no shame in them looking Negro, Bessie," Abraham scolded her, overwhelmed, as he often was, at how deeply he loved her, and knowing in his heart that he had already taken everything from her and her children. "Your heritage is theirs, too. Ignorant fools don't make it otherwise."

"Don't matter," she'd said. "It's a gift from God. They gonna be safe from the evils in this world."

No matter that Bessie's fear had eased away, Abraham remembered the man on the horse and his determination to take Bessie back into slavery. If he had come, others might, too. So Abraham refused all trespassers on the farm. When others wandered onto his land, seeking fellowship or trade, they were met with an angry Abraham, holding his musket and threatening to kill any man who refused to leave or who might return, despite warning.

"You can't drive every man away who comes here, Abraham!" Bessie had scolded him. "Someday, our boys will need to find womenfolk, and they ain't gonna find them growing in the fields."

Abraham spat.

"Can't let no man see you here," he told her. "Don't know what's to happen if they did."

"I'll stay in the cabin, Abraham," she said, wanting to know her sons would find love and companionship someday.

"I told you a long time ago I'd keep you hid if it was needed," Abraham told her. "But I won't see you hid away from a world that ain't good enough for you. The world will just have to stay where it belongs – the hell off our land!"

One day when Bessie was hanging wash on a line beside the cabin to dry, she spied a visitor ambling meekly up the road. Abraham and the boys were working in the fields. Bessie was alone.

She looked at the man, knowing it was too late to hide away. So she stood and waited.

"Ma'am," the man greeted her and asked, "Is the man called Abraham here?"

"No sir," Bessie answered, deciding on a lie to protect her children now that she had been seen. "I work for him, though. He's about here somewheres. You might want to go though. Mr. Abraham's not been happy to see strangers since his wife died."

"Oh," the man said, Bessie noting an air of desperation in the man's mannerisms. "I'm real sorry to hear it, but I need to see him."

"What about?"

"Well, Ma'am," the man said, "I don't know how it is, but I see this land doing well. There's crops in the fields, and it looks like Mr. Abraham has found a way to get water to those crops."

Bessie wondered at the man's meaning.

"Maybe you don't know it," the man continued, "but the rest of us around here ain't doing so well. Without the rains coming, our crops have died."

"Oh."

"We got nothing to feed the livestock with neither. Most has died."

"You didn't store nothing up for hard times?"

"Did and been through it," the man said. "This ain't the first bad year. Don't know how you folks have managed."

"Mr. Abraham's a wise man," Bessie said, suspicion growing in her mind. "A hard worker, too, along with his boys."

Then Bessie saw something she'd never seen on a white man's face before: tears. And for a moment, Bessie found deep in her heart some satisfaction at the sight. During her life she had seen rivers of tears fall upon the faces of her own kind, men and women alike, brought forth by the abject misery and terror they had been subjected to by the subjugating white man. She had never seen a slave who hadn't cried; had never seen a white man who had. Then she thought of her husband and her children and felt ashamed. "They ain't no different than this man here," she thought, and she pushed her feeling aside. "I won't hold no man accountable for the sins of others."

Bessie watched as the man struggled and wiped his tears away.

"I'm sorry," the man said. "Two of my own boys died this year. We got no food. I tried to sell my land, but ain't no one willing to buy. I come to tell the man named Abraham I'll give my land to him for enough to eat and keep what's left of my family alive so's we can get out of here to someplace better."

Thinking of her own boys, Bessie's heart ached for the man.

She was about to offer words of comfort when a vengeful Abraham suddenly burst from the high corn growing in their field. His musket was raised and ready to fire at the man. She saw murder in his eyes and knew Abraham would not hesitate to kill if he thought it right.

"Abraham!" she shouted. "Don't you do it!"

Because he loved her so, Abraham had seldom failed to heed his wife's admonitions, yet here, now, he felt her very life might be in danger, this stranger before him having confronted her. If this man had seen the posters somewhere with Bessie's description, word might get out, and Abraham might find another man someday soon, like the one he had murdered to set Bessie free, returning to his land to take what Abraham, where the law was concerned, had stolen.

So Abraham wanted very much to kill the man. Yet Bessie had spoken, so he lowered his musket and considered instead how to finesse the man away from what he had seen.

But finesse was beyond Abraham's skills, so he said, "I don't want no trespassers on my land. I'd as soon shoot a man than suffer him coming where he don't belong."

Abraham pointedly leveled the musket at the man and looked very much like he was going to shoot. The man stood, beaten before he'd arrived, and so ready for – perhaps welcoming – whatever might come from the barrel of Abraham's musket.

Abraham saw the defeat in the man's eye and lowered the musket. He spat and said, "But this woman here says not to shoot you. She's got a kindness in her heart I ain't got in mine. So you ought to reckon she just saved your life. But you get on out of here, and don't come back."

Abraham raised the musket again for emphasis.

The man turned, his defeat now absolute. Wordlessly, he began to walk away.

"Mister," Bessie called out. The man turned. "Where's your farm?"

The man told her and kept walking, his head hung low.

"Abraham," Bessie told him sweetly, "we gonna help that poor man."

"Why on earth?"

"He come here beggin' for his family," Bessie said. "Ain't no man with a good heart oughta have to beg his way outta misery."

"Bessie, have you forgot what men have done to you?"

"No."

Bessie gathered her sons then and put them to task. At their mother's urging, they hitched two wagons up to horses and loaded the wagons with grain and corn from the family stores.

Abraham protested.

"We got more than we need," she told him.

"We got enough to sell and make some money's all."

"Money don't do no good where your conscience is concerned. A dollar don't buy a sweet child's life. The Bible has a word or two to say about charity, too."

"I don't like it."

Bessie considered. "How is it we have so much, yet to hear this man tell it, folks are hungry hereabouts?"

"We," Abraham started to say, then stopped. He knew why.

"That man said he'd give you his farm just for food."

"I don't want his farm."

"Me neither. But we ain't gonna let him or his kin starve."

Bessie told her sons to take the wagons to the farm the man said he owned.

"When you get it there, you tell him to take what he needs. Then you ask him who else needs what's left, and you take it to them."

Abraham knew his sons had not yet been in the company of folks outside of their own family, and he feared what they might say. So he called them to him and admonished them before they left.

"You can't never tell no one that your momma is your mother," he said. "When you take that wagon, you don't say nothing about it. If they ask, your momma died."

"But why?" one had asked.

"Because all men have wicked hearts, and we don't want none of that wickedness falling on your mother's head."

Dutifully, the sons of Abraham and Bessie did as they were told, taking the wagons and keeping the secret. Every day after that, Bessie commanded her sons to milk the cows and take what they would not use themselves to the farms and families that needed it.

And so the reputation of the honorable Teague family was set in stone. In the next season, rains came, and farms prospered; hunger and loss faded to memories of bad times; but none forgot the kindness of Abraham Teague, his sons, and the woman who did his wash.

In the next prosperous season, Bessie bore the sixth son of Abraham Teague, their last son, Zachariah Teague. Little Zachariah was not strong, but sickly and small, unable to thrive like his older, stronger brothers. Many times during Zachariah's first years, Abraham and Bessie stood beside the child's bed, weeping and mourning, certain he was soon to die. Then Bessie would reach down and hold Zachariah to her bosom, tearfully telling the child she loved him and that he was meant to live to be a great man.

At these times, Zachariah would find the strength to look up into his mother's eyes, rebound and take nourishment, gaining strength for a time. Then the malaise would take hold once more, and the boy would wither and seem near death. And Bessie would raise him once more from the brink, holding him and willing life back into her child, for despite all that she knew of the cruelties of life and the ease through which the living passed into death, she would not accept that such things should touch her child and take him from the prosperity he deserved.

In his fourth year, Zachariah finally bent fully to Bessie's will and began to find strength in his frail form, growing fast and leaving the malaise behind. Bessie and Abraham rejoiced.

Bessie died suddenly, once the health and strength in Zachariah Teague had become certain. She wasn't old. She wasn't sick. She wasn't hurt. She was just sitting on the porch, smiling and singing a song to Zachariah as he napped in her arms. Nearby, Abraham watched mother and child, full of love for his wife and pride in his growing family, his fears almost forgotten. Then Bessie stopped singing. Her eyes shot wide open, and she fell over, spilling the sleeping Zachariah from her arms.

Before Bessie, Abraham had never had cause to love another human soul, nor, he was certain, had another human ever loved him. He'd loved God in his own angry, grudging sort of way, but he'd only come to it because he'd found a secret delight in the poetry of the King James Bible and delight also in the promise that God would judge and punish his tormentors someday.

But Abraham did love Bessie and in his heart had made her his wife. And, he knew she had loved him, for all his faults. She was taller than any man he'd met that had mocked him for his size, yet from her lips came only tender words of love and, when she found him less than he should be, harsh words of correction.

"You don't stand around here and sulk and spit 'cause you feeling sorry for yourself," she'd scold. "You a good man. You a good man, Abraham, and you give me my life back. Don't you think I'm sittin' here wasting a second of it giving one thought to them that set me to servitude. Now you stand up and be counted in this world, and don't let what's befallen you keep fallin' on you neither. You don't give no man that power over you. You better than that."

Abraham had been shocked to hear such rebuke. To his mind, he'd never felt sorry for himself, but fought all things that would *refuse* to let him be counted in this world. Yet Bessie found his hidden sorrows, rooted them out of him and made him cast them aside, for her sake if not his own. She taught him to see beauty and to laugh, even at himself – a thing he had never done before her smile filled his world.

She bore him beautiful sons filled with her spirit, and he loved them because they were so much like her. Yet Abraham had never forgotten the bargain and its consequences. He'd made the bargain even in spite of the God he thought he loved, and it had given him more than God had given him, though it had come from evil. So no matter how good life with Bessie had been, he knew retribution was only a matter of time, and his heart knew fear as much as it knew love.

Then Bessie died, as the bargain demanded.

Zachariah awoke as he fell from his mother's arms and stood looking at her form lying on the porch, even as Abraham ran to them.

"Momma?" the boy said. "Momma, you sleeping?"

Abraham took the boy into his arms and hugged him hard, tears in his eyes.

"Momma's gone to rest, my boy," he told his son. "You go get your brothers from the field and bring them back here."

Not understanding what was happening, Zachariah did as his father asked, running to the fields to find his brothers.

Abraham sat beside his wife and cried.

His grief was suffering worse than any he'd ever felt, worse than all the pain that had come to him through the infection that had almost taken his life and worse than the agony of the healing knife that the man by the stream had used to cut and sear his putrefied flesh – and which had branded Abraham Bessie's true killer.

As he waited for his sons, Abraham considered, briefly, trying to assuage his own conscience, that the bargain hadn't been all bad. Hadn't Bessie lived a life better than she would have had? She'd had many good years, free and living a life that had given her joy. But the bargain's terms crept back into his mind. The bargain wasn't against just her life – the evil Abraham had reckoned with would now lay claim to her soul, and what horrors that meant for his beloved wife, Abraham did not know.

"Bessie, now you see what I done. I'm sorry. I shoulda been a better man. I should have been worthy of you, but I was afraid to die."

As his boys gathered around him, Abraham said, "Your momma is in Heaven now. You boys kiss her goodbye."

Confused and frightened, not yet understanding what death was, they each kneeled down in turn and kissed their mother.

Abraham decided a ceremony was needed for his boys and to set his wife properly to rest. There was a place upon his land, a low hill rising above the fields. And on that small hill stood an ancient oak tree. This he determined would be Bessie's monument and resting place. He hoped against hope that from there her spirit might look down upon them.

He made his boys work with him, building a litter to place Bessie on for the journey to the hill. When it was finished, he and the boys lifted her body onto the litter. He got his horse and tied the litter to the saddle. Then in a slow procession, Abraham Teague led his boys and his wife to the hill.

Abraham began digging Bessie's grave near the oak tree. His oldest son, William, asked, "Why are you making that hole?"

"Your momma's to rest in it," Abraham told him.

"Momma don't want to get into no hole," William told him. "When is she going to wake up and come home?"

"Your momma can't wake up no more," Abraham said, continuing to dig.

"She's just tired," said Thomas, the second oldest. "Wake her up."

"She can't wake up no more," Abraham repeated.

William was sixteen, Thomas fifteen. Both boys were taller, stronger than their father. Yet for their years, they did not know human beings might die like beasts and did not believe it could be so. William jumped into the grave beside his father and ripped the shovel from his hands.

"She's going home," he said angrily. "You're not putting her in no hole."

Thomas neared the grave behind Abraham. Abraham felt the violence festering within them and remembered the bargain.

"You will have your sons," the devil had said. *"They will love you. No matter the man you are, they will worship you."*

Abraham rejoiced in that moment, remembering the words as if they had just been spoken. Here now was rebellion that had been bargained against! His mind shouted with hope. Let them rise against me, and the bargain fails!

"Your momma is dead!" he shouted, tearing away at his own heart. "I'm going to bury her and spit on her grave for it!"

He grabbed the shovel back from William and stared at him hard, willing his sons to strike him down. Behind him, Thomas grabbed him and lifted him forcefully from the grave, knocking the shovel from his hand.

William leapt from the grave, and Abraham's two oldest sons took him by his arms and dragged him to the base of the oak tree. Abraham was glad. They would fight him now and kill him even in defense of their mother. Their love for their mother would set them free!

But then their hands became gentle, and they lowered Abraham against the tree, all violence eased from their minds. Though the devil remained unseen, he had stayed true to his word, pulling Abraham's cherished children from their own wills, playing them like puppets upon hidden strings. Their anger returned to worship and obedience to Abraham.

"Rest, Father," William said. "Rest, and we will dig Mother's grave for you."

"We honor you, Father," Thomas told him. "We did not understand."

Abraham wept, utterly defeated, feeling himself the eternal fool. But that was not Abraham Teague. His own spark returned, stifling his tears and spurning despair. He was Abraham By God Teague, though his defiance was now conflicted by devotion.

He stood and wiped his tears angrily away. He thought then to step forward and fight his children over their mother's body. Make them fight.

Make them rebel. But he settled his purpose and stood silently by instead. He would not take from his sons the memory of doing their mother a final, unmolested honor.

"Let them bury her," he decided. "Then I will beat rebellion and hatred back into their hearts."

Abraham prayed that he could remain true to his purpose. But he loved his Bessie and his children so that he become confused in the task. Rebellion, he determined, would not be enough. They would need a history of their family to place them in the world; knowledge and meaning – a philosophy to be whole spirits true to themselves. Rebellion alone, he thought, could only be another denigration, another taking of their souls.

So in the years that followed, Abraham revealed to them all he knew about their beloved mother, shared with them her thoughts, her love and wisdom. He told them that she had been a slave and that they – her sons – had given her so much joy that they'd erased from her heart the suffering those agonizing years of servitude had brought to her. He told them that they, like their mother, had the blood of Ham flowing in their veins, telling them that it made them like her, and because of it they would be finer and stronger men than any who walked the earth. He impressed upon them that this knowledge must forever be a secret because weaker, lesser men would force injustice upon them if they knew it.

"The secret," Abraham told them, "makes you strong, but revealed, other men will use it to lay you low, a thing they cannot do otherwise."

His sons learned the lessons, took heed of their father's words, and rose into the world with their mother's spirit branded fully upon their hearts. And whenever Abraham saw the lesson's take hold, he would rise against his sons, beat them, and show them whatever petty cruelties he could, seeking to set them against him, to free them from his bargain.

Selfishly, in his deepest heart, he hoped he could provoke them to rise up and murder him. Perhaps then, he, too, might be free.

But the devil's strings would pull and pull, and the sons of Abraham Teague forever loved and worshipped their father.

CHAPTER 2
A MURDER IN 1897

Gideon Teague was the last son of the last son of Abraham Teague, and though his grandfather had once plunged a knife into a man's heart without a second thought, murder did not come natural to Gideon. Even his younger self, brooding and hate filled as he was, had not harbored a bit of intent that could rise to violence. Yet now he eyed the heavy stone that had captured his attention, reached for it and held it, figured its weight and the deadly nature it could be put to. But he was not his younger self. Death had come and instructed him in the faithlessness of hate, it being a transient and fickle thing, trifling and laying deceit against the man who held it. Death was permanent, unalterable. He had learned the lessons of Death, and the lessons took hold, wrenching the hard hate away from his heart. Regret and sorrow followed, nearly consuming him beyond the measure his hate had held for him. Then purpose had come, driven by contrition. Maybe contrition was the best he'd deserved, but love had come, too, giving him strength alongside purpose. No, hate had never been strong enough to put murder in his heart. But love was stronger than hate, and for love he would do what killing needed to be done.

Yet he paused. Maybe he would have thought better of it, feeling the weight of the stone as a lethal, living force. Unleashed, it could never be brought back to heel. His grip loosened, slightly. Then his quarry spoke, finally seeing – not the doubt, but the resolve warring with it on Gideon's face. The man stood, frightened, his defiance shaken from him. He ran, and Gideon's grip tightened on the stone. Like a hound let loose for the hunt, Gideon followed without hesitation. The man fell and screamed, begged. Gideon answered. The time for mercy had passed. He raised the stone and brought it down hard against the man's skull with all his might.

The sickening crunch of bone vibrated through the rock, flowed through Gideon's hands and up his arms. Nausea gripped his gut, and he thought he would vomit. The man's forehead had become a bloody pulp, yet the man did not die. He rose like a shot and took to flight once more, begging, promising. Gideon followed, holding death in his hand, and in his heart, once more, hate. Seething hate.

* * *

A malevolent, seeking eye wandered the land. The consciousness behind it was neither spirit nor demon, but an incarnation unto itself. It knew little of its origins, but its memory spanned the ages. Within its dominion, it held great power. To a man dying beside a stream, it could offer renewed life and reward the desires held within the dying man's heart. Yet gifts such as these would come at a deadly price, upon bargains struck foul, and only upon resentments held so deeply that a generation would be sacrificed in the taking.

The dying man meant nothing to it, and the gifts it could bestow were nothing more than trifles. A bargain struck, the man would be forgotten, and the creature would lay claim to the innocent generation that followed. It had struck many such bargains since humans first filled their hearts with desire – and resentment. In the molded destruction of the innocent, it amused itself and fed upon the despair that followed.

Yet a soul susceptible to its offerings was hard to find, no matter its influence. Other forces were at work in the world, pitted against the creature's desire. So the souls it found ready for its gifts were few. No matter. It was patient and seeking, ever seeking.

Somewhere close, it spied an emotion that held promise, and the creature flew to it. In a tiny remnant of forest, it sensed a man about to do murder. It entered the man's mind, unseen, seeking. But it found the vessel unsuitable. The man had found the things he desired – the murder merely at hand to keep those things as they were. The creature could not offer what already existed, and it thought to leave. Then it sensed a thing in the man, a lineage. The creature recognized the blood, for it had sweetly taken the blood of the man's preceding generation. The creature felt desire then, strong at hand. Yet it had no hold. A generation was what it took, and the next was denied to it by the terms of its bargain and forces it did not understand.

Still, its desire was strong for this generation, too. So, when the murder was done, it set its sight upon the murdered soul, and through that soul, it thought, might its claim fall at last upon the blood of a later descendant. It mused then that it had found a secret to take more than the bargain had given. That it had taken so long to see that this was possible enraged it so that it would make the murdered soul suffer for its oversight.

CHAPTER 3
THE NIGHT ROAD

The man lay in a great cavern, lit afire, suffering torments as certain as those pronounced by the Puritan preachers of old, in sermons he had read and mocked within his halls of higher learning, living in the conceit of his superior knowledge. Yet the preachers' words had held their sway, and in agony, he knew now he was nothing, neither righteous nor strong, but a helpless soul cast adrift in a sea of flame, Godless and alone.

He had never known a greater fear, fearful no longer of failure in life, but of eternity in death.

Then he was no longer alone. Near him, he saw a man lit red by the flowing fires. The man stood untouched, unhindered by the sulfurous, burning brilliance that burst from every crack, every crevice, and every opening in the floor and ceiling. The man was old, yet large and strong. He smiled, and the man who thought his agony complete felt even greater agony ripping through his heart, his very skull screaming in horror.

"You are mine," the old man proclaimed. "You will live again, but for the tasks I set before you. You have no will, no purpose but mine. I am forever now your master. Fail upon the night, and you will return here to me, and I will make all of this a cherished memory against the new sufferings you will feel."

Dread consumed the man, and then the memory of the smiling demon and his cavern of flames was gone. . .

. . . and it was night.

Cool night.

Interminable night.

The man was young, twenty-five, but beaten old. He staggered from the brush onto the road, not certain how he'd gotten so far from town, not knowing from which direction he had come or how he had travelled. Ironically, he well remembered that amnesia like this had become a constant in his life. He often awakened in a stupor, with the last of the liquor oozing from his pores, leaving his skin caked over in a stinking, slimy sweat, memories of the preceding hours lost to him.

Once on the road, he sat and reached into his vest pocket for his flask. He found it and pulled the cap free. He tilted it up to his lips, but already felt by the weight of it that it was empty. Still, he tilted the flask higher, hoping some small drop or two might be left to fall onto his tongue. But there wasn't even a wisp of vapor to comfort him.

Carefully, he put the flask back in his vest pocket and looked down the road, first in one direction and then the other. He wanted a drink. Which direction, he wondered, would get him to it faster, which direction would lead him back to town? In the dark, he could not tell east from west and certainly could not see far enough to make out any landmarks of note.

Thinking he wanted that drink very badly, he stood and said aloud, "I shall not go east, and I shall not go west. I shall go left."

He chuckled at his joke and pivoted to his left, beginning a slow, steady pace down the road.

He had a thought that he was forgetting something. Something important that had happened to him. But straining to remember what it might be was too much work, and he decided nothing was worth remembering if it made his head ache for the effort, though his head had not actually begun to ache.

Overall, he decided he felt good. Not only did his head seem clear and free from any pain, he noted that his hands weren't shaking in the least. And as he walked, his desire for drink seemed less and less urgent. After a while, he realized he did not care about getting a drink at all.

"I am the renewed man!" he shouted into the night, feeling once more the strength and vigor that had abandoned him these many months, since he had first taken succor in the bottle.

Succor indeed! His father had driven him to it. Faithless, heartless, fickle Father. But there was something more to Father as well, the man knew, resenting the knowledge. Father had wealth and resources, resources that had been stripped from the man, leaving him to wither in the field.

"What good is fortune without fealty to your own blood?" the man asked the air. "Am I not your legacy? Am I to be so callously cast aside, for mere want of profit?"

His father, he thought, was a bloated ignoramus, uneducated and foul. Yet somehow, knowing nothing, the man had built a shipping empire and kicked down the more amiable doors to society, though certainly not all or even most. Oh, how he lorded his money and his power and his slight society over his son, remembering nothing of humble origins. Walking now, leftward as he was, the young man thought how he had been abandoned for nothing more than trying to stand on his own two feet, to make his own place in this world, independent of his father's resources, though those resources were needed to light the spark, to grease the wheels, and make adjustments to an otherwise hostile world. And why shouldn't they have been provided freely, or more freely than they had been, so limited in time? Time. More had been needed, but the oafish tired old fool believed he was the minister of wisdom, pulling tight his purse strings before his miserly allowance had borne fruit.

"You brought me to ruin, Father," the man muttered, feeling sorry for himself.

He wondered then in which direction he might actually be travelling. He thought eastward might be the desired path, back to Father, back to his resources. Surely, he would be forgiven one failure, his effort having been so keen and pure. Yet his reputation had suffered despite his intentions, his actions having been less than keen and far from pure. He reasoned, however, that all had been his father's fault, guilt not lighting upon the man himself or marking him by his own accord.

"It is Father's doing," the man thought. "All of it. I am clear of the thing."

Nevertheless, much would have to be hidden if his homecoming were to be as he had begun to hope.

"I must go east," he thought, his scorn for his father fading against the backdrop of the old man's wealth. "I need a new beginning, a new star to set my sights upon."

It could not matter to him that his travel would be on foot. Thanks to his father, he had nothing, not even enough money for a broken-down horse, let alone a seat on the eastbound train. Perhaps he would undertake some honest labor along the way, enough to secure passage to New York and, with luck, back into Father's better graces.

With nothing more to guide him, he walked the night road for some time. Finally, a greyish, predawn light began to ascend the horizon, and the man rejoiced.

"East! Left is east!" he shouted. "Fortune favors at last!"

He began to whistle a tune. Then he was gone, faded from the night road, an ethereal spirit returned to his torment in the cavern of flames.

Night came again, and the man stumbled from the brush onto the road.

"Oh, my," he thought, feeling some degree of disappointment in himself. "I found my drink, it appears, and here my wanderings have come to rest once more."

He remembered nothing after the first light on the eastern horizon. Some kind spirit, it seemed, had provided him with kinder spirits along the way, erasing memory once more. No matter. His course was set, and this setback would not deter him.

This time, he took left as east and began his trek through the night, back toward the dawn. And with dawn, memory was again lost, and he arose the next night alongside the road, in the brush.

He walked briskly to the road this time, feeling that something was terribly amiss. A drunken reverie he could believe, and lost time did not mean no time had passed. But here, on the third night to awaken in the same place, along the same road – that was simply an impossibility.

"Westward then," he determined, feeling a rising panic, which he tried to mask from himself with a new joke. "I go right to see if that is right."

And right he walked through the night until he came upon the small town of Salud, a familiar sight at last.

He quickened his pace.

The street was empty, the buildings quiet, with only the faintest flickerings of lantern light in a few second-story windows. He strode past the general store and the shops along the thoroughfare. He wanted desperately now to see another living soul, but all slept, in town or in homes outside the town, not ready to return until the morning came. Well, he could be patient. He found the one shop for which he alone had the key. He found the key in his vest pocket and turned it in the lock. He did not notice that the door had not actually opened, that he hadn't heard or felt the key turning. Yet he passed through the door and entered the dark space beyond. There, he found a familiar couch and lay down, deciding to sleep until the morning came. Sleep, however, would not come. Instead, he lay awake, scared, hoping for the first sounds of life outside the door to his old shop.

The sounds did not come. Instead, he slept with the dawn and woke in the brush beside the road, miles from town.

He found nothing amusing in left or right or east or west now. His thoughts of his father were cast aside, the more urgent business of piercing the veil before him pressing hard. He was certain there had been no drink, no lost memories to account for his predicament. He was deathly afraid as he began his long walk back to Salud, fearful of the unknown.

Nightly he made the journey, alone and frightened. After a time, he would awaken in the brush and fade into the ether and torment before he could even reach the road, his journey stopped before it began.

At times, another would rise from his sleep, from his dreams of violence. When the dreams came, guilt followed. The other one would find the guilt too much to bear, and reason it away with anger and hate. At such times, the man's awakenings beside the road, in the long night, would take form once more, and he would wander to the town, not knowing that time had passed as it had.

Over the years, during those times the other one would rise with guilt, turned to anger and hate, the man was sustained in his wanderings. Memories, some previously lost to alcohol, returned to him. He remembered Gideon Teague and a scuffle with the man. He did not remember how it had ended, but he felt an unbridled hatred growing for him. Somehow, that Teague fellow was to blame for all of this. Perhaps his whore wife as well. They had planned it, this thing that had brought him beyond ruin and into sentient oblivion.

He decided, parted as he was from the living world, he would bring death to one that would hurt Gideon Teague and the girl. The girl. He couldn't rightly remember her name, but he remembered her father. He would find him. He would make him pay for Gideon's sins.

It had taken a long, ceaseless walk through the night to find the place where the father lay, slumbering drunk, the bottle resting on his bed stand.

The man found the barrier of the doors and the walls to the house had not been an impediment to him. He merely walked through them. The sensation gave him a thrill of power. Whatever had become of him, this was the first moment he took pleasure in it.

As the father slept, the man laid hands upon his throat and tried to strangle the life from him. Yet nothing happened. His hands found no purchase against the flesh. The father slept, oblivious to the man's murderous intent. The sense of power faded, and the man wept beside the bed of the man he wanted desperately to kill.

Time and again, given renewed form in the guilt and anger and hate the other one felt, the man returned to the father's bedside with the same result. Then he had a thought, and the thought became new power, new joy.

Instead of strangling the father, the man pressed his forehead against the forehead of the sleeping man. To his surprise, he could hear and see the fractured images of the father's dreams. A lost wife. Lost daughters. The father grieved in his sleep. The man pressed in, driving his hate into the father's dreams. Suddenly, the old man woke, startled and looking frantically about the room. The young man sat next to him and watched and laughed.

In the nights that followed, sustained during a cycle of guilt and anger and hate, the young man came and entered the father's dreams, pushing him hard toward the images of grief and planting a desire. Finally, after many such nights had passed, the desire took hold. The father woke from his sleep, mourning fresh death, deeply feeling the loss of his loved ones. The father, consumed with sorrow, reached for the bottle beside his bed and drank. With the bottle empty, the father lay back in his bed, comatose, his misery numbed. The young man smiled and pressed his forehead against the father's once more, willing the old man to vomit up his grief. Unknowing, the father did just that, emptying the contents of his stomach, overflowing from his mouth and settling back with his choking breath into his lungs.

The young man watched as the father's eyes opened wide. The father thrashed and tried in vain to clear his lungs. Then the thrashing ceased, and the father joined his loved ones in death.

The young man laughed. The grief would come to Gideon Teague now, and the whore he'd set his hopes upon. The man had found his purpose, and it felt sweet and strong.

Once the father had been found, buried, grieved and mourned, the man's hold over the night grew stronger. In his hate, he began to understand that his being was tied to Gideon Teague's. With Gideon's sorrow, the man freed himself from the night road and held dominion over the night itself, going where he pleased. Yet time passed, and Gideon's sorrow eased, and the man felt himself weaken, his hold over the night becoming tenuous and uncertain. This he would not abide.

CHAPTER 4
1908

On a cold winter's night, Hap Teague awakened at ten minutes to midnight. His bladder was painful and full. He rolled free of his covers, bracing himself against the cold. He leaned forward on the bed. The pressure in his bladder made him wince as he pulled his waiting boots on over wool socks. The air in his room was frigid, and even in the near-dark he could see his breath escaping as a floating grey mist. He buttoned his union suit up to the neck and moved carefully to the bedroom door. With the warmth of his hands, he had melted a glob of lard into the hinges earlier that day. Then he tested the door several times, opening and closing it against any possibility of creak. Now, he opened the door silently and stepped tentatively out into the hall. The floor would squeak some. There was no getting around that. Besides, night noises were common, and small squeaks would not rustle his slumbering parents. Only creaking, opening doors would do that.

Hap walked through the hall, down the stairs, into the parlor. He stood there for a moment, listening for movement from his parents' room. Then he moved into the kitchen and walked to the back door. Hap had sneaked in and melted lard into this door's hinges, too, when his mother took her afternoon nap. She never saw him do it, but she noticed the result. Hap had watched her marveling at the door after sunset. She'd seemed fascinated with the no-noise that it made.

He opened the door and stepped into the night air. The pain in his bladder hampered his elation. The cold made him want to turn around and go back inside. Yet his sense of anticipation grew, and he loped eagerly to the outhouse.

The outhouse door creaked loudly. He had failed to plan for that, but it was too late now. He stepped onto the wooden decking. Inside, he discovered he had to urinate so badly that starting to go was impossible. For a brief time he was afraid he'd gone too far. He had drunk cup after cup of water, so he would wake up in the middle of the night. Now, his guilty body shut itself down and wouldn't let him pee.

"What if I can't pee at all?" he thought. "Would I just build up and bust open with it?"

He imagined his fatless flesh bulging with gallons of urine. He saw it burst free inside of him and wash yellow liquid over his organs like floodwaters over the riverbank. The beginnings of a reluctant flow eased his fear, but it took a long time before he felt any relief. Finally, he was empty – and free.

"Now!" he thought, triumphant. "Now I will know the secret of it!"

Hap was twelve. He had been planning for this night for three days on the promise of a ghost. It wasn't a scary ghost like he'd heard ghosts were supposed to be or like the ones he had imagined in the darkness of his room late at night, lurking just beyond the shadows, an unseeable malevolence taking the form of the dead. It wasn't like the ghosts in stories he'd been told of spirits so aligned with Satan that their single, unholy purpose was to slaughter children as bloody offerings to the fallen angel, the lord of demons and ruler of Hell. Hap's ghost wasn't evil at all. His ghost smiled and promised the secrets of life, to be given to Hap alone, for Hap was a special being upon the earth.

"There is more to you than milking cows and living as a slave to the land," the ghost had told him. "There is greatness in you, and I alone can show you what others cannot know."

The ghost had come gently to him, standing beside his bed in the darkness, once the house was moved into the silence of night and his parents slumbered peacefully beyond his door. Hap himself had slumbered, too, dreaming peacefully of chores and riding horseback around the farm on a sunny day. His dreams drifted away, and Hap became conscious of the pillow against his face and the warm blankets holding the cold night at bay. He kept his eyes closed, hearing what had taken him from his dreams, a soft rapping against the floorboards next to his bed.

As he came fully awake, fear gripped him, icy adrenaline racing from his stomach out to his limbs. He thought of those malevolent spirits he imagined in the darkness, come now to find him and tear away his soul.

"Open your eyes without fear," a voice whispered beside him.

The voice was soothing, kind, warm like the blankets against the cold.

Hap opened his eyes and saw the ghost. He had come dressed in black, a fine suit making Hap think of English gentlemen he saw illustrated in magazines. The ghost held a black cane, its handle gleaming gold in the dim moonlight, the thing that had been rapping against the floorboards.

For a moment, Hap saw all of the malevolence of his imaginings, a hateful visage looming above him. The icy fear shot through him once more, and he was about to scream. Then the ghost smiled, and the malevolence faded away, quickly forgotten. The smile bared the ghost's teeth and contorted its face into a friendly form, comforting, even familiar to Hap.

"See?" the ghost said, mirth taking control of its voice. "Nothing to fear, young man. I come only to give you sight to see, a secret to know who you really are."

Hap smiled back at the ghost.

The ghost had come nightly to visit Hap afterward, telling Hap he was special and that soon, very soon, the ghost would tell him how and why.

"We must meet beyond the confines of this room," the ghost told him. "The night for it is not far away now. I will tell you when the time is right, and you must come to me. Then I shall reveal it, and you shall know."

Finally, the ghost told him to come to the road three days hence, when the moon was full.

The ghost did not come after that, but Hap had laid his plans. He'd felt guilty doing so. If Father or Mother knew, they would call on Reverend Casey for sure, convinced the ghost was an angry spirit to be cast away in the name of the Lord. But they hadn't seen his smile. They hadn't felt the warmth of his voice or felt the greatness of the promise he had made. Hap did not know what stuff ghosts were made of, but this one couldn't be from Satan. There was no smell of fire or brimstone about him, not that Hap knew what brimstone was, but he decided it must be the smell of rotten eggs.

And the promise! What could it be? He would share it when he had it. He would share it with his mother and father, and they would be happy for it, and that it had come from a ghost would be forgotten after it was brought.

Hap looked from the outhouse down the road. Far off, shining in the silvery light was the ghost. Hap wondered. What is his name? Why hadn't Hap asked him?

It was a clear night, the moon close and brilliant, pushing the darkness away into the shadows. It was just shy of one degree, and Hap's face began to hurt. He contorted his facial muscles, trying to find some relief from the stinging air.

"It's so cold," he thought. He hadn't considered the need to bring gloves or his coat. The night had not been this cold at any time in his memory. He had sometimes come to the outhouse at night, when the call dragged him from his sleep and he'd forgotten to replace his chamber pot. Never, ever had it been this cold. Never, ever had he needed more than his union suit to keep the cold tolerable.

But this night, his hands began to hurt, and he shoved them under the buttons of his union suit, against his belly, finding what little warmth was left there. Holding his hands thus and grimacing against the freezing air, he thought to go back inside to get his coat, but he'd risk waking his parents if he did. And he'd risk the ghost's fading away into the shadows, the secret kept and lost to Hap forever.

Hap looked down the road. The ghost beckoned him, waving him forward. Hap's breath stuck like fungus, frozen to the peach fuzz under his nose.

Tentatively, he took his first steps along the road, toward the ghost. As he did, the ghost turned and began walking away, farther down the road. Hap panicked. Had he waited too long? Was the secret to be lost?

He began to run after the ghost. As he got closer, the ghost turned and smiled, waving Hap onward. Then the ghost turned away once more, moving – floating? – farther along the beaten road.

Hap ran faster, but he did not seem to get any closer than he had been, so he began to run as fast as he could, his hands free from the union suit, swinging with his stride. His ears were on fire from the cold, his hands numb. Amazingly, he began to sweat from the effort and warmed a bit from his chest. His union suit grew damp. But his ears still burned. His face was in agony.

"It's like I'm in the fire and can't get out of it," he thought, wondering if he was getting frostbite. He'd heard of folks losing fingers and toes to the extreme cold and feared he might be one of them if he persisted. He slowed and looked back toward home.

As Hap hesitated, the ghost stopped and turned back to him, waiting, smiling.

Seeing the ghost had stopped, Hap continued forward. He caught up and stopped beside the ghost, breathing hard, panting to catch his breath.

"You've demonstrated your worth," the ghost told him. "Few could do what you have done to find me and hold me here by the sheer force of will."

Hap could not speak. He was overtaken by a fit of coughing, induced by the frigid air.

"Fear not this trifle you are feeling," the ghost smiled. "I will bring you back to the warmth of your room, safe and sound."

"The secret?" Hap managed to gasp, finding no warmth in the ghost's promise now. He was scared.

"One more task," the ghost said. "Once you have proven yourself in this final test, the secret shall be yours."

"What is it?" Hap cried, tears flowing and freezing against his cheek.

"Your mother," the ghost told him. "Your father. They stand in your way."

"Way? Of what?"

"The next task will be easy for you," the ghost continued. "They sleep now. I will see that they sleep deeper. And when I return you to your warm bed, you must get up once more and do this thing."

"What thing?"

The ghost smiled and let go of his cane. It stood without falling. The ghost reached into his coat then, producing a long blade, a sharp knife with a pearl handle – the same knife that once plunged into the festering flesh of Abraham Teague.

"You must kill them, Hap," the ghost smiled again, his voice soothing and sure.

Despite his agony, Hap stared at the ghost, astonished by what he had been told.

"I won't!" he screamed. "I love them."

"Oh, but they don't love you, Hap. That is why they are in your way. That is why you must use this," the ghost held the knife out to Hap. "This is why you must use this blade, which I brought especially for you, to kill them."

"No!" Hap tried to scream again, but it was no more than a whimper.

"You must. If you cannot agree to this one thing, Hap, I shall leave you here. I will have no choice. I will not take you back to the warmth of your bed."

"I won't!"

"YOU MUST AGREE!!!!" the ghost took on the malevolent aspect then that Hap had first seen from his bed, before the smile, before the mirth.

Hap fell to the ground, silent but shouting in his mind, "NO!"

The ghost was gone. The blade lay on the dirt road beside Hap.

"Pick it up," Hap heard. "Pick it up and you will be warm and free."

Hap managed to stand up. Feebly, he kicked the blade away from him and began hobbling toward his house. He was a mile away.

Hap staggered and tried to run some. Even his feet had begun to freeze under his boots and wool socks, making every step uncertain. He tried not to fall, but he fell several times, picking himself back up, fighting to make it home. The ghost had driven him away from his warm bed and had tricked him into this terrible injury. But no matter what the ghost said, his mother and father loved him, and he would fight to return to them.

The effort was monumental. Hap held the loving image of his mother and father in front of him to keep him from giving up. Finally, Hap clapped up the back steps of the house, feeling great relief, despite the pain. He tried to reach up to the door handle, but his fingers would not grasp it. Then he tried using the palms of his hands, putting as much pressure as he could against the handle, and it began to turn. Suddenly, he stopped trying. He realized Satan was working through him. No matter that the ghost was gone, no matter that he'd kicked the knife away, what would he do when he got inside? Would Satan force his hand?

The ghost had tainted him. Why hadn't he known it before? Reverend Casey had told him and the entire congregation all they needed to know to see Satan's work, but he hadn't seen it. The ghost was a demon sent to blind him, he decided. The demon kept him from seeing the hand of Satan forcing him to this wickedness. Things of the Lord would not cause you pain, but things of Satan were made to burn your soul.

Hap panicked. How could he go in the house now? How could he bring the Devil in with him to get after Mother and Father? He let his frozen hands drop from the door.

"I can't go in," he thought. "I've been ruined by Satan, and I went willing."

Hap sat on the steps and started to cry. He was scared because his feet were numb and the sweat under his union suit had frozen and was eating into him. His fingers hurt terribly from the cold, and he wished he had his gloves.

"I'm being licked by the flames of hell," he decided.

It almost occurred to him to go into the barn to seek warmth among the cows and the horses. But the ghost was with him still, and it pushed the thought away. So Hap sat and cried until he fell from the steps and onto the ground beside them. He'd already fallen into his last sleep when he fell, and he died in the hard cold night.

CHAPTER 5
BURIAL

In the frozen night not far from an ancient oak tree atop a low hill, just above the fields where crops were planted in the springtime, Sam Smith leaned on his shovel and watched a bed of glowing red embers. He had tended the embers and kept them smoldering over the earth for two days, contained in a rectangular barrier of rock, hauled and laid for this very purpose. Sam was fifty-three, but well-muscled and as strong as a man of thirty. But he was tired. Not from the hour or the cold, but from three hard days of grieving. Lanterns lit the ground outside the embers' glow. There was no snow to speak of on the hill, but frost permeated every bit of it, except for the ground contained within the rocks, beneath the embers.

He looked to the base of the oak tree. There, Gideon Teague sat rigidly against the trunk, staring soul-struck into the night. Beside him, bundled and covered in his favorite blanket, the body of Hap Teague lay waiting for burial. Hap's name was Eugene, but since he was a baby, he had been so happy his mother Alma called him Happy Boy. Over time, she shortened Happy Boy to Happy, then finally to Hap.

Hap stuck.

For a moment, Sam thought he saw a man standing beside Gideon, dressed in black. Something gold flashed in the flickering light of the lanterns, then it was gone, and the image of the man was gone, too. Sam

41

blinked and squinted, staring to see if what he had seen had actually been there.

"Nothing," he thought. "Just too goddamned tired to see straight. Too goddamned tired to think straight, too."

Sam looked away from Gideon, back to the embers.

"Well," he whispered. "Time's enough, I guess."

Sam took hold of the shovel and moved toward the bed of embers. He scooped out a shovelful and walked with it a short distance away, adding the still glowing embers to a pile of ashes that had burned over the ground in the preceding days, scooped away and replaced with new fire.

He worked for a while this way, scooping, walking, and dropping embers into the pile. Eventually, the ground where the embers had lain was cleared, leaving scorched, blackened, and smoldering earth. He lay the shovel aside and took up a pickax, using it to roll the rocks away, toward the pile. They rolled with blazing violence against the frost, hissing and raising angry steam into the air.

Finally, the earth lay bare and ready. Sam raised the pickax and struck the ground.

He was raising the pickax for his second blow, when he felt the hand of Gideon on his shoulder.

"No, Sam," Gideon said. "I'm to do it. I'm to look after my boy."

Sam looked into Gideon's eyes. He was struck by the contrast in what he saw: a blank, hollow stare that seemed to see nothing, yet at the same time a fierce determination.

The sight unsettled Sam deeply.

"The boy needs rest," Sam thought. "Not this. Not now. He ain't right enough yet."

"Let me dig a bit," he told Gideon. "You go sit a while longer. I ain't gonna be able to keep it up all night anyhow. You'll take over when I tire. Can't just one of us get this done."

Sam tried to smile, to reassure Gideon it was going to be all right. Then suddenly, he felt a cold chill at the back of his skull, colder than the frigid air, alive somehow and hate filled. With it came a voice, pounding into him, driving the kindness he'd felt for Gideon away: "He is my charge now, Old Man!"

Sam dropped the pickax and whirled around, holding his hands up in defense against the violence he'd felt in the voice. There was nothing there but a grey mist, no doubt rising, he thought, from the hot earth.

"Jesus," Sam sighed, almost laughing at himself. "So goddamned tired, I'm getting scairt of things that aren't there."

Gideon was reaching down for the dropped pickax. Sam's kindness returned, and he put his hand on Gideon's shoulder.

"Let me do it, son."

Something pushed hard against Sam then, throwing him back and away from Gideon. Sam stumbled and fell to the ground, searching frantically for the unseen enemy in the dark. But what he saw was more disturbing, more frightening than the invisible hand raised against him. He watched as Gideon bent down and grabbed the pickax, raised it high over his head, and drove it fiercely into the ground that would become Hap's grave.

The Gideon Sam knew, no matter his grief, would have reached down to help Sam up, to make sure his friend was all right. But Gideon did not even notice Sam was there anymore. He raised the pickax again and again, driving it into the earth, making, aside from his sharp exhalations of breath, no sound.

Sam sat up and watched dumbfounded. Slowly, he backed away, uncertain whether Gideon's hand would strike only the earth.

Finally, he stood and backed even farther away. He was confused, and afraid. Deathly afraid, but of what, he did not know. Feeling shame, great shame, he ambled toward his horse and slowly put his boot in the stirrup. Once in the saddle, he kicked, and the horse began walking away from the tree, away from Gideon, and away from Hap. Sam took one last look back. Gideon didn't seem to notice Sam was leaving, or Sam at all.

Behind Gideon, the spirit stood, delighted and grinning. Such wonderful power flowed into him, charged anew by the strength of Gideon's sorrow. He had not been able to lay his hands on a living being until this moment, when he threw the old man aside, like a feeble child.

"I will have more of this!" the spirit thought. But another thought came upon its heels, barely formed, not quite understood. For a moment the spirit looked upon the blanketed body of the boy. Hap? Yes, his name had been Hap. He looked, too, at Gideon, furiously attacking the earth with his pickax, to dig the grave and lay the body of the boy into it. The spirit's exaltation dimmed, and for a moment it felt an old, lost feeling. Sadness.

He saw nothing like himself rise from the boy's body. It was dormant. Dead. He himself was the author of the boy's death, and the barely formed thought brought with it something akin to regret. Then the spirit watched as Gideon's effort slackened. For a moment, Gideon stood leaning on the pickax, resting and bewildered, looking around the dimly lighted hill for Sam Smith.

The spirit felt its new strength fade then; its awareness of the night surrounding it flickered, fading. Sadness, regret for the child – even as these things came to the spirit, its essence began to dissolve into nothingness, its hold over Gideon lost.

"NO!" The spirit cried out and fought the fading of the night, subconsciously aware and fearful of the tormenting chasm to which it would return. It grasped desperately at thoughts of hate, seeking jealousy to sustain it.

"Foul child," it raged. "Paltry, needful little stout. How should you deserve the devoted father, the loving mother, when such things were deprived of me!?!"

The spirit grew its hatred for the boy, cultivating it with its renewing strength, found within its hate.

"I will make you despised and hated by my own hand," the spirit declared, setting its gaze upon Hap's covered corpse. "I shall turn your father's devotion to poison, and I will choke his life from him upon your memory!"

Its hold over the night returned to it fully, and it drove its will back into Gideon. Gideon sought no more for Sam Smith; instead, he grabbed the pickax harder than before and began driving it back into the smoldering earth.

* * *

44

Sam put his horse in the barn, alive with shame. To drive it out, he'd begun to tell himself there hadn't been a man dressed in black. He told himself there hadn't been a voice or hand raised against him, coming seemingly from the ether itself. He told himself he hadn't been afraid. Gideon, he told himself, just needed to be left alone, to work things through.

Sam Smith was not a man given to fear. Had he not been trying to shove his shame down and out of his thought, he might have considered, might have realized there was more than a disembodied voice and ghostly hand working upon him. He might have gleaned there was some power in an evil thing that could take hold inside of a man's mind and drive into it a fear so strong it could dash all courage aside. He might have thought, too, that such a force might be driving itself into the soul of Gideon Teague even as Sam walked up the steps of his home and into his parlor, certain now that Gideon was just working through his grief.

Inside, the parlor stove had nearly burned through the coal Sam had lit there before he had gone with Gideon to finish the work of Hap's grave. The air was chill, and he saw his breath when he exhaled. In the dim light of the kerosene lantern, he saw his wife sitting on her favorite sofa, holding, he thought at first, vigil for his return. Then he saw that something wasn't right. He saw her head and neck arched backward in a way that sent a sudden shock into him. She wasn't asleep, but rigid, her muscles tensed from head to foot. He moved quickly to her side and saw her eyelids were open, but only the whites of her eyes showed. A white foaming spittle dripped from her mouth and down her chin.

He shouted her name, but his wife did not move, did not change, did not look to see him. Frantically, Sam put his hand over her chest and, with some relief, felt the gentle rise and fall of her breath. He ran to the kitchen, found a towel, and raced back to his wife, wiping away the spittle and shaking her gently. She remained as rigid as a board. Sam thought an apoplexy had taken her and feared the woman he loved was lost to him now, passing over to the other side.

Sam did not know what to do. He couldn't put her in the carriage and ride to town, to see the doctor. Whatever ailed her, the cold would surely kill her if he took her out into it like this. He did not want to leave her alone, either, to go for the doctor himself.

Gently, he picked her up from the sofa and carried her rigid body up the stairs, to their bedroom. He lay her down and covered her with the blankets and then lay beside her. He stared at the ceiling, wondering if she would die lying next to him. "If she is to die," Sam thought, "I will be with her to the end." After a time, Sam's exhaustion took hold, and unwanted sleep drove his thoughts and consciousness away.

When morning came, he looked to his wife. Her eyes were open, seeing again, the pupils looking forward. He shook her, gently. The rigidity had left her. Sam sat up and put his hand against her cheek.

Gently, he whispered her name.

"Ellen."

She looked back at Sam. For a moment, he saw recognition in her face. Then she opened her mouth wide, as if screaming, but there was no sound. When the muted scream subsided, she lay motionless again beside him.

Sam rode hard into town, finding the doctor and rousing him to come quickly to his home. There, the doctor examined Sam's wife.

"Well," the doctor told Sam. "It's the damnedest thing. If it's apoplexy, I haven't seen one like it. There's no paralysis. She's not talking, but she's not trying neither. I think she can see."

"What then?" Sam asked.

"Well," the doctor told Sam, "some kind of fit, maybe. She's been through a shock, the business with Hap. Women don't take it so well as men folk do. Hysteria might be to blame. I say we give it time. Give it time, and it will pass."

Sam was relieved. Give it time, and it will pass. But the years slipped by, and it didn't pass. When it finally did, it was with a fury that brought true fear into the heart of Sam Smith.

CHAPTER 6
A MIDSUMMER'S NIGHT

1916

Hap's father, Gideon Teague, wondered as he did every night at how loudly the floorboards creaked when he walked on them. Every step sent a shrill shrieking throughout the house. Could he ever have slept through such a noise? He'd challenged himself to ease his way through without raising the sounds, time and again, night after night, in summer, in winter, in fall, and spring. For eight years he'd made it into the hall in the earliest of morning hours and walked and stepped and tip-toed in every conceivable variation, in socks, in boots, barefoot, stepping hard, and stepping soft. Every step creaked. Every tipped toe shrieked. But he never gave up the wonder and the tests and trials. Long ago he'd accepted that he could sleep through the screeching noises, but he still tried to pass through in silence and disprove what he knew.

No matter the squeaks, he never heard Alma stir. He wondered at that. To his hearing, every creak was a crack of thunder. From one end of the hall to the next, his movements sounded to him like a storm raging through the night. But nothing stirred, and Alma stayed wrecked.

Early on, Gideon saw that Hap's death had hit Alma hard, wrecked her, maybe forever. She spent her life and days reeling from it. Moments would come in which she would find some short-lived philosophy of hope, but her mind would challenge it. So hope came fleetingly when it came and then it settled back beneath her darker thoughts. She moved when there was cause and did those things she was expected to do. She cooked. She washed. She spoke when spoken to. If the cue was right, and if she recognized it, she would smile as the occasion called for and seem herself again. But her husband saw that she wasn't herself. He saw that her smiles were like hope, which if thought upon would crumble. Her face got old, her expressions slack. She skinnied up like a cancer had taken hold, but it hadn't, and he knew that she would live and she would wait until living and waiting were done.

Once he wondered if Alma had come back to him. Two years after Hap had died, on a cool March evening, he had lain in bed beside his wife, wondering at how hard she had taken Hap's death and wondering if she could ever be the same again, the same as she was when she would cock her head at him and smile, full of love and happiness. That night, he lay staring at the ceiling and listening to Alma breathe deeply, sleeping her sleep of death. He had started to doze when he felt Alma's hand slide across the bed, under the covers, reaching out to touch his chest. He gasped when he realized her touch, the first he had felt from her since Hap's passing. Silently he lay, trembling, wishing, hoping for Alma's love.

He felt the covers move with Alma as she slid across the bed, moving her leg over his legs and coming to a rest on top of him. He felt her eyes looking down at him, but he could only look up, away from her. Then he felt her begin to move, her naked body rubbing against his, up and down until he became erect. He did not look, but he felt her smile as she reached between his legs and pulled him inside of her. He hoped, but dared not hope, as she began to make love to him. When he came he groaned and continued looking away. She lay there then, on top of him, and soon he felt her head resting on his chest. She slept, and he lay there thinking of Hap and how he had wrecked her. Then, in the night, after she had rolled from him and back to her side of the bed, he'd gotten up, as he did every night, and walked into the hall, testing the floors and beginning his nightly ritual.

It was the only time they had made love since Hap, but Alma had gotten pregnant, and Gideon watched her progression with child, watching her grow during the months that followed. One day, as he slept at the kitchen table, exhausted from another sleepless night, Alma had given birth to their new son, whom she named Gabriel to do honor to the Teague family. Alma had not come to him since, and he saw that she stayed wrecked, no matter Gabriel's love.

This night, six years later, Gideon stepped into the hallway in wool socks, and creaking boards marshaled him to the door to Gabriel's room, Hap's old room. He reached his hand up and held the bells he'd attached at the top of the door. With his other hand, he turned the knob, which creaked. He pushed the door inward; scrupulously neglected hinges groaned. He let go of the bells and stepped into the room, shuffling now instead of stepping. Tiny sliding steps took him to the bed, and in the hard heat of this July morning, his son lay sweating atop soggy sheets. Gideon watched as Gabriel's tiny chest rose and fell with sleeping breaths. He reached down and gently placed his hand on top of the boy. His hand rose and fell. The tactile confirmation of what he saw calmed him, and he let go and sat on the edge of the bed.

"Hap," he whispered. "I need you to work the wheat fields today. Have the men get the water flowing like it should. There's something..."

His voice trailed off, and the conversation died. He struck up another, muted moment.

"By God, Boy! That woman of yours will have a boy, no doubt!" He congratulated Hap and predicted a fine grandson. "Me, son, I always thought I'd like to have a little girl, but then that don't always do you much good on the farm. Well, some. But to make them really work a farm, you gotta put more man in them then's good to have. You're like to have more than your share though. Have you a few girls in there for your old dad to bounce on his knee...."

His voice trailed off.

Another inspiration came.

"You should take Gabe out and teach him to hunt some," he whispered. "I'm so busy with the farm now, I can't teach him like I should. Can you do it for me, Hap?"

Gideon smiled at his oldest son, but the image died, and he dropped his head and stared at the floor.

"Hi, Daddy," he heard.

"Hello, Son."

"Whatcha doin' in my room?"

"I just wanted to see you, Gabe. Daddies do that sometimes."

"I seen you in here before, but I pretended I was asleep."

"You're a rascal."

Gabe giggled.

"I heard you talking."

"I talk sometimes."

Gideon felt his son's hand light on his shoulder.

"I love you, Daddy."

"I love you, Gabe."

Gabe's hand dropped away. Gideon heard Gabe's breath deepen. Tiny snorts followed. Gabe slept.

Gideon got up and put his hand on Gabe's chest again. Satisfied, he shuffled back to the door and held the bells while he pulled it shut. He walked down the hall without testing it and opened the door to his bedroom. Alma was settled and sleeping, and in the bright moonlight that filtered through their window, he could see her face. So long ago, when he watched her sleep, she had tossed, turned, and snored some and jolted. She drooled, and she farted. Sometimes on summer nights, she slept naked, and he marveled at how a woman with such a fine figure could scratch absently at her pubic hair and roll over and fart.

"Well," he remembered thinking, "they are human, too."

He also remembered that no matter how she moved and slept in those early days of their marriage, she looked content, even when she was engaged in the hard work of sleeping and dreaming. For years now, since Hap, she'd slept with her mouth pulled into a frown, like her lips were bent over a fence rail and forced down. Her eyes never closed all the way anymore, and her half slits stood in constant guard against any dreams of happiness. She never moved. She never jolted. She never looked content.

Gideon stared at her. She lay skinny and tight on top of the bed, blankets thrown to Gideon's side. Her feet curled into her nightgown, and her arms were thrown out in front of her. She didn't sweat. She lay dry cold despite the heat and sopping air. Her hair was white, with a few defiant strands of red shouting that she shouldn't be old yet, that she shouldn't be done yet. Yet she was old and done.

Hap wrecked her, he thought.

Gideon threw the blankets that were piled on his side of the bed to the floor, and he slid in, sinking some where he stopped. He lay on his side. Alma's back was in front of him. He reached a gentle hand out and placed it on top of her hip. Her flesh recoiled and shrank away. Yet she seemed undisturbed. She didn't move except for the flesh and bone surrounding Gideon's touch. There she seemed to close and curl away.

He took his hand away, and the flesh flowed back to its original, emaciated shape. It was what he expected. Hap wrecked Alma – wrecked her hard, he thought. Gideon had hoped, but he knew she would never come back. Alma was wrecked hard and gone, and just this bone sack remained, taking up space and haunting the house, a witless wraith trapped between heaven and earth and dumb to both.

"How wrong a life can go," he thought. "I fought so hard. I took steps. I took steps."

As he faded to sleep, he saw Alma reaching out for him, smiling.

"Gideon, I'm so sorry," she said. "Bear with me. My heart is in the coffin. I'm locked inside with Hap. I can't get clear of his grave to see you."

"I miss you, Alma," his dream self said. "I still love you."

"I can't leave Hap alone in his grave," she answered. "Pardon me. You should want me there, too, to give him comfort. You can't give him comfort no more."

"I want to. You can't either."

"Oh, I can, Gideon," she said. "I hug him, and I hold him all through the night. When he can't breathe, I say, 'Shhhh. Mommy's here.' When he wants a slice of pie, I say, 'Shhhh. Mommy's here.'"

"I lost you both, Alma," and in his sleep he cried what he wouldn't cry for when he was awake.

"He's quiet," so many had said of him. "Like a stone sometimes. Struck dumb, maybe. Or heaven knows it, some just have a hard heart beating inside of them."

"Alma, we have Gabe," he cried. "Alma, he's here, and he's alive. He needs you, Alma, more than Hap needed you."

"Gabe is for you; I'm for Hap."

And in the barn, Hap was three, and he watched his daddy heaving pounds of hay with a pitchfork, into stalls and into troughs and onto piles about the barn.

"Daddy, I can frow hay," he said, sure of himself and ready to work.

"Can you, Hap?"

"Yes, I can, Daddy."

"I wish you would. I'm so tired, it's getting to where I can't pick it up no more."

"I can pick it up, Daddy," Hap said, and Hap grew up, a young man, alive, strong, and full of hopes and dreams. He stood outside the barn door where Gideon couldn't see him.

"Daddy, I can't get the door open," Hap said.

"I know, Hap. You went out too early."

"I didn't mean to. Let me back in. I want to throw some hay."

"I want you to."

"I want to help you, Daddy."

"I want you to, Hap."

"Why don't you let me in, Daddy?"

Gideon wondered why he hadn't moved. He tried to reach his hand out to the door, but the hand was gnarled, and desiccated skin shrunk around bone. He tried as hard as he could to reach after Hap's voice, but his elbow cracked and crumbled into dust. His arm from the elbow forward fell lifeless to the ground.

"Daddy, I'm scared out here. Let me in."

"Gideon Abraham Teague, you never did cry for that boy of yours," they said. "You stood by and let Alma do all the grieving until it dried her up and shriveled her to the bone."

"Gideon," they said, "you got to bury your own in this world and move on. Wheat don't grow, and cows don't milk themselves and bring it to your table without you do the milking and bringing. Get up. Work. Your grieving will let up."

"Gideon's a hard man," they said. "Gideon's a hard man, like his daddy."

"Daddy, I want to come in."

"I know, Hap." Gideon wanted to explain why he couldn't help Hap open the door, but he'd forgotten the secret of it. If he could remember, he could unlock the door, let Hap in, and see how Hap had grown – and all would be fine. They could still be happy.

But he couldn't remember the secret.

"Daddy, I'll stay dead if you don't answer for it."

"I'm trying, Hap."

"Daddy, I don't want to be dead no more."

"I don't want you to be, Hap."

Gideon grew substantial again, the flesh back on his bones, his elbow back in place. He reached down into his pockets looking for the key. If he could find the key, he could open the door.

"Daddy, I'm dying again."

"I know, Hap. I'm trying."

"Daddy?"

"I'm looking for it."

"Daddy?"

"I'm trying, Hap."

Somewhere down in the bottom of his pocket, he felt the tip of the key, then it slipped away.

"Daddy?"

"Trying, Hap."

He curled his finger into a hook and scoured around in his pocket, but the key had fallen through a hole in the fabric. Gideon understood the key had bounced into the hay.

"Daddy?"

Gideon started rooting through the hay. He found a doorknob and discarded it. He found a horseshoe, a dog's tooth, and some balls of lead. He threw them all away.

"Daddy, I'm almost dead again."

Gideon began digging harder in the hay, and he was buried under it when his fingers touched the tip of the key again. This time he wrapped all of his fingers around it and held it tight in his palm. But the hay had gotten deep over his head, and he was trapped beneath. He clawed and dug skyward, but rats began biting at his legs and toes, dragging him deeper under.

"Daddy, I can see my bones."

Gideon was frantic. He threw big handfuls of hay aside and stood up above the pile. The key was in his hand, and the rats turned into tiny mice, barely felt. He kicked away the mice, and nothing impeded his run for the door. He looked at the door, but he couldn't see a hole for the key.

"Daddy, I'm getting et on by maggots."

"Hold on, Hap. I got the key."

He remembered then that the keyhole was at the other door, on the other side of the barn. He took off running for the door and seemed to fly the last few feet, coming to a stop right in front of the lock. He thrust the key in and turned and saw that the door hadn't been locked at all. All Hap had to do was walk in through this door, and he wouldn't die.

"Hap!"

Gideon threw the door open and ran out and around the barn. When he reached the front, he saw a tumbling darkness lying just past the barn, extending into everything his eye could see. Gideon saw a tiny smattering of dust blowing in front of the door, and he knew it was Hap – all that was left. The rest of him had to be out in the darkness.

"Hap," Gideon said, and he started to leap out into oblivion, out after Hap.

He felt a hand hold him back. It was Alma, standing young again behind him.

"You can't go, Gideon," she smiled. "I already went. Can't both of us go in there – there's no room. Hap will drown sure if you follow me."

"But you're here."

"I'm in there. Hap is there, too. We're dead together."

"I want to save you."

"You can't."

Alma grew skinny and old, then her arms dropped off. Her legs collapsed into dust, and the rest of her fell into the legs. Her dust blew across the dust that was Hap. The wind blew hard then, and the air was filled with dust.

Gideon tried not to breathe, but he had to, and he took his wife and son into his lungs.

Unseen in Gideon's dream, out in the darkness beyond the barn and living freely in Gideon's mind, a man stood dressed in black, holding before him a shining black cane with a golden handle. The man smiled at Gideon's misery, feeling content in a way he had never felt when he was alive. The smile began to fade as Gideon started to fall into a deeper sleep, free from dreams. The man held the cane high over his head and willed the deeper sleep to depart, hurling Gideon headlong into darker dreams of death.

CHAPTER 7
GIDEON'S SORROW

Gideon's clock ticked predictably past 3 a.m. The minute hand continued its arc around the clock face until the hour hand neared IV. The minute hand reached XII, and ticking gave over to the banging hammer against the bells. Gideon opened his eyes, feeling no rest. He swung his feet over the bed and dropped them to the floor. He stared at the clock, and what measure of hate he had in his heart, he poured out on the clock, contesting its will. It kept banging.

Cling, cling, cling, cling, cling.

He stared and knew no matter how strong and loud it sounded, he would win. It would wind down, get slower, weaken and stop clanging altogether.

The clock died.

Gideon reached down for the chamber pot on the floor next to the bed. He stood and held the pot in one hand and pulled his penis free with the other. He urinated, but briefly. His nighttime haunts took him through squeaking doors and out to the outhouse several times a night, where he would relieve himself and wonder how it was that his son had died. Every time he pretended that a force of will could take him back to that night, back to Hap.

In the earliest days after Hap died, Gideon sometimes carried a wool blanket outside with him, thinking about the promises of faith.

56

"Just that of a mustard seed can move a mountain," he reasoned, "so I got enough to look to my boy. I only need a second."

Sometimes he carried the blanket *and* a mustard seed with him as he wandered between the house and the outhouse, talismans to bring agony to bay, the seed so tiny in his hand that he must have enough faith beneath his great doubt to rival it.

So he thought.

Once, the doubt was as tiny as the seed, and faith made all things possible. He walked out into the cold air, and he worked it in his mind that Hap was going to be there, standing at the outhouse, just before whatever events took place to kill him.

"I'll see him as I get closer," he thought, walking through the dark night, forcing knowledge that Hap was there.

"I will see him just now, and I will cover him with this blanket and save him."

Gideon walked. He closed in on the shitter and looked for life. He looked for the living form of his boy. Nothing appeared but the dead wood that made up the walls and floor and the whole building over the hole. For months, Gideon carried the blanket and the seed. Faith raged, unbounded by reason or thought or knowledge or experience. Faith raged, faith demanded, and faith knew.

But Gideon's sight saw nothing new.

Faith flagged, and doubt found a foothold in affliction.

"What have I done to put off God," Gideon wondered, "what to demand this test of me?"

Then he remembered, took a sudden, startled breath and remembered and knew. The old guilt surfaced with the remembrance and warred with Gideon's sorrow. But still he begged as though his sin could be washed clean.

"Dear God, I will work my life to seeing what you want me to, but taking my boy is too much for me. I can't get through it, God. Oh, Heavenly Father, just bring my boy to me, and I'll do all you ask of me. I will repent my sin. I will do whatever penance you demand. I'll live in a cave and think of nothing but you. I'll eat worms, I'll walk on fire, and I'll crawl on my belly like a dog for you, and I'll love you for lettin' me know my boy is happy and free somewhere. It's not too much for me to bear, Lord, but losin' my boy is."

Gideon trod on through the nights, mustering faith and accepting that it was some flaw in him that killed Hap. Find the flaw, he thought. Drive it out. Accept the Lord.

"I love you, God! I live for only you, God."

But God saw the lie. God knew that Gideon laid plans only for his boy. And God saw that Gideon did not regret his sin, did not regret murderously crushing another man's skull, did not regret pounding the stiffened corpse into its shallow grave beside the road, left to rot. And when guilt came, tempting regret after all, Gideon fought the guilt with anger, leveled at the man he had killed, fought it with hate for the man for what he had done. Gideon still would not see it as sin.

"I'm in worship of the flesh, not the spirit. God sees right through me."

Gideon knew he'd always had doubt, and God had sent this test to root it out of him, bring it up whole and expose it to the light.

"I don't see no sense in you!" he shouted. "There, I confess it. Burn it out of me, God. Send me right to hell, and I'll praise you to every licking flame, with no hope of redemption. I'll keep faith now. I just need you to show me my boy, God. That's the only sign I need. The only little sign."

Gideon reasoned the sign he needed was as small as a mustard seed, too. It would be the tiniest of things in God's power to show Hap mercy and leave him to life. And the thought of how easy it would be for God started to work on Gideon, and he started to hate God. He hated God for some time, then he stopped hating.

"You ain't even there," he told the moon one night. "Never was. I was a fool to love you, and a bigger fool to hate you. Go your way, and I'll go mine."

He abandoned the blanket and the seed. But he still roamed at night. He let out of bed and traced Hap's steps. Then he'd come back in, sleep a while, wake up, trace the steps. Then he'd come back in, sit at the table, sleep a while with his head in his hands, then trace the steps. Then he'd come in and work his way down the noisy hall and into Gabriel's room, Hap's old room, and he'd put his hand on Gabriel's chest and feel life in the boy. Then he'd slide into bed next to Alma and wake at 4 a.m., tired beyond life and tired beyond years.

* * *

The pee wasn't much. Not much left for the pot. Some dribbled on the floor and became part of the sticky stain that never got cleaned. Alma left it to shame him, and Gideon loved her for it. A measure of hate was a measure of life, after all.

"I took steps," he said. "It never should've come to this. Never should."

He put the pot down next to the bed. Alma would fetch it later.

Alma, rising before him, had lit the tiny flame in the lamp on Gideon's stand against the wall. He walked over to the stand and twisted the knob up high. Light trickled out into the room and flicker lit his face. He dropped his hands into the bowl of warm water Alma had placed there, and he brought the water up in cupped hands and pressed it to his cheeks and eyes. Oil and crusts flowed through his fingers, down his elbows, and some back into the bowl. He looked into his mirror. He saw some grey in his hair. Not much. The stubble on his chin was white. The skin under his eyes was puffed up and threw shadows across his cheeks.

He grabbed his cup from a shelf and dipped it in the bowl. Then he took his brush and dipped it in the cup and worked up a lather on the soap inside. He lathered his face and poured what was left back into the bowl.

The straight razor scratched away the white stubble, and in that regard at least, time moved backward. He looked slightly less old with the stubble stripped away, slightly less tired, slightly less lost. He dried his face and wet a washcloth in the bowl, washing from neck to crotch and ass. He liked the smell of shave soap on him.

He got dressed and stepped out into the hall. Floorboards screeched and groaned under every footfall, and he went to Gabe's room. He threw the door open. It squeaked, and the bells at the top of the door jingled.

Gabe rose up at the noise and rubbed his eyes.

"Upsy daisy," Gideon cajoled. "Rise and shine! Day's a wasting."

"Daddy, it ain't day yet," Gabe answered with irritation, as he did every morning, with every "upsy daisy" and "rise and shine."

"Sure, it is!"

Gideon rushed after Gabe and grabbed him on the bed.

"Daddy!"

Gideon stopped and looked his son in the eye with all seriousness.

"Daddy, what? Don't."

"I got to."

"Daddeeee, don't do it!"

"No choice. I can't help it."

"Nooooo!"

Gideon tickled Gabe just under the ribs. Gabe laughed and squirmed and tried to get away.

"Stop, stop, stop, stop, stop. I'm going to pee!"

Gideon stopped. He'd made Gabe pee his union suit once, and Gabe had felt so shamed Gideon wouldn't tickle past warning anymore.

"Well, you better get you outside and pee where you're supposed to," he said. "We don't need no pee drawers in the house."

"I'm not going to pee!" Gabe encouraged.

"Just the same, get yourself up and ready. Your mother's got your breakfast cooking, and ..."

"... and we got work to do."

"You're a rascal. That's what I'm supposed to say."

"I beat you to it. Now you gotta do what *I* say."

"You keep thinking that, boy. It's good to dream."

Gabe laughed.

"Okay, come here," Gideon stood and held his arms out to his son.

Gabe stood up and went to his father and hugged him around the waist, pressing the side of his face into his father's belly. Gideon thought it was the sweetest treasure.

Downstairs, Alma had been busy. Eggs cooked in a skillet over the fired up stove, and bacon-spattered grease sizzled hot over dry scorched metal. Smoke erupted in tiny puffs with every spot of grease landing on the stove, while melting grease pooled and cooked at the bottom of the skillet, making shrinking bacon strips float and tremble and brown. Coffee brewed and sent its aroma throughout the house. Gideon inhaled as he descended the stairs and thought briefly that the only constant in this world was the smell of bacon and coffee in the morning. Men came into the world, walked through it and died to that smell every day, and their sons took it up, too, their women bringing it forth as sacred as life. The smells spoke of comfort and care, fixing the body and lighting the mind.

Alma had been up since just past three a.m., lighting fire, gathering eggs, and pulling bacon out of salt, beating the bearing cask, shut up again against decay. She cracked, she sliced, she coaxed tired and sputtering embers into angry hot air. She scooped, she grinded, she shuffled and dragged. She'd been out into the dark night, and she'd given the cold house its first hints of light and life.

Gideon came down the stairs and saw Alma in the kitchen lights: yellow bright shots pouring out of deep holes and slits in the iron stove; humbled kerosene smoke glows bouncing about the room. The spirit skewed his sight, and his vision of Alma showed her old and wrecked, moving purposely, true, but bearing all things against a weak and dying frame. Yet his love for her remained strong, a thing so powerful even the spirit couldn't break it through its years of trying, no matter what Gideon saw.

"Alma," he spoke.

"Gideon," Alma spoke.

"Smells good."

"Um, hmmm."

Alma was thirty-eight, but she was young in mind and body. Work, hard work, some said, wore a woman down and made her old before her time, but Alma thrived on work, took to it hard. She was strong, robust, and were the spirit to let the scales fall from Gideon's eyes, he would see she was as beautiful as she had ever been, and she had been the greatest beauty Gideon had ever seen. But what he saw was skinny and old and wrecked.

Gideon pulled a chair and sat at the table. Alma dropped a cup in front of him and filled it with coffee. He breathed the vapor in deep; aroma settled his lungs.

"It's good coffee, Alma," he said. "Good coffee."

Time was when he would have spoken words of love, but those words wounded her after Hap, he knew, harmed her and hurt her. So he left off of love and spoke only what they could see and touch and smell.

"Bacon smells good."

"Uh, hum," Alma answered, missing her husband's words of love, yet loving still the wrecked man who could no longer speak them.

"Gabe's up."

"Yeah, huh," Alma smiled, thinking of Gabe.

"Not so much work today. Sam'll handle most of it. Gabe'll milk the cows and feed the pigs and chickens. I'll tend the horses and maybe get Gabe to help me water some."

"He'll like that."

"Like work?"

"Havin' his dad."

"A mom's a better thing for a boy."

Gideon regretted saying it, but it was too late. Through the spirit sight, he saw Alma shut up tight as she dropped his eggs and bacon on a plate.

"I only meant you're a good woman, Alma. A good woman."

Alma put his plate down in front of him. Gabe came through the kitchen and out the door. Hinges squeaked; Alma stared. Gideon stood and went to the window and watched Gabe stumbling out to the outhouse. Gideon waited at the window while Gabe went in, spent his time, and came back out toward the house.

"Good morning, Mother," Gabe said, smiling just the way that Hap used to smile and looking for all the world just like him, too, but with only some difference in his eye and speech. Gideon couldn't pin it. Didn't care. He often thought how it wouldn't do to love Hap by loving Gabe.

Alma stalked by Gabe, stopped, looked down and smiled. Gideon knew it was a lie, but he'd never call her on it. Gabe needed the smile, and it couldn't harm the boy if he'd never known what the real one was like.

Gabe looked up and smiled and loved.

"Hi, Mom!" he said.

"Gabe," Alma said, smiling deeply and lovingly at the boy.

Alma went to the stove and filled a plate, brought it back to Gabe. She poured orange juice squeezed out a bit before and sent pulp and seeds oozing down the inside of his glass.

"Thanks, Mom!"

He reached behind his head and hooked his arm around his mother's waist, tugging her to him in a backward hug.

"I love you, Mom."

"Love you," Alma repeated, sliding free.

Gideon watched Gabe as he ate and thought how good it felt to be able to put food on his son's plate. His mind wandered, as it often did upon the spirit's bidding, on what would happen if the everyday was gone. In his mind's eye, famine replaced abundance, and he saw Gabe weaken. He saw Gabe lose what little weight he had, smiling a tepid reassurance to counter his father's fear. A month went by in that temporary world, and he watched Gabe waste away and die, emaciated, reduced, removed. Gideon lingered there for a moment, helpless and anguished, refusing to leave the imagined corpse; then he opened his mind back to the present. Gabe had egg yolk glistening on the side of his mouth, and he slurped up runny whites like a famished puppy.

"Where's that touch of class, boy?" he asked.

"Toucha what?"

"Class, Gabe. Eat like it's gonna be there a while. Chrissakes, boy, you're eating like a pig to slop."

"Sorry, Daddy."

Gabe wiped his mouth with his shirt sleeve and looked back at his father for renewed approval.

"You know how hard your mother works to clean them clothes?"

"What?"

"Jesus, boy. You got a napkin right there in front of you. Why are you wiping your mouth on your sleeve?"

"Sorry, Daddy. It was easier."

"Take time, boy. Someday, you're gonna have to sit at a table other than ours, and I don't think it'll do to have you slurpin' through your meal then and wiping your mouth on your sleeve."

Gideon smiled.

"What about when you're a daddy and you got boys? You gonna walk around the table wiping all their faces with your spit and sleeves?"

"Oh, I won't have no kids, Daddy."

"Sure you will," Gideon said. "Don't seem like it now, but you will. And you'll want them to grow up like I want you to – able to sit with other folks and not embarrass themselves."

"No, Daddy, I won't have no kids, so that part don't matter. But I'll be neater."

"That's a good boy."

Gideon watched. Gabe abridged his excesses and used his manners. Gideon imagined him walking in the barn and slipping in manure, falling back and piercing his skull against a hook in the wall. Gabe looked ahead with lifeless eyes, his legs splayed out in front of him, his butt off the ground, held high by the hook in his brain. Blood oozed out of his mouth. That the hooks were set to the wall above Gabe's height didn't quell the image. Someday, Gabe would be taller.

Gabe ate neatly. Later that day, Gideon took a hammer and nails and moved all the hooks in the barn up to higher perches, all above any height Gabe might get to in the next year or two.

"Daddy, how'm I supposed to reach that stuff?" Gabe asked when he saw Gideon hanging harnesses and tools back up on the hooks.

"Get you a stool," Gideon answered; then he saw Gabe falling off the stool and breaking his neck where he landed on the plow. "Naw, forget that. You call me when you need something down."

"Why can't I just get it? I did yesterday. I took care of it all, Daddy."

Gabe started to cry a little, like he'd been scolded.

"Now stop that! I got to see where things're goin's all."

"'Kay."

"Come here," Gideon said, holding his arms out for a hug. Gabe walked to him reluctantly.

"You don't trust me!" the boy bawled.

"I do, Gabe," Gideon said. "I just got to thinking a horse might brush up onto one of them hooks and get hurt. You wouldn't want Rosie or Gill to get hurt on one of them hooks now, would you?"

"It never happened, Daddy."

"Might though. That's the thing. You gotta be ready in life to think about what might happen and take care of it before it does."

Gabe hugged his father and said, "I can use the stool, Daddy."

Gideon grieved. "Okay, Gabe. But you use a ladder, not the stool."

"It's not right anyway," Gideon thought. "I took steps."

That night Gideon slid into bed next to Alma and thought to sleep. His clock ticked; the oak tree outside the house threw the tiny branches at the end of its mighty limbs against the house, scratching steadily along the clapboard siding. There was a slight smell of urine coming from the stain on the floor, and the moon reflected the sun's diminished light onto the bed, casting a distorted pattern of windowpanes over Gideon, Alma, and the tossed-aside blankets. Gideon watched the pane patterns change shape and creep across his torso. He imagined each line a sharp blade, peeling his flesh away or cutting downward through meat and bone, like a guillotine. He'd read once in a magazine about ancient Romans who would fall on their swords. He never figured out why, but he wondered how it would be to fall onto a long blade, with the metal plunging up inside his ribcage and through his heart. No matter its might, any heart would burst at that. And Gideon wondered how life, like a blade, had scraped so hard against his heart, lacerated it, shot steel against it, but could not make it burst dead like the Roman's sword.

"We live to die," he thought, and he knew he didn't mind dying, but he minded the hell out of others' doing it.

The panes traced their predictable paths and arcs, and Gideon got out of bed and pulled his waiting pants on. Barefoot, he trod sneaking loud down the hall, holding bells, and setting the unminded hinges to Gabe's door to life, screeching alarms against dying. Gabe slept, covers thrown to the floor. Gideon stepped to the bed and put his hand on Gabriel's waiting chest. The chest rose. The chest fell. Gideon sighed.

Outside, on the porch, Gideon sat where Hap had sat and died. In the hot and humid air, the thought of freezing here seemed a remnant of some forgotten dream. He thought if he could bring a single second of this hot air to Hap at just the right moment, then another second of it, and another, like bubbles of air thrown underwater to a drowning boy. . . Breathe one breath. Breathe another. Breathe again, and keep breathing until someone can reach down below the surface and pull the boy to light.

Sent seconds, he imagined.

He imagined sent seconds of hot air coming and going, surrounding Hap enough times to keep him living enough for Gideon to wake up and open the door, long enough for him to reach beneath the surface and pull his boy to light.

"I took steps," he thought. "This isn't my life that I picked. I seen it coming, and I took steps."

He could see his fields where they came up against the yard and next to road. He had them raised up and cut down year after year. Cut down, they always came back for him, thrived under his tender watch.

"How dead it is in winter though," he thought, thinking of the dead stalks, churned earth, and burning frosts. Frozen clumps of earth gave no hint that they'd ever yielded life so abundant, showed no promise of doing so again. But every spring the green would come, and the crops would sow, and the harvests grow. Since Hap had died, he saw every ear of corn, every stalk of wheat, every row of cabbage like the miracle of resurrection.

He padded barefoot across the dirt to the outhouse and stood in front of the door. What had Hap seen? What thought? He remembered how cold it had been, colder than he'd known for some years back. Why'd Hap venture out to it? What did he want to see?

"I took steps to bind us," he thought. "I killed to bind us. I took steps so as he'd talk and tell everything on his mind to me."

Steps taken never took. Nature was what nature was, and Hap hollowed for eternity the little bit of dirt he'd been buried to.

Spurred on by the spirit's will, Gideon started to walk down the road, his imaginary forces turning the road through time. He saw his father, big, brash, joyful, powerful – alive to the day like none had been since. Gideon became young like Gabe, scrambling after his father along the road. Father's hair was red like a torch, his skin copper white and freckled through with brown splotches and black moles. The vision shifted, and Father's massive arms held a team of horses back from their natures, Father standing atop a wagon and commanding, with outstretched arms, "Huh yah!" and "Git!", like rolled and cracking thunder. Gideon – young then and worshipful – sat next to his father and said, "Why don't you sit, Daddy?"

"Can't take hold of the earth sitting on your ass, Gids," Father'd said. "You gotta grab it and mold it and make it yours."

Gideon thought for most folks it was stupid not to sit where you might otherwise fall, but he knew his father was a force beyond reason or sense.

"Man goes through life sitting down for the ride might as well lay down and die," Zachariah Teague told his boy, sending a fast snap of his arm though the reins and to the horses, urging them faster down the road.

"Life's like these horses, Gids," Zachariah hollered over the noise of wheels and hooves and springs and boards. "You gotta see they ain't here for your benefit at all. Given to their own, these beasts would kick me right through the chest and send their hooves out the other side. I'm nothin' more than weakness and flesh. All I got is the mind to know they ain't my friends, and they ain't content to leave me be. They leave me be 'cause I took hold of them and molded them to my will. Without me, they'd be wild beasts. But so long as I got hold of them, so long as I hold on, so long as I got it in my mind that they are chaos constrained, I keep 'em from their nature."

Gideon marveled at his father's assaults on the living world. He'd learned that his father saw menace in everything except God, and God wasn't too eager to render up a life of ease to Zachariah Teague or any man who didn't see the living world for what it was. Gideon had heard his father's philosophies in a thousand places – in the fields, in the stalls, walking to church, riding to church, walking to town, riding to town, over dinner, behind the plow, in the hay loft, on the pews, at Bible readings, in the outhouse, in the woods, shooting for sport, shooting for food, fixing the roof, building a coop, and before going to bed. His father was there, preaching his seeing world, passing it all on to Gideon. In response, Gideon had been mostly mute, taking it in, confused some, seeing the light some, and wondering on the menace Zachariah saw in every thing in God's universe.

"This road here's a fine example," Zachariah shouted. "If I left it to its own, it'd rise up against me like a living thing. Ain't nothing living about it but that it sits in the universe, and that's got a great sense of how to crush a man. Some call it evil – Satan at work in the world. But I think if there is a devil, the universe would've run him off 'cause he'd have the supernatural powers to get on out of here. No one would stay here on this earth, Gids, without they didn't have a choice. This road here. I don't keep it up, and it will put me down. It will open up ruts and rocks and pitch you and me right off this wagon onto the ground. If we get lucky, we don't die from it. We don't get lucky, we do die from it. So I come out here, and I pull it flat with these very beasts and put it right, so you and I can come down it and stay living like we was a minute ago. The world changes in a second, Gids, from your trustworthy friend to death itself."

Zachariah gestured out to his thriving fields.

"We got plenty to eat now. We're going to make us some money, looks like, this year. But another year comes and drought takes it all away. The earth dries up, the crick muddies up then turns to clay. Crops die or never get up out of the earth, or you know you can't put them in the earth to begin with. Then you gotta wait to see. You gotta wait to see if your livelihood lasts it out. Cows die. Horses die. Oxen die. It goes on long enough, and people die, too. Only thing is it usually don't last long enough to start killin' too many folks. So people start thinkin' God's on their side and making it right. Well, I'm here to tell you God don't work that way."

Zachariah mastered the reins to put the horses into the coming turn they knew by heart anyway, pulling the wagon fast round the corner. Gideon thrilled at it, hanging on to the back of the seat. His father, meanwhile, braced his legs against the coming forces and stood firm against them.

"Daddy," Gideon thought to say. "When do we get to win?"

Zachariah howled laughter at the sun.

"We don't win, Gids. We die."

"But don't we?" Gideon couldn't decide exactly what the last part of his question was.

"No! Don't never think it neither! You go to thinking you're gonna win something, sometime, anytime, and you're a fool."

Zachariah pulled his team up to a halt. He sat down and put his arm around the boy.

"Listen, Gids. There's a secret we have. I ain't gonna let on until I think you can keep it. But it's a gift. It's a gift of life what raises us up above the rest of the people on this earth. It raises us above all men. Now I'm swearing you to a secret now that we even have a secret. You don't tell no one that. Not even your mother. She don't know it, and nobody knows it but me and my daddy, and he's gone to grave before you was born."

Gideon looked into his father's eyes. He'd never seen those blazing blue eyes piercing into his like they were now. Most often, Gideon thought himself a bit of furniture his father spoke to, never thinking it would answer or dwell upon the words. But now, Zachariah demanded a fealty from him that made him feel loved by his father.

"I need you to swear it right now, Gids, that you say nothing about we have a secret ever. And when I tell you what it is, you have to swear then that you'll tell no one but your sons."

"I swear it, Daddy!"

"Good. Now I'll tell you what the gift given by the secret is. It's knowing that the world don't make sense. Other people are fools living through it with tiny little brains. You can't count on a one of them to know right from wrong, love from hate. You and me, we're special. We're above the rest of them, and someday you'll know why."

"Are we royalty!?!" Gideon asked-exclaimed, knowing suddenly that he was a prince to be discovered.

"Not like people think royalty is, but, yeah, I think you could call us that. Now you don't tell though, not without you're tellin' your own boys someday."

Gideon swore it.

"Here's what the secret tells you, boy," Zachariah said. "There's this whole universe out there, and people think it's some part of God's design that everything has a reason and a purpose. People die, they see the hand of God. People's farm fails, and God has a purpose. Little children fall flat to the earth without ever seeing children of their own, and God took them home. God's everywhere, and He's doing everything. And if it seems like something He wouldn't do, that's Satan. The devil's workin' his way, but God *let* that happen. Like Job took it all in and obeyed God, they all see it's the way it is. They lost the sense to see right from wrong themselves without they see God's hand in it. Preacher says, 'Noah cursed Ham,' and folks see it's fine to put another human being to the yoke the way we do an ox. Noah curses Ham, and everyone thinks he's Noah now to keep on cursing. They whip and they lie with women don't want it, and they raise up their own like the sons of Ham."

"Daddy, I don't know what you're saying."

"I'm saying the true hand of God is the world provin' it ain't got no mind to think."

"Daddy, I don't know what you mean."

"I mean you see the sun right now when you look up, don't you?"

"Yes?"

"What would you say if that sun of ours just broke loose and set off out into space and left us cold and dark?"

"It can't happen."

"Why not?"

"Wouldn't make no sense."

"That's exactly why it can. Sense is something we give to things, Gids. We see sense in why a human being is a human being, but the sun wanders off into space, and what do we got? We got people that don't think like you and me. People kill. People lie. People cheat, steal, covet, bear false witness. And other people who you just love when you know them get all the bad that's heaped up upon the world. Don't make no sense. Babes die in their mammas' arms, and folks can't become what they are 'cause something's hanging over them all the time. Some got the chance, but not the awareness, or they got awareness without the care, and that's a worse tragedy."

Zachariah Teague carried on in a similar way for another hour, though he picked up the reins and started to drive his team toward town again. Gideon listened. Gideon wondered, looking down at the road and trying to see the menace in it. He couldn't muster malevolence in the image, so his thoughts wandered off far from his father's proclamations.

Years later, something had changed. Gideon grew, and the world shifted. Father shifted. No longer master, Gideon saw his father mocked by his own words, saw him shrunken and obscured against the world.

The wagon rides had continued, necessary rituals during the time it had taken for Father's transformation from icon into rube. Gideon couldn't say when Father had changed, and couldn't remember once thinking his Father more than a man, seeing him now as something less. Father's zeal with the wagon was the same, but to Gideon it had become a comical undertaking by an insignificant man with insignificant ideas and insufficient knowledge of the world.

On the way into town, Gideon worked his body, reacting to the jolting and twisting of the seat beneath him, his muscles live-forged into compensating springs. Without realizing it, he saw the ride through his father's eyes, the way Father had once explained it to him. He mused, with some minute expenditure of thought, that the rutted road below was waging an indifferent battle against man's will to see it tamed to the wagon's wheels. Indifferent, and despite the work that his sinews and reflexes had set themselves to, Gideon rode quiet and somber. Too much of what his father said and did confused him, proffered always as if there were some wisdom or meaning waiting for easy discovery. Gideon found no discovery. The effort to see it wore him down.

Absently, Gideon contrasted his acquiescence to his father's fevered, fighting spirit, warring with all things. Now Father pitted himself against the earth and the road, once more engaged in the endless confrontation. He wasn't driving a wagon so much as locking himself in a death-grip with the dust. Ruts and bumps threw the wagon upward, dislodging and catapulting Father from the solid wood decking. Father reveled in it, taking the blows as vanities, anticipating, correcting, and overcoming as his feet settled back down onto the boards, forced by his will to keep their chosen place in this world.

Gideon had only seen his father thrown once. They had been riding to the O'Dell farm to buy horses when a rut Father hadn't seen to master tossed the wagon high above the road. Gideon remembered Father almost motionless in the air, sideways above the sideboard, reins in hand, though most of his body was outside the wagon. Father hung on, vainly demanding continued obedience from the horses though he had been dethroned and had no power left to command.

Gideon watched bemused as gravity grabbed his father and pulled him to the angry ground below. Father's right thigh hit hard the sideboard, and he somersaulted, coming down to the earth on his shoulder; then he slid back under the wagon, for he had, even in absolute defeat, refused to release the reins.

Somewhere out of Gideon's sight, the man lost, or in a moment of disintegrating defiance, released the reins, and the wagon thundered past him. Gideon looked back to his father's broken form in the road, thought for a moment, then reached for the brake handle and pulled it harder and harder until the horses finally, impatiently stopped.

Gideon stood and looked back again, but then realized the horses and the wagon could come back to life in an instant. So he jumped from the wagon and stood clear of it, staring back at the sight which was his father. He wondered if the older man was dead. He wondered if he should approach to help injury or confirm death. Instead he stood and waited.

Eventually, Father began to roll on the ground, emitting a low hard groan from deep inside his chest. He rolled over to his belly and pushed himself up from the dirt, and the groan turned to an angry grunt, then a cry.

Father slowly stood, hunched forward in pain. He leaned with his hands on his thighs and blood oozed down his right arm to his hand and soaked into his pant leg. His face was bruised and bloody. He took a step, right leg first, and fell back onto the road, swallowed down into a wide, deep rut.

And Gideon heard his father cry. Not in anger, not in defiance, but in defeat. The sound satisfied Gideon immensely.

Father had lain there for some time. Gideon stood motionless. He wondered how he would work the farm by himself. He realized there was much that he didn't know, and he wished he had some of Father's knowledge to ensure his ability to carry on.

Eventually, Father rose up, a piece of him at a time. A hand to the ground, pushing up an arm. The other hand, the other arm. Knees assayed the dirt below, and then Father rose with a frightening groan. He began to walk, limping nearly to the point of falling with every other step, but still he moved back toward the wagon. His face was twisted in agony, and tears left light streaks down through the dirt that caked his face. The cry was gone now, and defeat in the groan became defiance once more.

Father limped to Gideon and stood before him, looking down at his son.

"This is the best it gets, boy," Father said. "The whole world, every piece of it will kill you if it gets the chance. Well, never stand for it. You'll lose, that's sure. I will lose, and don't think I don't know that. But I will rise up with every breath in my body to say it's otherwise."

Then Father had climbed into the wagon, cowed only by the insistence of pain and the need to heal. For the first time, Father sat for the ride.

CHAPTER 8
THE TAKING OF ALMA'S LOVE

Alma Teague watched her husband through the panes of their bedroom window, lit to life under the bright shining moon. She was still young and full of life, tried and tired only by the nightly hauntings of the man she loved. Her hair was a fiery, defiant red, with just a strand or two of white trying to make its stand against resilient youth. She watched silently over the top of Gideon's head as he sat on the back porch, lost in thought and hopelessness; she watched as he moved to the outhouse and took to contemplating some deep meaning in its weathered grey boards; she watched as he turned to shuffle down the dirt road, with no possible destination in mind in these early morning hours.

Hap had wrecked him, and among the many reasons she hated Hap, she hated him all the more for wrecking her husband. The hate troubled her. She didn't want to feel it, not even for Hap, whose flawed lineage no doubt took him from this earth.

"We're even then," she thought, not for the first time. "I should let go the hate. You've paid, little boy. You've paid for your father's sins."

But she couldn't let go the hate, hate for the dead reaching hand, coming from beyond Hap's grave, dragging Gideon down to join him, taking him from her.

"How do I bring my Gideon back?" she wondered, a familiar refrain.

Time was when Gideon's day began just before 4 a.m. He would reach over and turn his ticking clock alarm off before it ever began, never needing it to rise to the day. He would joyously rouse Hap and usher him laughing into the kitchen where Alma had breakfast waiting, her own day starting during the final hour of Gideon's slumber. Gideon would take breakfast then with Alma and Hap, laughing and sharing his love for them. Funny, Alma thought, but she couldn't remember hating Hap in those happy days, her hate, no doubt, muted in the radiance of Gideon's love. Then Gideon would ride out to the fields and spend the long days working with Sam Smith, with Hap at his side, learning all that Gideon and Sam were eager to teach. As dusk fell, Gideon would return with Hap, and when the boy was asleep, Gideon would hold Alma and laugh and love her. Remembering, she ached at how much she loved that man, how much she had lost with the passing of the hateful Hap.

A part of him was still here. The old Gideon came to life when Gabe was near. But even then, Hap's jealous spirit pulled him away, found the good man's brief joy too much to bear and turned him into a fearful creature, hiding against the very light he sought in Gabe.

She watched Gideon walk. Still large, still strong like his father had been. A good man. A loyal man. How could she have known these strengths in him would be his weaknesses, too? The good man so loved the hateful Hap, stayed loyal to that love, stayed loyal and lost to her.

Hateful Hap. As she remembered it now, she tried to love him. She begged God to let her love him. But she couldn't. Even when she sensed so powerfully that the boy loved her, she was true to her hate. She would smile at the boy, but it was a lie. She would hug the boy to comfort him when that was needed, as it is needed in all little boys, but she could feel her flesh curling away from the embrace, even as Hap took strength from it.

Then Hap was gone, Gideon gone, too.

"Yes, dull woman." She felt a wisp of fetid air behind her neck as she continued to watch her husband through the window. Then came the words, the mocking words. "I have taken him from you."

"Leave me," Alma said, goosebumps rising and moving down her shoulders, along her arms. She refused to turn. She refused to look at the spirit she knew was there. Long ago, she realized that to look upon the spirit, to hear his words, to consider him gave him strength. She shuttered her mind, locked it tight against him.

"I am always with you," the spirit said, mocking. "Your hate gives me life. Your hate binds me to you."

Alma was silent. She deliberately brought forward thoughts of Gabriel, and feelings of love radiated from her heart. A smile crossed her lips, and she felt the spirit's presence fade, weaken, and disappear.

Gabriel. Gabe. The light of her life and a living joy she couldn't have imagined, not after Hap. But Gabe was hers, always hers. When Gabe came, her hate for Hap remained, but she had less reason to think of him. Hap was gone, and life was as it should have been. But for the goodness in her man, but for the loyalty in her man. But for the spirit and its cloying sentiments.

She tried very hard not to think upon the spirit. To consider, to wonder at its part in Gideon's wanderings was to conjure it, to bring it to her, to give it a doorway to enter her consciousness and violate her being.

She did not remember the first time she saw the spirit because locking her mind to keep it out locked memories inside of her, as well, memories of the things it had done and the things it had changed in her. But, were she able, she would remember it had frightened her once, badly, coming to her as she lay in bed beside the sleeping Gideon, consumed with grief over the death of her father.

She had been staring blankly at the ceiling, remembering the dear man who had raised her, all alone after her mother had died. She remembered how her father had fought for her, even if the fight had been ill-considered and poorly made. She thought about the losses he had suffered in life, yet the man had persevered, keeping home and hearth safe for his only daughter. Finally, she had given him joy, returned when she married Gideon and brought his grandson into the world, his beloved Hap, *her* beloved Hap.

But as she lay, loving and grieving for her father, thankful that Hap had given him such pleasure in his later years, she heard a rapping sound coming from the corner of the room. Her eyes had wandered to the sound, and there sitting on the chair in the corner, the spirit sat in black, his gold-handled cane rapping against the floorboards. The spirit smiled, a grotesque imitation of gentleness and kindness. But Alma knew the spirit, and she began to tremble in fear, reliving the horror the ghost had wrought upon her when it lived.

Unthinking, forgetting the man could not be here, could not be alive unless Gideon had failed her, she shook Gideon hard beside her and screamed. Yet Gideon slept.

"Oh," the spirit said, "your Gideon slumbers. He will not be your salvation."

Alma's fear grew as Gideon continued to sleep an unnatural sleep, dumb to the waking world. She screamed again, yelling, "Gideon! Gideon!"

Yet Gideon would not rise.

"I am no longer the weak flesh that came to you before," the spirit said. "I am eternal. I may not be denied."

Alma's fear grew then beyond herself. She feared for Gideon. She feared for her beloved Hap, near and alone, as helpless as Gideon, if the man, whom she had not yet considered an echo of death, should stand to do them harm.

Her fear turned to anger then, hatred for the man who she thought was dead, but had managed to find his way, unheard, into her home and bedroom. If Gideon could not rise to fight him, she would. She tried to roll from the bed, to her feet, to attack the man with whatever weapon she might find.

But she could not move.

"I told you," the spirit said, rising from the chair. "I am no longer bound by the weakness of flesh."

Smiling, the spirit walked to the bed, leaning its cane against the frame. Then it climbed onto the bed and lay upon Alma, covering her body and plunging its face against hers. The spirit had no weight to it, and but for what Alma saw, it was as if nothing was there.

She screamed, this time with a fear deeper than any she had ever known.

She never knew how long she lay, violated by the wretched man, now a wretched spirit, tormenting her as she lay helpless and alone. But her consciousness finally left, taken from her, pulled deep within herself, the only way to hide from the evil thing that had come in the night.

When dawn came, Gideon was lying beside her, smiling.

"Morning," he told her. "I made breakfast. Hap's up."

She stared at him dumbly. Worried concern replaced Gideon's smile.

"Alma, are you all right?"

"No," she said to her husband, uncertain what to tell him, so she told him nothing of what had happened. "I was thinking of my father."

"Oh, my poor Alma," Gideon said, stroking her hair. "I miss him, too. He was a good man."

Gideon kissed her softly.

"I love you," he said.

Alma rose then, looking at the empty chair, looking for any sign of the spirit. But it was gone, replaced by the morning light. Gone, too, was her love for her son, Hap, replaced by a growing hate, a hate growing so strong she forgot that she had ever loved him.

The spirit had never come so powerfully to her again, but it continued to appear, sitting through the night with her, smiling, its malevolent will thickening the air, making her feel as if she were suffocating, paralyzed with terror. Over time, its visits became fewer, then it had stopped its nightly visits entirely.

Life returned to normal. Almost. She still had her love for Gideon, but now only hate for Hap.

Then Hap died, and with Gideon's great sorrow, the spirit returned. But this time, she had found a way to sometimes barricade her waking mind against its coming. All memories, thoughts of the spirit faded from her consciousness, rising only on those now rare occasions when the ghost stood beside her, taunting her until she could work her mind against it.

But in those silent regions of her subconscious, a part of her wrestled and fought against her true knowledge. It wasn't goodness or loyalty or Hap that wrecked Gideon – it was the spirit, come to the Teague household for Gideon on the night Hap died. It had laid a brooding darkness over Gideon then, given life in the wake of Hap's death. In her subconscious mind, Alma Teague was brutally aware that, while differently from Gideon, she, too, was changed by the spirit. Her every effort to keep it at bay, to keep it from her waking thoughts, rendered her waking thoughts dumb to its purpose.

But there in the darkness, in those places her conscious self would not walk willingly, the spirit lived, wishing her to know that Gideon's suffering was by his hand, wishing her to know he had taken her love for Hap away from her, replacing it with his own jealous hatred for the boy. So she watched her husband, knowing, but pretending for her own sanity not to know, that there was more to be seen than a wounded man wandering through the night. There was the enemy, too, a spirit of evil driving every wandering step.

The spirit gone now, she thought that Gideon would hate her if he knew how she had hated Hap. Maybe he did know. Maybe it was her hate, not his love for Hap that took him from her.

Gideon hadn't looked at her the same since Hap went away. Some part of him that would sacrifice anything for her died with Hap. So long ago, Gideon had been a roll of the dice. In him, she sensed anger, confusion, and, yes, even in Gideon, hate. But she saw beneath all of that. There, struggling to reach out into the world had been the good man, the loyal man, unformed, half-finished until he'd come to her, loving her. Love had taken him from the precipice.

But, no, she thought. Tragedy followed him. Love had saved him, perhaps, from being less than what he became, but tragedy had hit him hard, making him see the uselessness of his anger, the falsity of his hate. Her love, maybe, kept him from the darkness, but he had needed the darkness to see the light.

She watched out the window again. She'd already found a way to forget that the spirit had been with her moments before. Instead of considering it, she watched Gideon walk farther down the road, lost, the darkness of Hap extinguishing his light. Yet with Gideon, at least, there was some sense to be made of his wanderings: Sorrow for Hap, though protracted over years beyond sense.

More puzzling to Alma was Sam Smith's wife, another loved one lost to the ravages of Hap's death. Ellen Smith had been the strongest, smartest woman Alma had ever known, in enmity once with Alma and her father, but over time the greatest friend she had ever known, apart from Gideon himself. But as Hap had taken Gideon from her, he had taken Ellen, too, on the very night of his burial, condemned to her own wanderings. Even as Gideon paced the night, Ellen paced mindlessly through the days.

CHAPTER 9
THE LOYALTY OF
SAM SMITH AND ALMA
TEAGUE

It was goddamned strange, Sam Smith thought, making breakfast as he did every morning for the only woman he had ever loved.

Too goddamned strange.

But he had loved his wife Ellen with all his soul, so if strange was all that was left, then strange it would be for as long as it took.

Not that there hadn't been hope. During that first terrible night, while Gideon laid Hap to rest on the hillside where that ancient oak stood vigil over the Teague lands, Sam thought it certain Ellen would perish before the dawn. It was a miracle to him that she did not, but coming in the stead of his beloved wife was a silent, vacant vessel, looking for all the world like his wife, yet bereft of the slightest hint of who she had been. In her was no recognition, no hint of thought or emotion. But he learned if he took her arm, she would walk where he led, even seeing, she must have seen, stairs, which she descended or climbed, knowing where to place her foot to avoid a fall.

When he began feeding her at their kitchen table and giving her drink, she would chew and swallow and drink, taking what sustenance she was given. She moved as she needed to move to allow Sam to dress her and bathe her and to take her for long walks out of doors by his side.

Then one morning hope came on the heels of terror. Sam awoke, and Ellen was gone from their bed. He feared maybe she, like Hap, had wondered into the cold and deadly night. He cursed himself for having slept through her rising, and in a panic, he raced down the stairs, headed to the back door in the kitchen to find her, hoping with every step she had not followed after Hap. But when he entered the kitchen, she was there, dressed and sitting at the table. From that day forward, she would dress and undress herself, use the chamber pot or outhouse, and eat her own food when Sam served it, with knife, fork, and spoon. But hope faded, for every movement was governed, not with the bright will of his beloved, but by something unseen behind the vacuous, dull eyes left behind.

Sam stayed with her through the days and nights for a long while, but even in the winter, the business of the farm demanded his attention. The daytime called with work to be done, deals to be struck. Loans, purchases, preparations, contracts, and obligations – all demanded his time. Gideon, poor Gideon, had become useless in his grief, and Sam bore it all. Yet there was Alma, sweet Alma, who would come to the house and tend to Ellen, seeing she was safe through the days when Sam was gone.

"Alma and me is all that's left to see us through," he often thought, finding a growing anger in his belly for Gideon and his weakness. "That boy's lost what guts he had, and I thought better of him."

Sam loved Gideon like his own son, and that fueled the anger more. But nothing could be done. He'd yelled at Gideon to find his manhood, to rise up from his sorrow and see to his own. But Gideon only stared at him. So Sam struck Gideon, because it was all he knew. But Gideon accepted the blows without a fight or comment. Finally, Sam gave up and grieved for his wife and the boy he'd half-raised as his own.

"Alma and me both lost what was ours," Sam thought. "But Alma's a fine woman, strong and loyal. Maybe we can see it through."

Yet all of it was goddamned strange.

Hope had come once more, fleetingly. Spring came in the fifth year after Hap had died, and Sam worked hard to keep the farm alive. But every morning, he cooked and ate with his wife, as he had through the years, thinking it was all too goddamned strange. Then, one particular morning, he looked at Ellen and thought it would have been better for her to have died. For the first time, his loyalty flagged. His wife was lost. Gideon was lost. They were all that had kept him here in the first place. And he was tired.

"I'm not so old that I can't pick up and leave," he thought. "I don't need none of this. Money never kept me here, and I worked my whole life. I can go work somewhere else and leave this strangeness behind, let it wither all its own. Ain't nothing I'm doing making any difference."

At that moment, his wife looked up from her breakfast. She looked at Sam for the first time in years and saw the man she had loved. And she spoke.

"Sam," her voice was a whisper. "Forgive me, there's a thing to be done. But it's taking so long to do it. I will try to come back when I can."

Sam cried. He jumped up from his chair and tried to embrace his wife, but in that instant she was gone again. Yet she stood and walked out of the house. Dumbfounded, Sam followed. Purposefully, but again the vacuous being she had become, Ellen walked through the fields. Sam thought to stop her, but gave up on it and simply followed. It was as he'd thought before his wife had finally spoken: nothing he could do would make any difference.

Ellen walked until she began to ascend the gentle hill that rose up to the base of the old oak tree, where Hap was buried. She came to the tree and stood next to it, raising her hand to the bark and resting it there. For an hour she stood, and Sam saw she did not move. Eventually, he turned and left her there, going back to the house. He found Alma waiting in the kitchen with baby Gabriel in her arms.

"Sam?" Alma asked. "Where is she?"

"By the old oak," Sam said. "She talked to me this morning, Alma."

Alma's joy was instantaneous, for she loved Sam's wife, too.

"Sam! That's wonderful!"

"Well, no," Sam said. "Not really. She's gone again. It was just for a second."

Alma frowned.

"What did she say?"

"Nothing that made sense," Sam told her. "But now she's out there holding her hand to that tree. Can you go to her? I have work to do."

"Of course, Sam."

"It's just you and me, Alma," he said. "Lord only knows what's become of her and Gideon."

But Sam's loyalty was renewed by a few whispered words. It was goddamned strange, but goddamned strange it would be for as long as it took.

* * *

Though Gideon wandered restlessly through the nights, days were another matter. He would share breakfast with Alma and Gabriel, then for a few short hours, he would do small chores with Gabriel, obsessing over the boy in a way that made Alma wonder if Gabriel would not be better off without those hours, during which Gideon invariably imparted his nervousness to his son. But the hours were always short, and soon Gideon would become insensible to the day, nodding off in a chair or wherever he might lie down for a moment's rest. Then Gabriel was back at Alma's side, expressing his tugging concern over his father's lost grip upon the day.

"Oh," Alma would calm the boy, "you don't need to put no worry on your father's ways. He's awake all night while we're asleep, so it's natural he sleeps some during the day."

Then, while Gideon slept and the morning's dew was just leaving the earth, Alma would cajole her son into a happier mood and prepare him for the playful, laughing trek they would take to Sam Smith's house. Along the way, they would run and shout and throw rocks at trees and into the creek. When the summer was high, they would play hide-and-seek in the rows of corn, and when winter's snow covered the fields, they would throw snowballs back and forth. Whenever the two were together, Gideon's sorrow was forgotten in the work of play, and Gabriel was a happy boy.

But always their destination was the home of Sam Smith, and when they were there, Sam would hug little Gabriel and kiss Alma's cheek and thank them for sitting with his wife while he went to take on the work of the farm and the business that sustained them all.

And when Sam had left, Alma and Gabriel would sit silently for a time with Ellen at the kitchen table, where the woman would sit staring blankly into some unseen world, oblivious to the one and those about her.

One day, Gabriel's boyish restlessness would not sit, and he rose from his chair and jumped into the woman's lap. For a moment, Alma had thought to pull him away, to leave Ellen to whatever place her mind had gone. But some resentment took hold in Alma then at the woman who had left them, and she thought to let the boy intrude, to undo the sanctified solitude the woman held against them. The resentment surprised Alma, for she had loved Ellen, but she knew at that moment she felt more than pity for her: she felt anger, too.

To Alma's great surprise, however, while Ellen's blank stare remained unbroken, she reached an arm around Gabriel and hugged the boy tightly against her. Alma watched as a tear dropped from her eye. Alma cried then, too, silently so as not to unsettle Gabriel's effort. She watched as Gabriel wormed his way within the Ellen's hug and stretched up to kiss her on the cheek.

From that day forward, Gabriel would sit in Ellen's lap, and she would hug him but remain otherwise dumb to their world. When Gabriel would crawl down from her lap again, the woman would rise and begin her long walk to the old oak tree on the hill, with Alma and Gabriel following. Whenever they followed, Alma remembered how she had once been terrified of the shrewd woman, treading lightly whenever she was near. In Alma's heart, she had feared the woman would easily pierce the secret she and Gideon had kept from her, rebuke Alma, and turn her out. And Ellen *was* shrewd, and she *was* wise, and she pierced the secret so early on that Alma thought all was lost. But Ellen looked keenly at Alma in that moment, searching.

"Does Gideon know?" she asked quietly.

Alma could only answer, "He's always known."

Ellen had reached up and gripped Alma's shoulders tightly then, looking intensely into her eyes. Alma felt weak and afraid. Then the woman pulled Alma to her and hugged her ever so gently, kissing her on the cheek.

"Then the lie is how it shall be," Ellen said. "It's too late to cut you or Hap out of my heart now anyway. I love you both, dear girl."

CHAPTER 10
THE WISE MAN FROM THE EAST

Gideon continued down the road, pressed to his wandering by the spirit's hand, his mind pushed backward and trapped within memories that would sow regret, sorrow, and despair, all for the spirit's taking. Through his mind's eye, Gideon watched the memories unfold, staged in exquisite detail, nearly as real in sense and feeling as when he had lived them. But now, helplessly, Gideon watched, knowing his own part in the play was that of villain and fool.

Zachariah Teague drove his wagon into town, with Gideon, his silent, sulking son beside him. He brought the horses to a stop in front of Nate's General Store. Gideon watched his father leap from the wagon and hit the earth, making, impossibly, no impression or noise. Then Zachariah reached up for Gideon, a reflex that had lost meaning some time ago – and which currently stood as an offense to Gideon. But some part of Zachariah forgot the offense and reached upward anyway, realized, then abandoned the bond he had absently sought.

Gideon well remembered the days when his father would lift him from his seat, high into the air, and then swing his small frame down to the ground beside the wagon. Gideon had once loved the feeling of near flight enough to look forward to the moment most of the week. Then there it was, enjoyed and gone until the next trip to town. Now the feeling was simply, forever lost in the ether of memory.

Gideon leapt from the wagon as well, failing at his father's ease, hitting the earth clumsy and off balance. Dust rose and drifted like a miniature storm front. The failed approximation angered him. Much angered him these days, and he sought power in that anger, anticipated it. The anger, he hoped, would hold the world at bay and wrap him up, protected from all the things he did not know.

Reluctantly, Gideon followed Father into Nate's, where Father performed his weekly, and to Gideon, irritating ritual.

"Zach," greeted Nate, who turned to see Zachariah's hulking image darken his doorway.

"Nate."

"What can I do you for?"

"'Bout ten pounds of flour, hundred pounds of salt, and I'll give you the rest once you get that bagged up."

"Right," said Nate. "How're ya, Gideon?"

Time was when the little boy Gideon had been would eagerly respond, "Fine, sir." Now, his answer was to look off at the shelving across the room. Nate turned back to Father, leaving Gideon to his shelf watching.

"How's that wife of yours, Zach?" Nate asked, picking up a scoop and plunging it down into a barrel in the middle of the store. He brought up a pile of white powder and dropped it into a canvas sack.

"Doin' woman's work and livin' by the Word."

Nate laughed a little and plunged his scoop into the flour three more times. Then he plopped the bag on a scale.

"Nine and three quarters."

"That'll do her," said Father.

"Always seems silly to me," Nate laughed again, "you buying flour from me when it's your wheat that made it."

Father chuckled. "I like the way you bag it, Nate. Makes for better tasting bread."

Both men laughed, and Father slapped his friend on the back, saying, "I need to order up a new harness for the plow, too. Old one's hanging by a thread, and it ain't gonna take much to snap it. Can't grow no harnesses in my fields, neither."

Nate laughed harder, and Gideon sighed. He hunched his head and shoulders forward and walked out of the store. Father would be some time in town, he knew, and he had a place he wanted to go. Father would scold him for leaving, but Gideon parsed a portion of his anger to act as a shield against it. He had at least three hours here in town, and Gideon would not see it wasted next to his father, nor in pursuit of his father's affairs.

Gideon walked off down the street to the town's newest building, near the end of the block. The golden black printing on the glass door read "Oniate County Press" and inside was Gideon's wise man. Here Gideon would spend the day, hearing of things that mattered – things his father would never understand or come close to knowing.

Seeking hints as to what lay inside this day, Gideon pressed his face against the dark blurred glass, peering through to inconsistent shapes – his fellows, standing anxiously upright or leaning in feigned indifference. No matter their postures, Gideon knew each stood paralyzed with an irrepressible anticipation. What was to come, they all knew, was beyond knowing – a gift given, to them and them alone, to see the world, not as it was offered to others, but as it was supposed to be.

Gideon turned the door handle and proceeded through the threshold. On his right was a tall counter running the length of the room, making a short corridor between the counter and the wall. Gideon recognized the young men who waited inside, all from church and school, but his pulse raced at seeing one among them who did not belong.

Girls were not allowed in the worlds of men, but there, in the corner, standing proper and alert, lacking the self-consciousness she should rightly feel, was Alma Malone, her hair a rich red and tied tightly about her head, held in place with the secret clips and pins whose functions were truly known only to women and growing girls. She stood staring with a slight smile ahead, over the counter, toward the workings of the wise man from the east. Milling about, more proper to place, were Tom Harkins, Joseph

Beck, David Williams, and Jesse Yeats. Except for Alma, whose gaze and smile remained immutably directed toward the press and the man stooped over boxes of type, each nodded in silent camaraderie with Gideon. Gideon nodded likewise, though the sight of Alma Malone had begun to work a sweat through the pores on his forehead.

Alma had been forcing the same sweat from his brow since they were children, from the first time he saw her walk into church with her mother and father, some twelve or more years before. But he had never stood this close to her, never shared the same room with her without a crowd to insulate and protect him. To muster enough indifference to mask his fear now would be a trick, perhaps beyond his powers.

Needing his indifference to appear near absolute, he adopted the leaning posture favored by Harkins and Yeats. Let Beck and Williams stand and betray their interest; he, Gideon, would do nothing that might convey to Alma his intense interest in her, nor anything she might rightly perceive as undertaken for the benefit of her notice.

So Gideon leaned and looked over the counter toward the deft mechanizations of the man from Harvard, the educated and respected denizen of the east, holding court among the less sophisticated Ohioans – Henry Scott Douglas.

Douglas savagely plucked points of type from their assembled rows and thrust them back into service in arrangements that would carry the writer's – Douglas's – ideas and reports to the larger county population. He worked fast, efficient, humming some tune from eastern shores that was as foreign to those who waited as Douglas's Academy. The assembled acolytes knew nothing of Harvard or universities beyond a vague understanding that such places imparted wisdom and position to those who attended, lending Douglas an unassailable pedigree of knowledge and birth.

In Oniate County, however, few others were impressed with Douglas. Few cared where he came from, and most mocked the things he had to say. His paper, were it not for his family's unlimited and free-flowing resources, would have fallen to financial ruin, never lasting the year he had been in actual operation.

Douglas, Gideon heard, had come to Salud about a year and a half before, a man dressed finely to all proper appointments, leastwise by the accounts of those who claimed to see him arrive. Behind him followed impressive crates, which took two freight wagons to transport from the train station. From the start, Douglas put local tradesmen to work, sawing and assembling the frame and structure for his new office building. After the structure itself was up, the interior workings of the office, cornices and trims of exquisite and intricate design, followed his first freight wagons into town. They came carved and ready for cutting and fitting. Furniture followed, and, after six months, couches and chairs and tables from the finest of craftsmen had taken positions around Douglas's printing press, the former fineries stained proudly by Douglas, who sometimes wiped his inky hands upon their fabrics and surfaces. The staining was deliberate, designed to give favored aspect to the workaday business of the written word and lay low the most extravagant and expensive symbols of idleness. Idleness and gossip would find no respite here – only the real business of information and philosophy, combined to create the proper man.

The young men, all born within six months of one another sixteen years prior, were prone to boisterousness when assembled as they were this morning – but here, they knew, the assertions and postures calculated to divide young men from their parents could find purchase only in silence, a necessary precursor to perfected disdain.

Alma's rebellion was the more exquisite, for here she asserted herself outside the boundaries laid down for her entire kind. As a girl, a woman born into the world seventeen years before, she was flaunting expectation – putting her very position, future, and life at risk.

Gideon's male counterparts seemed to understand Alma's error and its irretrievable character. Gideon sensed that cloaked beneath their affected indifference was a sliver of hostility, a living thing, crouched and ready, upon opportunity, to shut and slam Alma into her place – perhaps even below that place in overcorrection of the affront. To this, Alma was oblivious, but in Gideon, it aroused conflict. His own hostility toward Alma, which was as tangible and ready as his fellows', warred with a rival urge to protect, an urge absent in his friends. Gideon sensed, on some level, that he wanted to drive his fist into Alma's face, to undo her smug expression of expectation. But the fear he felt, the sweat that seeped out onto his forehead, argued it otherwise. From the top of his chest to his failing knees, he felt drawn to Alma and overwhelmed by her.

Silently he leaned with these desires in conflict, until, at last, he resolved that he would die to protect Alma from any harm that threatened. His friends, whose violence toward Alma he sensed lay barely beyond action, stood now an ever-present threat. They were his friends, these young men. He liked them. Maybe he loved them. But he would fight them if they laid hand on Alma Malone.

Thus resolved, Gideon resumed his vigil, his anticipation of Douglas's words.

"Our great poet," Douglas said, huddled over his type, his back turned to his audience as though he were alone and speaking to the open spaces of his office. "Our greatest poet, William Shakespeare, gave utterance to the finest admonition ever bestowed upon a writer: 'Brevity,' he said, 'is the soul of wit!'"

Douglas placed great emphasis on "soul" as he swayed over his type, like a serpent seeking where it will strike. His index finger and thumb shot down into boxes and trays, plucking and placing type in machine-mirrored image of the words Douglas had penned to paper the evening before.

"Brevity," he repeated, "is the soul of wit!"

This time, his emphasis lay upon "is," and he turned to his assembled guests as he said it, confronting them with a smile that said, "There now. I have revealed it to you, this word 'is.' You may take it, my gift to you."

Gideon stood confused, and all of his energies now were dedicated to not betraying any outward expression of it.

Douglas's smile endured, and his prolonged gaze sought out recognition, a dawning ideal in the faces before him. He found muteness in pause, and returned to his plucking.

"Setting to type one's own words," he continued, "is the author's finest discipline, for every letter he writes he must later labor to assemble. Every author should be charged with setting type to all that he has written; thereby lost would be the outward flourishes of the pedantic, the trite mechanisms of the foolish, and the redundancies of the dunces."

Though his back was turned to him, Gideon sensed something like beaming in Douglas's mannerisms, some favored fealty to his just chosen words.

"The letters I choose today," Douglas explained, "are the assembled components of my thoughts yester eve. In my mind, I perused the facts I had learned, the opinions I had come to, and these raw materials I took, and for their expression, I dipped my pen into my most favored bottle of ink, and I scratched down the conclusions of my mind.

"Ah, but such conclusions cannot be shouted out to the reader, my friends. They must be cloaked in an understanding of the audience mind, and they must be crafted to move that mind in the favored direction. Set down the words like a noisy hunter trekking through the woods, and they will find no flesh to fell. Their targets will flee for the hearing, and such words will languish in an empty forest, unseen, unheard, and unknown.

"So, given that within every author is the writer's vanity of being heard, the process of thought and expression becomes complicated by the obstacles to being heard – and, moreover, obstacles to being listened to. For it is not enough for the author's labors to find a readership; these labors are meant for more. They are meant to affect the world the author lives in and writes in. They are meant to change the effect of the world by changing the people in it."

Gideon noted how pleasing the sound of Douglas's words were, though their meaning lay just beyond his reach, forcing him into a struggled effort to remember what words had been spoken, when they had been spoken, and the order in which they had been spoken. It seemed incumbent upon him to secure the order of these things and then put to them some species of math he did not quite know – to bring the speaker's intention to a quantifiable solution.

For Gideon, despite his efforts, and his sometimes belief that he was on the precipice of revelation, the math would not come. Yet he heard in Douglas's speech a diction that was lyrical and mesmerizing. This, Gideon found, was enough to keep him listening and willing to believe what he could not understand.

Douglas turned to the assembled, his lips pulled back into an impossibly patient smile. He beamed. He looked. He listened. The assembly averted their gazes from Douglas to the wooden boards beneath their feet. Douglas waited another moment, holding his toothy invitation out for the taking. No takers. The smile faded, and he looked up to his ceiling as if seeking – seeking something, something the assembled could not see or hear.

"Today," he suddenly proclaimed. "Today, we walk."

Douglas stepped to his writing table and pulled a rag from it, wiping the wettest of the ink from his hands and fingers. "Yes," he said. "Today, we will walk and be amidst the serenity of the natural world, if we are able. With our minds thus at ease, we may yet glean some truth mingled about the properties of this day."

Douglas took his hat from a hook on the wall and stepped toward the barrier, the counter that kept the assembled from his world among press and print. He found the secret opening and pulled a hinged section of the counter open and walked through, pushing his hat down over his head as he closed the counter gate behind him. At the door, leaning to the side, was a shiny black cane, with gold inlayed about the handle, an ornate finish to the slick and sheer run of the wooden shaft. The bottom, the part to strike the ground, was capped with a brass sleeve. Douglas grabbed the cane, turned to the assembled, and paused for a long smile. Gideon averted his gaze to the cane, to avoid the smile and its implications, its burden upon him. But like the smile, the cane too seemed to demand something of him. The cane seemed to shout something out to the world – something about the man who held it and the boy who beheld it. Gideon could not make out the words.

CHAPTER 11
REVELATIONS

Henry Scott Douglas opened the door to the Oniate County Press and, with a gesture of his cane, ushered his acolytes through the threshold. Hesitantly, the young men, not knowing precisely what was expected of them, shuffled out onto the wooden walk beyond, the boards squeaking against the gathering assemblage of shifting weight. Alma followed, her only hesitation made necessary by the dawdling males in front of her. She shifted her weight happily from one leg to the next, swinging her arms in some joyous rhythm only she could hear. Outside, she walked around the small herd obstacle the young men had become and moved up the walk to the east. Once positioned a respectable distance from the boys, she pivoted back toward the office and waited for Douglas to emerge.

Douglas obliged, pulling the door behind him and turning his key in the lock. Once turned, he plucked the key and deposited it into a waiting vest pocket. Then he spun around and started as he nearly collided with the young men, whose milling had begun in earnest no farther than a couple of feet outside the door.

Douglas recovered and smiled, unnerving the boys, whose milling intensified in response.

Gideon deliberately moved in Alma's direction. Alma, in turn, took notice of Gideon's movements and cocked her head in fascination. She looked directly into his eyes, her own eyes seeming to Gideon greener than the whole world of spring, flecked through with living highlights of pollens and bees. Impossibly, she smiled. More impossibly, Gideon returned the smile. Can it be, Gideon wondered, this easy?

"Death!"

The exclamation frightened Gideon's smile away, and shocked Alma's away, too. Their locked gaze broken, each turned back to Douglas, whose sudden shouted "Death!" came unbidden and unwelcomed, breaking the first moment of intimacy young Gideon ever shared with the woman he was now certain he loved, for all time to come, Alma Malone.

"Death!" again smiled, queried, harried, taunted Douglas, jabbing the brass tip of his cane down onto the boards of the walk. Twice he jabbed the brass against the boards, twice startling the assembled into rapt attention. "Gentlemen, we are standing on it!"

The milling boys, who were looking down, looked up at Douglas, trying to pierce this new revelation – their only hint, however, Douglas's broad smile. Bemused they stood, but for Gideon, whose world had fallen into a keener focus; meanings even greater than Douglas's hinted precepts were opened without warning, coming with the sensation of Alma's searching hand in his. So confidently it had come, there, as Gideon stood looking to Douglas, with his back to Alma and his entire world once more, in that moment, entrusted fully to the eastern wise man. He did not immediately comprehend it, and an eternity of confusion seemed to pass between the first sense of the first finger touching his palm and the full sliding grip of Alma's hand in his.

The revelation was complete when she squeezed Gideon's hand and pulled his arm, turning Gideon to her and reclaiming his gaze from Douglas, demanding it for herself. Her head cocked again in a gesture Gideon would someday find as familiar and necessary to life as every breath of air, a gesture he would learn to coax and encourage because, in a way that he understood proved him connected to the greater truth, the very sight of it made him feel as though he were reaching skyward to the certainties of fate and heaven – for Alma Malone was the force for which he would live every day, the force that connected him and made the unknown knowable. If, he would often

96

think, this woman, my Alma, can make me feel as wedded to her soul as she does just by tilting her head, imagine what the unseen can make me feel.

Alma was joy beyond all joys in that instant, and though Gideon had been wrong about fate and heaven, had he not seen one day that Hap had wrecked Alma, had he not himself been wrecked by the death of his son, he and Alma would have lived out their lives together, sharing between them, uninterrupted, a rare, unending joy, until death came to take living and joy away.

"These dead boards," Douglas rapped twice more on the wooden walk. "They lie beneath our feet, a rotting testimony to mankind's propensity to destroy nature."

Douglas elongated the second half of the second syllable of "destroy," making a lilting "oyyyyyy" out of it. Gideon's math only half figured the sound, his keenest ciphering now dedicated to bringing Alma fully into his world.

"Man!" Douglas spat-smiled his wisdom and disgust. "Man does not live with the world he inhabits – he kills it, and he keeps killing it."

The boys had looked up finally, to see Douglas's zeal, his wisdom unfold. They knew something of death, these boys, for each had slaughtered and gutted and cleaned and cut and sawed any number of animals, food for the day, meat for the salt, and sustenance for long winters each had already seen. They raised, they fed, they named and led cows and pigs and goats from their first wet decent from the womb through the seasons and growth and hard shots to the back of their heads, raised and bled the newly dead. Death they knew, father-taught from their earliest years. Now Douglas to them cried a new wisdom familiar to sense.

In unknowing affinity with the other young men, Gideon's mind flew to an image of his parents' farm. His parents were inexplicably absent, and in some unwritten detail of the imagining, he understood a barrier to their return, and the farm was his and his alone. But no, there was some reticence there. He reworked the imagining and left his mother to sew unseen in a small room off of the kitchen, door closed. Adding a sliver more to set the scene, his father was dead, not to be seen or challenging to Gideon's imagined world. In the kitchen, a joyful Alma sat at the table, expectantly.

Gideon himself, out in the cold and near the pig pen, had hung and bled a pig, slaughtered fresh for his new bride, which Alma had suddenly become. He took pride in the gift he would soon present, showing Alma that he would provide all of her earthly needs.

He squeezed Alma's hand, but tore himself from her gaze and his imagining, looking once more to Douglas. He as yet remained oblivious to Alma's complete disinterest in Douglas and his proclamations.

"These boards we stand upon," Douglas continued. "Not so long ago, they stood majestically among their fellows in the forests of this land, the truest denizens of nature, beauty and inspiration to the earth. In their sacred boughs nested eagle and owl. Their leaves fell to the earth and composted to make a living soil. From them sprang life and air so pure that a man breathing among them could find sustenance for a lifetime. Instead of that sustenance, that sacred sustenance, a lone man stands in the nurturing atmosphere of the forest, which each of you should learn to know and cherish. And instead of finding in his heart the need to protect that forest, given to him from heaven above no less, the man conceives destruction. In the mighty maple and spruce, birch and buckeye, ashes and walnuts, he decides to lay waste, to decimate, but not to one of every ten, but ten of ten, all of a hundred, and he brings a wrecking destruction to the thousands, leveling the forest into a clearing for farms and homes and hearths and cities and tiny towns like our own little Salud."

Douglas rapped his cane on the boards once more.

"Death is all that is left when the man is done. He takes the still living, slowly dying limbs and trunks and branches of the individual trees, and he builds from them mills. Inside he assembles saws and hooks – machinery to complete his murder of the trees. Soon sad and dying trees go in, and boards come out, matched with the blacksmith's nails to take the new, dead shape of the man's imaginings. They become walls and benches and shelves for stores, and pieces not so well-fashioned for walls and poles and framing become boards cast off once more, but now as the servants beneath our feet, dead supports to hold us up from the mud and offal of man's living in the closed spaces, the tiny reeking spaces of the town."

Douglas rapped once more.

"Here stood paradise. Man saw it, took it, and replaced it with death. And we are the poorer and sicker for that man's imaginings. The forest? It is gone. Even if we were to wait a hundred years, leaving the earth to its own, the forest would still not have time to return as it was. One lifetime of a man. Two lifetimes, three and four, and the forest would still be slowly, ever slowly just beginning to heal the scars upon the land."

Joseph Beck found voice.

"But what would we do if we didn't build places to live?"

"Indeed!" Douglas answered. "Indeed, what?"

He smiled to bring the inquiry to immediacy. He searched the faces of the young men, seeming to exclude Gideon and Alma from this gaze, they having removed themselves from the more tightly packed coterie.

"What?" echoed Jesse Yeats.

"Indeed!" Douglas pointed a finger skyward, indicating the proper question had been asked. The coterie looked up in unison, and Douglas's smile faded, replaced with a slight shaking of his head. He had acolytes, to be sure, but he seemed less than pleased with their caliber.

Meanwhile, Gideon was losing interest in Douglas, that interest near fully replaced with his newfound love. But Alma had come to Douglas, so she must have, thought Gideon, some continuing devotion to the eastern wise man. So he half-listened to Douglas, leaving the more agile portions of his mind free to contemplate the tangible and less encrypted developments between him and Alma Malone. What, he wondered, brought her to Mr. Henry Scott? What knowledge did *she* seek? Was it akin to his, which is to say, was it the need to piece some meaning from Douglas's confusions?

"'What' is but the question," Douglas said. "I am not here to offer up answers, for that sullies the question!"

Douglas smiled. "We walk!"

Douglas began striding purposefully up the walk, past the acolytic coterie and toward Gideon and Alma. He tipped his hat to Alma, with a happy "Good day, Madam," and walked past, to the end of the walk and onto the dirt road at the end of town. The young men followed, passing Gideon and Alma in Douglas's footsteps. All noticed Gideon's hand in Alma's and so refrained from bumping her as they passed, which would have been their intention had Alma not found the protections afforded in Gideon's willing hand.

Gideon and Alma followed a short distance behind, Gideon's attentions divided between Douglas and Alma. Alma's own focus was intent on Gideon alone, though Gideon ascribed to her a deft ability to fully comprehend Douglas while keeping her eyes to him.

The young men shook their shuffling and strode purposefully after Douglas, whose brisk pace quickly took the group farther and farther out of Salud. Alma and Gideon began to fall slightly behind, but Gideon tried, here and there, to catch up, maintaining the self-imposed illusion that Douglas still mattered to them.

"Our great nation," Douglas expounded, gesturing with his cane a wide arc.

"Not so long ago," Douglas danced his way into oratory, spinning toward his audience, twisting back away, bouncing and skipping and whipping his cane about in fanciful interpretations of his words, the grandeur to which he spoke. "No, not so long in the least, the people of this land pitted themselves, one against the other, a conflagration of opposing ideals. To the South, men rose to the ideal that one man had the right to own another – the right to own that man, that man's children, and to determine for that man what his life would be, what work he would do, where he would go, when he would go, what accouterments he would wear for his master's amusement, what scraps he would call dinner, and even what women he would couple with, if, indeed, he was allowed to couple at all. A Southern man, too poor in most accounts to enjoy the privilege he fought for, would nonetheless pour his life's blood willingly out from his veins and arteries and into our American soil, making of himself a Christlike sacrifice for those far richer and more decadent than he could ever hope to be. This dying man was a slave to the idea of a slave.

"Here, however, among us, our own people of the North rose to the ideal of national government – a government that could decide whether a man and a state could decide for themselves what their ideals would be. The Southern man fought to control a man, and the Northern man fought to control a state. But a state is just another word for a man, albeit an assemblage – many the man. The Southern man wished to control the men living on their plantations, the Northern man the men living in their states."

Remembering now, these years later, Gideon mused how, to the young men following Douglas, the easterner, the newsman, the editor, the Harvard graduate, the dancing cane man seemed ancient and wise. But to any observer long enough to the land, it would have been obvious that Douglas was barely older than the young boys he led, barely wise, perhaps less wise than the boys, he having filled his head with philosophies and literatures, histories, Latin and Greek – tools for hammering a world into shape, without the benefits of years and apprenticeship.

Douglas was then all of twenty-three years on this earth, Gideon was sure, never having known the need to work or to wonder whether his next hunger or whim would be satisfied. His inky ostentations, his affected distains for wealth and finery were funded by inexhaustible wealth and fineries. He never knew what it was to be worried or desperate, to face the knowledge that a drought or flood could end the entire world as he knew it, and end his very life at that, or worse, slowly end the lives of those he loved and cherished and worked for, he the helpless, anguishing witness. He knew too much, Gideon reflected, for a man who knew so little, and hadn't the experience to know even that. He, more than the boys, believed himself worldly and wise, a prophet perhaps.

Gideon remembered then how, two years or so later, when Gideon confronted Douglas, the town drunk by then, but not really the town's at all, so just a strange drunk that didn't belong. Douglas had lain nearly unconscious on the dead boards outside of Claymore's, where men went for the occasional drunk, and Douglas for the more perpetual variety. Gideon pulled him to the wall and sat him up against it, leaving a wet trail on the boards from the urine that was soaking through Douglas's pants. Gideon looked at him then, with a measure of hate, to be sure, but a measure of kindness as well. The kindness, however, came from the one thing that unexpectedly bound Gideon to the drunk, a treasure to Gideon that overcame the more natural course that hate might have laid down for him.

Douglas, Gideon slowly realized between the time of his awe and final distain for the man, had a compulsion to justify himself, to build fantasies about his worth in the world and to write himself larger than drink and ignorance would allow. He was above all things a coward, Gideon knew, but there was still in him some spark of living that wanted to try to be more than he was. For that, Gideon admired him a little, and even wished him well.

Whatever would come of that spark, however, could only lay some distance into the future. There, on the urine-soaked boards, Douglas had devolved into the simplest confusion of human contradictions. A seed, maybe, Gideon thought, with the potential to grow into something useful, but for now just weak potential lying in the mud. Yet weak as he was, Douglas was an enemy, too, a threat to be dealt with accordingly, no matter Gideon's bond to the man, no matter Gideon's kindness or tepid admiration.

Gideon remembered how he looked Douglas in his half-closed eyes. Douglas muttered, "A kingdom for a stage," and laughed the muted, unaccountable laughter that spills out of drunks between bouts of vomit. Gideon slapped him.

"Shut up, Henry."

"Hey, you."

Douglas roused for a moment and seemed to see Gideon for the first time.

"How dare you hit me. Oh, hello, Gideon. Come for your lessons?"

Douglas tried to muster himself to answer the call, to speak his philosophies to the student sitting at his knees.

"This lesson's for you, Henry," Gideon said.

"Oh, you mistake me, sir."

"You mistake you, sir."

"I will tell my father how you are treating me."

Gideon realized Douglas had lost whatever recognition he'd had of Gideon and now threatened a nebulous foe he had conjured out of his haze. Gideon had felt sympathy for Douglas then, invoking the name of his father. Whatever Douglas's father had been in his life, to Gideon's eye it had worked a ruin upon the man.

"Aw, fuck." Gideon thought. There would be no reaching Douglas in this state, so Gideon picked the drunk up and slung him over his shoulder. Urine started soaking through Gideon's shirt, wetting through to his skin.

"Aw, fuck," Gideon said again, and he started walking east on the boards, to carry Douglas out of town and into the woods.

"Today, we walk, you ignoramus," Gideon told the muttering, former editor and writer of the defunct Oniate County Press, who moaned in response.

"Hey, there, Gideon!" shouted Joseph Beck, who walked then out of Claymore's to see his friend with their former mentor slung over his back. "You taking him off to drown him out our misery, the horse's ass?"

"Gonna talk some sense to him," Gideon threw back. "Gotta let the drink work out of him first."

"You should drown the sonofabitch."

"Find your Christian heart, Joe," Gideon shouted back over his shoulder. "My meaning's to tell it to him like it is and send him packing."

Joe Beck laughed, "Ha! You are going to drown him. Don't worry none. I ain't gonna tell."

Gideon laughed, too, despite his irritation with what he thought was an unnatural amount of urine soaking his shoulder and beginning to seep down his arm, chest, and back.

"I ain't gonna drown him, unless he don't listen to what's been said."

Joe Beck caught up with Gideon and the limp burden across his back.

"No one's to blame you if you hurt him," Joseph was serious now.

"Don't want to hurt him," Gideon answered. "But I'm gonna convince him it's time to leave back to his own."

"Hope he goes," Joseph said. "He's a blight upon the land."

Gideon laughed.

"He is a blight at that," Gideon said, and people in the town had stopped by now to look at Gideon's progress out of town.

"Sack of potatoes you got there," he heard someone laugh.

"Sack of shit's more like," and a small crowd erupted in laughter.

"He ain't corruptin' no youth no more," said another. "Youth's wised up some."

More laughter followed, and Joe Beck said, "Let me know how it turns out."

Gideon felt Joseph's hand on his shoulder.

"He really is a stinking ass."

"Talks kinda pretty though."

Gideon and Joseph laughed hard, and Gideon nearly dropped Mr. Henry Scott for the weakness the laughter brought to his knees.

But on the day Alma's hand first found his, Douglas was still twice wise in his eyes, and he and Alma followed the natural denizen of eastern shores eastward from the town, down a road edged on either side by the outer boundaries of crops, crops grown high in this fortunate and wet – but not so wet as to lay a flooded waste upon the land – summer's season.

"One mighty army rises upon on the earth in defense of slavery," Douglas continued, gesturing again with his cane to indicate his proclamations encompassed all the lands that surrounded them, through the incalculable miles that led to the Gulf of Mexico, south; to the Atlantic, east; the Pacific, west; then off to the northern border that separated America from the British colonies that had become the Dominion of Canada. "Another army rises to destroy that brand of slavery and to impose another. The opposing forces clash in the greatest tumult this nation has ever known, but from the maelstrom it is revealed that man has but one driving instinct: to enslave."

Douglas drove ahead, with the young men in tow. Gideon and Alma started to fall farther behind. Ahead, to their left and away from the road, lay a small island of trees, remnants of the forest that once was, before settlers set down stakes and began clearing the land for homes and farms, livestock and barns. Gideon could not know then that the course of his existence would be decided in that small island of the natural world.

"Look 'round now, my fellow thinkers," Douglas had whirled to face them again. "Surrounding us even now is evidence of man's compulsion to enslave!"

"We ain't had no slaves here," Tom Harkins spoke. "We was a free state all along."

"No!" Douglas smiled. "Not individual slaves to labor in our stead, but a whole landscape enslaved to man's bidding! These crops, these farms – no part of nature here, but land enslaved to the same willful man who first stood alone in the wood to see death instead of life!

"These farms are not what nature intended for the land. But the land is bound to them now, servant to the will of man – all men. Generations placed the land under man's yoke, forced it to take the very root of man's selected sustenance into its soil. Forced it to endure manure and plow. Once this land selected for itself what composts would offer nourishment, grew only those seeds dropped by it and creatures that made their honest living working in harmony with the land. The land was an equal, living to the tasks it set for itself. But now, here, man condemns it to everlasting drudgery."

"But we got to have farms to eat!" Harkins expressed an uncertain incredulity at what he thought Douglas was suggesting.

"Indeed, we do need to eat," Douglas smiled now to show them they were on the brink of some new knowledge. "The question is, do we need to do so in such a way? Does a man need to enslave the land to live upon it?"

Douglas took to his stride once more, the young men following, Tom Harkins now driving ahead to be nearer the wise man. There was a challenge forming in his mind, and he drove closer that he might be next to Douglas when a coherent expression of it finally broke through.

"But farms ain't everywhere," Harkins finally said. "We got forests all over. A few farms don't change that."

"Lambs awaiting the slaughter!" Douglas exclaimed. "That's what the forests are! Like cattle in the stockyard, waiting certain death at the hands of man, the butcher!"

Douglas, losing sight of his own admonitions, had become the noisy hunter.

The group passed the old bit of land left to its natural growth, but Alma's hand began to pull back on Gideon's, slowing him and putting Douglas and the now doubting acolytes a growing distance away.

Alma stopped completely, pulling Gideon to a stop with her. She cocked her head, locked eyes with him, and then looked once more to Douglas and his crowd of young men. She saw that they were all looking ahead, no notice given now to her or Gideon.

Suddenly, she bolted for the trees, dragging Gideon along with her. She was laughing.

"Don't you know Gideon Teague how long I've been in love with you?"

The question shocked Gideon, but felt natural, too, expected. In his mind's eye he saw images of Alma through the years he had known of her, and he realized that every time he saw her, he saw her looking at him – intent, Gideon thought now, on building a meaning between them. Every time he had looked away. Had he held her stare, he would have seen her head cocking to the side as he had for the first time today, but years ago. He would have found succor in the discovery, as he had today, and longing, too.

But no matter, for he felt their souls join now in a way he knew would never change, never fail.

Their feet stumbled over dead branches and kicked up leaves and debris. Alma dragged him deeper into the wood.

"I seen you looking at me," Alma said. "And I wanted you to. My word, Gideon Teague, I've been in love with you so long now! I dreamed about you, too. You have the prettiest eyes I ever saw, and I know looking at them that you have to love me, too."

"I do love you, Alma," Gideon was surprised at the words and surprised to know they were true and had been for as long as he could remember. "You got eyes so pretty I can't even stand it."

Alma stopped and locked her pretty eyes on his. She reached out with her free hand and took his other hand in hers. Then she pulled his arms around her and raised up on her toes to kiss him. Gideon returned the kiss and put his arms around her waist, holding her close.

"I dreamed it that there was only one way to make you mine forever," she said. "And I believe the dream because it told me where to find you today. The dream told me where to go and to wait for you there. And you come like I knew you would."

"You were waiting for me?"

"I seen you go in there lots of times now when you come into town with your father, so the dream told me that's where I had to go, so as you would finally look at me for more than a second, so as you would talk to me and hold my hand."

"You weren't there to hear Mr. Henry Scott?"

"I don't know nothing about that man, but that you go to see him. But I dreamed I would have to see him to see you. So I went there, and I waited, just like in my dream."

Alma rose and kissed Gideon's lips once again. Gideon felt a flowing warmth and desire fill up from his belly into his heart and lungs. He began to breathe in small, hitching breaths, trying to control his sudden breathlessness without sounding like he had just run full steam from the barn to the house. Gideon thought it more than he could bear, and then he felt Alma's hand slide down the top of his pants, searching.

"Oh, God!" he exclaimed, uncertain if he felt shame or not.

Alma laughed.

"I dreamed that, too!"

Alma took her hand from Gideon's pants and looked at the wet semen on her fingers. Smiling, she wiped her hand on her dress.

"I dreamed this, too," she told him, and she reached for the back of her dress, undoing the buttons that held it to her waist. To Gideon's amazement, she let the dress fall around her feet, around her black laced shoes, and beneath it she wore nothing at all.

Gideon gasped, seeing for the first time in his life a woman's hips and thighs. The shining patch of red pubic hair held him in amazement.

His father had taught him long ago how to bring livestock together to mate, and from that he thought he might have some understanding of what was happening, though no one had ever told him people might do such things. He was certain, however, that there was sin in what they were doing. Confronted by the sight of Alma's naked waist, though, he knew that he did not care.

Alma stepped out of the fallen dress and reached down for it, laying it out on the ground.

"I seen it so many times how to do this with you," she said, and she started to unbutton her blouse. Gideon did not know what to do other than watch.

The blouse came off, and Alma laid it out next to the dress, making a covering on the forest floor. She turned her back to Gideon, and he saw the laces of her corset and the corset itself following the curve of her back. He marveled at the perfect shape, and let his eyes fall down the back of Alma's legs. He could not catch his breath.

"Unlace it," she said to him, looking back over her shoulder. Clumsily, he reached for the laces and untied them.

"Now loosen it."

Gideon followed the command, and Alma pulled the corset down past her butt and to her feet. She bent down to hold it and step out of it. Gideon thought he would faint.

Free from the corset, she turned again to face Gideon. He had never seen human breasts before, and Alma's were a sight beyond his imagining. They lay perfectly in front of him, separately falling off center, gathering perfections of flesh. Her areolas captivated him as much as her eyes had captivated him earlier that day, and her nipples seemed no less to him than the beautiful flecks that filled her eyes.

"Oh, my God, Alma. You're so beautiful!"

She stepped up to him again, fully naked now but for her shoes, and kissed him once more. He hugged her and felt her nakedness though his clothing.

"Come on, now," Alma coaxed. "I dreamed it. Now you take your shirt off."

Gideon fumbled as best he could, trying to undo the buttons. He gave up and pulled the shirt off over his head, still buttoned. Alma gasped in turn.

"You're so handsome," she said, reaching out to touch his chest, her own fascination nearly as complete as his.

Alma sat down then on her dress and unlaced her shoes, placing them beside her dress. "Come on, Gideon," she laughed. "Take your pants off like I done."

Gideon wasn't certain whether to do as Alma commanded or not. Shame crept up in the back of his mind with a measure of insistence nearly as strong as Alma's. But he reached down and unbuttoned his trousers, letting them fall. They gathered over his boots, and he realized that being so near to Alma's nakedness made him forget how to undress himself.

Gideon dropped down and sat next to Alma, finding knowledge again in the workings of his own clothes. He pulled his boots off, and then his pants.

"Lay back," Alma said, pushing him down on her dress. Then she moved on top of him.

He saw mosquitoes land on Alma and bite, but she didn't seem to notice them. She put her hands on his chest and moaned loudly, Gideon drinking in the moving sight of her breasts and hips and thighs.

"Oh, Gideon!" she exclaimed, exhaling hard. "I been in love with you forever."

"I've been in love with you, too, Alma," Gideon answered, meaning what he said but saying it because he could not find any other words for what was happening to him.

Mosquitoes buzzed in his ear. They landed biting on his arms and on the inside of his legs, too, raising an aching, loathsome itch. Alma was equally plagued, her perfect breasts marred by the black and bloating bodies that lighted on her. He watched as one of the insects on her shoulder bloated past being black, showing through a crimson red. He fixated on the insect until it finally split open and spilled blood down Alma's arm.

More and more of the insects landed on Alma, feeding and then flying off again, replaced by more that fed and flew in turn. Gideon wanted to reach up and brush them away but saw them bursting open in his mind like the one on her shoulder. So he lay with his hands to his sides. Alma suddenly could take no more of the biting, and she sat up, brushing the mosquitoes from her breasts with disgust. Gideon reached up to cover her breasts with his hands now, feeling bumps growing and hardening under her skin. She reached around and brushed her behind, which Gideon knew must be suffering the insects as well.

"I didn't dream about these mosquitoes, or I'd've picked another place!" Alma laughed and settled back down with her hands on Gideon's chest. Gideon held her breasts again, the back of his hands a new feeding ground for the insects.

Alma's rhythm slowly increased, getting faster and faster. Finally, she dropped down against Gideon fully, holding onto his shoulders and looking into his eyes.

"It's done now," she said quietly, looked up from his chest. "You and me are together now forever, one and the same."

"Forever," Gideon echoed.

"We gotta get married."

"I'll marry you, Alma."

"I love you, Gideon Teague."

"I love you Alma Malone."

"Alma Teague, soon enough."

"Alma Teague."

"I'll give you sons, and we'll make a wonderful life for ourselves."

"We will."

"We'll have a farm, and you'll tend the fields."

"Yes, we will."

"I'll raise the babies up to join you and help grow crops and raise the cows and pigs and chickens and goats. And I'll cook and clean and keep the house so as you feel like a king when you come in from your work."

"I'll dream of it all day."

"And someday our babies will grow up, and they'll have babies, and we'll live with them and watch them all grow up, and we'll be so happy."

"That's how I see it, too."

"I love you, Gideon Teague."

"I love you, Alma Malone."

"Gonna be Teague."

"Gonna be."

CHAPTER 12
LOST LOVE

Gideon and Alma lay side-by-side, enraptured by and reluctant to break from their physical closeness. But the insects became more than they could bear. Alma rose, dancing a jig and slapping wildly at the mosquitoes. Gideon stood, too, joining Alma's frenzied dance, angry that the piercing parasites had taken from him the most exquisite moments of his life. Lying with Alma's head on his chest awakened in him a feeling more precious and more satisfying than his first physical act of sex.

He knew his fate had been sealed with the simple sensations of Alma's breath and resting hand against his skin. He opened his heart and his soul fully to her in those few resting seconds and understood he would sacrifice everything to her. Instead, the sacrifice drawn from him was his blood, not for Alma's gain, but to sustain an insufferable legion of flying little pests. There was a purity Gideon felt tainted by the rising welts that plagued him, and he thought of Alma's blood, too, flying around them now in the bellies of the loathsome creatures.

"Our blood is probably mixed in them," he thought, "joined in their bellies and flying off to breed more misery."

"Oh, I hate these mosquitoes!" Alma exclaimed, reaching down for her dress. She stepped into it and pulled it up over her waist, crushing and smearing insect bodies against her skin. Gideon reached for his pants and pulled them on with the same effect.

"Help me, Gideon," Alma said, handing him her corset and holding her arms up high over her head. Gideon gently slid the corset down over Alma's arms and chest. She turned around, and Gideon pulled the laces, tying them behind her. He was sad to see the flesh he had bonded with hidden now, but grateful to see Alma covered against the onslaught he could not stop. He pulled his own shirt on over his head and smeared and rolled more guts and blood against his skin for the effort.

He and Alma sat together then in the moist dirt and debris. Alma slid into her blouse and buttoned it, while Gideon pulled his socks over his feet.

"Gideon," Alma said, "I know I was right to do this, to bring you to do it, too."

"It was right, Alma," Gideon answered. "You're a part of my soul now."

"Oh, Gideon! I always was. This was meant to be, you and me."

Gideon leaned over and kissed Alma, ignoring the buzzing mosquito in his ear. "I will not let them destroy this for me," he thought, willing himself free of the distractions imposed by the ever-present insects.

"I love you, Alma."

"I love you, Gideon," Alma answered. "But how do we go about doing what's next?"

"What's next?"

"Why, Gideon Teague! We have to get married."

Gideon wondered. He might be old enough to marry Alma, but how would he take care of her once he did?

"We gotta figure how to live, first," he said.

"Why can't we just go and live on your farm?"

"It's my folks' farm. I don't know that they'd let me live there with a wife."

"They will. Once they see we're going to help them work the farm and make life easier for them. Plus, your father won't live forever. He'll know he needs you to take over that farm someday. Needs you to stand by close, I'd imagine."

Gideon wondered. He hated his father and couldn't see clear to undo that hate, though he wasn't at all sure why he hated his father or why the hate couldn't be undone.

"I'll have to think on it, Alma," he said. "It might be more complicated than we can see right now."

"Gideon, I know you'll make it work," Alma told him. "I dreamed it all. You and me and our children living on that farm while your parents grow old, and someday we care for them. That's why they'll let us live there. We're their futures."

"What about your mom and dad?"

"Gideon, don't you know my momma is dead?"

Gideon wondered. He remembered seeing Alma with her mother and father in church for years, then just Alma and her father. He'd never figured it was because Alma's mother had died.

"Oh, Alma. I'm so sorry. I never knew."

"She died five years ago, Gideon Teague! You didn't hear?"

"Never did. I'm sorry though. She was a nice lady. Gave me an apple once."

"She knew I loved you," Alma spoke wistfully. "I told her when I was little, 'I know the boy I'm going to marry, and that's Gideon Teague'."

"You really did?"

"I did. And my momma told me you were a handsome boy and like to grow up into a handsome man and that your daddy had a farm and you would have it someday, too."

"I never knew."

"Oh, my momma knew. She said you were a fine choice, and she'd see to it as best she could you and me would get married someday. But then she died and joined all my sisters that died, and it was all up to me."

"You had sisters die, too?"

"They was all real little. I'm the only one that grew up. I was the last one Momma had."

"What about your father?"

"Oh, he don't know nothing about this. But he's been telling me I do need to find a man to marry someday soon. I think he had some fellas in mind, but none of them is for me. You're the one for me."

"Will you tell him that?"

"I will now."

Gideon wondered and began pulling his boots on. Alma pulled her shoes on and laced them tight.

"Will you tell your daddy?" she asked.

"That'll take some figuring," Gideon told her. "Me and him don't get on so well. My mother probably thinks I'm too young to get married, but I'll square it for you, I will."

"I trust you, Gideon," Alma smiled.

Gideon stood and helped Alma to her feet. Then Gideon heard something moving among the trees. Reflex made him keen, and he protectively pushed Alma behind him while he pierced the shadows and growth to see what had made the noise. He recognized, glimpsed half hiding behind a tree not too far off from where he and Alma had lain naked, pieces of Henry Scott Douglas.

"What the hell?" Gideon exclaimed.

He pounced instantly across the debris-littered forest floor and on top of Douglas. Douglas had spied on them, sat there peering through Alma's modesty and seeing what only he, Gideon Teague, was allowed to see on this earth.

Gideon threw Douglas to the ground and sat on top of him, ready to punch the wise man's smiling face into permanent misery. Douglas instinctively covered up, but before Gideon's fist was in motion and before Douglas covered his face against the anticipated blows, Gideon saw Douglas was bruised and battered and bleeding already.

"Please don't hit me!" he screamed. "They beat me real bad. They beat me, and I'm just hiding here so they don't kill me! I didn't see anything on purpose!"

Gideon paused and looked down at his whimpering mentor. His reflective awe was completely gone. He thought, "Why did I ever think he was worth listening to?"

He thought back to his first encounter with Douglas, just three months before. Gideon had sat alone on the dead board sidewalk at the edge of town, avoiding his father's company and determined not to lend a hand to help in anything his father might be trying to accomplish. He looked absently to the west, wondering if he had the courage to light out to California and make a name for himself there. As he sat and pondered, he heard someone stepping up behind him: Douglas. Douglas sat down next to him then, holding a leather-bound volume in his hand.

"You look west because you understand the need to seek wisdom," Douglas had told him. That was more than what Gideon had actually been about, but it sounded noble, and so Gideon accepted the mistake and told himself Douglas had been correct: Gideon *did* seek wisdom, and not the sudden riches and power he'd been fantasizing about, with which he would return to Salud and wield effortlessly to demoralize his father.

"Uh huh," Gideon affirmed, though he hadn't the slightest idea who Douglas was and had yet to hear the history of him.

"It is not to be found in a place, young man. Oh, you have to go west, to be certain. But the journey is an inward one. The miles, the trek, and the arrival – these things sit merely as catalyst to the truest undertaking, which is within."

"I know all that," Gideon replied, not knowing anything of the sort.

"You'll need guidance," Douglas said. "Come to my humble press when you have occasion to wonder, and your wandering shall begin there. In time, you'll be ready for the journey and ready to find that piece of truth you'll need to challenge the world."

Gideon took it as a power he could gain with which to challenge his father, though he wasn't certain what he needed to challenge precisely, beyond his father's actual existence, which was an affront to Gideon. Once wisdom came, he suddenly believed, he could unseat the old man, take his power from him, and make it his own.

Douglas had opened the volume then.

"You are like young Prince Hal," he said, "into whom William Shakespeare breathed life eternal. Harry's undertaking is your undertaking. His revelations, your revelations. His wise artifices, your own."

Douglas read, "Then should the warlike Harry like himself assume the port of Mars. And at his heels, leashed in like hounds, do famine, sword and fire crouch for employment."

Douglas closed the volume up suddenly and smiled.

The smile bothered Gideon, but the words sang. Gideon did not know what they meant or what meaning Douglas thought he should find in them. But it was something, and in the something Douglas seemed to suggest Gideon had undiscovered strength, resilience. So Gideon started his vigil in Douglas's Oniate County Press office, listening to uttered bits of prose and poetry, hammered home with Douglas's insistent smile. Out of this, Gideon believed, he would find his true self.

Douglas had similarly gathered Harkens, Williams, Yeats, and Beck to his counter wall, where they listened and believed in the nothings that Douglas propounded on them.

Gideon hadn't realized it, but as he was making love with Alma, his unsettled mind was working to reconcile his image of Douglas with the wise man's weakening sway over Gideon and his friends. As he'd sought out the meaning of his soul in Alma's breasts and eyes, he realized that Douglas's words, until today, had been pleasant and perplexing sounds, but no more. Today though, Douglas had put meaning to his words, and his acolytes suddenly understood him. The new words indeed contained a power that the previous, meaningless words had promised, but failed to unfold – a power to undo the fathers and legacies given to the young men without their choice. And they had beaten Douglas for finally giving what they sought, rejecting that power and its rejection of the only lives they knew.

Gideon's reflection became pause, and eventually Douglas uncovered his face, with a dawning gratitude that the beating he had endured would not continue by Gideon's hand. As Gideon watched Douglas drop his arms away, he sensed Alma moving behind him. Then he saw her run past him through the woods and toward the road. The shame of being caught, of being seen, sent her to flight, and Gideon was left sitting on top of Henry Scott Douglas without a clear idea in his head about what to do next.

"I'd thank you to stop sitting on me like I'm your porch stoop," Douglas said finally, breaking Gideon's silent confusion.

"I oughta beat the hell out of you," Gideon answered, and Douglas winced at the prospect. "What the hell are you doing watching folks out in the woods without them knowing you're there even?"

"Well, I wasn't watching so much as stumbling upon," Douglas explained, trying to recapture some measure of his former dignity. "You see written on my face a brief history of my last few minutes of living. One moment, I was talking to your friends, lending to them some appreciation for the natural, unblemished world that might yet find redemption in young, enlightened minds; the very next moment the ruffians turned on me."

"Well, what the hell are you sayin' to them? Their whole lives is built on a lie?"

"Be that as it may, I rather understandably took to flight and stumbled on the scene here. If my arrival was indelicate, it was because I have been the fleeing victim of an equally indelicate assault," Douglas said.

Gideon sat silent on top of Douglas, wondering what to think or do.

Douglas broke the silence: "I have to ask, just how long do you intend on sitting on me?"

Douglas's question brought Gideon back from his confusion, and he started to let Douglas up. But he thought better of it and repositioned himself firmly on top of the man. "So you was running away. That still don't explain why you was hiding and watchin' Alma and me. You coulda said something, or just walked away. But you stood there watching."

"I wasn't watching," Douglas proclaimed. "Oh, indeed I saw some movements of the flesh, but I couldn't help but see that since you chose to indulge your lust right in the middle of the path I was taking. And don't think I'm not hurt by it. Yes, your companions beat their fists across my face and kicked me about the midsection – that is at least honest critique. You, on the other hand, left the argument entirely untended and elected to engage in a more primitive intercourse instead. A man has some pride, and you've wounded mine, sir!"

Gideon sensed Douglas was trying to amuse, but the amusement didn't lie, and Gideon raised his hand as if to strike him. Douglas flinched. Satisfied, Gideon let him up.

"You don't go saying nothing about what you seen here," Gideon instructed. "You got no business talking about it. That there's my woman, and if you so much as slander her, I'll wallop you."

Gideon truly wanted to defend Alma's honor, but he felt some secret delight in being caught, too, and at the prospect of word getting out about it. He'd like to see the look of admiration on his friends' faces when they spoke to him, like he'd achieved a rare stature in their eyes. But he remembered the violence his friends had felt toward Alma, their resentment. He would do nothing to rekindle the danger she'd been in – so he raised his fist to Douglas again, for emphasis.

"Oh, relax, Gideon," Douglas told him, brushing dirt from his trousers. Neither his cane nor his hat was to be seen. "I've certainly been in the world long enough for your secret tryst to be something less than remarkable, and so I shall make no remark. I don't even know the girl, and I suppose I've known very little about you or your friends. Indeed, to beat a man up because you don't like what he says! Why, if it had been a fair fight, the outcome would have been different, I assure you. I proved myself a pugilist of some notoriety at Harvard."

Suddenly, Douglas's mood changed, and he looked plaintively to Gideon.

"I only tried to share some small portion of what I've learned with you," he said. "I had the privilege of an education, you see. I doubt any of you here will have similar opportunity. So I left comfort and security and headed here, west of home to give some little bit back of what I've had. I don't know how I gave offense."

"You didn't give me no offense," Gideon felt sorrow for the man. "You just didn't give me nothing either."

"You boys were my last hope. My paper doesn't sell, so no one is reading a word of what I have to say. Oh, I continue to labor at it. I have hope, you see, that I'll manage to light a spark somewhere, in some seeking mind. But no one is interested in the taking. I've accepted that now. I'd chalk it up to illiteracy, but I suspect it's because nothing I know has currency here. I'm more the antique Roman in the things I have learned. I could converse with the dead philosophers of Greece or Rome, because I have learned their language and their ideas. But here, in the living world, I've landed my knowledge bankrupt."

Douglas hung his head low. Blood dripped from his nose, and he wiped it with his sleeve. "All that I've learned, all that I've known and seen – these bits of my life have come to ruin here."

"It ain't been ruin," Gideon said, wondering if he could find Alma now. "You made me think some."

"Did I?"

"I expect that you did."

"Maybe we could talk some more. Maybe it is my turn to listen."

"Maybe later. I have business I need to tend to now."

Gideon smashed a mosquito against his ear, and turned back toward the road, leaving the wise man to his misery and seeking Alma's trail.

CHAPTER 13
BREVITY'S END

When Gideon reached the road, he realized that he hadn't the slightest idea where Alma lived. Her father, he knew, was the blacksmith and farrier. Everett Ray Malone had been to Zachariah Teague's farm many times to shoe the farm's horses. More than a few of those times Gideon helped get the horses ready for Malone's visits and stood by for the shoeing. But he'd been sullen with Malone and had handily avoided conversation. He suspected, if he spoke, Malone would sense something guilty in Gideon's words, though Gideon could not quite put his finger on what he might be guilty of. Still, Gideon feared Malone would sense whatever it was, which might have something to do with Malone's daughter, Alma. So he only mumbled to Malone, and Malone seemed settled on that and engaged in no conversation beyond "That'll do her. Tell your father he can settle accounts next time he comes to the shop."

"Yeah, huh," Gideon would answer, ending the exchange of knowledge and leaving Gideon continuingly dumb as to the location of Malone's shop. Nor had Zachariah Teague ever taken his son with him when he went to the blacksmith's, visits from which Zachariah would unfailingly return drunk. Nor in all of his wanderings had Gideon ever stumbled upon the shop to know where it might be, though to Gideon's mind he had explored all that there was to be explored in the viable vicinity of Oniate County.

But Gideon thought now that it was to her father's shop and likely home to which Alma had fled. He looked west toward town, and then eastward, out to what farms he knew lay in that direction. But there was north and south to consider as well, and various intersecting roads which traveled off in those directions. Panic began to set in at the prospect of losing Alma this day.

"Why did you run off, Alma?" he said aloud in frustration. "I was looking out for you. You would have been okay there with me."

A strange sense came over him then that none of it had been real, that he'd imagined Alma and all that they had done together, the only real thing being the innumerable welts raised on his skin from the mosquitoes.

"Why didn't I go after her when she run off?" he castigated himself. "Why'd I waste my time sitting on top of Henry Scott? My duty was to her, and I let her down."

Dejected, he began walking back toward town. Then he decided there was some slight hope, at least, that she had run there. After all, that was where they had met, where Alma had sought him out. He picked up his pace and began to run. By the time he reached town, what started as a determined run had become a loping, lurching sort of movement, all that was left to him after the energy that came from his panic and adrenaline had begun to fail.

Zachariah Teague's was the first soul Gideon encountered back in town, his father loading the last, heavy bags onto the wagon for the trip home.

"Not sure why I even bring you into town with me anymore, Gideon Teague," his father chastised. "You ain't been a bit of good to me for work or making the trip easier since last year. I ought to let you walk home, 'cause you sure ain't earned the ride."

Gideon looked at his father, feeling his hatred of the man flowing back into his bones. His shoulders hunched; his speech died; and he looked to Zachariah Teague as the sole source of his separation from Alma. He wanted to find Alma, was desperate to find her. But he considered her lost for the time being, returned to Everett Ray Malone's rumored forge. Still, he took one hopeful look down the street of tiny Salud City, searching for any sign of his beloved. Unseen, Alma and her bond with him were already memories of a fading afternoon.

One bag remained outside of Nate's store, and Zachariah stepped back from it, leaving it settled on the dead boards where it lay.

"You pick this one up, boy," Gideon's father said. "You load it, you load it up right, and you tie this load, or you don't ride home on this wagon."

Gideon thought perhaps he didn't want to go on the wagon. He thought he wanted to continue his search for Alma. He could inquire, ask, and find someone who knew where Everett Ray Malone's shop was to be found. But he would have to unhunch, find his voice, and extend bits of himself to other folks in the discovery. Then what? March to the mythical forge? Find Alma? Doubtless, there would be an encounter with her father in the finding. What would the man say, do, discovering Gideon's frantic search for his only living daughter, his only family living left to him? Gideon envisioned something falling short of welcome in the encounter and decided it could not happen this way.

He considered walking home then, rather than submit and share the wagon ride with his father. But the farm was miles away, and Gideon had no desire to walk so far. He would find himself walking in the dark at some point, and a part of him still found fear in the open air of night.

So he moved with an angry step to the sack, a hundred pounds at least. But Gideon was filling out with his father's frame, and even the still growing shadow of his father imparted enough strength in him to render the sack quick work. He threw the sack on top of the rest of the load and found the rope hanging from its hook on the side of the wagon. Painfully aware of his father's eye, he tied the load and sullenly climbed into the seat and sat.

Zachariah inspected the load, keeping his disapproving eye on his son. He cinched the rope tighter with a hard pull, shaking the wagon in rebuke of the boy. Then he swung himself up into the seat. To Gideon's surprise, his father remained seated and snapped the reins, riding silently beside him.

As they rode out of town, Gideon's memory sought out any power the day might have given him against his father. He recalled the smatterings of Douglas's philosophy, and worked up how it might be wrought against Zachariah. There wasn't much to work with. He did not have a respect left for Douglas's words, but he thought it imperative that he say something to hurt his father's pride.

"Brevity is it," he said finally, staring ahead at the horse shitting in front of him.

"What?" Zachariah asked, likewise staring at the horse and watching its lifted tail fall after the last of the manure dropped to the ground.

"It's Shakespeare," Gideon shouted, as shouting was required over the noises of the wagon and horses. "He's a writer."

Zachariah was silent. Then he laughed so loud that the wagon sounds faded from hearing.

"Shakespeare's not a writer!" he howled. "Leastwise, he ain't one that's living."

"He is, too!" Gideon protested. It never occurred to him that Douglas's poet wasn't alive and writing words that made no sense right this very moment somewhere east of Oniate County. Yet his father was projecting a knowledge that was another affront to Gideon. "Will he take everything away from me?" he wondered.

"Ain't so," Zachariah spoke, gut laughing so hard that Gideon's hate welled up and forced a tear from his eye.

"He is! I heard it from the *editor*, and he's a writer, too!" There was power, Gideon thought, in the word "editor," a force that could be wielded in this battle with his father.

"If you mean that pipsqueak little city shit that's moved here to print the most ignorant paper that's ever been writ, he's been the poorest of teachers."

"He's a wise man! He went to Harvard!" Gideon shouted, knowing it for the half-lie that it was. Still, he needed something to raise against the old man, and if it took a lie, a lie it would be.

"Well, he ain't got Shakespeare right, if you're sayin' it the way he told it to you."

"That's what Shakespeare wrote! You don't know nothin' about it." Gideon accused, though he now suspected his father might know something after all.

"My boy, it ain't spoke like that," Zachariah's howling let up, and he halted the wagon, turning to look at his son.

"How would you know how it's spoke?" Gideon seethed.

"Brevity is the soul of wit," Zachariah said. "That's how it's spoke."

"How would you know?" Gideon repeated, finding himself bereft of better retort.

"Jesus, boy. Did you think I just dropped out of the womb and set about living my life in ignorance?" Zachariah was serious now, working to reclaim something he'd lost and missed with his son.

Gideon felt betrayed and cornered, defeated. "Well, maybe I forgot some of how it was said."

"Someone forgot. It's from a story about a son who loved his father so much he'd die to avenge his murder."

This was far more than Gideon had known, and the words now seemed set down to increase – not diminish – his father's power over him.

"Brevity is the soul of wit," Zachariah repeated, and he snapped the reins again, putting the wagon back in motion.

Father and son sat in silence again. Half a mile went by. Gideon seethed. Zachariah, as Gideon's memory speculated, was given to thinking about what had been lost with his son and how much he missed it. He stopped the wagon again.

"Son, I don't know what's become of you over the last season or so," Zachariah said. "Well, no, that ain't true. The same thing came over me when I was your age. Mark me though, I wasn't taken to sloth like you been. I got a hate for my father about the same time I figure you got a hate for me. But I knew work had to be done, and I done it. You don't want to lift a hand, though it's how your own life is kept going."

Gideon, certain now that he was losing this battle, conjured up the image of Alma telling him she loved him; he wished he could burn the image into his father's mind, to hurt him with it.

"I thought I took steps so it would be different with you and me," Zachariah continued, looking, searching, trying to find some part of the boy who had adored his father. "I never beat you. I took you with me everywhere, and I tried to put everything I know into you, so you might take the world on wiser than I did. I figured I made a bond with you, and that'd keep you from growing into this time of hate, but I guess it's natural. All boys go through it. Can't be avoided."

Zachariah leaned back in the seat and put his feet up on the board, looking to heaven though speaking to his son.

"Time was when your mother and I tried to have more sons," he said, his words carrying memories back into the present. "Well, it didn't work out, and your mother, she nearly died trying a couple of times. So I gave up the idea of having more of my own to work the farm, and I put all of my energies into you. After a while, I thought it was good that I only had one son, because I thought I loved you more than I could have shared with others. Well, now, that ain't completely true. You did have a brother that lived some, but he died about a year or two before you were born. Broke your momma's heart, and mine, too. I loved that boy, and I buried him with my own hands, and I mourned that loss, and I still mourn it. But you can't expect nothing more out of the world but misery."

Gideon sat upright and looked at his father.

"I didn't have no brother! I never seen a grave or nothing!"

"Didn't mark it. He's gone. Nothing to be done for it, so I buried him and put all I had into you."

"Buried him! What was his name?"

"I don't speak it. He's in my heart, and he's mine alone now."

The two sat quietly. Time passed. Zachariah snapped the reins.

When they neared the farm, Zachariah stopped once more.

"Two things," he said, looking to Gideon. "First, your brother's name was Gabriel, and I loved him. Second, *think* about the things folks try to tell you. Think about this: 'Brevity is the soul of wit' is four words longer than it needs to be, and 'Brevity is it' is one word too long, but a good try at making it mean what it says. So good on you, boy, even if it was an accident. But you could shorten the whole thing up by saying 'Brevity pleases,' and then it would say what it means to say and be what it means to boot."

Zachariah snapped the reins. Gideon seethed.

* * *

Zachariah pulled the wagon into the barn and halted.

"It's been too long now that I give you to work through this time," Zachariah told him. "A farm is no weak-willed mistress to be trifled with."

Gideon started. Were these words of his father filled with *true* knowledge of Gideon and Alma?

"The farm, it keeps us living, but it demands every part of us to keep *it* living, too," Zachariah continued. "There's no give in it at all. It takes, and it takes, and we gotta give, or we die. Do you understand that, boy?"

Gideon stared at his boots in response.

"I give you all the time I can give you," Zachariah said. "I wish now I'd've pushed to have more sons, because you're turning into a powerful disappointment. While you're off sulking and nurturing your hate, I'm working this land pretty much single-handed, and when I ain't I'm payin' hands and other men's boys to come and help in your stead. Money and livelihood taken from me to give you your time to sulk. It ain't right, and it can't be that way no more. Now I done willing sacrifice to you over the years, 'cause I wanted what was best for your life and your living. You remember I taught you to read, neglecting my own work so you could know some things about the world. I put you in school when I could have used you on the land, so as you could learn arithmetic and the world some, to hold you in good stead when it was your turn to own the land. And you were lucky that you had no brothers to help me while you sat by the table, studying your *Murray's Grammar* and learning figures, 'cause that meant that this land would be yours someday, without you having to share it with brothers and their eventual families. You had it all, boy, and I give it to you, and I give it to you willing. How many of your friends are by themselves to the land they live on? None that I know of. All have brothers who will have to share the land. And ain't too many of them got family that lets them go to school to learn. What I got for it is your hate and sloth, and you won't lift a hand unless I force you to it."

Gideon turned and glared at his father. Then he conjured up more of what Douglas had said that day, though he figured he didn't believe a word of it.

"A farm ain't nothing but a slave to people," Gideon said, looking to drive the belief into his father that he, Gideon, believed the nonsense he was repeating. It was dangerous nonsense, he considered, and it had gotten Douglas beaten for its utterance. Yet it was the best hope Gideon had of driving hard hurt into his father's heart. "This farm is a slave to you. Nature don't make farms, but farmers come along and tear down its trees and destroy the land, so there's no true nature for it!"

Gideon drove on, telling a lie that smacked of nobility, "That's why you don't find me working like your slave, 'cause I ain't gonna be a part of destroying what nature's give."

Gideon felt satisfied. The anger had poured from him with those words, and he saw an expression creeping over his father's face that intensified that satisfaction. Still, he thought of Alma and her dream for them and the farm, and he wondered if he had just failed her a second time in a single day.

Zachariah sighed and hopped off the wagon.

"You go inside now and get you something to eat," Zachariah told him. "When you're done, you come here to the barn, and you get on Sadie and ride her out to meet me at the top of the south field, under the old oak. I'll be waiting for you. Don't think to ignore me, either. You don't come, and I'll come get you. We got business to discuss."

Zachariah began untying the wagon's load, and Gideon dropped down from his seat. He thought briefly that it might be a good idea to help his father, for Alma's sake. But he decided against it. "Let the old man struggle," he thought, and he marched off to the house.

* * *

Gideon considered defying his father but decided Zachariah might just come after him like he said. Gideon had seen something more than hurt in his father's eye that made him believe he wouldn't like the outcome. So he saddled Sadie and rode out to the field. The sun was starting to set, and Gideon kept a sharp eye to the ground, looking for holes that might lame Sadie if she stepped wrong. Reluctantly, he rode up the hill, where his father sat waiting under an ancient oak tree, on his favorite riding horse, Old Gus.

Gideon rode up beside his father and stopped. Zachariah faced the setting sun and looked to it. Then he pulled Old Gus around to face the land and crops along the rolling hills of his farm.

"Did you eat?" he asked his son.

"I did. Momma made me a good meal," he answered, wishing his father to know his mother cared about him, even if his father did not.

"You got a full belly then?"

"I do."

"Good. Now you listen to what I'm going to say. That nature you spoke on earlier is a powerful life force, but it ain't got no more intelligence to it than you find in a rock, Gids. Left alone, it would grow bramble and bush, grass and trees, and that's true enough. It would hatch all the living creatures to kill and be killed to run through its growth and live their short lives. But there wouldn't be no people at all sustained in all of that, or leastwise not so many as you know.

"Think of ten people you love the most in this world – and don't worry, 'cause I ain't expecting you to count me among them. Now you think about most of them never having come into this world at all. That's your nature, unbridled. Alone, it won't sustain a society of man. If you doubt it, think on that meal you just had and where it come from. Corn? From this farm. Bread? From this farm. Meat? From this farm. Butter? Where'd that butter come from Gids?"

"This farm."

"But you see nature as being something holier than your ability to eat and live. Nature is all power. It's got no brains. But a man comes along, and he sees nature's great power, 'cause he does have a brain – he is the thinking part of this earth. He watches nature and learns from it. He's driven to put his intelligence to it, so it can be more than the stupid beast that it is. He makes his farm, like mine, laid out as far as your eyes can see right now. A man's farm feeds his family. His farm makes human life possible. Without the farms, no one eats.

"You ain't ever gone too long without a meal, and you have a full belly right now. But the fullness in your belly comes from this farm, and from my labor. You and I both know your labor's been held back from it. But my labor and this land make everything possible in your life. Even idiot bastards like your great teacher in town is made possible by my farm and others. Without we took hold of the land and bent it to our intelligence, that dumb sonofabitch wouldn't have the time to be thinking up his stupidities to corrupt the youth with. You take all industry, all commerce in the world. All culture. Ain't none of it possible without I took this farm and bent it to my will. Shakespeare would never've wrote without he had a full belly and needed to keep that belly full with the sustenance that comes from the farm. All of his words was labor took to to get him a piece of the farm. He wrote of noblemen taking to wars, and for what? To conquer lands to put people and farms on."

Zachariah paused for a moment, lost in thought.

"Well, as I see it, this farm is more noble than all those worldly exploits Shakespeare wrote about, because we got it without killing no one for it, without making widows and orphans for it, and without putting slaves on it to do the honest labor meant for our own hands. They done that in the south, but not here. I never took from a man what he wasn't willing to give and to get something for it in return. Just you look to the land here," Zachariah gestured with his hand as Douglas had gestured with his cane. "Do you not see that as the most beautiful spectacle on this earth?"

Gideon was silent, embarrassed that he had ever repeated the asinine words of Henry Scott Douglas.

"Nature is a beautiful thing once given over to man's intelligence. Combined with a man's mind, nature becomes a powerful force for life. That lends it more beauty and more meaning than anything I can think of – because I think human beings may be beat from the start in this life, but their will to live despite a killing nature all around them is maybe even more precious than their worship of the God that set it all into motion."

Zachariah pulled back on the reins, backing Old Gus up against the oak tree.

"Buried under this tree is your brother Gabriel," he said. "I put him in the earth with my own two hands right here, because he used to ride to this spot to have lunch with me. He would ride up from the house on Old Gus here, when Old Gus was his horse and just Gus. He'd bring the lunch your momma had made for us with him, too. As the Good Lord sits in Heaven, he was a joy to my heart. He would look at the land and say he wanted to grow up strong like me and work it like I did. He told me this was his favorite place in the whole world, and that made it my favorite place in the world, on account of him.

"So when the sickness took him, a sickness born from nature, I brought his coffin and the preacher out here. Your momma, she couldn't bear to see him buried, so it was just me and the preacher. The preacher said the words, and I give him a few dollars for the trouble. The preacher rode off, and I began to dig. But in my grief, I hadn't thought nature through, and I got down not far at all before this old oak raised its hand against me and my will. Roots tangled everywhere just below the ground, and I couldn't dig the hole I needed to put Gabriel's coffin in the earth. So I dug around and under the roots, deep as I could. Then I took your brother from his coffin, and I turned and twisted his little body through the roots and deep under them. And I twisted my own body down to give one last kiss upon his dead flesh. Then I put the dirt back in over him. I like to think he's a part of this old oak now, because sure enough, it took sustenance from him. Nature given to its own devours us, but I believe Gabriel devoured some of it back and became a living part of this tree.

"He was only ten when the sickness came, but that's ten years of precious life that I thank mighty God for giving me. That ten years was made possible by this farm. Without my hand upon the land, that precious little boy would never have had ten years of living and being my joy and taking joy in me, like I know he done, like you done, too, once. Maybe I was spared seeing the same hate grow in his eye that's grown in yours, but I'd take that hate and a thousand times more for one more minute with my boy."

Zachariah was silent then, leaning from the saddle to place his hand on the oak's trunk. He bowed his head and for the second time in his life, Gideon saw tears in his father's eyes. For the first time in a long time, Gideon wished to reach out to touch his father, and he felt ashamed. Then Zachariah took his hand from the tree and sat upright, wiping the tears angrily from his face. Gideon's impulse to reach after his father remained, but the man seemed untouchable again.

"That's what living gives you. Defeat. The only answer for it is to take life as hard and true as you can, knowing all is lost but fighting on anyway.

"My own father, he brought me here like I've brought you. He was a good man, and he taught me to read when I was little and there wasn't any school here. He said he wanted me strong and able, and that meant strong of mind as well as body. He had but two books in the house: the Bible and a book with plays by your Shakespeare. He told me the Bible wasn't to be trifled with, so he taught me to read from the Shakespeare. Well, I didn't understand none of it when I could finally read it, and my father said that was fine. 'You read something that tells you something,' he told me, 'and all you are is told. You read something that you don't understand what it says, and that makes you think.' Thinking, he told me, was the finest thing a man could do with his life. Maybe I should have taught you to read out of Shakespeare, too, but I buried your granddad with that book, so you learned from the Bible. Anyway, that learning was given me when I was little. Then time went on. I grew, and I looked to my father with hate, the way you look at me. Oh, I worked the farm, because my head wasn't full of whatever ideas you've been told instead of thought on. But I still put all of my hate upon him, and to this day, I can't say I know why other than nature seems to make it that way.

"Well, he was a man of thought, so he brought me here. He showed me all the farm and told me it was a great thing to have and to have been given. But there was my hate, and he told me it was a thing he could not abide. He told me I had to go out into the world and see more than this farm to learn what was worth my hate and what wasn't. So he threw a purse to me filled with about five dollars, as I recall. He said, 'You take that with you son, and you leave this farm. I don't want you here, and I won't take you here until you got an understanding of the world.' He sent me on my way then, told me he'd welcome me back when I had enough living to know what's what. But send me away he did. I left Salud and saw parts of this country. I worked lead mines in Illinois, slaughterhouses, and as a hand on other folks' farms. I lived in San Francisco and worked the wharfs, and for a time I even traveled with a band of actors and performed Shakespeare on the stage. None of it was what my own father had to give me here, and I lost my hate and understood something about the man that I grew to admire. So I come back, and I worked the farm with him until he died a couple of years after. We was reconciled by then, and I loved my father and wept when he died."

Tears started in Zachariah's eyes again.

"Well, now," he said. "Time's come for you to go."

Zachariah fumbled for a leather purse and threw it to Gideon. Gideon missed, and it fell to the ground.

"When you pick that up," Zachariah continued, "you'll find thirty dollars there. You look behind this tree, and you'll find enough of your things to carry with you. But it's time for you to go from my farm. You take Sadie with you. She's yours to keep now. Look that you don't have to sell her to fill your belly again."

Gideon sat stunned, uncomprehending.

"You're putting me out?" he asked.

"I am putting you out," Zachariah answered. "You're sixteen now. If you come back when you're nineteen, and you got no more hate for me, you're welcome back. But not a day before then. If you don't come back, I'll make other arrangements for who'll own my farm once I'm gone."

"Does Momma know of this?"

"Not hers to say. It's my farm, and she's living on it same as you – by my graces."

"I'll go tell her! She won't have it!"

"You can go tell her, but day forth from this moment, and I'll beat you if you set foot here, so as you want to leave and never come back."

Gideon's hate was overcome with fear.

"It's getting dark! You can't put me out in the dark."

"Darkness is a part of living. You go out into the world on nature's terms, not your own. 'Sides, daylight comes soon enough."

Zachariah kicked Old Gus then and began riding down the hill, back to the house. Gideon watched his father's form fade into the darkening field, and he wished death upon the old man. Then he saw Old Gus stumble and Zachariah pitch forward, over the horse's head.

Old Gus got up and fell. The horse made a scream Gideon had never heard from a horse before. He watched paralyzed in amazement as the animal tried to get to its feet again. Old Gus got part way up, but rolled and tumbled, its haunches landing on Zachariah's legs. Zachariah lay still, despite the crushing weight. Then the horse rolled off of Zachariah in another effort to stand, falling away from Zachariah's motionless body.

Gideon was a tumult of panic, surprise, and hate. But something deeper than his hate stirred, and he kicked Sadie and rode her hard after his father.

Gideon was certain Old Gus's front leg was broken. The horse lay on its side, its eyes wild with fear, holding the broken leg out in front of it. The horse screamed again and again, trying to rise, tearing its broken leg worse with every effort. Foam flew from the horse's mouth and nose. The animal looked like it was locked in battle against an unseen foe.

Gideon saw a round blackness on the ground in front of him. He steered Sadie clear of it. Some animal had dug its hole there, Gideon realized, understanding that the hole had trapped Old Gus's leg, jolting the horse to a bone-snapping stop. In the fall, his father had tumbled onto his back. Gideon could see the amber glow of the fading sun reflected in the old man's searching eyes. Gideon drew Sadie to a stop beside his father and hopped to the ground, kneeling beside him.

Zachariah tried to speak, but the sounds were shallow and muted by Old Gus's panicked flailing and screams. Over the sounds of the horse, Gideon thought he heard his father say "neck" and "breathe." Foam and dust flew up from Old Gus and drifted and spattered over Gideon and Zachariah.

Gideon's panic returned. He had no idea what to do about the horse or his father.

"What can I do?" he shouted at Zachariah, desperate for the old man's knowledge.

Zachariah made a noise that sounded like it might have been a laugh. He turned his eyes toward his kneeling son. Gideon thought he saw something said in that final, living gaze, but couldn't decide what it was. Then Zachariah's lips moved to speak again. Gideon dropped his ear down close to his father's lips, but he could not make out the words over the sound of Old Gus.

Gideon's panic broke again, and he scooped his father up with strength he didn't know he had. He saw Zachariah's head flop backward as he lifted and slung his father over Sadie's saddle. Gideon knelt, putting his face next to his father's.

"I'll get you help," he told him, but he saw Zachariah's breathing had stopped entirely. In the fading light, Gideon saw nothing more than death reflected in his father's eyes.

CHAPTER 14
THE BLACKSMITH

Gideon thought of his father's tears when he spoke of his buried son, Gabriel. Remembering those tears tore down Gideon's hate, and he wished he had reached out to touch his father when the elder Teague had reached out to touch the oak. With that one gesture, Gideon's whole world might have changed. But he withheld his touch, and his father had straightened, resolved, and died.

Now Gideon stood in his Sunday best, his father's coffin laid out in the parlor, in the house Zachariah had built with his own hands for the growing family he had envisioned but never had, except for Gabriel. Except for Gideon.

Gideon stood upright. He held his shoulders high and determined he would find his voice and make it one to make his father proud, to undo the hurt he had shot into his father's heart. His mother sat in the corner, the women from the farms and town huddled around her. The smell of baked goods permeated the house, and more food than they could ever eat before spoiling piled up on every table and surface that had room for another pot or pie. Biscuits stacked so high, they tumbled from the tables and onto the floor. Busy wives picked up the biscuits, brushed them off, and put them back on the pile. Women were in the kitchen, sweeping and cleaning, and firing up the stove to cook more food brought raw to the house. Faintly,

Gideon heard one of the women chastising another for bringing an unplucked chicken.

"People got grieving to do, and you want they have to pull feathers out of a bird all day long? Mildred, sometimes I don't know what."

"Don't take all day pulling feathers from a bird, Alice. Bird's fresh. You boil the water, and I'll pull the feathers. I swear, sometimes you make such a fuss."

Crowded among the food offerings, candles burned on every table and shelf, mingling the scents of candle, food, and death.

The men stood about, each having walked in single file to shake Gideon's hand and look at Zachariah's body before milling and telling tales about the dead man. Gideon shook every hand, gripping hard and looking into the eyes of every well-wisher.

"Your father was a great man," some told him. "I sure am sorry for your loss. Martha and me will pray for you."

Some simply said, "Gideon." Others nodded.

"Thank you," Gideon answered every sentiment, with a strength and resolve that were a struggle for him. "It means a lot to us, you being here."

Yet Gideon knew almost none of the mourners he said this to.

"I will hold my father in good stead," he thought. "I will do this for him and make him proud."

Gideon stood his vigil for more than two hours before Everett Ray Malone joined the line. Alma stood at his side. Gideon continued shaking hands, meeting every visitor with the resolve he had dedicated to his father's memory. But he could sense Alma's searching eyes on him, and he was acutely aware of her and her father. He started to be afraid. It had only been two days since he and Alma had made love in the woods, and a creeping certainty grew upon him that everyone who had come to pay final respects would sense the sin they had committed as soon as their paths joined again in the parlor.

In the short time since his father had been pitched head first from Old Gus, Gideon had reflected that Alma hadn't been the only sin upon his head. Knowledge that he had wished his father's death at nearly the same instant the forces of momentum coalesced to snap Zachariah's neck settled like quicksilver in Gideon's gut. It hadn't been the first time he wished Zachariah dead either, and for the life of him, he couldn't understand precisely why. Still, he sensed that a spiritual punishment was upon him, seeing his curse turned to power, just long enough to give life to his wish of death.

Seeing his father's dead eyes reflected in the fading light of day, Gideon understood that there was no power that he had, no course of action he could take, no lifetime of labor that could undo all that had happened in less than two minute's time. Suddenly, he stood alone, with his father's body slung over Sadie's back. Old Gus was quieting down, though not from calm. Instead, the horse's broken limb had asserted its power over him, breaking Old Gus's will. For an instant, Gideon thought to throw his hate upon the injured horse, a new depository for that which he had heaped upon his father. But regret took hold, and his first remembrance of his now dead father was of the old man's love of Gabriel and his tender taking of that lost brother's horse. Old Gus was something Zachariah had taken to cherish his memory of a dead son. So Gideon's hate turned inward, and he saw himself as the only source of evil that had befallen his father.

Slowly, gingerly, so as not to jostle Zachariah, he began to lead Sadie back to the barn. He wondered how it would be that he would tell his mother that her husband, with long years of living left ahead, had come to have those years cut short.

As he left the fields and drew nearer the barn, Gideon could see the kerosene lamps lighted in the house. Doubtlessly, his mother waited for the return of her husband and son. Gideon knew her only expectation could be of the cold indifference Gideon would present, and her husband's irritation.

"What have I made of my life?" he lamented.

Inside the barn, Gideon lifted Zachariah from the saddle and placed him in the hay. He knew then what Zachariah would tell him to do next, and his repentance demanded that he follow in kind. He led Sadie to the house and tied her to the porch. He went inside.

"Where's your father?" his mother asked, standing sentry in the parlor. She waited at times like this, when she sensed the friction between Zachariah and Gideon was at a head.

"Momma," Gideon started, and then he couldn't speak. His voiced choked and tears began to fall.

"Gideon! What's happened to your father?"

Gideon saw panic rising in his mother's face. She stood and demanded, "Gideon! Tell me!"

Gideon fought for strength, fought to do as his father would have asked.

"Momma," he cried. "Momma, I need you to stay here and wait for me. Please."

"Gideon!"

Gideon went to his father's gun cabinet then and took a rifle from the rack.

"Gideon!"

"Momma, there's something I have to do."

Gideon's mother, Ellen, moved quickly across the room and took hold of the rifle, trying to wrestle it from him.

"Gideon," Ellen shouted, "you are not going to shoot him!"

Gideon was confused. Then he realized his mother's certainty. She thought he intended to murder his father.

"Dear God!" he thought. "What have I become that this is what she thinks?"

"Momma," he said. "Momma, Daddy's dead."

"Gideon, give me the gun!"

"Momma, do you hear me? Daddy's dead! I'm not going to shoot him. Old Gus threw him, and Daddy's dead. I'm going to shoot Old Gus, 'cause his leg's broke."

Ellen let go of the rifle and fell to the dead board floor.

"Did you fight?" she asked, slowly taking in the words that said her husband was dead.

"No, Momma," Gideon said. "I mean, yes, we did fight. He was putting me out, okay? But he rode off, and Old Gus broke his leg in a hole, and Daddy fell. My God, Momma, do you think it of me? Do you think I could kill Daddy?"

Ellen Teague began to sob.

"Momma, I know right now that Father would tell me to put Old Gus from his misery. I'm going to shoot Old Gus, not Daddy! Oh, Momma, I'm so sorry!"

It was too much for Gideon. His father was dead, and his mother thought him a killer.

"Where is he, Gideon? Where is your father?"

"Momma, I'll bring you to him when I get back," Gideon said, and he was filled with a sudden rage. "You can check the body for bullet holes, too, and if you see a one, you can take this rifle right here and shoot me dead!"

Gideon stepped out into the night then and mounted Sadie, riding slowly, carefully back out to the south field where Old Gus lay suffering.

After Old Gus was dead, Gideon rode Sadie back to the barn. His mother had found Zachariah's body there in the hay, and she lay next to him, wailing out an angry, indignant, disbelieving "Nooooo!!!!!" She wailed and sobbed and ran her hand desperately through Zachariah's hair, as if the vigorous motion could bring her husband back to consciousness.

For all of Gideon's confusion, he took to his heart now his father's strength and will. He left his mother to her moments with Zachariah and took Sadie's saddle off, hanging it on its hook. Then he put the horse in her stall and grabbed an armful of hay, which he dropped into Sadie's bucket. He returned to the hay, working around his living mother and dead father, taking more armfuls to feed the horses. It was the first time he had fed the horses in over a year, he having left the task to his father's hand. Now his father lay dead, yet the horses still needed to eat.

And drink.

He went outside to the pump and began pumping fresh water into the trough. Emotion stripped him then of whatever other knowledge he had of what work needed to be done, and he returned to the hay to sit beside his mother. His task now, Zachariah would have told him, was to tend to his mother – and to Zachariah.

Instead, he confessed.

"Father had me come out to the old oak," he said, though Ellen seemed not to hear. Her hands were searching Zachariah's body for injury. It escaped Gideon that she was searching for signs that Gideon had killed him.

"We fought some coming in from town, but Father spent some time telling me things."

Gideon looked to the light of the lamp his mother had brought to the barn dancing on the boarded walls, throwing shadows about the hooks and tools and harnesses that hung there.

"Father told me I was a disappointment to him. He told me that you and him tried to have more sons, but that you almost died from it. Then he told me to eat and meet him at the old oak. After you fed me, I took Sadie out there, and Father told me about Gabriel."

Ellen stiffened.

"He told me he buried Gabriel in the roots of that old oak and that Old Gus was Gabriel's horse. He said he loved Gabriel and missed him terrible. But he said it was time to put me out. He said as I'm sitting here that his own father had put him out, too, and that he thought it was the only way I'd learn to think and understand the farm."

Ellen sat with her back to Gideon. She raised her fist then and struck Zachariah's chest. She struck him again, and Gideon reached out to stop her.

"Momma, don't! He's to rest in peace now!"

Ellen fought and struck Gideon with her free hand. Gideon felt some relief in the blow.

"Momma, Daddy rode on and Old Gus fell, and Daddy fell and broke his neck. Now that's the truth! But I wished it. I wished Daddy dead and then it happened."

Ellen's eyes widened upon the hearing.

"Why, you two stupid sons of bitches!" she cried.

"Momma, I'm sorry."

Ellen fell to silence. Her tears stopped. Gideon felt the fight go out of her hand. She stood and brushed the hay from her dress. Then she walked silently from the barn, and Gideon sat next to his father's body, alone in the flickering lamp light. After a time, he got up and took the lamp to the back of the barn where his father stored boards for repairing the outbuildings. He selected the best, truest of the boards and gathered them next to Zachariah's body. Then he gathered the tools he would need and built the first of the coffins he would have to build for those he loved.

* * *

Everett Ray Malone's hand reached out for Gideon's. The blacksmith's hand didn't shake Gideon's, however. Instead, Malone gripped tight and pulled Gideon closer to him. The gesture forced an unsettling intimacy, though there was measure of comfort in it, too. Alma stepped up beside her father and put her hand on Gideon's elbow. Father and daughter stood in front of him then, a unified, comforting presence. Each searched Gideon's eyes for signs of what he was feeling. He tried to hide, tried to stand strong, but tears began to fall.

"Alma, you go see to Ellen," Everett Ray told his daughter. Reluctantly, she let go of Gideon's elbow and joined the women surrounding Gideon's mother.

"Gideon," Everett Ray insisted. "Let's walk."

Everett Ray put his arm around Gideon's shoulder and led him from the house. They passed a dozen or so mourners on the porch, the men tipping their hats and saying, "Sorry for your loss" and the women wringing their hands and setting their faces in expressions that said they commiserated with Gideon's pain.

Malone strode purposefully out past the barn and on into the field, guiding Gideon along the way.

"Let's just walk for a bit," he said. "I think maybe you needed to get out of there for a little while, and I have some things I need to talk to you about."

Gideon's guilt returned. Were they to talk about Alma and what had happened between them? Had Alma confessed her love for Gideon to her father? Was there to be retribution now, here, in this time of mourning?

"Gideon," Everett Ray said. "Your father was my good friend, so I guess I know a few things about him that you're likely not to know. I guess I know some things, too, about his thoughts on you. You'll need to hear those things."

Gideon felt some relief that this did not appear to be about Alma. He could not figure how he would deal with that now.

"I won't mince words with you, boy," Everett Ray said. "You were a chore to your father's thoughts, and I expect you know that."

Gideon tried to stop, but Everett Ray forced his step forward. "No, now, listen. You're gonna hear it. You have to hear it."

As Malone forced him ahead, Gideon realized that Everett Ray was a smaller man than he was, though not a small man compared to others. Gideon understood in that moment, too, that he was stronger than Malone, and if he wanted, he could stop Malone dead in his tracks, and there would be no forcing Gideon to go where he did not go willing.

"I am my father's son," he thought. "I am as large and strong as he was now."

But Gideon didn't stop. Everett Ray had knowledge that Gideon needed, light by which Gideon could explore his darkened soul. He sensed, too, that Everett Ray meant him a kindness, even if it was to be hard wrought along the way.

"None of us gets too far along in this world without we learn something of death," Everett Ray said. "Every one of those folks in your house, they've each of them lost a mother or father, maybe both. Some've lost a child or more, too. Lord knows, I've had more than enough of dying in my life. Three young girls gone to the grave, and my lovely wife gone, too, living the joys of Heaven with our girls. But knowing that Heaven's beyond don't take the hurt out of it one bit, and I don't expect there's anything gonna take the hurt away from you either."

Gideon wondered. His hatred for his father had seemed beyond reckoning, though it had begun to soften when he witnessed Zachariah's sorrow for the lost Gabriel. Then Zachariah had stated his purpose, his intention to put Gideon out alone into the world, into the darkness. And Gideon's heart hardened again. Followed by the confusion of Zachariah's death, Gideon felt the hypocrite finding the too late desire to please, to aid and comfort the dead. "If hate is what I felt in life," he wondered, "can it be changed in death?"

He suddenly blurted out the truth to Everett Ray: "I don't know what I feel, Mr. Malone."

Malone stopped, pulling Gideon to a stop with him.

"None of us knows the true measure of our heart," Everett Ray told him. "Maybe you feel things that don't have any business being felt side-by-side. These things take time to sort through, Gideon."

"He was putting me out," Gideon offered, some defiance, some hate returning to him, finding voice. "He told me I was a disappointment to him, and he was putting me out! I think he wished I wasn't even born."

Gideon looked to Malone, expecting the man to confirm Gideon's belief. He understood that he needed the confirmation to fall like an ax hitting him square in the skull. Instead, Everett Ray laughed.

"It ain't funny!" Gideon was outraged. He expected Malone to dish out some words of hurt, hurt Gideon needed to feel. What he got was Everett Ray's laughter and a hard slap on the back.

"Why, it ain't nothing more than a family tradition for you Teagues!"

Gideon knew not what.

"Listen boy," Malone's rough and scarred hand found the back of Gideon's neck and squeezed gently, far more gently than could be expected from the forge-hardened flesh. "No, I can't call you a boy no more. You're a man now, and that's what this talk we're having here is about. Forgive me that – I still see you sometimes as a child, 'cause I've seen you as that all the time I've known you."

Gideon heard the words but thought it odd that Everett Ray believed he had known Gideon at all. What world did Malone live in that made him think there was a long-standing bond between them? Gideon felt a flash of resentment that this man could hold such a notion, and that he seemed to know more about Teagues than he, Gideon, had himself ever known.

"If you mean my dad's father put him out, he told me that before he died," Gideon said, though his resentment and outrage were muted by the fact of a grown man's acknowledgement that he was not a child. He understood there was something in those words that he had needed for a long while now, something he'd needed from Zachariah.

"Your granddad put more than your father out," Everett Ray said. "He put your uncles out, too – every last one of them."

Uncles? Gideon hadn't known any uncles. He had no knowledge that any existed. What secrets did Malone possess of Gideon's life?

"I didn't have no uncles," he insisted.

"Oh, not that you knew," Everett Ray's mirth fell back into somberness. "Your father was the youngest of six boys, and quite a bit younger than the rest of them. There was William, the oldest, Thomas next, then it was Gabriel, your uncle Gabriel and Michael, the twins. You must have seen their names in your family Bible."

Gideon had seen the names, carefully penned in ink on the first page of the book, but he'd considered them unknown ancestors, farther removed than uncles could be. So he had given the names little thought, and the knowledge to be gleaned from the "Born" and "Died" dates beside the names had escaped him.

"Last, before your father, was Gideon, who you was named after," Everett Ray concluded. Gideon was overwhelmed. He was named after an uncle? A man he didn't know? Had that imparted something to him? Had it made the way his father saw him?

"If I had uncles, how come I never met them?"

"Death took them, every one," Everett Ray said. "Let me tell you the tale about your family tradition.

"Your grandfather, he had a reputation for being aloof from most of the folks around here. Stuck pretty much to his self. Oh, he come to church regular, and he did all the business that needed doing in town, but to engage the man in conversation was to talk to someone who didn't much respect the fact that you might have something to say. If he spit when you spoke, you got more out of him than most folks did.

"Now, before you get to thinking I knew him, I didn't. I saw him here and there, and I spent some time on your farm here when I was a boy, when there was just the old house. But he never said more than a word or two to me, and that was only to tell me to get out of his way."

Everett Ray laughed, "Hell, I wasn't even worth his spit, so I didn't get that out of him neither. I ate at your family's table in the old house more than a few times, but he'd say grace and then every word that came out of his mouth was reserved for your uncles. He'd tell them where they'd done wrong during the day and how they had to do things different the next. He'd tell them how their thinking was wrong and how they were a disappointment to him and how he would take the strap to them if they didn't straighten out.

"I remember one time, I was at your granddad's table, and without a word of warning, he reached across that table and dragged William over the top of it, knocking food all over and throwing William to the floor. He put a whooping on that uncle of yours right then and there, and for nothing more than that he didn't like the way your uncle looked at him. Leastwise, that's what your father told me the reason was. But like I said, I didn't know him, and like I said, he didn't seem to know I was even there. Your father told me it was like that for him much of the time, too, like his father knew his brothers were all there, but that your father was just in the way somehow. Saved him a few beatings, he thought.

"Of course, that makes it sound bad about your granddad, but your father told me he was a good man, that he was doing his best to raise his boys up to know what's what. He taught them like a schoolmaster and guided them to everything they'd need to know to live in the world as the masters to what was around them instead of helpless to it.

"Well, as you might imagine, though, those uncles of yours didn't always take to the lessons, accompanied by beatings, as they were. So it was never long before they found it in their hearts to be disobedient.

"Now your granddad, he was a remarkably small man, but he somehow got himself a crop of boys who were giants. Bigger than you, Gideon, and you're sprouting up to be a pretty big fellow yourself. But your granddad kept them all in line and put a fear into them that he was to be reckoned with. In time though, each of them grew up to hate him for his presence over them. They couldn't make a move without he put what he thought was the proper correction to them.

"William was the first, and he was the first one put out. The way your father told it to me, your granddad took William out to that old oak you were at when your father got killed. And right there, your granddad threw a sack of coin to William and told him to leave out of here until he could come back with a grown up mind and understanding of the way things were.

"So William went. Then Thomas, too. And when William came back, the twins was put out for their journey away from home. Then Thomas came back, and it was Gideon's turn to go. The twins, they come home, too, but Gideon, he never did come back. Your granddad got a letter one day from a woman who said Gideon had married her and had died of some sickness or other. Your granddad buried that letter, your father told me, by the door to the old house, so he would think of Gideon whenever he come home and whenever he left it to start his day.

"After word came of Gideon's death, your granddad started seeing Zachariah and putting his worth into him. Your uncles, 'cept for Gideon, all lived in the old house with your granddad after they came back, and they worked the farm, each taking his share as the old man said they'd earned and deserved. Well, then it was your father's turn. He journeyed out to the old oak tree by your granddad's command, and he was put out, too.

"Now let me tell you, that old man put a beating on your father more than once when he thought he needed it, and your father had his own cause to be disobedient. But that sort of thing wasn't tolerated around here, and he was sent off to learn his way about the world, like his brothers before him."

Malone's words struck Gideon's heart. Family and history unknown to him were being revealed, had been known by this man who shoed his horses and who had known his father better than he, Gideon, ever could have. Gideon wondered at his father's secrets, resented that they had not been revealed to him until now.

"Then how come my uncles aren't still living?" he asked. "How come they aren't still working the farm? Why weren't they working it with my father?"

"Well, now, Gideon," Everett Ray said, "this country came to tumultuous times. I expect you learned this in school. When Mr. Lincoln became president, there was that great war I'm sure you heard about. The South and old Jefferson Davis decided it was to be a war with the Union, and a war it was.

"I fought in that war – joined up to fight for Union. Your uncles, except for Gideon, they got into it right from the start, leaving your granddad here on his own. Your uncles Gabriel and Michael, the twins, they told me he took it hard when they left. Said he had tears in his eyes and hugged them for what they thought was the first time in their lives. They took comfort in that, and it put a fight in them that they needed to try to live to see home again."

"You mean they was fighting not to get shot?"

"No. In the end, they was fighting not to let starvation or sickness take them," Everett Ray said. He paused for a long time then, tears filling his eyes. Gideon didn't understand what was happening.

"Gideon," he said at last, "I didn't fight in that war too long, but I saw men cut down right before my eyes, living the prime of their lives one minute and taken apart by hot lead the next. Well, the boys I was with, we got beat. We got beat and those of us that didn't get killed straight away got captured. We was boxed up on railcars and shipped off to Georgia, to a place called Andersonville.

"I don't have too much to say about that place but that it was hell on earth. We was prisoners, and the Rebels starved the life out of us. Most didn't die from starvation though, but from dysentery. Imagine falling down the hole in your outhouse – that was Andersonville.

"Well, your uncles Gabriel and Michael fought through most of that war, but they finally got beat and ended up in Andersonville, like me. They found me there, and I expect that's why I'm alive today. They fought some for me because I was your father's friend. They took to me like I was a part of the family, and they got me food when they could and give it to me instead of taking it for themselves sometimes. I'm ashamed to say I took it, too, though I knew they needed it as much as I did and that they'd fought for it, and I didn't. I hope you never know what men that's even on the same side of a war will do to one another, what men become when they're desperate enough. It's more than I ever wanted to see of this world. I have nightmares about it to this day.

"In any event, your uncles was built like bulls. They kept us alive for a long while because of that, but Andersonville was such that it cut down even them, until they was no more than skeletons wrapped up in skin.

"Gabriel died first, and Michael and I held him and give him what water we could scrape from the tent in the morning while he lay there weak and ready for his maker. Then he died, and the guards took him out like a heap of garbage. They didn't have no trouble carrying him, but Michael and me tried to fight them, to keep them from taking him. I don't know why. What would we have done with his rotting corpse? I don't know, but we didn't want that he would be thrown into a pile of corpses, down into the red mud like a lost soul thrown right into hell.

"We didn't have much fight in us though, though we give it all that we had to give. It was a shooting offense, too. We were as like to be killed for it as not. Well, we was pushed aside and laughed at instead, and they took Gabriel from us. It all happened again with Michael, only I was the only one holding him and fighting when they took his corpse away, too. That I had enough left in me to live to see today is because of them, and I'm shamed for it and grateful for it, too."

Everett Ray wiped the tears from his eyes and stood tall.

"So you see, I have it in me that I owe something to the Teagues, and I know what men came back from being put out. I know what men your granddad raised, and they was a lot to be proud of."

Gideon took it all in, imagining the faces of heroic uncles he'd never known. But he had been named after the one that died in obscurity, without a story beyond he had grown sick and died.

"I come home here to Salud after the war. I took some time to get strong again before I come, but I got strong, by God, and I come home with flesh back on my bones. I had it in me to go and see your granddad then, to tell him about Michael and Gabriel. By then he'd heard that William and Thomas had given their lives up to that war, too, though they was killed in the fighting and left to rot on battlefields far from home.

"Well, I walked from my father's shop out there to the old house, and I knocked at your granddad's door. He opened it, sure, but he didn't see that I was standing there. He looked right past me like I was a ghost, same as your uncles. I remembered your uncles telling me about his tears for them, and their determination to come back to him after the war.

"So I stood my ground and willed him to see me. I willed it that I would see what it was in him that they so loved and was determined to come home to. Well, you'll learn in life sometimes we can will all we will, and it will be for naught. That old man didn't look at me at all. So I said, 'I come to tell you about Michael and Gabriel. We was in Andersonville together. Your boys, they was the bravest, kindest men I'll ever know. They saved my life, too, and I'm here to tell you about them.' I said all that. But the old man he just turned around like he'd answered nothing more than the wind rattling at his door. He spit and went inside, closing the door against me."

Everett Ray was silent for a while, which was more than fine with Gideon, whose head was spinning at these revelations.

"I didn't know none of this," he said, sounding like he'd be gut kicked. He wondered, too, at a secret his father had sworn him to keep before the secret had ever been told, when he was a child and still a willing vessel at this father's knee. Was that to be revealed as well?

Everett Ray smiled.

"Well, now, your father made me swear to tell it to you if anything ever happened to him," Malone said. "That is to say, he wanted me to tell you if he hadn't had time to get around to it. He woulda told you one day, when he thought it would matter enough to you to be worth the telling."

"My grandpa," Gideon said. "He sounds like just the meanest cuss alive."

Everett Ray stood pensively, then began, "Now here's where it would be a whole lot better if your father was telling this, because I know it sounds just like you're saying. But that's all I saw, so that's all I can tell you. It puzzles me, like a piece of iron that won't hammer out right, even though I know it should. To my eye, he was an impenetrable bundle of hate and ire.

"But your father, he had a love and respect for that man that there's no explaining. He thought the greatest kindness any man had ever done to him was when that mean old cuss, as you say, sent him from his home and put him to the cold hearth of living on his own. That's why he aimed to do the same to you. He didn't want to do it, but he saw it as his duty to you when – now this is his thought, not mine – when he saw you weren't learning what needed learning to avoid being a hazard to yourself."

"Hazard?"

"Listen, Gideon," Malone said. "Your father and me, we spent a lot of time talking about our children. We shared our grief in those we lost, and we shared our joy at those we had. So I know a lot about his thinking on you.

"His greatest hope was that you'd come into manhood young and not need direction beyond that which he himself had given you. But you became sullen, and you started to look at him with hate and disobedience. You wouldn't do a lick of work, and you didn't understand the farm or the living it would provide you. Gideon, you didn't understand the gift that you were given, and he couldn't give it to you without you understood it. So he was to put you out like your granddad did him – because he couldn't see no other way. He thought it would clear away the chaff and leave the man he thought he saw in you.

"Now, like I said: I didn't see no more of your granddad than I told you here today, and I saw him as a mean old cuss, same as you hear it when I tell it. But I can't deny he raised up men on this earth that, given the need, I'd lay down my own life for. Gabriel and Michael were like those ancient men of the Bible, those that come to do the Lord's bidding and which fought great battles in His name. And your father was like my own brother. Your uncles other than Gabriel and Michael I saw only from afar, really, but all I ever saw or heard of them was that they was great men, too."

"I didn't know my granddad," Gideon reflected. "But he don't sound like the sort to raise up greatness."

"No," Everett Ray laughed. "No, he don't."

"Ain't it just possible he didn't raise up nothing that wasn't there?" Gideon asked. "Ain't it possible those uncles of mine were going to be great men or bad without their being beat on or sent out to the world?"

Malone spat. "Don't know. Hadn't thought on it like that before. It's a interesting question though. Might be worth talking about and figuring on some later, but not today. Today there's a question that needs more immediate answer: What kind of man will *you* be from this day forth, Gideon? Will you be a great man or a layabout? Or neither?"

"I don't know what you mean," Gideon said. All of this had been too much; he'd been given a wealth of knowledge about his family and legacy in just a half-hour's time, but that knowledge brought only questions and confusion.

"Gideon," Everett Ray said, "your father put it on me to come to you with what I'm asking you this day, if this day had to come. So consider this as coming from beyond the grave and it's your father speaking to you and not Everett Ray Malone. You got your whole life ahead, and you lost the one champion you always woulda had in it. So standing and deciding on just your own two feet, what will you do?

"You can turn your back on this farm and go out into the world with a few dollars in your pocket maybe and make whatever life you will of it. You'll be putting your own self out with what money you can sell this farm for. But you won't need to rise to greatness for that. Nothing to stop you from it either, I suppose. But if you stay on this farm, you'll bring it and yourself to ruin if you don't rise up right now and find it in you to be a great man, to be a Teague the way the Teagues I've known have been."

Gideon was incredulous. "I can't work this farm."

"Can't, or won't?"

"Can't! I'm not my father!"

"Then it will go to whoever's got enough money to buy it from you?"

"I didn't say that neither."

"Who will keep your mother fed and warm through the winter?"

"I don't...I hadn't thought..."

"She's a strong woman, but you think she's going to put this farm in order and make it work all on her own? And how do you think she'd pay you for it? You gonna give it to her? Make her pay rent? Or just let her live here on her own? Or you gonna stay and hope she figures it all out and gets it done while you sit around and wait for it to get done?"

"I don't know."

"Where would she go if you sold?"

"I don't know, I said!"

"You don't think it's going to work itself, do you?"

"Leave me be on this!"

"Can't do it. This is your father asking, like I said. He put me to it. You need to decide right now what you're going to do, because a farm don't wait on a man to figure himself out, and your father ain't here no more to keep it running while you figure it. You got crops in the fields, so what kind of man are you going to be, Gideon Teague?"

CHAPTER 15
RUMINATIONS

Gideon stomped away from Everett Ray. He was not ready for the confrontation the blacksmith had placed upon him, but there was no escape. He thought of Zachariah, who seemed to stand taller than Gideon ever could, with strength he would never have. He thought about Ellen, his mother, who looked at him now like he was the very hand of death. How could he square with her what could not be squared? Should his life be nothing more than willing sacrifice to his mother's comfort? What of Alma? He had made promises to her, and he thought maybe he meant those promises. But there was doubt in his heart. The promises tumbled out of him when he was flush with the newfound intoxicant of Alma's flesh. He'd thought then that he loved Alma and would do anything to keep her. Now, a death and two days later, he couldn't be sure he'd meant any of it. Did he still owe her the life he had imagined with her?

"Gideon!" Everett Ray called. "Gideon!"

Gideon turned and walked back to where Malone stood, on a small rise above the fields. Gideon stood in front of him, resigned. "I guess I gotta try."

"A farm don't take to try," Everett Ray said. "You need to know more in you than to try, 'cause here's a simple truth you better know right from the git. You will fail at this, Gideon. You do everything right, and failure's waiting for you, in some measure or other. Maybe it's complete failure, or maybe it's just some that you'll fail – but you're gonna fail."

"Damn you, Everett Ray Malone!" Gideon shouted. "I don't get what it is you want from me! You say I need to take over this land, then you said I'm going fall flat on my face if I do. What's being a great man, like you're telling me I need to be, got to do with it if I'm gonna fail no matter what I do?"

"Gideon, the greatness comes when you fail and stand tall in defeat," Malone reached up and put his hands on Gideon's shoulders. "That's what I'm saying. You're going to fail a thousand times in a thousand ways, and when a man sinks down and dies because of it, like it's easiest to do, he might as well not ever have lived. That's what I'm saying. You gotta take all of this on knowing when it's working and all is well, that's just a nice little stretch that you've found. And you gotta learn from it and try to find that smooth stretch as often as you can, taking what you've learned to find your way back to it.

"But all too often, you're going to be on rough ground, fighting for every mile, and you're gonna know that no matter how hard you fight, you ain't going to make it. That's when you're going to have to be a great man. All men fail, but only a great one keeps getting' back on the road, determined to make it to the end, smooth stretch or no."

"My father never failed," Gideon protested, though some instinct in him considered Everett Ray's words for truth. Maybe this was the very truth that had been eating at him for so long, a truth he'd somehow known and been afraid to face.

"Your father was a great man," Ray Malone conceded.

"The greatest," Gideon answered. The words fell from his lips like an admission of guilt.

"A strong man, stronger than most."

"The strongest, I think."

"Wiser than most folks ever get to be."

"The wisest."

Gideon felt as if he was suddenly seeing his father clearly, with the confusions which had been put on him wiped away. His hates lost their hold, and Gideon felt resentment and fear all lifted from his thoughts. What was left was just an unblemished image of Zachariah Teague, and Gideon felt, for the first time, the full measure of his loss.

"I don't want this," he wept. "I don't want to feel this!"

"So you won't take the farm on then?" Everett Ray pronounced, disappointment echoing in his voice.

"Oh, God," Gideon cried. "Is that all you can think about! I don't want my father gone. I don't want my father dead. I want to forget what I saw when his body rolled over and snapped his own neck. I want to never see that in my mind again, but I can't get rid of it! I see it over and over, and I don't want to see it no more."

Gideon realized the image was hateful for its destruction of his father, but even more hateful than that, the image wrote the history of father and son in immutable stone. Nothing could ever be changed. What was simply was and could be no more.

"I want my father back!"

Gideon didn't know how he could go on without the chance to make it right.

"I am lost," he cried. "I loved my father so, but I showed him nothing but hate."

"The farm, Gideon!" Malone insisted. "Gideon, you got to decide about the farm! There's no time for this now. You got to take hold!"

Such was Gideon's anger at Everett Ray's insistence, he might have struck him had he not understood it was Zachariah's will working through the blacksmith. Yet Gideon could not face the decision about the farm. Mourning had fully taken hold, and it demanded Gideon release everything he had been feeling, every regret, every sorrow.

"My father died believing I hated him," he sobbed.

"Gideon," Everett Ray's voice shifted, became soothing. "Gideon, your father knew you loved him."

"How could that be?" Gideon was without hope that Malone's words could be true.

"Father's don't take to raising kids thinking that particular road will ever be smooth," Everett Ray said. "We have our children knowing there's risk that they will die, and we are so afraid of that, but we love them all the same and guard against the darkness, we guard against death. But it comes and takes them from us no matter what we do – some of them. We know that, but we still risk it. We risk it because it's in us to raise you up and love that you're here with us, crawling and walking through this world.

"We have our sons and daughters knowing they'll grow up with imperfection marking their souls, but we try to ease the imperfections from them, or teach them how to live with what burdens are put on them. We have them knowing that they'll grow up thinking we've done them wrong somehow and that they might even hate us for all we done for them.

"Still, we have them kids, and we love them, and we'd die for them. Bein' a father, well sometimes that's just like bein' Jesus on the cross, and we know it. We also know we ain't got Jesus's unblemished soul. We fight and struggle, and sometimes we give you good reason to hate, though we're trying to do otherwise. We fight against ourselves, too. We fight ourselves when we see we ain't doin' right by you as well as we wished we could.

"But we have our imperfections, too. What I mean, Gideon, is it's a hard road to be father or son. Your father knew that. Your father and I knew each other like brothers. I know he loved you and was doing his best by you because you were his boy, no matter how hard it got between you."

"My father was a great man," Gideon said. "I never seen *him* fail."

But Gideon remembered his father broken in the dust, thrown from his own wagon and dragged to defeat. He remembered, too, how Zachariah had raised himself up from the road, beaten by his own will and moaning against the pain.

"Your father was a great man," Everett Ray agreed. "But the way he seen it, he failed plenty. He come home from his wanderings, never having faced down the Rebel army, only to find all of his family had been wiped away from the earth – his brothers all gone and dead while he was in San Francisco, strutting around on a stage, same as the coward that killed Mr. Lincoln. He saw his own father die mostly bereft of the things he worked for, his sons, save for Zachariah, all dead. To his mind, he failed by not being here to do something to save his brothers, or to risk death alongside of them.

"But he picked himself up and got along with his life. He married your mother, and she was a fine woman for him. Understood him. Made him strong again, and made him believe in hope. So he built a new house here on the farm to have it filled with family, but he only got one son. So he tried to turn that home and the farm to the task of protecting and raising that boy. But death came and took him anyway, and your father couldn't do nothing to stop it. He was like to give up then, I remember."

Malone suddenly stopped. His eyes widened and his face flushed red.

"Oh, my," he said. "I'm sorry, Gideon."

"Sorry?" Gideon asked.

"Did you...," Malone stammered. "I got to talking, and I just plain forgot."

"Forgot what?"

"You didn't know you had a brother, did you?"

Gideon looked down and kicked the dirt.

"I know I had a brother," he said. "My father told me about him the day he was killed. He told me how he loved him and how Old Gus had been his horse."

Malone sighed, relieved.

"I'm sorry, Gideon, that so much has come to you in such a short time. I was afraid I'd just . . . I was afraid this might be the first time you were hearing about Gabriel."

"I'm hearing lots of things for the first time," Gideon said. "Please, tell me more about my father."

Malone looked Gideon in the eye, seeming to take stock of how much Gideon might handle without breaking.

"Okay. But I'm going to ask ahead of time for your patience, Gideon," Malone said. "You're going to need more than you're accustomed to having before this is all settled, I think. More than you've shown already."

Malone kicked up some dust then and shuffled around, pacing and trying to decide, Gideon thought, how to proceed.

"Well, Gabriel died. You know that. It was hard on your father. It broke him. Things may not have been the same between him and your mother after that. But the good Lord saw their loss and felt for them, and He give them another son, and that was you, Gideon. So your father picked himself up again and determined none of his failures would be put on you or known by you because he wanted you to come into your own believing you was the only son he'd ever had or would have. And once you was in the world, he took that as true, forged it into his heart and hardened it against the losses and defeat he felt after Gabriel."

Everett Ray fell silent for a time, seeking words that would make Gideon understand.

"You put a seed in the ground, Gideon, and it's nothing," he said finally. "You tend to its needs, and it's got nothing for you in return but that it grows some and you can feel satisfied that it's making its way. Still, it ain't got nothing to give you for all your trouble but more trouble and work. But you keep at it, and when you give it enough of what it needs to grow up full, it comes into its own and bears fruit or corn or wheat or whatever it was in that seed to give once it had enough time to grow.

"That's what it's like having a son or daughter, Gideon. Your father, he saw you grow, saw that what rose up in you would be good and fine someday, but he knew that what had to come first from him was work with no reward. That ain't to say there was something wrong about you – you were just a son growing up to be a man.

"My own trade gives me burns and scars for my troubles. But I put labor to the hammer and forge, and I work the iron into what it will be once it cools to its purpose. And for all the fire and grief it gives me along the way, it becomes what I expected it would be if I stuck to it and put my effort into it. Once that happens, it's a thing of pride for me, and it gives me more than a trade – it gives me life.

"What your father felt from you, that fire of hate you was feeling, he knew that was part of what it took to be a father. But he took to it loving that heat and flame, because he knew your manhood lay on the other side of it. He knew one day you'd look him in the eye, man to man, and the two of you would go about the world facing the fire together.

"Your father loved you, Gideon, and whatever you see as having wronged him, he saw as the necessary flame. Well, he didn't get to see the other side of it, and you been pulled out of the fire too soon. That, Gideon, is gonna make it harder on you than it needed to be. So now it's up to you. You have to take what you was given too early to be sure about it; that's the humor of it, and it forces you to make a choice you aren't ready to make."

Gideon hung his head low and thought. Then he said, "Mr. Malone, you say trying won't scour. Then you say I'm going to fail no matter what I do. You tell me my father failed, even though he was a great man. Greatness the way you give it don't mean nothing then but to try. If you fail no matter that you tried, then greatness ain't got nothing to do with it. Try is all there is. It don't matter if you got greatness in you or not. So I can try to take this farm, and me being a great man or not don't make a difference."

Malone smiled.

"You got more than a bit of your father's ruminations in you, Gideon. That'd make him proud. But greatness does matter. Any man can try, but when failure comes to him, he's defeated and done if he's got nothing for it. A great man can try, and he will fail. But when failure comes to him, he don't let it take his will from him. He don't let it pull him from himself and the man he intends to be. He finds a way to turn it around and move forward. That's what you need to have in you to take this farm, Gideon."

"The way you tell it," Gideon said, "greatness can't be found until failure comes to a man, and I won't find whether I got it in me or don't until I fall on my face or get pitched from a wagon."

Everett Ray thought on it.

"Sounds about right," he conceded. "I stand corrected. Let's think on that then the way you tell it. You're hurting bad now because your father got himself killed."

At the mention of his father's death, Gideon's moment of clarity departed, and his grief renewed its hold.

"You got yourself a deep wound," Everett Ray continued, "and it's infected with guilt. What you got in you right now is your failure to set it right with your father. You got guilt for pitting your thoughts against him and having them so put when he got himself killed. It's good that you got guilt for that. It's the seed of redemption. But there's no other way to call it but that you failed. So now you have to decide whether you let that wound fester and mark all that you can ever be. Will it fester into failing your mother, too?"

Gideon stood silent, feeling the tears on his cheek.

"Gideon," Malone said. "Gideon, when your father rode off away from you and that old oak, he was in the middle of something. He come up with his way of putting things right with you, but it was only the start of something he intended to see through. He figured on it's being finished in a couple of years, maybe, but it ended in that field, a thing undone. I know he's dead, but that don't mean he has to have died with his purpose put to rest with him. You can stand up now and take on this farm, and all that he intended to do will be done. You have that chance to see to it he didn't fail and that you didn't fail behind him. But that can only be the way it is if you stand up right now and do what needs doing."

Gideon thought on it. He didn't want to take on the farm if his only reason for doing so was to be a mere extension of his father's will. He knew now that he loved Zachariah, but he was afraid of losing himself in a life he didn't choose.

"I'm not my father," he said.

"No, you're Gideon Teague, and death has come to you but fortune, too. This farm is yours now, and what becomes of it is up to you. It's your inheritance. His time with it has passed. Yours has just begun. So you think on the alternatives."

Gideon thought on his confusion and his sorrow, thinking it was like being mired in the mud. Then another moment of clarity struck him like a slap to the side of the head. With it came a revelation of simplicity.

He realized he had a power that he hadn't thought on before. It was nothing like the power he'd imagined just days before, sought after for no other reason than to lord over Zachariah Teague. There was no great mystery to be uncovered, no elusive truth lying just beyond his reach. He suddenly understood that everything and everyone could be lost, but that he, Gideon Teague needed but three things to live: food to eat, water to drink, and fire to keep warm. But for three things, he was absolutely free.

He looked Everett Ray in the eye.

"I expect this farm can feed me," he said.

Everett Ray looked at him quizzically. He said, "When times are good, it will feed you and more. Much more. And if you lay up enough stores for when times ain't so good, it will feed you then, too."

"The cistern stays filled most of the year, and we have three more wells for when it don't."

"I helped build your house and dig them wells with your father."

"There's wood enough around here for the stove and fireplace."

"True enough, but I don't get your meaning, Gideon."

"I don't want nothing to do with your greatness, Mr. Malone."

"Then you'll give up? Fail before you start?"

"I got nothing to give up on. I'll take over on the farm, and I'll start right now, though Lord help me, I don't know how I'm going to do it alone."

"You're not making sense," Malone said. "Not a lick of sense, but I ain't going to stand here and fight that you take it on my terms or your father's anymore. I guess it *is* enough that you're going to try."

"I don't even know what to do next," Gideon said. "My father did all of this himself, and I ain't him. So I gotta start figuring on it."

Everett Ray smiled, though Gideon sensed a great a sadness lay behind the smile.

"You know, I've been holding back my own grief because Zachariah put it on me to get you started on this. So I got some more to do with you, then I'm going home to mourn your father my own way."

"You got nothing more you have to do, Mr. Malone," Gideon said. "I made some sense of it now. I just have to figure out the doing of it."

"Not really," Everett Ray said. "Now you're going to need that patience I was talking about."

CHAPTER 16
THE LIE OF IT ALL

Gideon had not known it, but talk of the farm and greatness – all these were distractions, prologue to the truest of Everett Ray's revelations – the revelation that the world Gideon had taken for true was but a sliver of truth, the rest of it built up and laid down upon a lie.

The telling had begun after Gideon's acceptance of the farm. Everett Ray, finally settled with the idea that Gideon was to take the farm on his own terms, slapped Gideon on the back and set them to walking again, farther and farther from the current Teague home, draped as it was in mourning over Zachariah. Gideon did not know it, but the two were walking to the old house that Gideon's grandfather built as a young man, a house built on a foundation of hope – built for dreams and for a future that came but briefly before being lost. Sons lost, life lost, and a hardscrabble bit of land left to toil over.

Along the way, Everett Ray began to unravel the lie.

"You looked out your window while your father worked the land that was in your sight," Everett Ray said, looking straight ahead as he walked. Then he drew to a stop and looked intently at Gideon.

"Your father didn't have to work that land," he told Gideon somberly.

"I know. I should have done it," Gideon responded, chastised and impatient. He thought all of this had been settled. "I should have been the one in the fields."

"You miss my meaning, Gideon," Everett Ray said. The blacksmith pulled a twist of tobacco from his vest pocket and took a bite from it. He offered the twist to Gideon. Gideon hadn't chewed tobacco before. He hesitated, but then reached for the offered twist. He bit into it, took off a piece, and began to chew. He handed the twist back to Everett Ray, who tore away the end that Gideon had bitten before returning the rest to his pocket.

"You don't chew on it too much," the blacksmith said. "Just a bit, then stick it into your cheek."

Gideon did so, and the blacksmith set them to walking again. Gideon began to feel dizzy.

"Your father worked that farm like it meant something," Everett Ray told Gideon. "But he only did it so you would come and join him in it."

Gideon only half heard the blacksmith. His head was spinning from the tobacco, which had caused him to salivate fiercely. Then he realized he couldn't swallow for fear of what the sickly-sweet concoction would do in his stomach. He spit a stream of brown juice onto the ground. Some of the slimy substance refused to fall free. It dangled from his mouth and whipped around in the breeze, finally sticking to his chin and chest. His mouth filled up again almost instantly. Gideon wasn't sure what to do about it.

Everett Ray smiled and spat clean, practiced enough to avoid the stringy spittle that had stuck to Gideon.

"Every day," the blacksmith said, "your father struggled on what farm you saw outside your door. When you was younger, you worked it with him, learned some from it. You might even find you know more than you think you know about the farm because of it. That's what your father wanted.

"But, and I don't mean to keep harping on you, so don't take it that way, but you come into your time of rebellion, and you wouldn't help out without he forced you to it. He didn't want to force you though. So he worked it alone, for you to see. He worked it to shame you out of that house and into picking up the plow to be a true help. He wanted you working the land like you were a part of it. Only you didn't come to it, Gideon.

"So your father kept working that small stretch, for you to see it. He even hired some local boys to work it with him, to add to your shame. He wanted you to find it in your heart to come and help because the man he wanted you to become would have. He wanted to see it in you that you wanted to stand by his side before he would show you more. Leastwise, he needed you to know in your heart that it was wrong not to. He couldn't show you nothing else until you took that step as a man, not as the boy you had been. He couldn't show you nothing else until you wanted to help feed your family and earn your keep."

"What do you mean about showing me more?" Gideon's mind was divided between the sickening feeling the tobacco had given him and his curiosity over the blacksmith's words. He felt like he would vomit.

"Oh, Gideon, Gideon."

Everett Ray told him the burden of the farm would not be the solitary venture Gideon had imagined. Absent curiosity, it had escaped Gideon's notice that his father was not a lone laborer, working a disproportionate bounty from the earth. Zachariah Teague, Everett Ray told him, was a strong man but not so strong as to plow and plant and harvest the farm he owned single-handedly.

"Gideon," Everett Ray said, spitting another stream of tobacco juice to the ground. "Zachariah's land was too large even for twenty strong men to work to its full potential. Your father sometimes had as many as forty men working for him, particularly during planting and harvest."

The dizziness overcame Gideon, and he stumbled away from the blacksmith, vomiting and desperately trying to spit the tobacco from his mouth between bouts. When he was done vomiting, the tobacco was still strong enough to overpower the bile taste of the vomit. He continued spitting, trying to get the remains of the twist from his mouth. The dizziness remained, and Gideon vomited again.

"Takes some getting used to," Everett Ray told him, spitting. "Chew it enough, and you won't get sick from it no more."

To make his point, the blacksmith pulled the twist from his pocket again and extended it to Gideon. Gideon vomited at the sight of it. Everett Ray smiled and returned the twist to his pocket. After a time, Gideon began to recover, realizing he was terribly thirsty, but afraid to swallow anything that would carry the tobacco taste back into his stomach. His mind began to clear some.

"I never seen no forty men working on my father's farm," he finally told the blacksmith, trying to regain a measure of thought and dignity. He decided he had no intention of getting used to the tobacco, and he wasn't sure if he was angry with Everett Ray for giving it to him or grateful that the blacksmith shared it. "I seen some working with my father, but not that many."

"You never seen the men I'm talking about," the blacksmith said. Everett Ray explained that these men were an unlanded, migratory bunch. Some were second, third, and fourth sons to families with just farm enough for one son's inheritance. Some were men who had lost or never found their footing in other professions. Some were the poor sons of share-croppers who couldn't stomach what would be their unfair share in that scheme, preferring a meager, honest wage to the more meager illusion of ownership. Some were of more nefarious origins, laying low in the labor of the land. Still others were immigrants looking beyond the industrial hellholes that America had prepared to consume their lives in the fury of manufacturing and production. No matter their origins though, Malone told Gideon that any number had returned to the Teague farm time and again, finding something desirable in working for the great man that was Zachariah Teague.

"What in God's name are you telling me, Mr. Malone?"

"Gideon, your father was a very wealthy man. That farm you saw outside your back door all your life was just the tiniest bit of what he owned."

Everett Ray explained to Gideon that, though Zachariah Teague had never shared the knowledge with his son, he had built a farm unlike any other in Oniate County. To the small farm his own father had brought into the family, the only farm Gideon had known, Zachariah added new lands over the years. The whole farm now stretched over two thousand acres. Everett Ray revealed, too, that Zachariah Teague had become rich, reaping the benefits of a natural facility with farm management and an instinctive prescience when it came to finance, transportation, and technology. He had taken advantage all three to place what were, for the unimaginative, local farm commodities into the streams of national and international commerce. The product of his farm found its way by river and rail, and by ocean's steam and sail, to cities and lands far from Oniate County. Humble, proud; demure, forceful – Zachariah Teague's genius was expressed in contradictions. There were men, Everett Ray told him, who spent their whole lives pretending to have more wealth than their neighbors. Zachariah though – Zachariah spent his life hiding his genius and the wealth that followed it. Few, very few, knew beyond rumor that Zachariah was a man of means. Fewer still knew the exact size of his operation. His personality was such that he was able to inspire, in those trusted few, fealty to an ideal of obscurity that worked directly against man's boastful nature.

"Your father's working that farm you know," Everett Ray told him, "his laboring on it was for your benefit. He wanted you to watch and learn and to gain your own curiosity about how to manage on a small scale before he introduced you to a larger one."

"He never told me none of this!"

"You weren't ready, and he didn't want you to grow up spoiled, thinking you only had to take what was given rather than build for yourself."

"I did work that farm with my father!" Gideon protested, and it was true. As a boy, Gideon had been an appendage to his father, spending untold hours at his father's side, helping on the farm any way he could to earn his father's approval. It had only been of late that Gideon had retreated from the farm, leaving his father to seemingly solitary labor.

"But you stopped once you grew," Malone told him. "You stopped once you got it in your head that you had a choice. Your father saw it best to let you choose then, and to take measure of your choice."

Because he lacked something vital – some critical aspect to his being – Gideon had been duped. He had not been cognizant of any farm or wealth beyond the 160 acres that could be seen from the back porch and barn of the Teague home. Those things, that land and livestock within sight, Gideon had watched Zachariah Teague work with unyielding energy. Yet beyond lay the true work of the land, born upon the backs of men whom Zachariah paid for their labor. All Gideon ever saw had been an illusion, an act played out for his consideration.

Gideon felt himself an unutterable fool.

The revelation of the lie was much harder on Gideon than the revelation of his family's unspoken past. The hearing of it and then the slow understanding of it separated Gideon's body from his control, worse than the tobacco had. His legs gave out beneath him, and he fell to the ground.

"It isn't true," he moaned. "It's a lie!"

"It was a lie, Gideon," Everett Ray said, looking down over Gideon with a sad compassion. "I'm sorry to tell you of it. If it had come about the way your father intended, it might have filled you with wonder instead of what you're feeling now. It was a lie, Gideon, but it was a noble lie. It was a plan, Gideon. Planned for your benefit."

Gideon wondered that his sanity didn't break, wondered if it had, wondered if he was even hearing what he thought he was hearing. His world was an illusion. Some parts of it true, but most of it an illusion, making him believe in a reality that did not exist.

"But I saw him there, working the farm like it was our whole world – his world, my world, and my mother's, too."

"You saw what he wanted you to see."

"And you're telling me it was a goddamned lie!"

"It wasn't a *goddamned* lie!" Everett Ray's voice filled with its own brand of rage. "It was a beautiful lie, meant to save you, not damn you!"

Gideon thought of Old Gus. Like the horse, Gideon tried to stand, but flailed and fell back to the ground, as injured and helpless as Old Gus had been. He dug into the dirt with angry fists and threw it from him, grabbed more and threw that, too.

"Oh, the lie of it!" Gideon shouted. "That's the foundation for my hate! The hate was give to me – I sensed it but didn't know what it was! Everything I saw, everything was give to me a lie!"

"The lie was to save you, Gideon!" Everett Ray insisted. "You don't know the hearts of men. You don't know how easy we're corrupted when power comes to us too easy! Should he give you the world, the power of it over others without you knew the struggles and hardships most men face? Satan tempted Jesus with all the world – well, what if he had been the man to take it give to him the way it was?"

"Damned, heartless man!"

"Gideon, did you ever long for power in your heart? Did you ever long for riches and know what you would do with them if you had them?" Everett Ray implored. "We all long for things in our hearts that if we was to have them would ruin our souls."

Gideon shouted to the heavens, "I hate you Zachariah Teague. To hell with you and to hell with your farm!"

"Gideon!"

"What am I? A puppet to be played with? Was I a toy to be pulled about on strings by my own father?"

"It was no easy lie to tell, Gideon," Everett Ray said. "Your father made his own life harder than it had to be to work that lie."

Gideon could not see the world in front of him for all his rage. He had been lied to, toyed with, and made a fool of his whole life. Pressing in about the dark cloud of hate he was feeling, however, were reflections about himself that tried to lift the hate. He had sought so long for power with the single purpose of bringing it to bear upon his father, to bring him harm. Some separated part of his mind tried to tell him about himself. He'd sought out what he could, not to bring solace into his world, but to destroy it. Was the lie to protect him from his own weaknesses?

His disembodied reflection eased and then fueled his rage anew.

"Goddamn you, Zachariah Teague!"

"That's enough of that!" Everett Ray said. "I won't have you cursing the name of a great man."

"Great man!" Gideon shouted. "Was there anything he ever told me was true?"

"The lie was meant to show you truth," Everett Ray said. "If your father had given you the truth, it would have ruined you."

Unwillingly, Gideon thought of Henry Scott. He had come from riches from the east, casting about as lost as Gideon, only he did not seem to know it. In the end, he was a weak and pompous little man, cowering in the woods and silently watching as Gideon and Alma made love. What kind of man had he become knowing wealth and power stood behind him? Gideon watched as Henry Scott built up his own lie, a house of cards that tumbled down in the course of a single day. Had Zachariah Teague's cruelty been kindness after all?

"Jesus, Gideon," Everett Ray said, exasperated. "Your father put it on me to be patient with you, and I know you been told more than a man ought to have to hear in a day, but pull yourself off of the ground, and quit your damned crying. I had enough of it."

Gideon ignored the blacksmith. He rolled over on his back and looked up at the sky. Clouds lay motionless overhead, and Gideon felt as if time stood motionless as well. He had eternity to think about all that had happened this day, but decided he didn't need it. How many ways of thinking, how many philosophies had he adopted in the span of two days' time, one succeeding the other as fast as the one before it had come? How resigned had he come to conviction, only to see each conviction discarded upon its first test?

As he lay in the dirt, he imagined all of his confusion, his fear and anger draining from him and into the earth, like blood pouring from a slaughtered animal.

"It's like I got no life left in me at all."

He lay silent. He heard Everett Ray spitting and grunting impatiently. Gideon did not care. There was no benefit in belief, he mused, no point to purpose. So he was in no hurry to rouse himself.

He considered: "If what I know makes me who I am, who am I if nothing I know is true?"

He conjured images of Zachariah and regarded the man. He relived those times he saw his father fall broken to the ground, first from the wagon and then from Old Gus. The living memory of Zachariah, he understood, was as broken and inconsequential as his corpse. The man's thoughts, his purpose – there was nothing about him Gideon could latch onto, make his own. Zachariah Teague was as much a mystery to Gideon as his own namesake, that lost Gideon Teague who had died in obscurity in California.

He remembered how he had begun to see his father's image in his own reflections in recent years. Looking back at Gideon when he spied himself in mirrors and glass was a face that did not belong to him – he saw instead the jaw, the eyes, the nose and skin of Zachariah Teague. When he looked at himself, he mostly saw his father looking back. He saw nothing more than a younger Zachariah Teague, and that had troubled him. Was there anything of Gideon to be found in the image? It troubled him, too, that his voice, his mannerisms – everything about him seemed cast from his father's image.

"That's why I opposed him so," Gideon thought. "If I couldn't destroy his image, I had none of my own."

At the same time, Gideon remembered, there was something calming in the reflection, a stability. Seeing Zachariah in himself, he felt he was part of something greater than his physical being, an irreplaceable link in a chain of family and history, connected to and legitimized by an unknown legion of Teagues going back in time. And no matter his opposition to Zachariah, Gideon had counted on him. Gideon knew each day would start and end with Zachariah's loyalties to him intact, whatever travails Gideon had placed on him that day. His father would suffer him, feed him, teach him, and provided a home for him. As much as Gideon felt lost in his father's image, his father's image in him made him something to Zachariah Teague that no other person could be – his son.

"At least, I think that's true," he wondered.

But what had he been to his mother? He thought her the peacekeeper, that part of himself that he could not be. Where he could not find it in himself to express to his father regret or love, his mother did it for him. She was his bridge. She calmed his angry world where he desired to but could not. How he had counted on her! He took for truth that he was a part of her soul – without him she could not be who she was. Her life, her purpose was to see to Gideon's growth and protection.

So he had thought. Silently he had believed she understood his darkest depths, but saw the goodness in him so that she loved him despite the darkness. He counted on her knowing who he really was, what he would truly become. Yet in a single moment he learned that she could think him a murderer. She had seen in him something that did not exist, something too terrible to think on. In his wildest illusions of hate for Zachariah Teague, in his fantasies that destroyed his father, there was still no part of him that could bring physical harm to the man in whose image he was wrought. Angry words, yes. Calculated scorn, surely. Spite, most assuredly. But he was not a soldier in his hate – he could never bring aim to actual harm. Not to his father, not to any man. He was not, ever, in his heart a killer. Even the necessary slaughter of livestock sickened his soul.

He thought on himself a bit. When he sensed Alma might come to harm at the hands of his friends, he knew it was in him to protect, not to hurt. He knew when he brought the news of his father's death to Ellen that his course was settled on protecting her as much from hurt as he could, to take it all to himself and shelter her from it as much as shelter could be given. And when true harm had come to Zachariah, Gideon knew he would traverse heaven and earth to save him. That the crippling break of flesh and bone could not be undone left him powerless to save, not unwilling. Yet his mother had been so certain that Gideon was a killer, he saw himself reviled in her eyes.

"None know me," he considered. He thought, also, that the opposite must be true: "There is no one who I know."

He wondered what he would do with these thoughts. For all he believed outside of himself, he decided, in the end, there was only him.

"I could come to a conclusion right now," he thought, "and I will watch it fall apart with next words out of Everett Ray's mouth."

It occurred to him suddenly that every word Everett Ray spoke might itself be the lie. He had no proof the blacksmith was his father's friend, at least not in the way the blacksmith told it. Aside from a few names inked into the family Bible, he had no proof that he had had any uncles at all, or if he had, that their histories had been as Everett Ray told them.

"When I lift myself up from this dust," he resolved, "there will be no Zachariah Teague in my mind. I will be motherless, without history beyond myself. What I will know is only a thing that might be, not a thing that is."

He rolled over and got up to his knees, looking at a pacing Everett Ray Malone. He stood then, thus resolved, not knowing how impossible it would be to live life the way he'd just figured it.

CHAPTER 17
EVER THE FOOL

The moon still shone brightly, though true morning lay not too far off. Gideon wondered at how keen his memory had been this night. Alone on the road, barefoot and purposeless, he had walked and taken in, for the thousandth time, Everett Ray Malone's ruminations on failure and death.

Ever-present death.

Most folks, Gideon thought, learn to get by. They fold up memories of the dead like the letter his grandfather had gotten telling of Uncle Gideon's death, burying them out of sight but near enough that they were never really gone. Others curled up and died with the loss of child or kept restless watch like he himself had done all these years. Death, so common, and yet the loss of Hap was so particular with him the grief never found its resting place.

Hap, Hap. Happy Boy!

Gideon stopped walking, uncertain about what he wanted to do next. It was well past the time he should have returned home. Alma would rise soon. Gabriel would be up, and he should be there for the boy. Yet he felt compelled to move forward, to drop back into his unsettled past. He did not want to. He wanted to go home. Yet he felt drawn back down the road, back to the dead.

Unknown, unseen, but sharing fully in Gideon's remembrances, the spirit delighted in the wreckage of the hollowed man. Often, the spirit had thought to take the boy, Gabriel, and lay waste to him as he had laid waste to Hap, to complete Gideon's destruction. But the spirit stayed its hand.

"Take one more bite," the spirit chastised itself, "and there will be only the core to rot, not enough left of the man to suffer as he so sweetly suffers for me now."

Yet sometimes a piece of the spirit broke free of itself and wondered if it, more than Gideon, had been lost in the union that bound the one to the other. In every nightly wandering Gideon took, the spirit took it with him, beside him, feeding from him. When dreamless sleep came to Gideon, when slumber gave the slightest surcease from sorrow, the spirit weakened, flying during those times to Alma, taking some strength from her misery, too. But her misery was never as strong as Gideon's, never so sweet, and the takings were too light to hold him to the earth. In those times, the spirit faded, taken to a Lethe stream, away from its hate – back to its master and into its own hateful terror.

As a life, the spirit had been marked by ignorance and sin, and while ignorance alone could render regrettable the makings of the man, its marking could not hold or bind the man's soul. Yet the sin had been enough to see the man's soul bound to its master, to the evil all living creatures sense lurking beyond the light, a festering malevolence, alive and driven to destroy. As a life, the man's sin had turned its soul to prey, and in death, evil had found it and slain its better makings.

In that Lethe stream, bound in the darkness of death, the spirit recoiled at its driving purpose, wanting nothing of Gideon Teague or the draining away of the living man's soul. The spirit wanted nothing more than to die the true death and to be free of what it had become. The evil would overtake it at those times, rendering into fearsome flames the spirit's regret and desire for oblivion. Every thought of freedom consumed the man's soul in the burning fires. The spirit suffered unutterably, seeing its life through a flowing river of fire, dragged screaming to is end, with the crushing blows of Gideon's murderous stone against its skull.

Then darkness of night fell upon the living world, and Gideon would rise from those moments when unquenchable, dreamless sleep had taken him to his own Lethe stream. The spirit would return to him then, forgetting the fires, forgetting the regret and wish to die, and it would be consumed by the fire of hate instead, an unyielding hate for Gideon Teague and all things that might allow purpose back into the man's life. Again, the spirit would nurture Gideon's sorrow.

Rarely, though memory of the flames had departed, the spirit would wonder what it had become and stand on the precipice of its own sorrow. But then it would gaze upon Gideon and hate the man and drink his misery, the finest wine it had ever known.

Unheard by Gideon, the spirit cried laughter into the night, as Gideon thought he should go back to bed, sleep a little bit. But the spirit heard the thought, refused to fade, and it found the memory in Gideon Teague, pulled it to life, and Gideon, heard, was beckoned again by Everett Ray's voiceless words, and his mind wandered back in time.

* * *

"Gideon?"

Gideon remembered hearing the blacksmith and rising up from the ground, no longer angry, no longer broken. He'd felt free.

"Everett," he said, "you give me a lot to think on today." He brushed the dust from his trousers and wiped what was left of his tears from his cheeks and chin.

"Too much, I admit," Everett Ray answered. "And I'm sorry about that, Gideon. I truly am."

Gideon looked out to the west. Had he been sure at that moment that everything Everett Ray had told him was true, he would have begun walking in that direction, never to return. He felt the far away ocean calling him to it. He heard his namesake Gideon's spirit on the coastal winds, calling him to new life and solitude. Nothing, if Everett Ray spoke true, remained for him here. Like a calf falling from the womb, he decided he was with sight for the first time. It was time to stand on his own feet, newly born and free from Zachariah, free from every lie and love he had ever believed in.

But it nagged. He had been such a fool, if Everett Ray spoke true, yet he could only be a bigger fool if he were to believe this stranger, this man who claimed so much that Gideon had no reason to believe but for its telling. "Will I walk off now for hearing a few words?"

He looked hard to the west. He longed for it. But sometime hence, he thought, he would look back to this moment and wonder if he'd been the fool again.

On the road, in the moonlight looking back, remembering, Gideon wondered what would have happened if he had taken that walk. Would Hap be alive today? What things had he brought to Hap's life that lead to the boy's frozen corpse? Alma would have raised him, maybe married, maybe not. There was to be a shame for it, sure, but shame is not death unless the shame is in continuing to be a fool or living a lie.

"I loved that boy like my own," he thought. "I love that boy like my own."

Back in time, he decided he could not trust Everett Ray's words enough to leave. Maybe there was more to be learned. Maybe his mother's scorn had come from grief, and maybe she did not think it in her heart that it had been in him to kill his own father.

"If I go and let my world be undone, will I ever have a world to call my own?"

Still, the temptation was strong. But he drew something from his earlier philosophy of the day. He needed but three things: food, water, and a place to be warm. In truth, these were hard things to find. Here, he had them. If he set out, now, with the clothes on his back, he would have only warmth because of the summer sun and humid nights. Shortly, he would find himself searching for food. He envisioned himself without resource, stealing wheat and corn from fields along the way – sneaking hens from farmhouses in the night, slinking to it like a coyote, hiding from angry farmers who had less reason to love him than Ellen Teague. His clothing would wear out, with no one to sew up the holes and patches. He would have to find work, on farms perhaps, working harder for strangers than he had been willing to work for his own father on his own land. A bigger fool he would be than he was, and for the first time he understood that nothing would come to him without struggle. He felt shame for all that he had refused to do, not for the disappointment it brought to Zachariah, but for the ignorance he had shown of himself.

Gideon resolved then to stay – for now.

"I'll see what's what," he thought, then to Everett Ray he said, "Everett, you put it in my head that I been lied to and made the fool for my whole life."

Everett Ray started to correct him: "No, now it was your own..."

"Everett, I heard enough for the time being," he interrupted what was sure to be another exposition upon the weakness of his character. He'd had enough of that talk. "I heard a lot from you, and your story is that I've been the fool – that I been tricked and lied to all these years, but I'm telling you I consider it possible that your words are the lie. To my mind, it may be that you have something you want of me the way you say my father wanted something of me and lied to get it. So you tread careful now. What I learned is suspicion is my only friend. If what you say is true, I should have been given to suspicion of my father. If what you say isn't true, suspicion will counsel me to be wary of it. What I know is not to give respect to any man unless I seen it tried and true through my own eyes first."

Everett Ray's eyes grew wide and his face reddened with anger. "You calling me a liar? You thankin' me for takin' on your father's duty to you by telling me I'm some kind of deceiver? You think this has been easy for me? You think it's some kinda task I took to for profit?"

Gideon laughed as hard as Everett Ray had laughed at Gideon thoughts earlier that day.

"Everett, what kind of fool will I be if I take as Gospel the word of a man I hardly know telling me the man I did know – my father – was a liar?"

The blacksmith started to say something, thought on it, and started to laugh with Gideon.

"I guess you'd be a goddamned fool at that!"

Everett Ray's humor irritated Gideon; he thought for a moment that he would tell the blacksmith what he had done with his daughter, to see the look on Everett's face knowing *he'd* been the ignorant fool, that Gideon knew something about Everett's world that the blacksmith hadn't known.

"Bring shame to you," Gideon thought, "and put us on equal footing."

"Alma's a pretty girl," Gideon said, abruptly.

"She is," the blacksmith answered, oblivious to Gideon's purpose.

"I seen her in town the day my father died."

"She told me she was looking for you," Everett Ray said, a tenderness in his voice. "My girl likes you, Gideon."

Everett Ray seemed to take comfort in the telling. The blacksmith thought it something innocent, and he approved. Gideon's heart sank, and his purpose died.

"I am the fool all over again," he thought, wondering at what he had been about to do. Maybe there was something in him after all that justified his mother's doubt. He had nearly sacrificed Alma to place his vanity in opposition to Everett Ray. To what end? He remembered Alma's tender touch in the parlor – her comforting presence. That she had it in her soul to offer that to him, yet he would cast her aside for a moment's satisfaction in bringing Everett pain.

"My father was right to give me the lie," he decided. He decided, too, that Everett Ray had been speaking some measure of truth, at least. Yet the blacksmith remained to Gideon nearly the mystery the Teague's family past had been. As Gideon knew him, Everett Ray was the blacksmith and farrier Zachariah Teague trusted his horses to. Gideon had been aware, too, of his mother's annoyance whenever Zachariah returned from his visits to the blacksmith's home. These arrivals were late night, noisy episodes, during which Zachariah Teague was invariably drunk. But Zachariah took to drunkenness like he took to the wagon's reins, commanding it, determined to work it to his will. This increased the cacophony. Doors slammed, boots were thrown at the walls – his mother was lifted high in the air in mid-scolding. Zachariah laughed through it all. Once he barged into Gideon's room and shouted, "I can wait you out, boy! You'll come to it! Damn if you won't!" And Zachariah laughed and slammed the door after him. Gideon did not know what to make of it, but he was afraid to challenge his father at these times. Often, his mother's scoldings settled into their own brand of laughter, and Zachariah and Ellen Teague would tear around the house, making more ruckus than Gideon ever heard between the two. At these times, he sulked under his covers and felt his resentment growing.

So that had been the effect of the friendship Zachariah shared with Everett Ray Malone. It fueled Zachariah's certainties and unleashed his humor. The other side of that friendship, Gideon had never seen, but he decided that he believed the blacksmith and his father likely shared the abundant exchanges of thought that Everett Ray said they did. And there was Alma. Whatever else Everett Ray Malone was, he was father to Alma Malone, and Gideon resolved he would not fail her again, leastwise not to pit himself against the blacksmith.

"I like Alma, too, Everett," Gideon responded, his previous purpose abandoned. He thought about his mother, then, and the fact that he had stepped out of his father's wake, leaving her alone to the task of shepherding the final respects. "Even when it is my purpose to remain true," he thought, "I stray."

"I have to go back home," he said. "My mother's all alone to it. I should be there."

"Sure enough," the blacksmith said. "But there's one more thing for us to do first. It might even put it in your head that I'm putting truth to you."

* * *

Gideon hadn't been to the old house in some years. It was where his father had been born and raised. He remembered riding there with his father when he was much younger. He remembered seeing men there, and his father talking to them and pointing and giving orders. To Gideon it had been nothing more than the noise adults made, the meaning of it beyond his grasp.

It was not much of a house. It was soundly built to be sure, from logs that likely grew on the land before it had been cleared. But it was small – a tiny cabin. Gideon couldn't picture living in it, though the builder, doubtless Gideon's grandfather, had had dreams enough to stack the walls high, so he could build a standing porch that looked slightly down on the farm around it. To either side, plank-sided lean-tos had been added. Gideon reflected now that these were to add living space for his father and uncles. Even with the added lean-tos, however, Gideon couldn't imagine how all of the Teague men could crowd into and live in the place, particularly in winter, when the weather would make it too hard to escape outside for long. Gideon wondered about his grandmother. Had she lived there, too? In all of his life, Gideon never heard his father utter a word about his own mother. But then, Zachariah Teague was full of secrets.

As he and Everett Ray approached the house, Gideon saw it was unchanged, though the roof over the log section appeared to be newer than the rest of the cabin. To either side of the cabin, however, things had changed considerably. The old corn crib had been converted to a bunkhouse. Solid siding now covered the once open slats. A couple of windows and a chimney had been built in, too. On the other side of the cabin, the small barn had been converted for living in as well. Where large doors had once stood at the end of the building, to allow livestock in and out, a wall had been erected in their place, with a small entry door. Stalls that once opened outward from the sides of the barn were fitted over with solid planks. Smoke rose from a chimney. The smoke smelled of pork.

"I ain't been here in a long while myself," Everett Ray said. "Zachariah told me about it, but I had no cause to come here. Your father has his barns and horses scattered where the old farms were, so I'd go to those places to shoe the horses. He's got some of his men living here, but most are scattered about the old farms. He stayed fond of this place, though. Wouldn't let it go to rot and made it part of his operation."

Everett Ray led Gideon to the cabin porch and beat his fist against the door.

"Sam!" he shouted. "Sam Smith!"

At Everett Ray's second call, a stocky, black haired man opened the plank door. Gideon saw the man's hair was flecked through with bits of gray. He had a white beard, kept short.

"Who the hell calls him!?!" the man answered, making no effort to hide his annoyance. Then he recognized Everett Ray.

"Blacksmith," the man said. "What brings you out here? I thought you'd be at Old Zach's wake."

"I've been," Everett Ray answered, making no effort to hide his own annoyance. He seemed bothered at the man's calling Zachariah Old Zach. "I have some business here that Mr. Teague put me to."

"What business?" Sam asked, spitting. "Don't need no horses shoed here."

"I'm here to introduce you to Mr. Teague's son, Gideon Teague."

Sam spat again. Dust rose up where the spit hit the earth. Gideon wondered if the spit had landed anywhere near the buried letter.

"I am sorry about your father, boy. I've been working this farm for him for five years – and not because his is such fine country. I done it because he was a good man."

Gideon met Smith's words with silence, sharing Everett Ray's irritation, annoyed with the man's addressing him with a dismissive "boy."

"Mr. Teague told me if harm ever came to him to bring Gideon to you," Everett Ray said. "You're the boss around here, I guess, but now this is Gideon's farm. He's going to need your assistance in getting a grasp on it."

"Well, now, there's news, ain't it?" Sam said, pursing his lips. "I knew Old Zach had a boy, but never did see him here working a lick."

"Ho, now," Everett Ray said, taking a tone Gideon had not heard from him before. "Best to mind your place, Smith. How Mr. Teague saw fit to raise his own ain't your business. I'm told you're a good man with the farm, so let's not get us off on the wrong foot here."

"I'll thank you not to call me 'boy,' neither," Gideon spoke, finding that after all his thought and outpouring, his rage still sat, easily exposed. "I expect you work for me now, and I'll not be called out like a child."

Gideon was surprised he had said it, but if Everett Ray's words were true, he expected that he spoke true as well.

"Take hold!" Gideon heard his father's voice, saw him standing high atop the wagon, willing his horses and the road ahead to bend to his will. He felt his father's spirit rising like instinct in him. "Let this man start by calling you boy and all is lost, Gids! Take hold!"

Smith spat. "You expect I work for you, boy?" Smith laughed. "You go on expecting whatever you like, but I don't work for you. And you, Blacksmith, last I looked, you were doing what work I put you to. Now you come here putting it to me that you're speaking on Old Zach's behalf. Any man can come up here and tell me he's here for Old Zach and knows his business, but that don't make it so. Old Zach put it to me otherwise. I'm to take this farm over in his stead and see it keeps making food and profit for Mrs. Teague, and he didn't say nothing 'bout I'd be working for his runt."

Gideon watched as Everett Ray turned deep red at the insult, but the blacksmith took a breath. Instead of hitting the upstart Smith, as Gideon suspected and hoped he might, Malone settled himself and started over.

"We're on the wrong foot here," Everett Ray said, forcing a small laugh. "Now look here, Smith, I been about as close to Mr. Teague as kin. Grew up with him and shared the same table as boys, right here in this cabin, so I do know his business, and the first of what he told me should something happen to him is that you're a good man and to trust you to know something of what's to be done. So let's step back and do this from scratch, eh?"

Everett Ray held out his hand. "Mr. Smith, my name is Everett Ray Malone, not Blacksmith. I shoed horses around this farm for my friend, Zachariah Teague, not because I was working for you or needed work from you. Doubt it if you will, but I don't recall you ever paying me a lick. Zachariah done plenty for me as his skills were to put it, and I done plenty for him as my skills put it. If you misunderstood that arrangement 'cause you knew what horses needed shoeing, Zachariah and I should have put you straight on that. I apologize that we didn't. Makes for misunderstanding now that don't need to be."

Smith spat, stepped down from the porch and kicked the dirt. He refused Malone's offered hand but took measure of the man who had come to see him.

"All right, we'll start over," he said. "I been around Old Zach for a few years myself, I guess, and I run the better part of this farm for him for a long while. I expect I know his mind better than you, leastwise about this farm. And here's what he told me: If it ever come to it, he wanted me to keep running this farm for his wife, and to get his no-good son to do some work on it if that could be done. So whatever you think he wanted you to do or to tell me to do, you just forget it. Old Zach wasn't my friend, and I never broke bread with him when he was a little boy who didn't know no better. But he trusted me, and I respected him. So if you're like kin the way you say, you'll respect him, too, and leave me to my business."

Malone dropped his hand, and his face reddened even more than it had a moment ago. Gideon clenched his fists and thought if Everett Ray would not strike the man, he would. Gideon stepped toward Sam Smith then. Everett Ray put his arm in front of Gideon, however, and held him back.

"Be patient, son," he said to Gideon. "Mr. Smith don't mean no offense, but thinks he's telling it the way it is."

"That *is* the way it is," Smith said, turning his back to Everett Ray and Gideon, stepping back onto the porch.

Everett Ray turned to Gideon and whispered, "You need this man, so hold back."

Malone stepped after Smith and said, "I got papers that say it's otherwise, Smith. I don't know what Zachariah said to you or when he said it, but I got papers that say I'm to oversee this farm for a time, and instructions that I'm to hold it for Gideon here. So why don't you come back and let's discuss this."

Smith turned.

"Why you dirty son of a bitch!" Smith shouted. "You got papers to what? Steal this farm away from Old Zach!?!"

"Zachariah can't be stole from," Malone shouted back. "He's dead! And I got his will and testament, and it don't say nothing about you, but it gives everything here to Gideon, after I look to it for a couple of years. Now he told me he trusted you. Are you to live up to that trust, or be put out of here?"

Three men had emerged from converted corn crib then, drawn into the house by the loud voices. They stood ready, a few paces behind Everett Ray and Gideon.

"Easy, boys," Smith told the men. "Nothin' here but a lot of hot air."

"I'm about to lose my patience with you, Mr. Smith," Malone answered the insult.

"I have lost mine!" Gideon shouted. "You're fired, Smith! You're fired, and you clear off of here!"

Smith laughed again, mocking Gideon.

"You men there," Gideon said to the flanking hands. "I'm Gideon Teague, and this is my farm. If you want to keep working here, you put this man out. I want no more of him."

The men looked to Gideon and began to laugh along with Smith.

"Who's the boy?" one of the men asked Smith.

"Claims to be that no account son Old Zach talked about."

At that, Gideon rushed at Smith, filled for the first time in his life with true violence. Everett Ray tried to stop him, but Gideon brushed him aside and flew onto the porch after Smith, his fists raised and ready to strike. Smith moved and, without Gideon's understanding how, slammed Gideon into the door. Gideon fell.

"Gideon!" Everett Ray yelled. "Stop it, Gideon!"

Gideon ignored the blacksmith and scrambled to his feet, throwing a punch at Smith's face. Gideon felt powerful compared to the smaller Smith, felt sure he would beat the man and send him away. But his fist hit nothing at all, and Smith's fist met him full in the gut, forcing the air out of him. Gideon fell again, and Smith kicked him in the ribs, knocking him from the porch and sending a crippling pain throughout his body. Gideon rolled in the dust.

The men laughed. Everett Ray rushed to Gideon's side and helped him stand, though Gideon felt too weak to keep his footing. Everett Ray held him up.

"Dammit, Gideon!" Everett Ray said. "We don't need to fight!"

Gideon could not speak. His breathing came in desperate hitches, his lungs incapable of filling with air.

"He'll need to fight if he comes out here again without I invite him and put him to work," Smith said. "You two be on your way. I don't care what paper you say you got that wills this place to the boy. I'm holding it like Old Zach wanted, for Mrs. Teague – and I guess even for this worthless lump of shit here."

Everett Ray took Gideon under the arms and began walking him away from the old place. Smith and the men went back in the house.

"Gideon," Everett Ray said while he walked the injured Gideon slowly back toward the mourning Teague house. "This ain't the way it was supposed to happen. I'm going to talk plain to you now, and I shoulda done it before we got here. Forget what I said. You don't know how to run a farm like this. Hell, I sure don't. You need that man. Your father wanted you to learn from him for a time, if the need rose. To learn what needs learning to run this farm. You didn't take that knowledge from you father, not full like you should've. So he expected you could get it from Smith for a time, until you could stand on your own. It don't look like that's going to go too easy now."

The men walked, and after a while, Gideon was able to breathe again.

"Take hold!" he heard his father's voice as clear as day, and the pain started to subside.

He turned to go back to the old place, determined to unseat Sam Smith and the men who had laughed at him.

Everett Ray tried to stop him, but Gideon broke free.

"I won't be beat by him," Gideon said.

"You been beat already," Everett Ray told him. "There's other ways to do this."

Gideon ignored him and kept walking. Malone sat in the dirt and called after him.

"Gideon, listen to me for God's sake!"

Gideon kept walking, his rage all-consuming now. But before he got far from Everett Ray, Sam Smith appeared on horseback. As he rode by, Gideon lunged after him, intent on pulling him from the horse. Instead, the bit hit him on the side of the face and knocked him back to the ground. Smith rode off, past Malone and toward the Teague home. Gideon rolled on the ground holding his face. He was bleeding profusely from his cheek.

Everett Ray picked him up again.

"You been spending too much time in the dirt today, Gideon," he said gently. "Calm yourself, and let's get back to your home. Lord knows what Smith is up to, but we need to see to it."

Gideon broke loose from Everett Ray's hold and bent down to scoop up a handful of dirt. He started to bring it up to his face. The blacksmith knocked it out of his hand.

"What the hell are you doing?" Everett Ray asked.

"Damn it, Everett," Gideon answered, tears in his eyes. "Just want to stop the blood with some dirt."

"Jesus, boy, that's the surest way to make it fester. Only a damned fool looks to dirt to stop up a wound."

The blacksmith pulled a clean patch of old flannel from his back pocket and handed it to Gideon.

"Here," he said. "Use this to see to that cut of yours."

Gideon dabbed up the liquid blood from his face and scratched away that which had crusted and stuck down his jaw and neck. The blood stuck pieces fell inside his shirt against his skin and stuck again, between fabric and sweat.

"Nothing for it now," he thought, and pressed the flannel patch to his wound to stop new blood. Eventually, the wound slowed and oozed, then it began to scab.

Gideon and Everett Ray walked mostly in silence. Eventually, they neared the house. Among the many horses and wagons and carriages crowded around the Teague's two-story home, Gideon did not see Smith's horse. He realized, however, that, while he had a perfect, up close image in his mind of the horse's head and the bit that struck his face, he couldn't remember exactly what the rest of Smith's horse had looked like. It could be any of the lone horses loosely tied around the house, to posts and porch and the sides of buckboards and carriages.

Gideon expected Sam Smith had had plenty of time to wreak what havoc he would wreak by the time Gideon and Everett Ray finally made it to the house. Gideon did not know what harm that could be, precisely, but the blacksmith seemed anxious about whatever it would be. So Gideon was anxious, too.

"But," he thought, "if Everett's words are true, there's no harm Smith can bring to me, other than he shows me his fist and boot again."

"He's here all right," Everett Ray said. "Guess we'll go inside and see to it."

The blacksmith picked up his pace and looked solemnly at Gideon, saying, "Try to trust me some here, Gideon. Trust I'm trying to do what I think is right, though the good Lord help me in doing it."

"Take hold!" Gideon heard his father's voice.

Gideon slowed. "Give me a minute, Everett. Wait for me."

Gideon was thirsty. He was beaten and weak, but he was determined to take hold and face Smith down with a different result this time. He left Everett's side and walked into the barn, striding purposefully past the horses in their stalls and past his father's wagon. He kept walking until he came out the backside of the barn, where the water pump was located. There was a pump directly outside of the house's kitchen, too, but Gideon did not want to be seen.

He began pumping the handle until water flowed. Then he let go of the handle and held his cupped hands under the fast fading flow. He brought his hands up to his mouth and sucked up the water, rinsing away, as much as it could be rinsed, the taste of tobacco and vomit. He spit and began pumping again, bending his head under the water while he continued to pump with one hand. He drank long droughts of water until his thirst subsided. Then he stuck his head under and washed his hair and face. He felt his strength return, and he stopped pumping and stood tall.

His wound stung him, and the pain strengthened his resolve.

"He beat me 'cause I wasn't thinking," Gideon thought, pulling his tie free. "Can't fight a man in Sunday's best."

In truth, before his encounter with Sam Smith, Gideon had never fought a man at all, or even another boy. While he had it in him to seethe, he hadn't had it in him to harm. Until now. Until Sam Smith.

Gideon removed his coat and hung it from a hook in the barn. Then he rolled up his sleeves and took a long look at Zachariah's wagon, idle in the barn. He pictured his father and his frenzied defiance, standing atop the wagon to face down whatever would come.

"Take hold!" he said aloud, and he marched back toward the house.

The blacksmith hadn't waited. While Gideon prepared himself for whatever would come, Everett Ray had gone into the house. Gideon heard fragments of his mother's yelling from outside.

"Devious!" "No account!" "Conniving!" "Son of a bitch!"

Gideon rushed inside.

There he saw Sam Smith standing silent and respectful in the corner of the parlor. The men had backed up against the walls, and the women gathered in force behind Ellen. Alma was at Everett Ray's side, holding onto his arm and staring harshly, defiantly at Gideon's mother. Zachariah's body lay in its coffin in the center of the room, with Everett Ray standing beside. Gideon noticed biscuits tumbling to the floor as if shaken loose by his mother's shouts.

"You haven't got a will, Everett!" Ellen shouted. "I have it. I read it. By God, I helped prepare it. So what are you after, Everett? Do you mean to get rich by my husband's death? Is it to be forgery before a man who called you friend is buried even? Or is it just a lie to take what isn't yours to take?"

Gideon knew not what. He stood just inside the door. He had been ready to act in some manner or other, but found his purpose lost in the confusion of the scene. What had taken place while he had cleansed his head for this encounter?

"Ellen," Everett Ray answered. "Ellen, I ain't done nothing here to harm you! Zachariah put it on me to see to Gideon's taking over the farm. I got papers!"

"You show them to me," Ellen demanded.

The blacksmith stammered.

"Ellen, I don't have them with me, of course! I have them kept safe."

Gideon's mother, veiled and dressed head to toe in mourning black, stepped across the room and slapped the blacksmith hard across the face. Alma tried to pull her father back and to stand in front of him, but the blacksmith pushed her behind him, accepting the blow.

"It's good for you to get it out, Ellen," he said, calmly. "I'm sorry Zachariah didn't make it clearer to you."

"He made it clear for me all right," Ellen challenged. "I have his will in the safe. You don't have anything but a lie upon your lips."

"Ellen, maybe he. . . " Everett Ray began. "Dammit, Ellen, he made his meaning clear to me!"

"Horse's ass!" Ellen slapped the blacksmith again. "I stood next to him. I showed him the inventory of property. I watched him set it down!"

"Ellen," Everett Ray, Gideon noticed, was beginning to sound desperate. "I got the papers!"

"Your lying is an insult here, and done over my husband's corpse. You'll rot in hell for this, Everett Ray Malone," Ellen said, calmly now, resilient, accusatory, and confident in her scorn. "You haven't even taken the dower into account to make the lie credible. Everyone here sees you're lying, Everett."

Everett Ray took a step back.

"My father doesn't lie!" Alma stepped forward as her father stepped back. "Zachariah Teague was at our house plenty, and I heard his talk! He said he worried for Gideon and wanted my father to look to him."

Alma's own fist raised in opposition to Ellen. Her father pulled her back.

"Alma, it's okay," he said softly in his daughter's ear.

"It's not!" Alma lashed. "All of you here know my father! He's a good man. He's a good man!"

Alma looked about for support. None came. Everett Ray put his hand on his daughter's shoulder and gently pushed her aside.

"Ellen Teague," he said, "your husband was like a brother to me. I loved him like he was my own kin. The Teagues always done me service, and my loyalty is to them. I spoke the truth about what Zachariah told me he wanted. I made it up that I had papers to smooth it over, so his will would be done. I've dishonored you by saying so, but I spoke the truth about what Zachariah wanted."

Gideon felt the breath go out of him, like another kick to his ribs.

"You leave my house!" Ellen whispered. "You never cross this threshold again, Everett Malone. You take your daughter, and you go from this house and never return."

The blacksmith turned to leave. He saw Gideon then, and tried to speak, but couldn't. He walked to the door, his head bowed. Alma kept her hand on her father's arm and locked her gaze upon Gideon. She did not speak, but he saw she felt he had abandoned her by standing mute.

Everett Ray and Alma Malone walked out the door. Everyone stood silent for a time, and Gideon heard the Malone's carriage working its way from the house and onto the road. The sound of the carriage faded and Gideon stood still.

His mother broke the silence and said to her son, "You had but one task today, and that was to honor to your father. Instead, you walked off and shook hands with an enemy. You conspired. You tried to steal what's mine. Mine for making a living. Mine for raising you up into manhood. I am ashamed to have raised such a wicked boy."

Gideon blanched at his mother's words, and his thoughts left him. He stood mute as stone.

Ellen stared at her son, full of hate.

The mourners silently worked their way to the door. Gideon held his mother's stare but willed her to see what was in his heart. He willed her to see the truth of this day, but he saw steady tears begin to fall down her cheek instead.

Outside, the sounds of carriages and horses filled the air, and dust blew inside the door. Gideon heard the mourners begin to argue about whose wagon or carriage was to go first. Gideon turned around and stepped outside, onto the porch. There he sat watching the mourners as they tried to leave. The mourners had come and left their conveyances haphazardly about the house. There was no orderly retreat, as the mourners found themselves stuck. Gideon watched the spectacle for the half hour it took before the mourners finally figured their way out of the tangled mass and started their way down the road. The yard stank of manure and horse urine.

Gideon still had the small satchel of money his father had given him by the old oak. He thought to saddle Sadie and follow the mourners down the road, to strike out west after all. Yet no matter how hard the duty, he had to bury his father. How the funeral would be now, with those who would attend scattered back to their lives, he did not know. He had brought dishonor to Zachariah Teague after all. His seething hate had found its final fulfillment. His honorable father would be buried without the honor and respects he was due.

Gideon wept. Then he heard the door opening behind him and the sound of boots hitting the porch boards. He didn't care who it was. He continued to look longingly down the road, thinking he could go after his father was buried. Go and never return.

"You looked like you'd been hit over the head when you heard that blacksmith admit to his lie," Sam Smith said behind him. "It's got me to thinking maybe you weren't in on it with him. Maybe you were a fool to his lie."

Gideon was silent. The fight was gone from him. His contest with Smith was built on a lie, like his whole life had been. There was nothing to take hold of here.

"My mother thinks it of me," Gideon sighed. "She was all I had left."

"I'm not sure I don't think it of you," Smith said. "Just that I got doubts now."

Gideon sensed Smith standing behind him for a long time. Neither man spoke.

Finally, Smith walked past Gideon and down the steps. He walked around the porch and pulled his horse free from the rail, mounting it and bringing the horse around in front of Gideon.

"I'll go and get some men," he said. "We'll load you father on the wagon and take him to the cemetery. You nail the lid on and get the wagon ready. The preacher's inside, tending to your mother, so I expect he'll come along and say what words need saying."

Smith rode off.

Gideon sat and wondered at what little he had left of his life. Malone's words, for all their conviction, were lies. It was clear there was some truth, that truth being about his own father's lie. There was a mighty operation at work all around him, but he had no part in it, had no knowledge of it before today. Alma seemed lost to him, too, though he was beginning to wonder if she was some part of the blacksmith's plan, claiming she had heard Zachariah's words.

"Malone was right that I would fail," he thought. "I had but one task today set in my own mind to be done as honor to my father, and I abandoned it before it was started."

Gideon felt weakness deep in his bones, but he finally stood. His only friend in the end, it seemed, was the one true enemy he had deliberately made this day: Sam Smith.

Gideon walked to the barn and hitched the horses to his father's wagon. He threw a hammer and nails enough for the coffin's lid into the back, and he drove the wagon in front of the house. He took the hammer and nails inside. His mother had left the parlor and was nowhere to be seen.

He stood above his father for the last time and looked at his dead flesh. Zachariah's face was gray, and his skin had sunk over his cheekbones. The body wore a fine suit.

Gideon tried to see some semblance of his father's life in the corpse, but the body offered nothing but the smell of death. Still, it was all Gideon could talk to.

"I hope you're in heaven, and you can see the shame I feel," he whispered. "I was a bad son, and I don't even know why. You made it sound as if you knew though. You made it sound like there was some forgiveness in your heart, though you were putting me out to find it. If you're looking down on me now, I'm begging your forgiveness. I seen into my heart hard enough to know I don't deserve it. I took all you give me, and I did you wrong for it. That's why you lied. I deserved the lie. I don't forgive you for it, 'cause I see it now that you got nothing to be forgiven. I want to take it back, but I can't. I want to follow you into the fields and work by your side, but I can't. But if you forgive me, I promise I will have grandchildren for you someday, and I will do my best to raise them up so as you would be proud of them. I will raise them up that they never need to be put out. I will take steps against it. I will keep them at my side and speak true to them. When they need a lesson, I will speak of you. And I will confess it how I failed you, though you would give me all the world. My words will do you honor that my deeds never did. If they grow up to hate me, I will bear their hate in your name. But before all of that, I will make myself a man you would be proud of. It's all I can give you now. It's all I ever could have given you, it being a gift of my own being."

Gideon bent down to lift the lid in place. Then he thought of the sound of the hammer driving the nails into the lid, and he set the lid quietly back down and walked out of the house and back to the barn. There he hitched Sadie to the carriage and rode it to the kitchen door. He went inside and into the kitchen. His mother sat at the table with Reverend Leyden. The reverend looked at him coming in the door and smiled compassionately. His mother turned away.

"Take hold."

"Mother," he said, but he could find no more words. Instead he took hold of her hand and walked her out of the back door. She resisted at first, then allowed him to lead her. The reverend followed quietly behind. Gideon helped his mother onto the carriage.

"Reverend," he said. "Please drive my mother to the old oak. She can show you where it is."

Ellen looked faint.

"I know Gabriel is buried there, and that's another loss you've had to bear," Gideon said gently. "But it was my father's favorite place, because he loved his wife and the son they had. Go there now and think of my father and that he loved you. I will come for you when it's time."

Reverend Leyden took the reins.

"Where to, Ellen?" he asked.

Ellen pointed in the direction of the old oak.

Reverend Leyden set off.

Gideon watched until they were far enough away. Then he went back into the house and hammered the lid onto his father's coffin.

CHAPTER 18
SINNERS WELCOMED

Gideon drove the wagon with his father's coffin to Gladdis Cemetery, about half a mile from the town of Salud. The cemetery stood atop a hill looking down on the town and surrounding farmland. A white picket fence enclosed the space with about a hundred crosses and headstones. Sam Smith and the same three men who had backed Smith at the old place rode their horses behind. Gideon silently objected to Smith's and the men's presence but offered no other protest. He had added enough to his mother's grief this day and would take no action to add more.

Ahead of the wagon, Ellen Teague sat beside Reverend Leyden in the Teague's carriage. There was no one else. There was no other family, no other friends. The wake was to have lasted most of the day, with burial to follow. But the blacksmith business had ended that.

As Gideon drove he wondered how his father would have driven the wagon to a funeral. He imagined it would have been one of the few times Zachariah would willingly sit. Gideon's mind wandered. There was too much to think about, and Gideon was overwhelmed. So he thought of nothing at all. Absently, he formed the words of a poem.

"Death knocks upon my door.

I will not answer. I will not go.

Again Death knocks.

I do not answer.

So it comes barging in."

Gideon stopped the horses near the cemetery's low gate. He set the brake and hopped down from the wagon. He stumbled a bit. One of the men on horseback laughed.

Gideon regained his footing and walked to the carriage and extended his hand to help his mother down. From beneath her veil, Ellen's eyes searched his. He sensed she was trying to understand him. All the things that had been heaped upon her, and now when she needed him most, he saw that she still could not be sure of her son.

There was nothing to be done for it but to take her hand. Whatever she decided, he realized very little of it would be in his control. Finally, she gripped the side of the seat and helped herself down, refusing Gideon's help. She walked past him. Sam Smith opened the gate for her, and she walked into the cemetery.

Reverend Leyden looked down at Gideon from the carriage and sighed.

"Give it time, son," he whispered. "Remain loyal. Be strong."

Then the reverend stepped down and stood next to Gideon, placing his hand on Gideon's shoulder.

"Look to the Lord," the reverend still whispered. "Repent of your sins, and you will find forgiveness."

The reverend walked by and through the gate.

Sam Smith gathered his men at the back of the wagon. They began to slide the coffin.

Gideon felt a surge of panic.

"Stop," he said.

Smith looked at him. "Can't leave him in the wagon, boy."

But the men stopped. Gideon worried. He had never built a coffin before. He used the drill to make holes in the sides, and he had put reinforcing blocks of wood on the inside, also with holes. Through those he had fished through rope and had tied the rope into knots that would not slip out of the hole. At least he was sure at the time they wouldn't. Now, he pictured these mocking men lifting the coffin by the four rope handles Gideon had made and the ropes slipping through, letting the coffin fall. Or, worse, he imagined the ropes holding and the weight pulling the side boards loose, causing the coffin to come apart and fall to the ground, with Zachariah's arms and legs spilling out. Or maybe the bottom would break loose, letting all of his father fall to the ground.

Smith walked up to Gideon.

"We gotta put him in the grave, boy," Smith said.

Gideon forgot the coffin for a moment, and glared at Smith.

"Mr. Smith, I've had enough insult for this or any other day," he said, quietly, so his mother could not hear. "I'm going to ask you kindly, this once, not to call me 'boy' no more."

"You're holding up Old Zach's funeral just to tell me not to call you 'boy'?"

"No. I'm not sure the ropes will hold."

"The ropes? Who'd you buy the coffin from?"

"No one. I made it."

"You made it yourself?"

"I did."

"You ever build a coffin before?"

"No. I seen a couple."

"Jesus, boy."

"You will insist on insulting me, I see."

"No insult meant. I can't help that you take it that way. Any man under twenty or so, I tend to call boy, like folks done me before I was twenty. Makes you feel better, you can call me 'Smitty.' I don't let most folks do that. Don't much care for it even out of the folks I let say it."

Gideon thought on it, let it go.

"I thought I made it okay. Now I'm not sure."

Smith looked at him and said, "Who taught you to work wood?"

"My father."

"Did you listen to what he taught you?"

"Used to."

"Then let's see if you listened like you should have," Smith said. Then he turned to the men. "Lift her up, boys!"

194

The men pulled the coffin. Two men grabbed the back ropes, and Smith walked over and took one of the front ropes, directing the third man to take the other.

Together, they lifted the coffin and pulled it free from the wagon.

Gideon winced and decided that he would find the opportunity to beat Sam Smith within an inch of his life sometime soon.

The ropes held. Smith looked over his shoulder back to Gideon and winked.

Gideon seethed, and the men carried the coffin into the cemetery.

* * *

The first morning after Zachariah's death, Ellen lay asleep on an ornate Victorian sofa that Zachariah had purchased for her from a New York furniture maker. It had taken five weeks to arrive, but finally word came that it had been delivered by train and waited for pick-up in a dusty warehouse next to the station. Zachariah recklessly rode after his purchase in his wagon, defying all the world as he stood behind his horses, grasping the reins like weapons. At the warehouse, he paid the freight and conscripted idle warehousemen to load the crated treasure onto the wagon.

Zachariah's ride home was taken as defiantly as the ride to the warehouse had been, he having little instant regard for the cargo in the back. When he reached the house, he brought his wife outside to see her new sofa as he uncrated it in the back of the wagon. He ripped the boards that formed the wooden box apart with a crowbar, looking expectantly for Ellen's expression when the crate finally revealed its contents. When the sofa was free enough to be seen, Zachariah saw the ornamental woodwork that bordered the cushioned back was cracked and scratched. Zachariah howled.

"Goddammit! Ellen, I swear, I saw a picture of this couch at Nate's and knew it was for you!"

Zachariah threw his hands up.

"This moment was supposed to be special for you," he said. "Ah, hell. I'll send it back, and you'll have a new one. By God, you don't pay for something only to have it come to you already worn."

Zachariah pulled the rest of the boards away and threw them to the ground. Ellen beamed. Gideon watched. His mother's smile grew as her eyes focused in the sofa's fine cloth and pattern.

"You don't need to get me another one, Zachariah!" Ellen said. "This one is beautiful the way it is."

"Are you blind, Woman?" Gideon's father protested. "It's busted up."

"It isn't busted at all."

"Get your spectacles on, Woman! It's plain as day. I'm sending it back."

"Don't you do it, Zach," Ellen said softly. "It is a beautiful pattern, and the scratches remind me that nothing in this world can be perfect."

"Jesus, woman, you need only read Matthew a few verses in to understand that. Don't mean you don't demand to get what you pay for."

"Zach, you bought it for me. I don't want perfection from you – just that you love me. This sofa says that fine."

"I don't understand what you mean by that, Woman. I do understand some merchant in New York got the money I sent for a new couch for the woman I married, and he kept the money and sent me a busted piece of furniture when my wife deserves the best there is."

Ellen did something then that Gideon had never seen her do. She climbed onto the back of the wagon and stood toe to toe with her husband. She put her arms around Zachariah's waist and looked up at him.

"Kiss me, and shut up about my sofa," she said.

Zachariah had been the essence of agitation the second before, but smiled unwillingly at his wife. He bent down and kissed her. She kissed him so deeply in return, Gideon sickened and left for the barn. The sofa stayed. On occasion, Gideon had watched as his mother ran her fingers along the scratches and cracks. He didn't understand it at all, but the texture of imperfection seemed to soothe her.

The night her husband died, Ellen Teague had retired to the couch and there sobbed through the early morning hours. Gideon found her there at 6 a.m., done in, unmoving.

"Let her have her peace," he thought, and he quietly stepped back outside. Gideon himself had been at the task of building the coffin all night. Through the deepening darkness and increasing chill of night, he sawed, he planed, he hammered and drilled. His muscles ached. His hands and fingers were bloodied and blistered. He wished he could collapse like his mother had on the sofa. He was as done in as Ellen Teague, but he had to keep moving. There was too much to do, though he had very little idea what actually needed doing.

In the barn, Gideon saddled Sadie and rode her to the church, looking for Reverend Leyden. The reverend was not there. The building was open, but empty of any living person. Gideon's ability to think was sapped by his fatigue, and the silence confused him. But after a considered effort, he got his bearings on the day. This was Tuesday. No services were held here until Sunday, and the church was not a house to anyone but God. The reverend's home had to be somewhere else, leastwise unless he slept and ate in the pews.

So Gideon rode from the church into Salud. The only person he had spoken to in town of late was Henry Scott Douglas, but Gideon had had his stomach full of that man. He remained ashamed, too, that on his last day with Zachariah, he had used the words of Henry Scott to unsettle his father. Worse than the shame was the guilt Gideon felt alongside it: Without those words and the way Gideon had used them, Zachariah might well be alive right now, a hated but living presence.

No, he would never again seek anything from Henry Scott.

Knowing nowhere else to turn, Gideon rode Sadie on to Nate's store. As he rode, he unwittingly nodded at times, experiencing short dreams before jolting back awake. In these instant dreams, he saw the image of Henry Scott Douglas standing tall like the giant in *Jack and the Beanstalk*. The giant Douglas reached down to Gideon with a helping hand. Trusting, Gideon reached for the hand, which grasped his arm and began to crush it. Then the jolt. Then more moments of tenuous consciousness.

Gideon found Nate in back of his store, unloading a wagon full of barrels. The storekeeper pulled the barrels to their side and rolled them onto a long ramp that was hitched to the back of the wagon. Gideon wondered if he was dreaming again when he saw Henry Scott helping Nate. He watched as the editor caught a barrel on the bottom side of the ramp and held it so it rolled slowly down.

"Henry," Gideon said, trying to decide if he was talking in his sleep. He saw Douglas's face was badly bruised.

"Gideon," Douglas said. "How do?"

"This don't look like philosophy to me," said Gideon. He realized his words were real. He was awake enough, too, to understand that he felt more than disappointment in Douglas – a strong resentment had grown in place of his former admiration.

"Of course, it is," Douglas answered, winded from his exertions. "Laboring among the low, one sees more clearly what sentiments will allow a man to rise above."

Nate laughed. "Henry, you ain't done a lick of labor high or low yet."

Nate seemed to look past Gideon then, searching for Zachariah.

"Nice to see you, Gideon," he said. "Where's Zachariah?"

"I'm alone," Gideon answered solemnly.

"Well now," Nate said. "I don't get to see you much without your father's with you."

"Nate," Gideon was reluctant to speak in front of Douglas, but his business was too urgent to wait. "Nate, my father's been killed."

"My God!" Nate set the barrel he had been tipping to its side back upright. "Oh, dear God, Gideon. I'm sorry."

Douglas lost his hold over the barrel on the ramp then. It rolled free and fell to the side.

"Careful, Henry!" Nate hollered at his helper, his amusement at Douglas's words gone.

"My condolences, Gideon," Douglas said, stumbling from the ramp in the process and falling backward over the barrel.

Gideon said to Nate, "I'm trying to find Reverend Leyden. I don't know what's to be done."

"Well, he's like to be home this early in the morning, Gideon."

"I don't know where he lives."

"Oh, Gideon," Nate said. "Are you sure Zachariah is dead? You might need the doctor, rather than the reverend."

"Nate, I'm sorry, but my father is dead. His neck broke from a horse."

"Oh, Gideon," Nate sat down in the wagon, stunned. "I love your father, son. Tell me he ain't dead and you're playing a prank on old Nate."

"I wish it were a lie," Gideon began to lose his voice. He fought the cry that was trying to escape him and couldn't speak. He was taken at Nate's sorrow. He remembered how kind Nate had been to him before Gideon had grown and lost his own kindness toward Nate. A visit to Nate's had never passed without Nate's sneaking him a couple of pieces of candy while Zachariah pretended not to look.

"Nate," Gideon said, finding his voice again. "I need help. I don't know where the reverend lives."

"He keeps a room above Claymore's," Nate whispered, barely to be heard as he sat and stared between his legs. "Oh, my friend. My friend."

"He lives above the bar?" Gideon could not hide his surprise and disapproval.

"Jesus ministered to whores," Henry said, trying to pull himself to his feet for a speech. Instead, he lost his footing and fell from the sidewalk into the dirt, his speech cut short.

Gideon wept over Nate's grief.

"I'm sorry, Nate."

"Go on, Gideon," Nate whispered, embarrassed at the tears that had begun to fall to his cheeks.

Gideon pulled Sadie's reins and began walking her toward Claymore's. Henry found his feet again and called after him.

"Gideon," the editor/laborer said. "Gideon, Jesus wept, too."

"Jesus, Henry," Nate said. "I ain't known you more than an hour, but I want you to shut up more than anyone else I know."

"I just want him to know . . . " Henry started but trailed off. Even he had begun to realize he had nothing to say.

* * *

Gideon tied Sadie to a post in front of Claymore's. The door was closed and locked.

"It's not respectable for a reverend to live above the saloon," he judged. But he had nowhere else to turn. He knocked on the door. No one stirred inside, so he walked to the side of the building and found the stairway leading to the second floor. His feet felt like lead, but he mounted the stairs and began the walk up. When he reached the top, he found a brass nameplate on the door: "Reverend Edward Leyden." Below the nameplate, scratched into the wooden door were the words: "All Sinners Welcomed."

Gideon knocked.

"Come in," he heard the reverend's voice, loud as it was from the pulpit on Sunday mornings. Gideon turned the knob and opened the door. Inside, Gideon found the reverend sitting at his desk, pen in hand, writing. The reverend put his pen down, and turned to see Gideon in his doorway.

"Gideon Teague!" the reverend exclaimed. "Welcome."

"Thank you, Reverend."

Gideon's expression gave away his distress.

"What is it, son?" The reverend stood and gestured for Gideon to take a seat. Gideon missed the gesture and began talking as quickly as he could, telling the reverend that his father was dead and he did not know what to do.

"Sit down, son," Reverend Leyden said, gently. Gideon looked about the room and noticed the furniture for the first time. Five single chairs stood in a circle, each chair facing the others. Aside from the reverend's desk, there was no other furniture in the room. Gideon made his way to the closest chair, entered the circle and sat down.

Reverend Leyden took a bottle and a shot glass from his desk. He filled the glass and handed it to Gideon.

"I don't drink, sir," Gideon said, remembering his disapproval at finding his reverend lived above the saloon.

"Most times a man shouldn't," the reverend said. "But this is one of those times a drink is required."

Gideon took the glass and looked at it dumbly.

"Drink it, son."

Gideon started to sip the whiskey, but the smell of it made him shudder.

"I don't think I can drink it," he said.

"Drink it down fast."

The reverend poured another shot glass.

"Like this," the reverend said, tipping the glass back into his mouth and swallowing the whiskey whole. "Not usually a morning drink, but when occasion calls for it."

Gideon imitated the reverend's gesture. His whole body shuddered. The reverend refilled his glass.

"Another."

Gideon tipped the glass and swallowed. The liquid burned his empty stomach but warmed him as well. The sensations dulled his fatigue. Gideon felt almost sensible.

The reverend refilled the glass.

"Last one. Then we'll talk."

Gideon drank. The whiskey found its way to Gideon's brain and quieted his grief somewhat. He was grateful for the relief, as little as it was.

The reverend entered the circle of chairs and took a seat across from Gideon.

"Now son, I want to you start from the beginning. Tell me what happened."

Gideon told his story, leaving nothing out. He confessed his hate and his mother's certainty that Gideon had murdered his own father.

"Son," the reverend said. "I am not here to judge you. I am only here to help, but I need you to tell me the whole truth about last night. Does your mother have reason to believe you harmed Zachariah?"

The reverend had an expression that Gideon had never seen before. The reverend's whole face seemed to say Gideon would find no rebuke here, no matter what he might say.

"I don't know what you mean," Gideon said, wondering what more he could tell the reverend.

"Gideon, I just need to know so I can do the Lord's work in good faith. Did you hurt your father?"

"I did hurt him. Everything I said hurt him. I meant it to."

"Gideon, let me make my meaning clearer," the reverend said. He smiled at Gideon the way his father had smiled at him whenever he had hurt himself as a boy. The smile held no derision or amusement – only love. Empathy.

"Gideon, did you bring physical harm to your father?"

Gideon finally understood, but he was surprised to find relief in the question rather than offense.

"Reverend, I wished my father harm, but I did not harm him, unless thinking made it so."

Reverend Leyden nodded. "Okay, then, Gideon. I needed to know that. I expect there are hard times ahead, and I needed to know the truth. Rest assured son, the Lord will forgive you for whatever thoughts you had – you only need to repent of them in your heart."

Gideon sat quietly. He did not know what to say. He wasn't certain of repentance or forgiveness.

"Have you bought you a coffin yet?" the reverend asked.

"Bought one?" Gideon's looked at his blistered fingers, worn hard through his night's labor. Had he done his father a disservice building a crude coffin by his own hand? "Folks buy coffins?"

"The undertaker can sell you one, simple enough. We can go see him when we're done here."

"I built one last night," Gideon spoke as if it were another confession.

"Oh, I see," the reverend said. "That's fine, Gideon. That's a finer thing than buying one. You did right by your father there."

"Thank you," Gideon said, feeling the strongest measure of relief since Zachariah's death. Gideon reflected then that it was the whiskey that made him feel this more than anything else. He wondered briefly if this was the kind of relief people found downstairs.

"The first thing we need to see to then is your father's wake," the reverend told him. "Bill Evans the undertaker can help us with that. But the most important thing for you to do is see to your mother. Where is your father now?"

"In the barn. I put him in the coffin this morning."

"Good work, son. Did you put the lid on it?"

"No," Gideon said. "I expected a funeral."

"That's fine. We don't want to put the lid on it yet, unless your father is in a state that can't be looked upon."

The reverend's last words were a question. Gideon answered that his father looked fine.

"You can't tell that his neck is broke at all," he said, marveling at the truth of it. Shouldn't an injury that could kill a man scream out that it was there and what it had done?

"All right, then. I'll go to Mr. Evans and make arrangements. There are things you will need. I'll have them delivered. Now, be clear here, I will put these on your account. You'll have to pay for them."

Gideon thought about it. He had only the money his father had given to him as he was putting Gideon out. He doubted it would be enough.

"Your mother will have your father's accounts in hand," the reverend explained, seeing the worry in Gideon's face. "We'll take care of it later."

The alcohol worked with the reverend's words, settling Gideon's worry.

"Now, I need to know if you will have your father buried in the cemetery. I don't believe that the Teagues have a family cemetery at home."

The reverend's words indicated his belief that the cemetery was the best place for Zachariah. So Gideon agreed.

"We'll make sure of that with your mother," the reverend said. "But I think it is best. It is very hard for folks to get on with life when they see their departed every time they step out of their door."

"But we'll want to see him," Gideon said, second guessing his agreement.

"And you will," the reverend said. "The cemetery is close enough to get to, and your visits will be preceded with deliberations that will do honor to your father's memory. Buried at home, there's no time for reflection, only sorrow."

The reverend explained that there was little else for Gideon to do.

"I will arrive at your home later today, with Bill Evans," the reverend told him. "Mr. Evans will prepare the house and your father for the wake. Have your mother set out his best suit of clothes. That's a woman's work, and you should not do it for her, Gideon."

"Okay."

"If your mother agrees to the cemetery, the grave will be dug today. I'll make sure folks know the wake begins tomorrow. I can get the word spread pretty fast, so you don't need to worry about it."

"Okay."

"It's summer, Gideon," the reverend looked somber now. "We can't have more than a day for the wake. Do you have family living far off?"

Gideon thought a moment and realized he did not know.

"I don't think so."

"Good. We can make it a short wake then. Funeral after."

"Okay."

"You ride home now. Tend to your mother."

"Okay."

Gideon left and made his way down the stairs from Reverend Leyden's rooms. He mounted Sadie and began his ride back to the house. As he left town and began down the road his fatigue returned, intensified now by the whiskey. He began to sleep several times but was jolted awake again by the rhythmic movements of the saddle. He leaned forward, with the thought of resting his chest on Sadie's neck, but the saddle got in the way. At one point, he was startled back from sleep when he began to slide sideways from Sadie's back.

"This won't do," he thought. He pulled Sadie to a stop and led her from the road several yards to a large oak. There was shade and quiet under the tree, and Gideon decided he would take a short nap there, regain his thoughts and get back to his mother. He sat with his back against the tree and nestled into the trunk. There was no place to tie Sadie's reins, so he looked at her and willed her to stay. Sadie stood still.

"I'll just sleep a short while," he thought. His head slumped forward, and he saw Reverend Leyden standing in the center of the circled chairs. In each of the chairs sat a demon, rendered into dream life like inked etchings he had seen in books. The demons poked at the reverend with pitchforks, laughing. He saw the reverend accepting the stabbing tines and regarding the demons with warm concern. Then Gideon saw a pitchfork in his own outstretched hand. His arms thrust forward, and he stabbed at the reverend with the pitchfork. He saw that his arms were not like the etched demons' at all but shining red and fully muscled. The reverend began to bleed, and he looked at Gideon.

"Why?" the reverend asked. "I would have forgiven you."

Gideon saw there was hay on the end of his pitchfork, which soaked up the reverend's blood.

"Because you would have forgiven me," he said.

* * *

Gideon woke to the buzzing of mosquitoes and the sound of a carriage passing him on the road. It was dusk. In the fading sunlight, he thought he recognized Reverend Leyden in the carriage, riding back into town. Sadie was gone.

"Oh, no!" he thought. "I've slept the day away."

He rubbed his eyes and took a deep breath. The humid air made him cough. He stood up in a panic. He was supposed to be home to tend to his mother and meet the reverend. Instead, he had lain against the tree trunk for what must have been ten hours, at least.

He ran out onto the road, hoping to catch the reverend. But the carriage was fading from view, and Gideon stood alone on the road. Dust from the carriage settled around him.

"No matter how hard I try, I can't do right," he said aloud. There was nothing for it but to begin walking home. He struck out and darkness fell. There was no moon to light his way, and he was afraid.

It was some time before he came to the house. He saw a single lamp lighted in the parlor. He went to the barn and managed to light a lantern in the darkness. He found Sadie fed and watered in her stall. All of the horses were fed. The stalls had been cleaned. Zachariah and his coffin no longer lay in the barn.

"Shit."

Gideon had a terrible thirst. He drank at the pump, washed his face, and went into the house. He found his mother sleeping on the sofa in the same position she had been in when he left. The parlor was draped in black cloth, and the fragrance of flowers filled the room. The coffin stood in the center of the parlor. Gideon saw Zachariah's body was dressed in his Sunday suit. Everything had been tended to in his absence.

"Shit."

Hungry, he went into the kitchen. The stove was cold. He found a couple of biscuits on the table and ate them. Then he went to the sofa and sat beside his mother. He smelled death and slept.

Gideon woke earlier than usual. His neck hurt. The lamp still burned near the window. The coffin lay quiet in the middle of the room, and his mother still slept.

"I will do right this day," he thought.

Carefully, so as not to wake his mother, Gideon left the parlor and went into the kitchen. He cleaned ashes from the stove and went outside to the wood pile. He grabbed an armful and took the wood inside and set it next to the stove. He lighted a fire with kindling and began feeding the smaller logs into the stove. Once the fire was certain to continue burning, he went to the henhouse and gathered the eggs. Inside, he set these on the table and cradled them between his hands until he was certain they would not roll. Then took a clean bucket to the hand pump outside the kitchen and filled it with water. He set the bucket on the stove. He found bread and butter and jam in the cabinet, and set these on the table. Then he grabbed the coffee pot and took it outside, filling it with water at the hand pump. He brought it inside and scooped coffee into the pot and put it on the stove. Then he went outside again and down into the root cellar, coming up with a large potato. In the kitchen, he peeled the potato and shredded it. Then he found a cast iron skillet, put it on the stove and dropped a scoop of lard into it. Once the lard melted, Gideon cracked open the eggs, put them in the skillet and then dropped the potatoes in. All in all, he was proud of his effort. He had never cooked before, but wanted to care for his mother as much as he could this day.

The noise had awakened his mother. She opened the kitchen door and seemed confused by what she saw. Gideon smiled.

"I made breakfast for you, Mother," he told her.

Ellen looked at him and regarded the stove and the crackling food. The smell of coffee had begun to fill the room.

"I don't believe I'm hungry today," she said. She walked by Gideon then and out the kitchen door. Gideon looked out the window and saw his mother walking toward the barn. He ran after her.

"Mom! What are you doing?"

"Have to tend to the animals. Work has to be done."

"Mom, I will do that. You go inside and eat."

"Not hungry today," Ellen said, but she stopped and looked at Gideon. "I don't want to go inside," she said.

"Go and get ready for Father's wake," Gideon told her. "I'll take care of everything else."

"I don't want to go inside," she repeated.

"You don't have to do no work," Gideon insisted. "I'll do it all."

"I don't want to go inside," Ellen said again, and she kept walking toward the barn.

Gideon wanted to follow, but knew the food would burn and catch fire if he didn't tend to it.

"Mother, come eat! Or tell me what you want me to do."

"You've done enough, Gideon," his mother answered, her back to Gideon. "You've done enough."

Gideon watched as his mother disappeared into the darkness of the barn. He went back inside and ate what he had cooked. Then he cleaned the kitchen and went to his room to find his Sunday suit.

Bill Evans arrived with Reverend Leyden early. Gideon found them in the parlor when he came downstairs. Evans was placing candles about the room.

"Gideon," the reverend said. "We missed your presence last night."

"I fell asleep next to a tree," Gideon answered. Then he thought the reverend should bear the blame of it. "The whiskey you give me made me sleep."

"Oh," the reverend answered. "I'm sorry about that. But you looked like you needed something to ease your mind a bit. Where's your mother?"

"She's in the barn."

"Gideon, you shouldn't leave the chores to your mother ever, but especially not now."

"I couldn't stop her."

"Well, then," the reverend said. "We all deal with grief in different ways. If she needs the work to ease her mind, we'll leave her be for now.

Meanwhile, let me catch you up a bit. Mr. Evans has had the grave dug overnight. Summer's heat don't let a soul keep too long in the parlor. I got word out, and folks should be here today for your father's wake, and then the funeral. You're the man of the house now. You're to stand by the door and greet the mourners as they come in. Remember, you're the man of the house now. This is your duty. Your mother's to be looked after. Mostly, the women will do that for you. We'll go to the cemetery then and have the service. Your mother says anyone who wishes may come. I'll say some words, which I hope will do your family justice. Then we will say our last goodbye to the departed."

"Okay," Gideon answered.

"Gideon, then life must go on. It will be up to you to shoulder the work around here."

"I will."

"All right then," Reverend Leyden smiled at him. "You help Mr. Evans until folks show up. Then you know what to do. I'll go see to your mother now."

"Okay."

The reverend left and Gideon watched as the undertaker busied himself around the parlor.

All had gone as the reverend said. Gideon stood by the door and greeted every soul that entered until Everett Ray and his daughter Alma Malone came to the house. Without knowing or intending it, he did everything wrong after that, and the funeral took place that very day, without Zachariah's friends and neighbors there to say goodbye.

* * *

Graveside, Reverend Leyden began to speak. His voice boomed as if he were speaking to the large crowd that had been anticipated, yet there stood by the grave only Gideon, his mother, and four men Gideon despised.

"The Lord gives each of us a measured time in this world," the reverend said. "In that time, each of us must find our way, but the Lord our God is there with us. He inscribes upon us the capacity to find joy – if we have the wisdom to seek knowledge in his Word. Our joys are written just as the Word of God comes to us, in our family Bibles. There we write down our celebrations of marriage and of birth. In the Teague family Bible, we find Zachariah's joy. His marriage to Ellen Gardner, his beloved wife. The births of his sons, Gabriel and Gideon. It is upon such joy that a man finds the foundation of his life, the purpose behind his toil. Family. A man's success is never measured by wealth – it is measured by his willingness to sacrifice for his joy. For his wife and children, he toils in the fields. He plows the earth and plants his harvest. There is no leisure in it, no idleness. It is for a man to express his love and loyalty for his family in his labor. It is a tireless pursuit. The earth will yield its bounty only when it is mastered by the constant and unwavering hand. Even then, hard times lie ahead. Yet he must remain constant. It is the same with a man's family. There is the joy of life, but comes to a man as well the sorrows of death. Yet he cannot waver. He cannot waver in the firm hand he brings to his children. He cannot waver in his fealty to his wife. No matter how constant though, no man can hold onto this life when his time has come. In life and in death, he must entrust the lives of those he loves to the hand of Almighty God."

Gideon's attention began to drift. His situation was hopeless. Zachariah was about to be covered in the earth. His mother would not acknowledge him. Whatever legacy that had been left to him was undone by Everett Ray's machinations, and Gideon still didn't know what those had been. His mentor was a fool. And Alma, sweet Alma, looked betrayed when Gideon stood dumbfounded in the face of her father's lie.

"I will go west," he thought. He still had the sack of coin his father had proffered when he meant to send Gideon away. Then he considered he had lost nothing that was not already lost.

"Hadn't my father put me out?" he reflected. "Put out, I lost my father, mother, and home already. I had nothing to offer Alma but my few dollars and a horse and saddle. She would not have me, I think, without the farm. She made it clear she was counting on living with me on the farm."

Gideon regarded his mother and thought he loved her. He could go now, and nothing would change. She would take his memory as disappointment to the grave. A bitterness rose up in him then.

"Well, let her! If she thinks such things of me, then let disappointment be her reward in this world."

But Gideon loved her. And his father had loved her.

"Do I stay for her sake? What of it if there is nothing I can do, nothing I can change? She has all the money in the world now. She will think I stay to get it from her. I cannot abide that! I will not live under her suspicion!"

Yet only three days ago, he felt her love for him. It had taken his father's death to unsettle that love. If only she could know, understand that he did not harm Zachariah. If only she could know his hate was not hate at all but the natural order of things. Zachariah had known it to be true! Zachariah confessed his own hate!

"What if I can make my mother understand that I was just like my father in my hate?"

Gideon turned his attention to Sam Smith. Would his mother need protection from this man? He seemed to hold the key to everything Zachariah had built. Without Gideon to protect his mother's interests, would Sam Smith come like a thief to take it from her?

Gideon realized there was no answer to his dilemma save one. "I will simply ask my mother if she wants me to stay. The future then will be her doing, and I will be absolved of it."

Gideon rested on that. Let his mother decide.

The reverend concluded his service. Sam Smith and his men rigged the ropes to lower the coffin into the grave, and would have done so, but Gideon stepped forward to stop them.

Take hold!

"You men," he said. "I thank you for your help today. But this is my father. It is my responsibility to see him buried."

The three hands looked to Sam Smith. Smith shrugged.

"Have it your way, boy," he said. "Don't see how you're gonna do it by yourself though."

Smith and his men left the cemetery and mounted their horses. Smith called back, "Mrs. Teague, you want we should leave?"

Ellen looked startled and called back to Smith, "No, we must bury my husband."

Gideon walked up to his mother then and whispered in her ear.

She looked to Gideon then and answered, "Yes."

"Go, Smith," Gideon said. "This is my family, and I will see to it."

"You may leave, Mr. Smith," Ellen echoed, and the men rode off.

"Gideon," Reverend Leyden interjected. "Maybe you should let those men help you."

"I will see to it without the likes of them," Gideon answered. "Take my mother home. I will follow, but I will be late."

"May I trust you act with true repentance in your heart?" the reverend asked.

"You may trust that I love and honor my family," Gideon said.

Ellen joined the reverend in the carriage and turned it around to ride home. Gideon waited until they were out of sight and began walking into town. He had not revealed the true scope of his plan to his mother, or she surely would have said no.

CHAPTER 19
REUNITED

Gideon found Nate at home above his store. Nate was surprised to find Gideon at his door.

"What was that business with Malone?" he asked pointedly. He had been at the Teague home when Ellen confronted the blacksmith and had left with the other mourners. Gideon realized he was drunk.

"A misunderstanding," Gideon answered. "Listen, Nate. My father was to be put in the grave by a bunch of hired men."

"Buried already?" Nate asked. Tears fell from his eyes.

"No," Gideon said. "I wouldn't have it. Nate you were my father's friend?"

"I was. I am. He was a fine man."

"Well then it's for you to bury him with his son and friends. Not for some no account loudmouths to do it and dishonor his memory. I come for you and Everett Ray to help me bury him next to Gabriel."

"Everett Ray," Nate spat. "I don't trust him after today. He done Ellen wrong. Maybe you did, too."

Gideon ignored the accusation.

"I don't know what Everett Ray was about," Gideon said. "But I know my father would go to him when he wanted friendship."

"That he did. I did, too. We were friends, the three of us."

"So will you help me find Everett and come with me to bury my father?" Nate wiped his face with his sleeve.

"I will."

Gideon rode with Nate on the storekeeper's carriage, down a road Gideon had somehow missed in all his wanderings about Oniate County. The road led directly to the blacksmith's home and forge. Gideon was amazed. The road was so close to town that he could not fathom how he had failed to find it.

Everett Ray was drunk in his cabin. Alma was there, too, worrying about her father.

"My father didn't deserve your mother's anger," she said immediately as Gideon entered the cabin with Nate.

"I don't know what he deserved," Gideon answered. He felt enmity growing between Alma and him, wanted to speak, to say something gentle to stop it. Finding hate in his Alma would be a tragedy as great, he thought, as his mother's suspicion. But his emotions were wrung dry. He could not be upbraided by yet another woman today, so he spoke harshly. "Mind you, I'm not here on that business."

"What then?" Alma demanded, standing between her father and Gideon. She seemed certain Gideon meant the blacksmith harm.

"I come for my father's friend," Gideon said.

Everett Ray looked up. Gideon was not certain just how drunk the man might be.

"I'm sorry, Gideon," he said. "I thought I was doing your father's will."

"Maybe you were," Gideon said kindly. "But no one's will should be done on a lie."

"I wronged your mother," the blacksmith said, full of self-pity.

"Dammit, Everett!" Gideon yelled. "There's business that needs doing! Like I told Nate here, my father was to be buried by hired hands!"

"The work of the world is done by hired hands, Gideon," the blacksmith said. "We're all hired hands."

"Well, then let me speak it plain. I don't like these men that would have buried my father. It was Sam Smith and his men. I don't like them, and I won't have it! He is to be buried by his friends. Am I wrong to count you among them?"

The blacksmith stood, angry.

"I am a friend to all Teagues," he yelled back. "Even now!"

"Well, if you loved my father, get off your ass and come with me! I will see him buried with his son, Gabriel."

Everett Ray looked Gideon in the eye. His balance wavered.

"Drunk!" Gideon thought.

"I am honored to bury my friend."

Gideon looked from the blacksmith to Nate. Two drunks now to bury his father. Yet Gideon decided Zachariah Teague would approve.

"I am honored to be accompanied by his friends. We will not see him buried by jackasses."

Alma's growing hate eased and died. She cocked her head at Gideon and smiled.

Gideon did not know what to say to her, so he said nothing. Her smile faded.

The men took shovels and picks from the blacksmith's shed and put them on the carriage. Everett Ray saddled a horse and together Zachariah's living son and his two closest friends rode to the cemetery. They found Zachariah's wagon and his fiery team standing still idle by the cemetery gate. Gideon had worried that his father's horses might have bolted away with the wagon in his absence, but they remained contentedly hitched. Together, the three men lifted Zachariah's coffin from the graveside and carried it to the wagon, sliding it onto the back. Then the blacksmith tied his horse to the picket fence and joined Nate and Gideon on the wagon. They rode the wagon together over road and field to the old oak. Everett Ray tried to stand during the ride but fell over the seat and onto the coffin. From the back of the wagon, he laughed.

"Guess you gotta be Zachariah to stand on a moving wagon without busting your ass!"

Nate laughed in turn.

"Never figured how he managed!" Nate exclaimed. "All the times he rode standing up, it ain't right that he broke his neck when he was sitting in the saddle."

It was starting to get dark when they got to the oak with the coffin.

"Better get started," Everett Ray said. He hopped off the wagon and grabbed a pick. He took it to the base of the tree and swung the pick into the earth.

"Can't do it there," Gideon said.

"Why not?"

"Roots. We'll bury him out here a ways."

Gideon picked a spot and broke with earth with a pick. Everett Ray joined him. Nate grabbed a shovel. Gideon and Everett Ray would break the earth, then stop, allowing Nate to shovel the broken dirt from the grave. It took several hours. During their labor, the storekeeper and the blacksmith worked out the differences that had grown between them in the Teague home.

"I was only doing what I thought Zachariah wanted," the blacksmith told Nate. "The lie came to me when that horse's ass Smith challenged me on it. I didn't need Gideon here fighting no challenges from him."

"Can't say you done right," Nate said. "Can't say you done wrong, necessarily, either. I guess you didn't mean no harm in it."

The two men cried together for a time. Gideon waited patiently for them to finish.

The job was made harder by the darkness, and they were forced to break through roots extending from the old oak more than once, but the men were determined. They finished about midnight.

Together, Gideon, Nate, and Everett Ray stood at the back of the wagon to rest.

"I hate to bury a friend," Nate said. "Zachariah was a good man."

"Knew him all my life," Everett Ray said. "Loved him like a brother."

"Well," Gideon said. "Let's do it."

Everett Ray and Nate grabbed the rope handles on one side of the coffin. Gideon, who was larger than either man, grabbed both handles on the other side. They lifted the coffin and set it next to the grave. Then Gideon grabbed ropes from the wagon, which he rigged to lower the coffin into the grave. Again, he worked one side of the coffin, handling two ropes while the storekeeper and blacksmith handled one each on the other side.

"Gideon," Nate said. "Looks like you're to be as big and strong as Zachariah."

Gideon did not answer.

Once the coffin settled into the grave, Gideon pulled the ropes free, and the men filled the grave. They stood silent for a time. Both Nate and Everett Ray had sobered up hours before. Everett Ray thanked Gideon.

"Things went bad today," he said. "I didn't intend things to end like they did."

"I believe you," Gideon answered.

"Sometimes you try to do right, and it don't work out."

"I know."

"I appreciate you bringing me here to help. It will rest easier with me knowing I took part."

"I wanted his friends to bury him."

"You did right," Nate said.

"I think so," Gideon answered. "But you have to keep the secret of it."

"Secret?" Everett Ray asked.

"My mother isn't taken to you right now, Everett," Gideon said. "It won't do for her to know you buried her husband."

The blacksmith was silent.

"I don't mean no harm in saying it, Everett," Gideon told him, commiserating. "She isn't taken to me much right now either, and that's because of what I done, not you."

Nate said, worriedly, "But folks will want to know he was buried."

"We'll fill in his grave at the cemetery before we call this a night. Let folks think he's buried there."

"Why?" Nate asked.

"That grave will be for folks who want to pay their respects," Gideon said. "This grave was for my father. I think he would have wanted to be buried here, reunited with his son, my brother. No need to confuse the issue for folks."

"It's a lie, Gideon," Everett Ray said. "We had enough lies, don't you think?"

"I need this one for it to rest even between my father and me," Gideon answered.

"Well then," Nate said. "Let's go bury the empty air."

CHAPTER 20
THE STINGS AND SORROWS

While the spirit's influence over Gideon forced him into a malaise of worries over imagined harms which might befall his son, its influence over Alma did not extend so far. She did not fret in the slightest over falls or famine, objects blunt or sharp, kicking horses or disease. She let her son Gabriel play fully in the world, discovering all its wonders and joys, as well as its stings and sorrows.

So on those days she and Gabriel scrambled along after Sam Smith's wife, drawn as she was to the old oak tree to stand in silent, tactile communion with it, Alma would sit nearby and place no constraints upon Gabriel's zeal and quest to climb upward into the tree's highest boughs. Sometimes, if she was dressed right and in a playful mood, she would kick off her shoes and climb up after him. It wasn't quite so easy as it would have been in her younger days, but Alma remained youthful and strong, and when she would see Gabriel hesitate to go higher, she would laugh and climb past him and urge him beyond his fears.

Other days she would sit while Gabriel climbed and wait out the vigil Sam's wife kept, vaguely aware that she was sitting near the grave of her once beloved son, Hap. On one such day, she sat and watched the woman standing blankly with her hand upon the tree's thick trunk. Suddenly, the woman's face came to life. Expressions of triumph then tears flashed across her face, though her hand never left the tree's bark, and Alma knew somewhere, somehow, the woman was full of life. After a time, though she was amazed at what she had seen, Alma felt tired. She watched Gabriel up high in the tree and smiled. Then she lay down in the shade and dozed, dreaming of the Gideon of old.

* * *

The stage stood empty in the darkened theater. Standing alone in the last row, thinking how long it had taken to get through the door and inside, Ellen Smith stood and cried.

"You have to be there!" she shouted. "I couldn't have come so far to find nothing in the end! Come forward, damn you!"

Nothing.

Darkness.

Silence.

Ellen fought her tears away and regained her composure, angry, defiant. She would not be seen as weak, even by her own eye. The world might try to shutter and cloister women against the harsh dominions of men, but she had never acquiesced to that world. If she had, she would not have been capable of undertaking this journey, like Odysseus venturing into Hades, ready to face down whatever stood between her and her purpose.

Yes, she was like Odysseus, she thought, far from home, her own voyage as harrowing, if not, as yet, quite so long.

What force had set her adrift, she did not know. Perhaps, she considered, it had been nothing more than her own will, awakened by a moment of sight. Hap, innocent, happy Hap had perished, and she grieved hard for the boy. And as Sam and Gideon set out to put his poor body to the grave, she had wept tears like never before, finding no weakness in them, but the fiercest strength of her love. As she wept in that powerful, dark grief, a veil had been lifted from her sight, suddenly, showing her visions no mortal was meant to see.

She saw Hap running through the cold moonlit night, lured away from the safety of his home by a scheming spirit dressed in black. Seeing the scene play out before her, she found hate for that spirit and wished to strike out against it, to lay waste to it and save poor, sweet Hap. Innocent boy. Beloved child.

The veil lifted further, and she saw the spirit, too, had been lured and set to this purpose, lured from death itself. The spirit, she saw, was a pawn and a fool, lifted from the grave by a darker creature than the imaginings of men could dare to conceive.

She knew fear then, but the veil had been fully lifted, and fear would not stop her mind's eye from regarding the creature. Devil, demon, or something else perhaps, it had killed the boy she loved, and she would confront it.

Then the thing lifted its own eye and regarded her. She felt its surprise at being seen and sensed something within it akin to fear at that moment. She had done a thing no living creature had done in countless millennia – she had found it and saw it in its true form. Its retribution was swift. It struck out against her with the full force of its malevolence, washing over her mind with waves of hateful energy, and she was lost . . .

. . . for a time.

It had failed to destroy her. Her will prevailed against it, but her whole spirit passed through the veil, freed to roam in a netherworld between the living and the dead, kept from her living self.

In that netherworld she wandered alone, in darkness at first, yet with time, she began to see within the darkness. She became aware of a small meadow, brought to her attention by the sounds of the brook flowing through it. Darkness became light, and her awareness became sight.

She found herself standing in the meadow, regarding a man lying on his side beside the brook, his hand dipped into the water to drink. Were her senses such as they had been in her body, the thing she sensed now would have been the smell of infection and death. The man, she saw, was injured and overcome with fever. She was certain he was going to die. Then she saw the fearsome creature come to the dying man's side in human form, offering sweet life in the face of death.

She understood the deal that was made and understood, too, that the dying man was the father of Zachariah Teague.

"Oh, weak, selfish man," she thought. "You have sacrificed your blood to the devil himself!"

She drifted then, seeing the foul bargain collecting the soul of Zachariah Teague, her angry, innocent son Gideon bearing stark witness as his father was taken from his life. She allowed herself the time to weep for both husband and son. "Poor Gideon," she thought. "In my grief and ignorance, I blamed you. Forgive me!"

She saw the same spirit that had taken Hap to his early grave rise in the night and latch itself onto Gideon Teague's living spirit, like a leech feeding on the blood of its host, draining and weakening Gideon's will until none was left to the man. The sight of it enraged her, and were she able to bring thought to action within that void where her consciousness roamed, she would have brought herself against the thing, tearing it from Gideon's mind. But such power was not hers to command – only sight was given to her in that place. So she watched and began to see the spirit rising like an automaton in the night, wound up and set into motion by the dark creature that had struck out against her and which had, long before that time, bargained for the life and soul of Zachariah. In her heart, pity grew for the spirit. Despite its purpose, it was a thing lost to its own will.

There was only one true enemy here, and she seemed powerless to stop it. Then she sensed another presence, powerful and alive in that place, yet somehow, she gleaned, it had been rendered dormant, collected and kept by the evil being behind all the misery that had beset the Teague family. She recognized the dormant spirit behind the presence. It was Zachariah Teague.

Her mind began to seek him then, sought to speak to him, wake him if such a thing could be done. But the void was an expanse of boundless proportions. She sought, but she could not find the man she knew would fight for the soul of Gideon Teague.

It occurred to her then not to seek the man, but to find the place where they had first bonded, long ago and far from the home they had made in Oniate County, Ohio. She concentrated long and hard, trying to recall the details of the place, willing herself through its doors once more to find her first true love, Zachariah Teague.

She did not know how long it took for her imaginings to become as real as a thing can become in that place, yet in a moment of triumph, she realized she had stepped from the streets of San Francisco and through the doors of the theater where Zachariah Teague had once played upon the stage.

She called out, yet the theater remained empty. She beat back her tears of frustration and willed the presence to come before her. Slowly, the gas footlights began to shine, dimly lighting the stage. Yet it remained empty. Her will weakened momentarily, and she looked to the floor in grief. When she looked up again, a man stood on the stage. The man did seem to resemble Zachariah, but she knew in her heart it was not him. Who then? What trick?

The man spoken then, questioningly, inquiring, "Mother?"

Ellen froze. While she had no heart to beat in this place, she felt it begin beating hard nevertheless, as if it were leaping from her chest.

"Mother!" the man repeated, this time sure of that which he spoke.

The man leapt from the stage and ran to Ellen and embraced her, weeping.

Ellen stood, uncertain, dumbfounded.

"Gabriel?" she whispered.

"Mother," the man said. "Yes. I'm here."

Ellen pushed the man away, thinking the creature had found a way to confound her, to pull her from her purpose. The devil, she thought, may assume a pleasing shape.

"My son died a boy," she accused then. "Not a man. You are not my son."

"Oh, Mother," the man laughed. "How long ago did I die? Did you think I would forever be a small boy?"

Ellen took measure of the man. Maybe he was twenty-five by the looks of him.

"You are not young enough or old enough to be my son," she said flatly. "Not old enough. You are not my son."

"I grant you, Mother, I have not remained a child. But while I did not remain a boy when I moved on from the world, neither do we grow old in that place."

"What place?" Ellen interrogated. "What place would an innocent child go when he dies?"

The man paused and seemed to consider.

"Well, I don't know. But it was pleasant enough that I thought to stay."

Ellen considered the problem confronting her now would not be resolved, though in her heart she wanted very much to believe that Gabriel Teague, her son, was speaking to her in this theater where she had met his father. Yet she was a suspicious woman. She would not be taken in or grant even provisional acceptance of such a thing without sure proof of it.

So she changed the subject.

"I am here to find Zachariah Teague," she said. "You are not him."

The man who called himself Gabriel sighed.

"You will not let belief take hold?"

"And find you a spirit sent to damn me? Keep me from my purpose? No, I will not."

The man smiled. "Such a thing to find my beloved mother, only to hear her doubt I am her son. Yet, I see where you might doubt. But we have a common purpose, so perhaps we can let the issue settle itself, and I will not, when you find it true, shame you by reminding you of this doubt."

Ellen heard the words "common purpose" and considered. Was a different sort of trap being laid, she wondered?

"You seek my father," the man calling himself Gabriel said. "So am I. Let me tell you a tale, Mother. I remember being sick in that body of mine, sicker than I'd ever been. And I remember your tears and Father's tears, and but for that, the whole world fading around me, until darkness settled over my sight. The pain was gone. My spirit lifted to a place I cannot describe."

"Try," Ellen tested.

Gabriel considered and said, "Well, it was like sitting on the porch on a warm summer's day. Not too hot, but just warm enough to bring some sweat to the skin, and for that sweat, sweet lemonade sat in a glass beside me, endless, with chips of ice from the icebox keeping it cool to drink. All my chores were done, and there wasn't a thing I had to do but look out at the world and know it was good. The sky was blue. Birds flew by. A little breeze would come along here and there and cool me down a bit and rustle the leaves in the trees and stalks in the field. Gus stood tied to the porch rail, ready to ride wherever I wanted to go, if I got a mind to go anywhere at all that is."

"What else?"

"That was it, pretty much," Gabriel said. "Didn't seem to need more at first. Then, in time, I got to feeling my father should be there with me because he should be free now to join me. Only he didn't come. And I got to missing him more and more. So I got up and started looking for him. Then I came here and found you, looking for him just the same as me.

"Only something's not right with that. I don't feel you'd be free to join me on that porch, Mother. I got every sense telling me your time hasn't come, and I don't know how it is that I'm even seeing you. I'm not a ghost come to haunt my old house. I'm just looking for my father."

"Why wouldn't Zachariah be there to join you?" Ellen asked, finding doubt in her doubt. Despite her instincts and good sense, she wanted to believe it was Gabriel before her.

"He's dead, Mother," Gabriel said. "No longer bound to the earth. Yet he did not come to me, as I know in my heart he would, if not kept from it."

Ellen decided to believe for a moment in Gabriel as an ally, her son, perhaps his brother's salvation. It might be folly, she knew, but perhaps she had no choice. So she told Gabriel of the bargain struck for the life of Zachariah.

"Oh," Gabriel hollered. "Foul thing! My father does not belong to it."

"No," Ellen answered. "He does not."

"His father made a contract for his soul," Gabriel said. "Heartless man!"

"Listen to me," Ellen said. "I know something of contracts, and two may not bind a third who is not privy to the bargain."

"My father never agreed to such a thing!" Gabriel exclaimed.

"He is ours by right," Ellen said. "We must take him, bring him back to us, but I do not know how."

Gabriel considered and said, "We are bound by more than heaven and earth, my father and I. Our souls have been mingled in the old oak where we shared our meals together, the meals you provided for me to take and share with him."

"He buried you under that tree," Ellen said, tears welling up inside her as she came more to believe this man was Gabriel, her son. "But he was buried in the cemetery. He is not bound to you there."

Gabriel looked sad for a moment, then said, "But he is, Mother. My brother buried him there."

Ellen laughed at herself because the revelation made her realized her son, Gideon, had lied to her, and she was, for a moment, angry with him. Such a foolish thing now, she thought. His disobedience, however, may be his salvation.

"How is it a tree can bind you?" Ellen asked. "It is just a tree."

"It is a force, Mother," Gabriel said. "I cannot say what force it is, but I feel my father through it."

"Then use it to find him!"

"Let us both go, Mother," Gabriel said. "He could not find his way to me, even bound as we are in the roots of that old, loyal oak. We must go to it together."

"Then let us go."

And in that instant, Gabriel was gone, and Ellen remained alone. Fear gripped her heart.

"Gabriel!" she cried. "Gabriel, I am still here! Come back to me!"

But there was only silence – for a time. Then the footlights at the stage grew brighter, then brighter still until the light was nearly blinding. Ellen shielded her eyes, yet tried to see through the brightness, too, seeing a shape forming upon the stage.

"Gabriel?" Ellen whispered, hopeful yet doubting as the new form did not resemble her newfound son.

"No, Child," a woman's voice answered. "*Your* child has been sent forth to find sweet Zachariah."

Ellen sensed – but could not see through the brightness – a smile form on the woman's face, compassionate and sad.

"I apologize," the woman on the stage said, her voice strong, powerful, comforting. "But you cannot look on me the way I am, for there is a power upon me, given me to right the wrongs against me and mine."

"Who are you?" Ellen demanded then, though finding herself in awe at the sight before her.

"Oh, dear Child," the woman answered. "I am a mother, like you. And you are tender to me because my son loved you and was blessed by you."

"Your son?"

"My baby, my child. Zachariah."

Again, Ellen tried to see through the brightness, but her vision was lost in a fog of light.

"Zachariah?"

"My child, my baby boy, taken from life by the foul thing I have set it on you to see. I am Zachariah's momma, Bessie. All my boys, my Child, my Zachariah and all his brothers, was taken from their lives by a wrongful deed done by their father, long ago."

With all she had seen and experienced in this netherworld, Ellen could find no doubt in the words the presence before her spoke. Her mind raced through the implications.

"I saw the bargain as it was made," she said finally. "By the brook in the meadow."

"I gifted you that sight," Zachariah's mother said from the lighted stage. "Gave you the mind to see the thing we must overcome – and more."

"You brought me here," Ellen said flatly. "Took me from my life."

"No, Child. Your life is yours. I gave you knowledge to see things that can only be seen in this place. I have given you what you need to save poor Gideon."

Ellen considered, her suspicion finding voice once more. She said, "I saw the bargain. Your life was an offering in it as well. Perhaps you do the bidding of your master now."

At this, the brightness of the footlights grew impossibly brighter, blinding Ellen. She covered both eyes with her hands, yet the light drove through the flesh of her hands and eyelids, sending a fiery red light into her mind. Then at once, it faded away. The woman uncovered her eyes and saw the stage now dimly lit, with Zachariah's mother, tall and strong, standing with tears in her eyes.

"Not just my life, offered, no," Zachariah's mother said. "My soul. And the souls of my cherished children. That's the bargain my sweet husband made. And that thing tried to make good on the bargain, to gather my soul after taking my life. But I would not go to it.

"I am not owned my man or spirit. Even in life, my body could be chained and shackled, but my spirit would not be bound! I am not bound now. I fought it, and it found a thing it could not overcome – a soul that's fought forever to be free. I fought, and I *was* free because it couldn't overcome my will. Here, something else gave me strength, but not in time to save my children, except for Zachariah. He remains here, to be found by me or bound by the demon. We both fight for him now, and the demon still struggles to bind him to its own bosom.

"I am here to save my children, and my grandchild, Gabriel, will help me do it. You, poor woman, are not a part of this. But family is family. Yours and mine remain in the world where I cannot save them. I have given you what you needed enough to do that. You will go from this place now, back to your body. Gideon is your charge. You know what spirit and demon ail him now. Save him. And be warned: My battle here to save my sons means the demon will fight harder now to take yours."

The lights dimmed into full darkness. Ellen blinked, first opening her eyes again to the darkness, and then to the light. She stood with her hand on the oak. The sun shone brightly, and she felt the warmth of the day. Overhead, in the tree, a child climbed and shook the branches. Alma napped in its shade, over the grave of her son, Hap.

The woman let her hand fall to her side. She looked up and saw the boy looking down at her, sensing she was there with him.

"Gramma!" he said.

Ellen put her finger to her lips to shush the boy, looking to see if Alma stirred. But the girl dozed steadily in the shade. Ellen gestured to Gabriel to climb down. He obeyed, and as he neared the bottom of the tree, Ellen reached up and took him in her hands, easing him to the ground beside her, where she hugged him fiercely.

"Gramma," the boy whispered. "You're here again."

"I am, sweet child," Ellen said, understanding the child must be her grandson, born to this world while she was lost in another. How long? How many years had she been gone?

"Tell me, sweet boy, what your name is."

"Gramma!" The boy seemed amused by the question. "I'm Gabriel."

"Gabriel?" Ellen whispered. Alma had named the boy after her own sweet child, just found and lost again in that other place, grown and seeking his father.

"Well, that is a wonderful name, dear child. I am sorry I did not know it. But I think I have been gone a while."

"Were you asleep?"

"In a way," Ellen answered.

And then she whispered her secrets to her grandson.

CHAPTER 21
ALL THE WORLD'S A STAGE

"I want you to stay, Gideon," Ellen Teague answered her son, after her husband had been buried and she began to conceive how the world should be moved without him.

"I had doubt," Gideon said.

"I *have* doubts," Ellen said.

"I haven't done as I should."

"That will have to change."

"I'm willing to take on the farm. Try to make the business work."

"I won't let you."

"I have to. You don't trust Sam Smith, do you?"

"I'm not sure I trust *you* yet."

"Then Smith's to run this farm?"

"Gideon, sit down. There are things you don't know."

"I know I have a lot to learn."

"That's true. But there's more to know than what's to be learned."

"I don't understand."

"Sit down, Gideon. Sit down and listen."

Ellen paced the parlor, trying to find the words Gideon needed to hear to understand his new place on the Teague farm. Without Zachariah at her side, she no longer had room to indulge Gideon's willful indolence.

Time and again, Zachariah had implored her to give the boy more time.

"He's a growing boy," her husband said. "Nature makes 'em want to spread their wings a bit and stomp the ground to be heard. He'll straighten up."

"I leave it to you then, Zach," she'd answered. "But I would advise you in favor of correction."

Now Zachariah was gone, and Ellen knew business would not stoop and bend to the whims of a misguided child.

Finally, she said, "Your father was a good man, Gideon. He was a smart man, too. He ran the work on this farm, sure enough. He managed the men, paid their wages, and saw to it that the work got done, from planting to harvest.

"He stood face-to-face with some of the most powerful men in this county and beyond. He negotiated the prices, whether we were buying or selling, and he always came out ahead. Oh, he could make an audience believe any illusion he wanted them to, and he could do the same if the audience were but a single man."

Ellen paused and looked directly into Gideon's eyes. Gideon wanted to wither beneath the stare, but held firm. He needed his mother to know he was strong enough for the road ahead.

"Now listen to me, son, and make sure you give credence to what I'm telling you. Whatever you may have thought, it wasn't your father who was in charge of the business that made this farm prosper. I was. *I* set the range of prices he negotiated. *I* picked the men he would see, and *I* decided what deals were to be made. I even selected the crops we would plant, because I predicted markets better than he ever could. I picked the audiences, and I wrote the lines. Your father – your father's job was to speak those lines. Gideon. *I* ran this business, not your father."

"You ran it?" Gideon almost laughed, forgetting how much he had wanted to earn a second chance with his mother. "But you're a woman!"

"And you're a boy of sixteen yet. In this world, that makes us even. In what's to come, that makes us partners."

230

Ellen sighed and stood with her hands on her hips, taking stock of her son silently. When she spoke, Gideon saw more of his considered father fall from grace.

"Have you wondered why I have no family for you to know?" she asked. "Did you think I popped up like as seed from the earth, solitary and alone? No, Gideon. I grew up in California. I grew up in San Francisco, and I knew privilege – as much privilege as a woman can know in this world."

* * *

As a child, Ellen Teague worshipped her father. Samuel Gardner was a businessman of considerable talent and wealth, and little Ellen thought he was a wizard. There was magic in the man, who saw the world and deftly wove his artifices and spells upon it, bringing all things to whatever purpose he divined. His elixirs were contracts, influence his incantations. Ledgers filled to the margins to show the efficacy of his wizardry, and Samuel Gardner had every material thing that untold wealth could secure to his name.

The one spell Samuel Gardner could never cast, however, was the one necessary to bring forth those things he wished from his wife's womb. Above all, Samuel wanted sons who would grow to run his businesses and continue the Gardner name. Yet his magic failed in this regard, and he had but one daughter, Ellen Millicent Gardner. Because he refused to believe his wisdom would not pass as he wished to the sons that never were, he took – reluctantly – his daughter on as his apprentice, though the apprenticeship was pointless at its inception. A daughter would never be a man and could never wield the wealth and power the apprenticeship taught to control.

Nevertheless, an apprenticeship it was, and in Ellen, Samuel laid down the foundations of understanding he would have laid down for his sons. With him, young Ellen lived in the ledgers and contracts that accrued the Gardner fortunes. Samuel shared with her his understanding of markets and commodities, stocks and investments. He schooled her on shipping and imports and exports. He taught her what labor could be exploited for the cheapest wage, and what talent should be rewarded to increase profits. He whispered to her whom to bribe and at what amount. He showed the necessary connection between politics and business, and how to ensure the man he wanted was elected or appointed. Through it all he reminded her that his instruction was a waste of time. Often he would stop midsentence, look at her and tell her she was only a girl and could only be, at best, a well-married woman.

"It is a shame," he would tell her. "You have more raw talent than anyone I've seen. You were born the wrong sex!"

Then he would forget that she was not a son, and the lessons continued. Over the years, Ellen Gardner learned more than most men could ever know about profit and corruption. Whenever she could, Ellen's mother would try to stop her daughter's learning.

"You will make her unsuitable for marriage!" Eloise Gardner would complain to her husband, who would agree.

"I should not show her such things," he would say. Then he would forget and begin again, continuing lessons that were meant for the sons he never had, with his daughter standing in their stead.

Yet the one lesson Ellen could not abide was the lesson of her sex. Every word, every limit placed upon what she had learned angered her. She was told she would never be set free to use what she had learned, never control or make a fortune because her only destiny was to marry well, become another man's property, and have – her father and mother hoped – sons who might take part in Samuel's empire. As her life was given, she would sit in her husband's parlor someday and manage nothing greater than a household, direct nothing more than servants to wash and clean and wait and feed. It would not matter if she were smarter than whatever man she would marry, and she would be expected to hide whatever talents she had learned, sitting mute and helplessly obedient.

But all that she had learned taught her that she would take the world she wanted, not to suffer the one she was given. She was Ellen Millicent Gardner, and to her, that meant she would not be beaten before she tried.

* * *

Ellen Teague told her son these things, remembering with deep bitterness how trapped she had felt, yet determined to avoid the fate being laid down for her.

"I rebelled," she told Gideon. "No one ever expected I would just walk out the front door, so no one noticed that I did. I just walked out of the house and walked for a mile or more, until I was on the crowded streets of San Francisco. Walking among the crowd, I tried to figure how I might use what I knew despite my sex. There was no answer. So I decided I would leave the City, strike out east, to the frontier between east and west, somewhere where society and position wouldn't matter. There, I would figure my way."

As Ellen spoke, Gideon remembered his mother's sewing room was filled with ledgers and papers that he assumed his father had thoughtlessly stored there. He remembered his mother pouring over the books, she, he'd thought, curious but without understanding as to what they could possibly mean.

"But I was afraid," Ellen continued. "I was afraid, so I returned home. But it remained my secret to sneak out of the house and roam the City after that. There, away from my father, I could think of a future settled my way, not his. One day I passed a theater, and I decide to go inside. I knew my father would never approve, and that's exactly why I went in. It felt like freedom.

"I was surprised to find there were actors on the stage, even though it was midday. They were rehearsing, and I watched, standing by myself in the back of the theater. I noticed the leading man right away. He had such an amazing voice and presence. He made me believe the character he played was who he truly was. A king! The leading man was your father, of course, and I myself set down to memory the very first words I heard thunder from him that day, so I would remember them always."

Then Gideon's mother herself spoke the words, deepening her voice and comically acting the words out in imitation of her husband so many years before.

"But tell the Dauphin I will keep my state,
Be like a king and show my sail of greatness
When I do rouse me in my throne of France:
For that I have laid by my majesty

And plodded like a man for working-days,
But I will rise there with so full a glory
That I will dazzle all the eyes of France."

Ellen finished and smiled, even laughed a little, remembering. Gideon stood amazed, feeling some echo of the rousing he'd felt when he'd first heard Henry Scott speak his confusing words.

"So," Ellen said, "from the first, I saw your father as a king! And he is that forever in my heart. I think I fell in love that very moment. As it would happen – a trick of fate – my king saw me through the darkness, standing as I was in the back of the unlighted theater. He said that I was a distraction to him.

"He said he had the hardest time remembering his lines because he wanted nothing more than to meet me. Your father was a magnificent actor. And there I was, a woman alone where I really should not have been. Maybe that is what caught his eye. I never asked him about that. But he was a man who cherished defiance."

Ellen was silent for a moment, remembering the day like it was within reach again.

"After the rehearsal appeared to be over, I left the theater. While I began the walk home, I heard a man's voice calling after me. It was your father. He had left the theater as fast as he could to find me on the street. I don't know what it was about him, but I loved him right away, even though his face was covered with greasepaint."

Ellen laughed, her eyes searching as though she were looking once again into the made up face of a strange actor.

"We found a café, and we sat and talked. Before the afternoon had passed, he asked me to marry him. Yes, it was that fast. And I agreed. I had no ulterior motive that I am aware of. I do not believe I said yes just to defy my father. To this day, I know in my heart that I was in love with Zachariah before he even spoke to me. He was, as I said, a magnificent actor. Had he chosen to stay on in that profession, I do not doubt fame would have found him, and his own fortune, too. Sometimes, I thought it a shame he did not.

If Zachariah Teague had a fate, I do believe that would have been it. But he had other thoughts, other things he believed in.

"He told me he was from Ohio. He told me his family had a small farm and that he intended to return to it. I told him I would go with him, but he asked me to wait. He said he had to settle things with his father first. I gave him my address and told him to send from me."

Ellen sighed. "I waited more than a year for him to send for me. His letters came regularly, and he told me the time wasn't right in every one. Soon, he wrote. Soon. Yet I did not doubt him, and the words finally came. He told me his father had died and the farm was his. Would I still come and marry him?

"I told my father and mother I was leaving to be married. They were angry. My father had found a proper man for me to wed, and he would not have me giving up comfort and prosperity to live in the dirt, as he said.

"I defied him, and I left. I came to Salud, and I married your father. And we did live in the dirt. A tiny cabin, a bit of land, and hard work were all we had. Then my father decided to disown me. But he sent me a tidy bit of money with the letter that said he would. He wrote that I had my inheritance to squander in the dirt, and that's all I would have from him ever again.

"Your father didn't know what to do with it. But I did. I surveyed our prospects, and I showed him what to do. God bless him, he was a charismatic man! He was a powerful negotiator, and he stood tall in the making of what we have. But I directed it. I directed where he would go and with whom he should speak. And I provided the capital.

"Your father loved me, Gideon. He did not treat me like I was just a woman. Maybe in front of other folks he did, but between us it was never that way. He listened to me. He believed in me. And he did as I told him to do.

"Over time, my father's money built upon itself, and we have had success for ourselves. But I directed it, Gideon. What we have is my doing."

"Why is it I keep learning that nothing was ever the way I learned it?"

"Because some secrets must be kept," Ellen answered. "If folks thought your father was doing a woman's bidding, they would not have done business with him. They would have laughed at him. So we never told a soul. I'm telling you now because I need to trust you."

"Why do you need to trust me?"

"Because I have no choice. Our interests are the same now. You want to be secure in the world, don't you?"

"I need to eat," Gideon answered. "I need water and warmth. That's gotta come from somewhere."

"Well, I think we can do better than room and board. But you're a boy. I'm a woman. No one will do business with us the way we need it done."

"I'm a man, not a boy," Gideon protested.

"Businessmen will see you as a boy. So will any opportunist. No, we will use Sam Smith. We'll let him think he's got the reins. But I'll send you with him wherever I send him, and you will report back to me everything you hear and see. You'll make sure he makes the deals I want him to make, the way I want them made. Smith will be our ally, but we can't trust him. You're my hedge against deceit. In your hands lies our security. As for our prosperity, I will direct it, as I always have."

Gideon's world was full of shocks. To his surprise, he simply let this latest one wash over him.

"Well, my mother is the genius," he thought. "And my father was the stooge. I'm to be the stooge now."

"Mother," he asked. "I asked you if you wanted me to stay because I needed to know if you love me and trust me. It seems now that you just have use for me."

"Gideon, I love you. But you are an irritating child. We will work to change that."

CHAPTER 22
GIDEON'S HAPPY SOUL

A year passed, and Gideon decided it was time to visit his father. So he woke early and got to work. He fed and watered the horses, milked the three cows he and his mother kept in the barn, fed the pigs, and drank heavily from the well pump. When he was finished, he thought to saddle Sadie, but decided instead to walk in the cool morning air.

He hiked the distance to the old oak, enjoying as he went the dawn's brilliant light sweeping over his fields and the long shadows flowing from his crops. He whistled a tune and squinted against the light, looking with pride at the corn and wheat he had planted single-handedly in the spring. The vibrant expanse of green and gold made him feel vital and alive. Yet when he neared the spot where Zachariah had fallen and died, he had to fight against the darkness that tried to invade his thoughts.

He had learned the trick over the last year of ignoring intruding thoughts of despair, pushing them down and covering them over with the sights and sounds of the living world. When the trick would not work as it should, he thought of the things that had to be done and how he would do them. Then he set himself to the work at hand and busied his body and mind until the darkness left him again. This morning his anticipation kept the darkness at bay. He wanted to see his father to tell him how much he had managed this year. He found the grave, fallen in somewhat since he had covered it with Everett and Nate the year before. He thought he might bring a shovel later and fill the depression in with new earth.

At the grave, Gideon sat. Shade from the oak covered him for the time being, and he watched as the sun rose higher in the sky. Eventually, the morning light touched his skin, and he took a deep breath.

"I've been busy, Father," he said, not to the grave beside him but to the clear blue sky. "I harvested your crops last year, and I planted the fields new this year. I did it myself, and I thought of you while I did it. I wished you were there with me."

A gentle breeze picked up. The heat of the sun had already broken the coolness that had been in the air. It would be a very hot day.

"My mother is a hard woman," he said, now looking into the depression of the grave. Gideon laughed. "She's put me to all sorts of work, directing my every move. We got Sam Smith to stay on. He does a lot of our business for us. He didn't know that much about it, but Mother shows him what he needs to know. I don't like him much though. We tangled a couple of times, even though I knew Mother wouldn't want me to. Still, he makes me so goddamned mad I can't see straight, calling me 'boy' like I don't mean nothing. So I took a slug at him more than once. But he's quick. Doesn't work out so well for me when I try to take him. He don't seem bothered by it though. He just knocks me on my ass and says it ain't personal, that he'd knock any man down that tried to slug him."

Gideon laughed again. "Actually, I guess I don't mind him that much. I just got it in my head I need to knock him on his ass once. Then I can let it rest."

Gideon stood and looked to the old oak, thinking of his brother Gabriel buried beneath its roots.

"When we buried you, Father, we broke through some roots digging your grave. I'm guessing by now those roots have grown back into you. That means you and Gabriel are together as part of this old tree now. That's why I buried you here. I put you and Gabriel together at your favorite spot. You're joined up again. If not in heaven, you are here."

Gideon told his father that Ellen was doing for him what her father had done for her.

"She's teaching me. Said I was more interested in it all than you were. She said that's because you loved her and trusted her so you didn't have to worry about it any. But she said I have to stand on my own two feet because she won't be here forever.

"I tell her she'll be here plenty long, but she ignores me. But you know she's a hard woman, I expect. She started by giving me a ledger and pointing me to the fields. 'You try your hand at the land your father tended,' she told me. She said the ledger was the key. She said to look to it to see what I had to spend, what seed I could buy, what feed for the horses, what labor I could pay, and what profit I should make for the year. Whenever I asked her a question, she said I was to look to the ledger. Learn the accounts. There's a few years of history in it with what you done. She told me look to that as a lesson book and then figure it on my own. So my life is ledger, barn, and fields. She said when I learn that, she'll show me about how to handle the rest of it, the whole farm.

"She sends me off with Sam Smith, and I'm to keep an eye on him. He strikes whatever deals need doing nearby, but only the way Mother tells him it's to be done. I expect he's honest enough. Seems like he wants to help. Still, I want to knock him on his ass, just so he knows I can do it. I'm to help him with harvest this year, run some of the men and fields. We'll see how that goes.

"Mother makes me read contracts, too. She explains what they're for and why we need them. She says never trust anyone when it comes to contracts, but to write your own and make the other side sign what you wrote, not the other way around. She shows me what goes in them and why, too, and says every word means something and has its consequences, so I have to know what's what. So I'm learning what needs done, I guess."

Gideon's thoughts wandered. What would his father want to hear from him if he were alive? Gideon realized he didn't know the answer. He could only guess, build up an imaginary image of his father and speak to the imagined man.

"I think I was in love," he said finally, feeling some confidence that his real father would have been interested to hear it. "I was in love with Everett Ray's girl, Alma Malone."

Gideon imagined Zachariah's ears perking up at his words.

"But there was that fight between Mother and Everett at your wake," Gideon said. "Everett said he was trying to do your will. I believe him, but Mother took offense, and Alma – she sided with her father.

"Of course, she did. Well, I got busy after that and couldn't figure how to get away long enough to go see her. She was in church every Sunday with Everett, but with Mother there and her and Everett not talking, I couldn't really get free to talk to Alma there either. But I kept thinking I would go see her after this or that got done, but there was always more this and that to get done. Hell, I didn't even get to come see you until today, and you're just here up the hill a bit. Anyway, before I knew it, Alma didn't come to church no more, and Everett told folks she went off to live with her aunt.

"So I never even said goodbye to her. I promised to marry her, too, on the day you died. Before you died, of course. Didn't tell her I wanted to get married while you was laying in your coffin, that's for sure.

"It felt like it was meant to be something between her and me though. I felt it since we was kids. She'd look at me, and I'd look at her, and it was like our souls were joined. I can't explain it better than that, but Mom said it was that way with you and her, so maybe you understand.

"I guess I would have lost her anyway though, even if you hadn't died. You were putting me out, so I'd have nowhere to go but out west. Couldn't expect she'd wait for me to have a pot to piss in. So I lost her anyway."

Gideon thought about it and said, "I don't know if I'd've cried over her. I cried enough over you getting killed, and when I stopped it was like I didn't have nothing left I could cry about."

Gideon sat beside the grave again and felt the humid air beginning to dampen his skin.

"I love summer," he said. "Winter's too much like death."

Gideon thought on what needed to be done early today.

"I have to go. You thought I was lazy. Well, I can't be that no more. You'd be happy with that. But here I am talking, and I don't really feel like you're here at all. It's like talking in an empty room."

Gideon stood. "I don't know if I'll come back for a while. I'm not sure how I feel about talking where there's no one talking back to me. But I love you, Father. I wish I could hear you talking to me again. I think the way I am now is how you wanted me to be when I got back after being put out. I think we could talk, and you'd like talking to me."

Gideon thought to say goodbye, but felt he'd be foolish to do so. So he started walking back to the barn, without a glance back to his father or the tree that grew into his brother's bones.

But somewhere in the unseen, as Gideon spoke, the spirit of Zachariah Teague had been in a fight for his soul. For all his strength and for all his will, Zachariah was losing the battle. The enemy was relentless and strong, undeniable in its claim. Then somehow, emanating from the boughs of the old oak and breaking through onto the spiritual battlefield, Zachariah heard the words of this son. Where he had been about to release his hold on the reins, to render his soul up in payment for the bargain Abraham Teague had made with a devil, Gideon's words found him and gave him strength. He grasped tighter, and the battle was renewed in earnest.

* * *

In the present, dawn began to break over the horizon. The spirit beside Gideon had faded away, back to its Lethe stream – and into its own remembrance and torment. Gideon's remembrance of death had kept the ghost keen and strong, but as the memories fell from grief to melancholy, and even to the proud memory of burying Zachariah beneath the oak, the spirit lost the full sustenance of sorrow and dissolved into the night. Some measure of oppression lifted from Gideon then, perhaps giving way for the fond memories of speaking to his father's spirit and reconciling with his mother. Those remembrances had not come to him in years, the bound, jealous spirit always forcing them away from thought.

In the distance, Gideon saw storm clouds revealed ahead of the sunlight. The night was gone. Wrapped too tightly in memory, he hadn't been able to break free to sleep.

"I never stay up the whole night," he thought. "Memory's never this keen."

No point, he thought, to think of sleep now.

He looked over the fields. Just a short walk, really, to see Zachariah's grave. He hadn't been there in years, but memory seemed upon him mercilessly now. So he started to walk.

Beside his father's grave, he sat. Then he looked at Hap's grave beside it and wondered that he had it in him to wander the night thinking of his son, but never wandered to his graveside to speak to the boy.

"Hello, Hap," he said. He heard thunder in the distance. "Sometimes death is all there is son."

Gideon wept, and memory tried to right his way.

* * *

Gideon hitched the horses and began the drive into town. All around him, Gideon saw life – crops crowding the fields, trees and grass giving shelter and sustenance to every type of animal. Birds called out, and unidentified creatures rustled through the brush. What a contrast, Gideon thought, between the wonders of this day and the isolating days of winter. From November through March, winter drove the earth to a barren expanse. In that time Gideon could see the treasured life of spring and summer choked and buried for miles around. In place of the crops that now blocked his view, the only features on the land were clotted grey lumps of earth. Gideon thought winter a cruel and depressing time, making all things – even the things made for comfort – difficult to bear. But for now, winter and death were held at bay. Three months of vibrant life remained before death overtook the landscape. Gideon took cheer.

Gideon set the wagon's brake in front of Nate's and went inside.

"How are you Gideon?" Nate greeted.

"Fine as can be, Nate. Beautiful day."

"It is at that. How's your mother?"

"Fine, Nate. Just fine. She's the terror of the Teague house, you know. And I am her humble servant."

Nate chuckled, and a loud banging came from the back of the store.

"Sheeeiiitt!" Nate hollered toward his storeroom. "Goddammit, Henry, what the hell are you up to back there."

"Sorry, Nate," Gideon heard the unmistakable voice of Henry Scott Douglas answer. "I slipped a bit. Got a grip on it now. Nothing to worry about."

"Geez, Nate," Gideon said. "Why do you still got Mr. Ass working for you?"

"Mr. Ass?" Nate was confused.

"Sure. First name Jack, if I remember correctly."

Nate laughed. "Yeah, Henry is a bit of a jackass, ain't he?"

"More than a bit, I think. Does he do anything for you other than drop stuff?"

Nate lowered his voice, "No. He's taken to drink, too. More trouble than he's worth most days."

"Then why do you got him here?" Gideon thought he would like nothing more than to see Henry Scott Douglas move on back to where he came from.

"Reverend asked me to keep him on," Nate said. "Reverend knows he's drinking too much. Knows he's a horse's ass, too. But Reverend Leyden has it in his head that Henry needs time to find the Lord and accept Him true. So the reverend says I'm to look after Henry's physical needs, while he ministers to the spiritual."

Another crash and the sound of cracking wood came from the storeroom.

"Goddammit, Henry!"

"Sorry, Nate."

"I think maybe the reverend is more interested in teaching me Christian charity, because I sure want to kick Henry's ass right out of this store," Nate told Gideon.

"No one could blame you if you did," Gideon said. "Ah, speaking of humble servants, Nate, my mother made a list for you. Any chance you could get this stuff put on my wagon while I walk around town a bit?"

"Sure enough," Nate said. "I'll have Henry do it."

"Then I'll check for breakage before I pay."

Nate chuckled. "I'll see to it everything gets loaded in one piece."

Gideon handed Nate his mother's list and told Nate there was no hurry.

"I feel like walking a bit."

Gideon left the store and wandered down the street until he stood in front of Henry Scott's press. There was a sun beaten, handwritten sign in the door. The paper was yellow and curling on the edges. It read, "Temporarily closed. The Oniate County Press will continue operations on . . ." and it gave a date eight months past.

"Behind schedule a bit, Henry," Gideon said. "Jackass."

Gideon's talk with Zachariah had left him thinking about Alma. He told his father he'd been in love with her. Was it true? He hadn't seen her since she'd left to live with her aunt, and he hadn't spoken to her since he came to get Everett Ray to help bury Zachariah. He sat on the sidewalk and tried to remember how it had been when they made love. His memory wasn't as keen then, in that moment, as it would be years later, but he could still conjure up the sensation of her head resting on his naked chest. It remained in his mind the sweetest moment of his life.

"I felt so content," he thought. "Until Henry Jackass came along."

Yet he hadn't spoken to her in a year. So had he ever loved her as he told himself he had?

He decided if he calmed his mind and thought only about her, the answer might come. It wasn't easy. Wagons, horses, and carriages rode down the center street. The smell of manure and horse urine was strong, and people passed behind him on the sidewalk in a constant stream, ringing and cracking the dead boards beneath their feet. Some said, "Morning, Gideon," and he answered, "Morning. Gonna be a scorcher." "That's for sure," some replied, with others answering, "Already is."

He managed, despite the noise of life all around him, to see Alma's image in his mind. The image troubled him. He felt guilt, he realized, and longing. Guilt for letting things lie, and longing for what seemed another loss. He remembered how it had seemed to him after burying his father that anything short of death was not a loss at all. Yet time went by. Things changed. Had Alma lost the love she professed for him? Was that why she left Salud? Had she waited and hoped, only to see Gideon's silent avoidance of her at church?

He should have spoken to her, he thought, regretting that his need to keep his mother's love kept him at her side. Ellen Teague had settled on

Alma's father as an enemy. If Gideon showed his hand, his allegiance to Alma and his continuing respect for her father would have torn his new world apart.

So he avoided Alma and forced his feelings away.

"When the time's right," he'd thought. "When Mother's anger fades."

Even now, his thoughts about Alma were a danger to him. If his mother knew, it might break the bond they had developed since Zachariah's death.

"Morning, Gideon," someone passing said.

"Morning. Going to be a scorcher."

"Already is."

Gideon stood. Everett's shop and home weren't too far from town. He could walk the distance in a short time. He had reason to believe he'd done service to Everett, bringing him to bury his father, the blacksmith's friend. Surely, Everett would not turn him away.

He set out to the Malone place then, his mind made up. "I will find where Alma is and write to her. I'll tell her why things happened like they did."

He wondered. "Will I tell her I love her?"

Gideon walked briskly. He felt alive.

"I will just make my mother understand," he thought. "She fell in love with my father and defied her family. I will tell her I am in love and want to keep my family all the same."

Along the way, Gideon began to doubt. Alma's affection for him may well have taken the turn his own feeling about Henry Scott had. Had she seen things in him that would have changed her feelings? He decided that he could not let doubt stand in the way. If her feelings had changed, he was determined to know it. If they hadn't, he was determined to give them reason to live again.

The Malone place sat just off a curve in the road. He passed the trees that were blocking his view of the place. There was no smoke coming from the shop. Maybe the blacksmith was making his rounds, shoeing horses for the day. He almost turned to leave when he saw a fat woman come out of the house and walk to the hand pump. She carried a bucket.

"Did Everett find himself a new wife," Gideon wondered. "Well, one way to find out."

Gideon began walking toward the woman. Before she saw him, recognition took hold. She was larger, fatter, but it was Alma! Home to visit!

"Alma!" he shouted, joyous at finding his love in front of his very eyes, in the flesh.

"Alma!" he shouted again. He began running to her.

Alma looked up, startled. She dropped the bucket and ran awkwardly to the house, closing the door behind her. Gideon laughed. His joy at seeing Alma was such that her reaction to him couldn't take it away. He found the bucket she had dropped and began pumping the handle on the water pump, filling the bucket for her. He carried the bucket to the door and knocked.

"Alma," he shouted through the door. "I'm so glad to see you! Please open the door. I filled your bucket for you."

He was met with silence.

"Alma," he said again, putting the bucket down. "Alma, I've been wrong not to see you. Things were hard on me when my father died, but that's passed now. Alma, I want to tell you I love you. Please open the door."

The door opened ajar. Alma's beautiful eyes met Gideon's, but they were filled with sadness.

"Alma, what's wrong?"

"Gideon," Alma answered. "No one's to know I'm here."

"But, Alma," Gideon laughed again. "I do know it. I'm looking right at you."

Alma closed the door again.

"Alma," Gideon shouted. "Alma, I'm sorry I didn't see you. Things were complicated. Your father and my mother were at odds. My father died. Things were unsettled. I had to work to set things right. Alma, I never stopped loving you."

The door opened again, fully this time. Alma stood before Gideon, large beneath her loose-fitting dress. She said, "You'll stop loving me now."

Gideon looked her in the eye. "Why would I?"

"Gideon, don't you see it?"

"You got fat, Alma. That's all. Why wouldn't I love you anyway?"

"Gideon Teague, I ain't fat! I'm going to have a baby."

Gideon could not hide his surprise. Alma started to close the door, but Gideon put his boot in the way.

"Alma, we have to talk then, don't we?"

"Why would you want to talk to me now?"

"I love you, Alma."

"I'm to have a baby, Gideon! Anytime now! Don't mock me."

"I'm not mocking you, Alma! You said it yourself, we're to be together. We made love."

"That don't mean you'll want a woman that got herself with child."

"Alma, I'll make it right by you."

"You'll make it right by me? Gideon Teague," Alma was angry. "How the hell can you make it right by me?"

"I'll marry you!"

Alma let go of the door.

"Poor Gideon," she said. "We can't get married now. That's passed us."

"You don't love me no more?"

"I never stopped loving you, Gideon. But you hurt me. That's what happened to me."

"Alma, I know I hurt you. I was wrong. But you're here now. I'm here. Let's do what we said we would do and get married."

"You'd marry me like this?"

"I will marry you like this."

"Gideon Teague, you're a fool."

"I'm a fool in love with you, Alma. I done wrong by you. Well, I'm done doing wrong by folks I love."

"You really love me still?"

"I never stopped loving you. I just got sidetracked for a while."

"Your mother won't let you marry me. I'm keeping this child with me. Gonna raise it."

"We'll raise it together, Alma."

Alma began to laugh and cry.

"Alma, what is it?"

"Gideon, I don't know what it is that you would ruin your own reputation to marry me. And your family's name."

"Well, what are you going to do if you won't marry me? You gonna hide in this house and keep your baby in a closet so as no one ever sees it?"

"I'll stay here, close to home. No one needs to know I'm here if you don't tell."

"I'll tell everyone that you're here, and it's only a matter of time before I do right by you and marry you."

"Gideon, you really mean it? You're not making fun of me?"

"I'm not making fun of you, Alma. Where's your father? I'll tell him right now we're to be married."

"He's out working. He won't like this, Gideon. He'll be angry that you know about me."

"He was my father's friend," Gideon said. "I expect he'll look on me as a friend as well."

Alma cried and laughed all at once. She stepped out of the door and hugged Gideon and kissed him like he was all the world to her.

"I loved you forever, Gideon Teague. If your mother and my father say it's all right, I will marry you and live with you forever."

Gideon kissed her. "Say you won't change your mind."

"I won't change my mind, Gideon. I loved you forever."

"Then you don't disappear on me. I've got some work to finish in town, and then I'll go home and tell my mother we're to be married. I'll say the blame is mine, because it is. I'll make her understand, and if she won't, we'll marry anyway."

"I won't ruin your life, Gideon," Alma said. "I love you too much. Without your family says it's okay, I won't marry you."

"My mother will be made to understand that I love you and won't live without you," he said. "Now you stay here, and don't go off to live with no aunt."

"There isn't no aunt, Gideon. That was said to hide me."

"I won't have you hid. And don't tell your father. That will be my obligation."

Alma looked more joyful than Gideon had ever seen.

"Gideon, you're saving me."

"You're saving me, Alma. You don't change your mind and go off."

"I'll wait for you."

Gideon left, running toward town and looking back over his shoulder. Alma stood watching after him in the doorway.

CHAPTER 23
THE GOOD MAN

"I never seen it happening like this today," Gideon thought, happily driving the wagon along the road.

He had tied down the load securely for the ride home, knowing in advance how he would ride. He drove the horses fast and stood tall on the wagon. The ride home was seamless violence. He jostled and bounced, flew up into the air, landed – all with the consistency of a flowing stream. There was no unbalancing, no fall or injury. He was more alive today than he had ever been.

"Alma Teague!" he shouted to no one at all. "Alma, I will marry you!"

At home, he unloaded the wagon, whistling. His mother came out to see him work, hands on her hips and watching him closely.

"What's got into you, Gideon?" she asked.

"We'll talk when my work's done here," he said. "I got news to share with you."

When he finished unloading the wagon and putting the horses away, he found his mother waiting in the parlor, sitting on her sofa.

"Mother," he said. "You may be disappointed in me when I tell you what I got to tell, but I see joy in it. I'll ask that you forgive what's to be forgiven and look to the future."

"Gideon, what on earth are you talking about?"

"Mother, I'm to be married to Alma Malone."

"Alma Malone?"

"Yes."

"Isn't she away with an aunt or something?"

"No. She's right here at home. Mother, I have to tell you that Alma and me . . . now this is where I'll need your Christian charity."

"Charity?"

"Mother I . . . Alma and me made love on the day my father died. Not after he died or anything, but that day, before it all happened."

"You made love to Everett Ray's little girl?"

"She wasn't little, Mother. She's a year older than me."

"You're sure she's who you want to marry?"

"I'm sure."

"Well, then, Gideon, I guess you'll make plans to marry. I expect there's no hurry in this."

"Mother, there is," Gideon mustered his courage. "Mother, Alma is going to have my baby."

"Your baby?"

"My baby."

"'Going to have,' as in she hasn't had it yet?"

"That's right. She's pregnant. Looks like she's ready to have it anytime."

"And you . . . you and she . . . on the day your father died?"

"I did. I'm sorry, Mother. I shouldn't have. But we were in love."

"You know what I think of Everett Malone, don't you?"

"I think I do."

"He tried to steal this farm away from me, using you to do it."

"Mother, I ain't exactly sure that's what was taking place."

"You been talking to him, have you?"

"No. No, not since father's funeral."

"That man was working through you, Gideon," Ellen said. "That's how I see it, plain as day. Now I'm looking at this news of yours like maybe he's working through his daughter to get to the same place."

"Mother, Malone, well, I think he might have thought he was doing right, though he lied in doing it."

"So you're taking up for Everett then?"

"Don't know that I'm taking up for him," Gideon answered. "I just don't know that I see it the same way you see it."

Ellen looked at her son.

"Gideon, the world is full of people who will play on your ignorance," she said. "You have to learn to see past these things. There are people set to steal what you have at every corner you turn. You have to be wise to it Gideon."

"I know, Mother," Gideon said. "But I don't see none of that in Alma's heart. I wish you could see her through my eyes."

"Gideon," Ellen said pointedly. "Your father died a year ago."

"I know," Gideon said, oblivious to any purpose that might lie behind his mother's observation. "That's what got me to thinking about Alma, I guess. Got me to thinking, and I went to Everett's house to ask him where she was. But she was there herself! And I asked her to marry me. Well, really, I promised her I'd marry her when we made love that day."

Ellen laughed.

"You approve then?" Gideon misread his mother's laughter.

"I do not," she said. "Gideon, you're being played a fool."

"Mother, no I'm not. I love Alma."

"Gideon, what do you know about babies?"

"What everyone does, I expect. It's like the farm animals. I know how it happens."

"And a year ago, she got pregnant with your baby?"

"I didn't know it until today, or I would have done something about it already."

Ellen laughed again. "Gideon, a baby does not take a year before it's born."

Gideon heard his mother's words. He thought he understood her meaning, and he realized that he had no idea how long a woman took to have a baby.

Take hold!

"I know that," he answered his mother's laughter dryly.

"Then you know for it to be your baby, it would have been born in April, or thereabouts. This is July, Gideon. July."

The import of it was immediately clear to Gideon. Alma had made love to another man. What man he didn't know, other than whoever it had been wasn't around. Otherwise, Alma wouldn't have to hide. In his mind he turned it around that she had betrayed him. She wasn't waiting for him at all. She was a loose woman, lying with any man who came along. Gideon had been just another of those men. Yet he had asked her to marry him. He had asked her to marry him though she carried another man's child.

But she hadn't lied. He heard her words. They were admitting what his mother had just told him. Marrying her would bring shame to him as a fool who took another man's child. She was telling him this. He thought then how she had looked at him in church, and how he had turned away, as though he had shunned her. He'd given her no reason to think anything but that he had abandoned her. It would need sorting out, he decided. Maybe he would not marry Alma Malone, after all. But he wasn't certain of anything yet.

"The first time we made love was a year ago," Gideon said, finally. "I didn't want you to think worse of us by telling you we snuck off often and did it again."

Ellen looked at her son hard.

"Gideon, are you telling me truthfully that this child of Alma Malone's is my true grandchild?"

"I am."

"You sound uncertain."

"I didn't know how long it takes to have a baby," he admitted. "I thought it happened the first time. I'm feeling pretty stupid about now."

Ellen sighed. "If this is your child, you must marry her, Gideon. Should have done it already."

"I didn't know."

"Well, we will have to figure out how it's to be done."

"We have your blessing then?"

"My acquiescence, not my blessing. Folks do foolish things. Can't get far in life pretending they don't. But I have reason to keep my eye on your bride-to-be and her father. Don't think I won't do just that, Gideon."

"Thank you, Mother."

253

"Don't thank me, Gideon. I'm not happy about it. I feel like you might be letting the enemy in through our own gates. But the way I see it, the only thing worse would be if you have a bastard running around and folks know about it."

Gideon laughed. "That's good enough for now."

His ruse was temporary, he knew, but he needed to sort through what he'd just learned. He wasn't sure if he felt anger, guilt, or both. In either case, he was certain that he felt regret.

* * *

Gideon couldn't let it lie long enough to think on it. He left the house after talking to his mother about Alma and walked quickly to the barn. There he saddled Sadie and began riding back into town. He'd ride to the Malone place from there, since he wasn't sure how else to get to the place.

When he rounded the curve and saw Everett and Alma's home, he saw the forge was afire. Smoke bellowed from the chimney. Everett was home. Gideon had hoped the blacksmith would still be gone. This could only complicate things.

"Could just ride by," he thought. "Sneak around the shop and knock on the door."

He thought it a good plan. He took a wide arc around the shop and tied Sadie up behind the house, out of sight. Then he came back to the door and knocked. As the door started to open, Gideon spoke quickly: "Alma, we need to talk."

It was Everett at the door.

"Gideon," Everett said, surprised. "Gideon, Alma's gone off some time now to live with her aunt."

Everett stepped outside and closed the door behind him.

"I thought you knew she left. I thought everyone knew."

Everett put his hand on Gideon's should and began walking him away from the house, toward the shop.

"I got some work to do today, Gideon, but you're welcome to keep me company for a while. It's been a long time. Smith don't call me out to your place to shoe the horses no more. Guess there's a couple of guys around here somewhere that shoe horses, but I don't know where they are. I thought I was the only one hereabouts."

Gideon walked with Everett and went into the shop with him. He wasn't sure how to approach the situation with Alma now. No telling how Everett would react.

"Fire's hot," Everett said. "Ever work around a forge before, Gideon?"

Gideon was too anxious to speak with Alma to play this game with Everett. So he got through it directly.

"Everett, I know Alma ain't off with no aunt. I seen her here earlier today. I seen she's pregnant, too. I got to talk to her now."

Everett's face contorted, and he dropped the tongs he had just picked up near the anvil. He stood dumbly for a moment and then walked slowly to the door. Gideon turned to watch him and was surprised beyond reason to see Everett pick up a shovel leaning next to the door. The blacksmith held the shovel out in front of him. Gideon realized that Everett at the very least was threatening him, and might be about to do him harm.

"My, but it's a complicated world," he thought. "Am I to be murdered now?"

"Gideon," Everett said. His face was twisted like he was in physical pain. The blacksmith seemed to struggle to find words, but grunted instead. Anger? Grief? Gideon couldn't tell what was coming out of his father's friend, but he realized he wasn't afraid. He was much larger than the blacksmith, and he figured he would be faster than the man, too. He kept his eye on the shovel and any possibility of movement put to it by Everett. He was ready to react, but he betrayed no tension or readiness at all.

Take hold!

"I hope he ain't as quick as Sam Smith, or I'm fooled and about to die."

Gideon realized Everett thought he was protecting Alma. Would he kill Gideon to do it? Any man might kill to protect his family, Gideon decided. There was real danger here. Everett took a step toward Gideon, and Gideon decided his best course of action lay in words, not violence.

"Everett, don't tell me you mean to beat my brains in with the shovel we used together to bury my father last year," he said.

Everett paused a moment and looked at the shovel like he was surprised to find it in his hands. He glared at Gideon and gripped the handle tighter.

"It's not the same shovel."

"Well, you gonna try to use this one to bury your friend's son with?"

"Gideon, Alma . . . No one can know about Alma."

"It's too late. My mother knows, too. Told her I'm going to marry Alma. Who knows who my mother told by now, planning for a wedding," Gideon said. "You gonna go about bashing brains in all over the county 'til no one's left that knows?"

The tension went out of Everett's body like a man in defeat. He threw the shovel down.

"I wasn't going to beat no one's brains in," he said. "Just trying to keep you from seeing Alma."

Gideon thought it otherwise.

"If I have children of my own," Gideon decided, "I would protect them as hard as Everett here would."

With that and the shovel down, Gideon decided he would bear no animosity toward Everett.

"Everett, listen to me," Gideon said. "I'm here to see Alma. We have things to consider, her and me. I made some mistakes with her, and I need to talk them through with her."

"*You* made mistakes with her!?!" the blacksmith shouted. "You made mistakes. So there was truth in that, at least. Oh, dear God in heaven, how many men has my daughter made mistakes with?"

Suddenly, the blacksmith shouted to the ceiling, "My daughter's a whore! A whore!"

Everett fell on his butt and sat, legs splayed out in front of him, bent over in utter despair.

Gideon walked by him and out the door. He had no earthly idea how to deal with Everett just now. So long as he wasn't set to hit Gideon over the head, Gideon decided there was no hurry in figuring it out either.

Gideon didn't knock on the door. He walked in and called for Alma. He heard her answer from a small room. He went through the door and found

Alma lying on a bed, with a damp rag over her forehead. She sat up and threw the rag into the water bucket Gideon had filled for her earlier in the day.

"Gideon," she said, smiling. "I thought I heard you talking with my father. Did you tell him?"

"Alma, we have to talk."

"Oh, no!" Alma's smile faded. "Your mother's against it?"

"Alma, I'll ask you to forgive my ignorance," Gideon said to her. "I'll put it to you straight. I thought that baby you're carrying was mine. I didn't know until my mother told me that it couldn't be mine after a whole year."

Despair crept over Alma's face as it had her father's a few moments before, and Gideon realized then that she looked very much like her father, the same way he himself looked very much like his father.

"I thought you understood that," she said, matter-of-factly. Gideon could tell she was reigning in emotions that were hard enough to crush her. "I made it clear I knew I'd be a shame to you."

"Alma, you got no shame in my eyes," Gideon said, surprised to hear himself say it, and surprised to know he meant it. "But I need to understand."

"You need to understand what?" Alma's voice took on an edge of anger. "I think it should be clear enough."

"Alma, I need to know what happened."

"Do you think I owe you that?"

"No. I just think I need to know it."

"Gideon, I loved you forever."

Gideon sat silently at the foot of the bed. Then he said, "Alma, I love you. But I have to figure on this. I can't make sense of what I'm to do without I know more."

Alma sighed.

"I thought you abandoned me, Gideon. I thought you abandoned me, and I wanted to hurt you even if you didn't know it."

Alma spoke and made Gideon see events through her eyes. She started with his father's wake, telling Gideon she had no idea what had transpired between him and her father. But she knew her father for a good and honorable man. Whatever had happened, she knew Ellen Teague was wrong to dishonor her father by calling him a liar. Gideon refrained, though he wanted to tell her her good and honorable father had been about to beat him over the head with a shovel, and might have tried if he'd thought the secret of it could be kept.

Alma said it had been a terrible shock to her to find herself banished from the home she had hoped to make her own someday by Gideon's side. The shock made worse, she said, by Gideon's standing mutely by as it happened, taking no step to defend her or her father's honor.

"Whatever he done," she told him, "he done because he thought it was what your father wanted. He done it to help you."

"And you," Gideon thought. Everett had more than hinted how Alma had liked him. Was it his plan to see Gideon set up only so his daughter would profit from it?

Alma said when Gideon had come to get her father to help bury Zachariah, she expected that he would make up for his silence at the wake. She expected he would come back to her and settle on how they would be together. But he never came. In church, when she saw him with his mother, Alma expected he would talk to her, take her to his mother and tell her they were to be married. Instead, he turned away from her. Week after week, Gideon did the same thing. Finally, she thought, he had sided with his mother. The Teagues would be in enmity with the Malones for all time forward.

"I gave myself to you, Gideon," she said. "I never gave myself to any man, and only gave myself to you because I knew it in my heart and soul we were to be married and spend our lives together. Then you abandoned me, and I was nothing but a whore, cast aside."

Alma cried. Gideon let her.

After a time, Alma's tears settled down, and she told Gideon about the day she decided to hurt him, to give life to the anger she felt over his abandonment.

"That man you regard so highly," Alma told him, her voice full of scorn now. "He saw me in town and began to talk to me."

Gideon felt a shock go up his spine, and he realized it was fear. Was Alma to tell him that Henry Scott Douglas was this child's father?

"He told me how sorry he was that he had seen you and me that day," she explained.

Henry Scott Douglas, cane in hand on a cool autumn morning, had told Alma that there was no shame in being seen, and no shame in what she had done, though she herself had not felt shame in it until Henry spoke of shame. He told her it was nature and life itself. He told her the whole of the human race would wither and die like a grape on the vine if men and women did not give in to what nature decided they must do. Then he asked her plainly if she would like to see where he printed his newspaper, forgetting apparently that she already had. Alma did not really want to see the place again – or Henry. She thought he was pompous and unattractive. But he was insistent, and he spoke of how it was a terrible thing that Gideon had had his way with her and hadn't been seen with her since.

His words stoked her anger with Gideon, and before she knew it, she said she would like to see how a newspaper got made.

Henry led her then to his offices and unlocked the door. He looked around and saw no one on the street. Then he took her inside and closed the door. He did not show her the press, which was set up beyond the counter, just as it had been the day Alma had come here in search of Gideon. Instead, he grabbed her behind the neck and kissed her, roughly. He tasted and smelled of whiskey. For a moment, it didn't matter, such was her desire to trade back with Gideon the hurt and shame he had set upon her.

So she allowed the reeking kiss and kissed Henry back.

It had only been a second, but the second set her mind right again. She did not want to hurt Gideon for all he had done to her. In her heart, she still loved Gideon, though he had abandoned her.

So she pulled away. But Henry did not allow it. He pulled her roughly to him and tried to kiss her again. She pushed back and slapped him across the face. Then she saw an aspect cross Henry's face she had never seen in any man before, and she was frightened.

She turned and ran for the door. Henry's hand flew from behind and wrapped around her face, pulling her backward. She bit his hand as hard as she could.

Henry screamed and let go. Alma turned and kicked at Henry, trying to drive him away. Instead, he stepped forward and punched her in the face.

"Then he grabbed my hair and pushed me over the counter there," Alma cried, reliving the moment before Gideon's eyes.

Alma was in shock, barely comprehending what was taking place. Then she felt Henry's hand under her dress, pulling and prodding until he found her naked flesh. She tried to turn to fight. He hit her again and pushed her against the counter, keeping one hand against her neck and smashing her face down while the other pushed his finger inside of her.

"I wanted to get away, to run away," she said, weeping. "But I was so afraid, I couldn't move."

Henry let go of her briefly, and she heard him pulling his pants down. She looked to the door, hoping to find help outside. But she saw the mottled glass on the office door was hard to see through. No one could see in unless he was pressing his face directly against the glass, and even then, he would see only distorted shapes.

Realizing what would happen otherwise, Alma turned and reached for the door. But Henry violently pushed her back against the counter. Helpless, she stood bracing herself on her palms. Henry grabbed the back of her neck again. He kicked her legs apart, pulled her dress up, and he forced himself into her. She screamed, but if anyone heard, there was no help from it. It was over faster than it started. Henry stepped back and pulled his pants up. Alma pulled her skirts down and turned to face Henry. She meant to slap him, but this time fear kept her from it.

"It was just nature, he told me," Alma said. "No shame in it, he said. But there was shame, Gideon. My whole life is ruined in shame now. I only thought to make you jealous somehow. I didn't know what he would do."

Gideon felt rage like he'd never felt rage before. For the first time in his life, the rage he felt had a true purpose, a true source. He wanted for all the life of him to take Everett's shovel and carry it to Nate's and beat the life out of Henry Scott Douglas.

"You're the only man I ever willingly made love to, Gideon," she said. "I should have got pregnant by you. Instead, this horrible man put me with child, and now the reverend wants me to marry him."

Gideon could not believe what he was hearing.

"Marry him!?!"

"I'm told that's what is to happen," she said. "I was resigned to it until you came to me this morning. I thought God had forgiven me and sent you to me. But you asked me to marry you because you don't know how long it takes to have a baby."

Alma looked intently into Gideon's eyes. He saw her raise her hand, and he knew she was going to slap him. He let her.

"Now you know it all," Alma cried. "That's why you won't want to marry me."

Gideon thought. He wasn't sure at all whether he would or would not marry Alma. He was sure he needed to know the why and how of her marrying Henry Scott Douglas.

"Who else knows about all this?" Gideon insisted.

"You know now. My father knows. The reverend knows. And that man knows."

"Tell me," Gideon said. "Tell me how it is that you're to marry Henry after what he done to you."

Alma told Gideon her father began to figure things out when she took sick.

"I sicked everything up for a time after he done that to me," she said. "My father asked me about it. I told him I didn't know. Then he asked me if I stopped bleeding."

"Bleeding?"

"Yes. My father had me and my sisters with my mother. So he knows a woman stopped bleeding when she's to have a baby."

Gideon was confused.

"Why were you bleeding?"

Alma cocked her head at Gideon and laughed.

"Gideon, you don't know nothing at all about babies, do you?"

Gideon smiled. He wanted to ease Alma's pain, even if it meant she could laugh at him.

"No, I guess I don't. Tell me."

"Women bleed near every month, Gideon, out from down there," Alma said, gesturing. "We get to feeling sick, too. But when we get pregnant, that all stops. Except the sick part. But it's a different kind of sick."

Alma smiled at him. "Don't feel stupid about it Gideon. I didn't know either until my father told me."

"I got a lot to learn, I guess."

"My father was angry with me. He hit me, Gideon, said I brought shame on him."

"You didn't bring no shame, Alma."

"Folks will see it that way."

"I don't. What happened then?"

"He asked me who the father was. I told him. I told him I didn't go to him willing, either. So he was like to find that man and kill him."

"Why didn't he?" Gideon thought that's what Everett should have done with his shovel instead of raising it against Gideon.

"He wanted to see the reverend. Said he couldn't figure what was right. So we went and saw Reverend Leyden at his place. He's got a special circle of chairs he talks to folks in."

"Been there," Gideon said.

"Why did you have to go there?" Alma looked concerned, like Gideon might have a secret *she* should know.

"Didn't know how to take care of my father's funeral. Went there for help."

Alma seemed relieved.

"Well, he talks to folks with worse problems there, too," she said. "So my father and me went there, and we told the reverend what happened. Reverend Leyden prayed with us. Then he told us the right thing to do was to have Henry marry me."

Alma told Gideon she had refused. But the reverend explained that was what God would want. Men and women with children, he said, had to be married, for their own souls and the souls of their children. Besides, he had told Alma and her father, it was the only way to keep Alma from shame. The only way she could hold her head up high in this community again.

"So he told us to wait, and he left. He came back with that man."

Alma said the reverend told Henry that she was pregnant and that he was the father. Henry denied it. Then he told the reverend he barely knew Alma and only at that because he caught her in fornication with Gideon. Henry said Gideon was likely this baby's father, and he was clear of it. Alma lied and said she had never made love with Gideon. She reviled Henry and would not have him soil Gideon's name the way he'd soiled hers.

"The reverend is not a stupid man, Gideon. He kept asking questions of Henry and tripped him up. When he was caught, he said he would never marry me. He said his father wouldn't have it. Said I was a whore, and he was from the richest family in New York and wouldn't have no bastard babies or a whore for a wife."

Alma told Gideon Henry stormed out of the reverend's home. There Reverend Leyden, Alma, and her father sat.

"Reverend Leyden said he'd work on Henry," Alma said. "I was to go home and wait for him to sort it out. He told my father if I got to where folks would tell I was with child, he should say I'd gone to live with an aunt. He told us he is a patient and persistent man. He said he would bring Henry to repentance, that he would get Henry to do the right thing."

Gideon thought on it.

"How long ago was that?"

"Oh, a long while now. Don't look like he's having much success, and I'm happy for that. My father wants me to marry him; the reverend wants me to marry him; but I don't want to live my life with that man. I'd rather live my life in shame."

Gideon thought on it. This wasn't Alma's fault. She never betrayed him. He had betrayed her, though it hadn't been his intention. But he could make it right. He could save Alma still and undo his betrayal. It was the second chance that never came in death. He reached out and put his hand on Alma's shoulder.

"Alma," he said. "My mother gives us her blessing. We can get married."

Alma cocked her head. "She ain't giving no blessing when she finds out what happened."

"Alma, I told her it's my baby, 'cause it's what I thought," he explained. "Then I told her we made love more than once, so the timing looks right."

"Gideon?"

"Alma, I will marry you, and that child will be my child."

"But it ain't yours."

"That child is here because of my actions. If I had been with you, this wouldn't have happened. So I bear responsibility. So I'm responsible for the child, and the child will be mine."

Alma wept. Gideon kissed her and told her he would take care of everything.

CHAPTER 24
THE REVEREND'S RUSE

Gideon found Everett in his shop. He was sitting on a stool staring at nothing.

"Everett," he called. The blacksmith turned to look. "I'm asking for Alma's hand in marriage."

Everett stared blankly at Gideon.

"Everett, did you hear me?"

"I did," the blacksmith answered. "She's spoken for."

"The hell she is," Gideon said. "Alma and I were in love before that jackass did what he did. I'll not have that son of a bitch take that from us."

"He's the father of her child, Gideon. That's the way it's got to be."

"Alma don't want it. Sounds like Henry don't want it either."

"So she told you then?"

"She told me."

"Well, Gideon Teague, as happy as it might make me to have you marry my daughter instead of Henry, how do you expect to square it? You gonna marry her, make a home, and have folks thinking you're the baby's father?"

"That's how I figure it."

"And if Henry tells folks he's the baby's father, what then?"

"He won't."

"You don't know that. He's a braggart and an imbecile."

"We'll talk to the reverend."

"He's got other ideas."

"We'll change them."

"And when the baby grows to look like his father and not a bit like you, what then?"

"Maybe the child will look like you or Alma, or your wife."

"Gideon, you're building a house with kindling."

"It's what I intend to do. I want your blessing."

The blacksmith laughed. "Sure, you got it. Can't get worse than it is."

"It's going to be fine, Everett. And don't you ever raise a shovel up to me again."

"Wasn't going to use it."

"I think you were."

"Maybe I was. Changed my mind anyway. Thank your uncles."

* * *

Gideon, Alma, Everett, and Henry sat in Reverend Leyden's circled chairs. Henry was a problem.

"I won't have it," he said. "I am the father of that child! No petty farmer is going to raise my son."

"Henry," Reverend Leyden said. "You've made it pretty clear you don't want to marry Alma and raise her child, boy or girl."

"I haven't exactly made up my mind. There's a great deal to be considered here."

"Henry," the reverend said. "Everyone is agreed except you."

"Well, I won't have it. I've gotten no respect in this town. Now it looks like I'm holding all the cards."

Henry was drunk. He had begun his spiral into alcoholism before he raped Alma, and it got worse by the day. Far from the would-be philosopher, he'd become a petulant and irritating drunk. He'd been beaten more than once since his rhetoric had deteriorated into petty insults. His face was battered and bruised more often than not. Gideon noted a scar on Henry's hand, in the shape of Alma's bite.

"Henry," the reverend said, "I pray for you every day. You've got the demon alcohol in you, and you won't break it without the Lord's help. But the Lord demands repentance. Think of this as repenting your sins. These two were to be married before you came along. Now they still want to fulfill their plan, though you've defiled this poor woman."

"My child," Henry insisted. "Why can I not get the respect that a father should have?"

"You still may someday," the reverend told him. "But you'll have to repent and change your ways first. And this will not be the child you'll be father to."

"I won't have it. No, I will go to the street right now and tell all who will listen: I am this boy's father!"

"Henry, the child isn't born yet," Reverend Leyden said. "Now you've done wrong by Alma here, and her father and Gideon, too. Could have been they decided to look after her honor by doing harm to you. I dissuaded them from that because I believe in your immortal soul. I wish to bring you to a better place in this world and prepare you for the next. But you must repent."

Henry stood. "I'll tell."

Reverend Leyden sighed.

"Okay, Henry," he said. "I have in my desk the letter I've written to your father. It tells all about the child, the mother, and your part in this affair. I've made it clear that financial support will be required to keep the family's name out of it."

Henry blanched.

"My father may not hear of this."

"Oh, but your father will, Henry. If you refuse to repent, it is all we can do."

Henry clenched his fists. He paced the room, stumbling on the corner of the rug and falling on his face. He stood up. His nose was bleeding.

"I will not stand between these two," he proclaimed, as though no one had exerted any pressure on him in the least. "Clearly, before this woman came to me, she had dalliances with Gideon here. More like than not, it is his child anyway. Yes, I will step aside."

"You'll need to do more than that, Henry," the reverend said. "You'll have to swear you will never tell another soul of it."

Henry wiped the blood falling from his nose on his sleeve and said, "The whole business dishonors my family name. I will speak nothing of it."

"And you will never try to see the child."

"What child? I know of no child."

"We're agreed then, Henry?"

"I agree that I have never spoken to you people, and you will agree you have never spoken to me."

The reverend smiled. "We're all agreed to your terms, Henry."

Henry Scott said, "Good day then" and left.

"Why don't you send him home, Reverend?" Gideon asked. "To where he come from? To his own people?"

"Believe it or not, Gideon, I love that man as a child of God. Maybe it is my conceit, but I believe I may help bring him to the Lord yet. I've had success with harder cases. Forgive me my friend, but it is what I do. But don't worry. I think he's too afraid of his father to risk my sending that letter."

"His father *should* know of it," Everett said. "But I understand what should be and what can be in this affair is two different things."

"I don't really know who is father is in any event," the reverend admitted. "My letter is a white lie, told to achieve a satisfactory conclusion to all of this."

Reverend Leyden looked at Gideon.

"Are you ready to do your part, Gideon?"

"I am."

"I will turn the pulpit over to you on Sunday then, as we discussed. But there is more to plan. Let me think on it, to make certain we get it right."

Gideon, Alma, and Everett met with the reverend twice more before the next services. Together, they rehearsed and memorized the lines that the reverend had set down for them.

"And now," thought Gideon, "I am an actor and a liar like my father, too."

Ellen was not at the church on Sunday. Gideon had begged her, told her not to come, explaining, without telling the untruth of it, what was to come.

"This is my shame, Mother," he'd said. "It is for me to undo it. I don't know that I can seeing you there."

That much was true. Gideon did not think he could lie again, when it would play his mother the fool. Not with her sitting there and watching him, regarding his words and thinking them through. She was a shrewd woman, and he loved her too much to lie to her in front of so many people, and he feared her too much to think he could succeed if he tried.

"I must be there, Gideon," she answered. "This is a family matter, and I am your mother."

Gideon persisted, however, and she'd finally relented. So Gideon rode to the church alone on Sunday, intent on what was to come.

The reverend did not preach. When his congregation was assembled in the church, he asked them for their patience and went outside. He reentered the church with Alma Malone at his side. He held his arm out to help the pregnant woman walk, and he led her to the front pew. He helped her sit, and he smiled at her.

"Welcome home, dear child," he said.

"Thank you, Reverend," Alma answered, her voice loud and confident. "I am very happy to return to the Lord's house."

There were murmurs in the congregation. All knew that Alma Malone was not a married woman, yet she had walked into the church very pregnant, and with no acknowledgement of shame.

In the last row of pews, Gideon sat with Everett. Reverend Leyden called Alma's father.

"Everett, please attend the front of the church to sit with your cherished daughter," he said. Everett stood and walked up the center aisle. He bent down and kissed his daughter on the cheek. Then he sat beside her.

"Gideon!" the reverend commanded then, his voice full of rebuke. "Gideon Teague, come and join me at the pulpit!"

Gideon stood. He had doubt. But he remembered his mother telling him how his father was able to sway an audience, whether it be a single man or a theater full of patrons.

"I am my father's son," he thought. "I have it in me to do as he was able to do."

Gideon stood beside Reverend Leyden, and the reverend said, "Gideon, you have told me that you have repented. Does that remain true?"

"It does," Gideon answered. "I have done wrong, and I am here to confess it."

"Then confess it, young man!"

The reverend stepped down from the pulpit and sat beside Alma and her father. Gideon looked at the congregation. The unexpected spectacle had induced them into a state of expectation. They were silent, waiting to hear Gideon's words.

"I have sinned," Gideon said. "I have repented, and I mean to do right."

Gideon searched the crowd, making eye contact here and there. In all instances, the other person averted his eyes. Gideon felt *he* was in control.

"All of you know my father died a year ago," he said. "I was courting Alma Malone at the time. She was a true and chaste woman, and I had asked her to marry me. But when my father died, I became confused. I didn't know if I still wanted to marry. Because she was true to me, Alma stood by my side those months after my father's death and asked me how she could help me get past my grief. I did not tell her I had doubts about marriage then. I lied to her. I told her she should marry me right away. But I told her I must lie with her first, to ease my pain over losing my father."

Gideon paused. There were gasps in the crowd. Gideon was pleased.

"She resisted, but I told her it was her duty to me. Because I persisted and because I lied, she lay with me as my wife, though we were not yet married. Then in my confusion over my father's death, I abandoned her. I stopped calling on her, which I had done before with her father's permission.

"I was a sinner, and I took Alma into sin with me. I lied to her to make it so. Because she was loyal and true, and because she wanted to ease my great pain over my father's death, she believed my lie and she lay with me, thinking I was to marry her right away.

"But I left poor Alma. I left her, but I also left her with child."

Sighs and gasps. Gideon heard whispered comments coming from every pew in the church.

"She came to me and told me of this, but I told her it was not my child. I sent her away. So she left to live with her aunt in Cleveland."

Gideon added Cleveland, deviating from the agreed speech. He thought it a good touch.

"When my grief over my father passed, I understood I had done wrong. I missed Alma and realized my love for her is eternal. So I sought the reverend's help. He counseled me against my sin and told me I had to make it right. I sent for Alma and had her brought here today."

Gideon looked down from the pulpit to Alma. She cocked her head in response and smiled.

"Alma, I repent in my heart, and before this congregation I confess my sin. I have asked the Lord's forgiveness, but now I ask yours. Will you forgive me, Alma Malone?"

"I forgive you, Gideon Teague, but you must do right by me," Alma repeated her rehearsed lines, written for her by Reverend Leyden.

"I intend to," Gideon said. "Before God and the good people of this congregation, I am asking not only for your forgiveness, but for your hand in marriage. I have asked your father's permission, and I have it. Alma Malone, will you be my wife?"

"I will, Gideon Teague," Alma answered.

Everett Ray stood up and approached the pulpit. He reached out and shook Gideon's hand. The reverend went to the pulpit and asked Gideon and Everett to sit with Alma in the pew. There was a cacophony of conversation in the congregation. This was an unexpected happening, and everyone had need to comment. The reverend spoke to quiet his flock.

"Good people, we have witnessed the Lord's work here today! A sinner has confessed his sin and has acted to undo the dishonor he tried to bring to his fiancé. I ask everyone who has witnessed this act of contrition to act hereinafter with the charity and forgiveness the Lord our God demands of us. Let us remember the words of our Lord and Savior, Jesus Christ: 'He that is without sin among you, let him first cast a stone.' We are all sinners, and we shall cast no stones here. Let us welcome Gideon and Alma back into our community, provided they do as the Lord commands and sanctify their repentance in marriage."

The crowd sat silent.

"That is all we have today," Reverend Leyden said. "The Lord's hand at work is better witness to His word than my poor sermon would be. Please go home now and pray over this. The good Lord will counsel you to acceptance and joy for what will be a holy matrimony."

The people looked confused, but one by one they rose and began to file from the church. Outside, carriages and wagons began their journeys home, and Reverend Leyden said to Gideon and Alma, "I think you'll be fine now. Believers are an interesting lot. We tell them it's in God's hands, and they're mostly adaptable to whatever you might have to say. Tell them it's what God wants but that it's going to take them to make it happen, and they're more the willing. After today, folks will think the two of you have come for their forgiveness over God's. It's not the right way of thinking, and I normally discourage it. But in this case, so long as folks figure you've been forgiven by their good graces, the forgiveness will stick. Oh, there will be a rumble here and there, but I believe you can get on with your lives now. It was a fine performance, Gideon."

The reverend smiled. "It nearly brought a tear to my eye."

"You were the author of it," Gideon reminded the reverend.

"Well, now, I believe you're right," Reverend Leyden laughed. "All a man needs to do is live sixty years or so, and he can set down a believable line or two."

"I thank you, Reverend," Alma said. "I do have a tear in my eye. I'm happy where I thought I'd never be again."

"Be happy forever, my dear," Reverend Leyden replied. "We will have the wedding soon as we can after this blessed child is born."

Gideon reached out for Alma's hand.

"Have that child, Alma," he said to her. "I don't want to go any longer than I have to without you're my wife."

It wasn't long after Gideon's scripted confession in the church that Eugene Samuel was born in the house of Zachariah Teague. The following Sunday, Gideon married Alma Malone and Eugene Samuel became Eugene Samuel Teague.

CHAPTER 25
HENRY'S LAST LESSON

The year that followed was a happy time for the newly married Teagues. Ellen's acquiescence turned to acceptance and then love of her grandchild, Eugene. Soon her love for Eugene softened her stance regarding Alma, and the two became friendly enough that Gideon did not fear for Alma's happiness while he was working. Work was most of Gideon's life now. With a wife and child to support, he took an even keener interest in the farm. He worked ten to sixteen hours a day. He spent most of those hours in the fields beside the men, where he watched and listened to learn the nuances of their work and thought. Sam Smith had told him, "You learn how men think, then you learn to see yourself through their eyes. Once you figure that, you'll have the secret to their respect. Remember, it ain't good that they love you but don't fear you, and ain't good that they fear you but don't love you. You have to figure how to make them love you while they fear you. Learn that, and you could run a kingdom, let alone a farm."

He spent the remaining work hours of the day at Sam Smith's side. Gideon and Smith had fought several times since Gideon's visit to his father's grave, with Smith beating Gideon to the ground every time.

"Nothing personal," Smith always said. "I'll knock down any man that tries to hit me."

The last time Smith knocked Gideon to the ground, he did not manage it until Gideon landed a punch. Smith seemed dazed, but Gideon was laid out in the dirt. Smith stumbled and sat beside him.

"Okay," Smith said. "Now it's personal between us, 'cause we're getting closer to the time you can beat me, Gideon."

"I know it," Gideon said, wiping blood from his mouth. "I think pretty soon I'm going to lay you out, and I'll be looking down at you, instead of the other way around."

Gideon chuckled. Sam Smith chuckled in response.

"So now that the time is near, I'm going to fight harder, 'cause I don't take knocking you on your ass personal, but I do take getting knocked on my ass personal."

"I'm learning your tricks, Sam," Gideon said. "You ain't got too many things left you can do without I see them coming."

"That's true," Smith stood and reached his hand down to help Gideon up. "So let's get to an understanding, and save us both some trouble. I'll concede it right now that you're going to whup me."

"Okay," Gideon answered. "So then what?"

"Then you don't have to whup me. You know you can, and I know you can. Save us both getting hurt proving what we already know."

Gideon thought on it.

"But I really want to whip you, Sam – for real."

"Well, Gideon, let me ask you," Sam said. "How are either of us going to get the men we got working to love us or fear us if we're spending our days beating the hell out of each other?"

Gideon thought on it.

"They'll laugh at us."

"Likely."

"Okay. So long as you admit I can whip you."

"You can. So are we through with this foolishness?"

Gideon reached out to shake Smith's hand. Smith took it, and the two men shook on it. It was their last fight, but a new, less amiable battle was about to begin.

As Gideon and Alma's first anniversary approached, Reverend Leyden died and so did his hold over Henry Scott. Soon thereafter, Joseph Beck came to Gideon to warn him of the drunken rumor their former mentor was spreading. Beck had been working for Gideon and Sam for a good part of the year, and Gideon had come to trust him enough that he let Beck supervise the operation out at the old Schick farm. After a long day's labor, Beck pulled Gideon aside and asked him if they could talk alone in the old cabin. Thinking it was something to do with the Schick place, Gideon invited Beck inside and lit a lantern. The men talked over a cup of coffee.

"I don't like telling you this, Gideon, but that horse's ass Henry Douglas is telling anyone that will listen to him that he's the father of your baby boy," Beck said. "I thought you should know it. He's a no account loudmouth, and I don't think there's anyone that believes him."

Beck looked at Gideon, and Gideon understood that Beck was searching for the truth of it in Gideon's reaction. Gideon laughed.

"That drunk has been looking for some way to feel important again ever since you and the fellas beat the hell out of him over his philosophy lesson," Gideon said. "So what, he's to make a name for himself claiming he's fathered someone else's child?"

"That's the way it's heard."

"Well, I know the better of it. But that puts a cloud over my wife and son. You sure that's what he's saying? That it ain't someone else he's talking about?"

"He mutters," Beck said. "But he mutters this clear enough. Says Eugene is his son and he's coming for him. Says you're an officious intermeddler, whatever the hell that means. Sounds kinda funny though."

"Well, Joe, I'm glad you told me this," Gideon made certain he betrayed no truth that might lie in Henry's ramblings. "That man's fallen on hard times. Christian charity says to forgive, but this ain't forgivable talk, given the start Alma and me had."

Gideon knew the whole of Salud was very much aware that he had married Alma *after* Eugene was born. He would use that as much as he could to show Henry's words were a lie, though the circumstances might argue otherwise.

"Well," Beck said. "I thought you should know. I know I'd want someone to tell me if that kind of talk was trying to follow me around."

"I'm glad you told me," Gideon said. "I'll have a talk with the man, see if I can't set him straight."

"I'd do it sooner than later," Beck said.

Gideon took to it the following day. He walked to town, taking the time alone to figure out what he intended to do. Henry, he decided, would have to go back where he came from, or anywhere else for that matter. But Gideon was determined to set Henry off far from Oniate County.

He found Henry in front of Claymore's in town. Henry was too drunk to understand who Gideon was, much less what Gideon had come to tell him. So Gideon slung the urine-soaked Henry over his shoulder and carried him east of out of town, to the very woods in which Gideon and Alma had first made love. There, Gideon intended to let Henry sober up enough for him to understand Gideon's demand.

It took some hours. Gideon sat with his back against a tree, slapping at mosquitoes. He wanted to take his shirt off to let it dry on a branch since it was soaked with Henry's urine. But he figured that would be an invitation to more misery from the insects, so he sat with the urine soaked shirt wetting his skin.

He tried to think things through. Everett's prediction was coming true. Henry was insisting on telling the world that he was Eugene's father. Gideon was amazed, really, that the man would confess it, given what he had done to Alma to father the child.

The shirt was finally dry. Henry sat up, holding his head in both hands.

"How 'bout a drink?" he said, not certain where he was.

"No more drink until we conclude some business, you and me," Gideon told him.

"Gideon." Henry said in recognition. "Where on are we?"

"In nature, getting et on by mosquitoes," Gideon said. "Blood sucking nature's all around us, you horse's ass!"

Gideon thought he would be calm. But despite his pity for Douglas, he realized his hate for the man was far stronger.

"Horse's ass." Henry repeated weakly. "Me?"

Henry spat, looking feebly at the ground.

"No, sir," he said. "Not I. Say, if we won't have a real drink together, how 'bout a cup of water? I'm thirsty."

"No doubt," Gideon responded, making no effort to hide his scorn. "You done pissed about a week's worth out of you already today and got most of it on me."

Gideon watched in disgust while Henry began licking his lips and making smacking sounds with his mouth. Eventually, he stopped and turned to look at Gideon with bloodshot eyes,

"Forgive me," he said. "I don't remember doing that. I don't even remember how we got here." Henry looked down again and sighed dejectedly. "I'm a broken man, Gideon. Broken all to hell."

Gideon felt his scorn subside then, great pity taking its place with Henry's sad admission. But his resolve remained. Henry had to go. Yet perhaps it could be done kindly. Maybe there was redemption lying in wait somewhere within the hollowed-out man that was once Henry Scott Douglas.

Then some of the old Henry returned, some of the former orator.

"Oh, poor Gideon," he said. "I feel for you. But you must understand that I have been through a confusing time. My father has cut me off. I have no more of the Douglas fortune to keep me solvent. I have been given to drink. And what has it all come from? It has come from my own misguided belief that I could and should raise up among the common folk all the philosophies I have learned of the world. Why should Socrates and Plato belong to the wealthy? Why shouldn't their ideas live in the world of men who hew the land and give life and sustenance?"

"Henry, I don't know who Socrates or Plato are, and I don't expect most folks around here care."

"No, Gideon! They don't! But I have been set upon by ruin for my efforts. I came as Prometheus, but I was judged for the fire I would bring!"

"Henry, I don't know what the hell you're talking about," Gideon said.

"No. You don't. But it doesn't matter. For I have learned that it is not for me to bring to this place, but to take from it. There is much I need to learn about humble origins, and I will make myself humble and despised. In that, I will find greater wisdom than that with which I arrived."

"You're already despised, Henry. I'm giving you a way out. Leave."

"No, Gideon," Henry stood up. Vomit caked his clothing. "I will admit that I have fathered a bastard. I will proclaim it from the rooftops. I am a part of this very land now! I have driven into it my own seed, and I will watch it grow."

"Eugene is my son, Henry," Gideon said quietly. "And it's time for you to go home, back to where you come from."

Gideon watched Henry closely and saw cunning return to the man's eye.

"I'm sorry about your father, Gideon," he said, trying to gain an upper hand in the conversation. Gideon seemed to hear an ever so slight hint of mocking in his tone. "You know, I've heard talk over the last few months. There are some around here who think you had something to do with your father's ignoble end."

Gideon tensed at the insinuation and felt the old hate trying to take hold. He tried to recall the pity he had felt only moments before. "He's just a stupid wounded animal," Gideon thought, "trying to bite to save itself."

"The only ignoble end here is what you come to, Henry," Gideon told him. "Now the only redemption for you, the only way back is for you to get on a horse and ride east. There's nothing here for you. No son. No life."

"Forgive me, Gideon," Henry continued, ignoring Gideon's words. "Of course, I know you did not kill your father. But those who do whisper that a man who could kill his own flesh and blood should not be trusted to raise a son."

Gideon stared silently at Henry, deciding he was more than a wounded animal after all. In him was a capacity to be cruel, as he had been to Alma. Yet Gideon remembered his own cruelties, all the hurtful words he had unleashed against his father, his wish of death upon the man.

"I changed," he thought. "I'm not that hateful scourge that I was no more. Maybe it's in Henry to change, too, given enough time and misery to see what's true."

Gideon sought some piece of forgiveness in his heart, refusing to be baited by the miserable drunk that Henry was trying to be. "Maybe Henry is my penance. Forgiving myself ain't enough. I got to forgive someone who don't seem like he deserves it."

Then Henry spoke again. He said, "We both know that boy is my son. The woman admitted it. But I have been part of a deception, and it has to end."

"The only ending here, Henry, is for you to go. Do it in peace, but know I won't let you stay here and harm my family. I'll give you a horse and a hundred dollars to see you on your way. But you will go."

"Poor Gideon," Henry said. "I will take you with me to the wisdom that comes from misery."

"I got misery enough, and most of it is already by your hand."

"Not my *hand*, I think," Henry laughed. "Oh, don't you see it, Gideon? We are brothers, you and I."

"Henry, in another hour, you'll be a despised drunk again. I'm giving you a chance to be more. You made mistakes. Stop making them. Leave."

"No, Gideon. No more drink for me. The reverend told me when I was ready I could defeat the demon alcohol."

"It has a hold on you. You'll be drunk in an hour."

"No. The reverend told me to put some faith in the Lord. He told me I could wrestle alcohol away from me if I look to it like it's the devil himself. He told me to fight every urge for it like I was fighting for my immortal soul. He said if I could think on it like that, and if I would fight it every single minute of every single day, I would be free. I want to be free, Gideon. I see my purpose now."

"You're telling me your purpose is to ruin lives?"

"Not ruin, Gideon! We will all fight the demons, together, and we will be victorious."

Henry looked to the ground and began to weep.

"The reverend said no matter what I did, he loved me and forgave me."

"Then here's what you do, Henry. You fight your demon alcohol by yourself. Go home. Write again. Think again. But do it where folks will understand you. Make a life for yourself. Find your father's forgiveness. And you let this lie lie. I won't have you bringing Alma's life to ruin."

"Alma!" Henry exclaimed. "She is a beautiful woman. But, Gideon, you showed me that she was not chaste! When I saw you were nowhere to be seen around her, I knew she was for the taking! So I took her! Nature makes it that way. I am driven by Nature, and Nature demands I raise my son up to see Nature in its true form. You would make him what, Gideon? Some backwoods ignorant farmer?"

"Henry, I'm a farmer, and I think that's fine enough a thing to be."

Gideon had thought to reveal to Henry that he was likely richer than Henry would ever be. But he realized Henry wouldn't take comfort in his son's being raised by wealth. More likely, Henry would return to drink and find a way to blackmail Gideon to keep his secret.

"It is not, sir! My son will be raised to understand the philosophy of Nature, not the dirt it resides in."

"Henry," Gideon said, thoughts of forgiveness beginning to wear around the edges, "I will beat the living hell out of you if you don't take me up on my offer and leave."

"So what? I've been beaten fairly regularly now. You have no power over me."

"Beating's likely to hurt a helluva lot more if you ain't drunk."

"Gideon, poor Gideon. A ruffian's gambit? I have no fear of pain."

Gideon wondered if that were true.

"Assuming I don't beat the living hell out of you, what will you do, Henry?"

"First, I will go to Alma. Poor Gideon, please understand she must choose me over you. I have refinements you will never possess. And I have planted my seed in her."

Gideon imagined it. His time with Alma was wonderful, but he sensed the secret pain she carried over what Henry had done to her. Gideon had worked to make her as free from that pain as she could be. Henry would make her relive it, destroy her life and happiness for whatever errant philosophy he embraced at the moment. His resolve thickened.

"Henry, I'm giving you your chance here. I'll give you a horse. I'll give you enough money to get yourself back where you belong. Take it."

"No, Gideon," Henry shouted. "I am the father of my child! I will raise him up to stand wise among men and to bestow gifts upon them!"

When Henry finished his proclamation, a change took place in Gideon, a new and sudden reworking in his mind. Never before had he been a true soldier in his hate, but with Henry's latest words, Gideon's primal consciousness finally heard and began to harken to the call of war.

The spiritual winds shifted, carrying the scent of Gideon's rising purpose to the savior of Abraham Teague, the ancient, malevolent healer of wounds and taker of souls. The creature was itself savage in thought, seeking new souls but searching also for one that had fought and defied its will – the soul of Zachariah Teague. That soul, that impudent, insignificant soul belonged to the creature, but had somehow – for a time – slipped from its grasp, filling the creature with untold rage. No matter. The creature would soon find its possession and, in rebuke of his defiance, lay down for Zachariah Teague suffering greater than any the creature had ever meted out before.

But for now, there was a new scent in the wind, new prey, perhaps, and the creature flew to it.

Gideon reached down and picked up a large stone he had been eyeing while the urine dried on his shirt. He held it and doubted. Then he conjured up the image of Henry Scott Douglas in his print shop, pushing and holding Alma while he raped her.

"What do you mean to do, Gideon?" Henry asked. His voice stammered. He understood.

He started to run. Gideon ran after him. Douglas was slow and clumsy. He tripped and fell. He rolled over and looked up, his eyes wide with fear.

"Gideon, no!" he screamed. "I'll leave! Give me the horse. I'll take your money and go!"

Gideon kneeled over Henry with the stone raised high above his head. He saw the dawning in Henry's eye and the cowardice that truly lay behind his conviction. He felt more pity, and regret that Henry would not let forgiveness rule the day.

"I don't believe you mean it, Henry," Gideon said. Then he smashed the stone against the top of Henry's skull. Blood erupted from Henry's head, but to Gideon's surprise, he did not die. He rolled over and scrambled to his feet quicker than Gideon thought possible. He started to run, yelling, "I'll leave! I don't need your money. Keep your horse! I'll walk to New York. You'll never hear from me again."

Gideon ran after him and smashed the rock against the back of Henry's head. Henry fell, convulsing on the ground. Gideon dropped the stone and started to walk away. Maybe Henry would live, take this as a lesson learned and go. He tried to believe it. He was sickened by what he had done. Then he saw in his mind Alma's body as it had been the day she made love to him in this wood. He saw the love in her heart and the hope she carried with it. He heard Henry moan and walked back and slammed the rock into his head three more times. Henry was dead.

Gideon covered Henry with leaves and branches which littered the ground. He wondered at what he had done – how he had found it in himself to do it. He hadn't come here with any intention of harming Henry. He was determined only to see him go. If Henry had shut his mouth, he'd still be alive.

"Crazy fool," Gideon said aloud. "What do you think? You threaten a man's family and remind him you raped his wife – what kind of ignorant philosophy could you get out of that?"

Gideon realized he had a terrible problem. Everyone on the street of Salud had seen him carrying Henry on his shoulder out toward these very woods. He'd joked with Joe Beck about drowning him. Now Henry lay there looking very much like he'd been murdered. It wouldn't take a genius to figure Gideon for his killer.

It was beginning to get dark. A plan began to form in Gideon's mind. He determined he could count on the cloak of night to help him in this business. He waited until the last of the light faded from the sky and began walking home. He did not stick to the road through town, but walked overland, through woods and fields. It was slow-going. He didn't make it home until after midnight. He went to the barn first and washed up at the pump. Then he went inside the house. Alma was awake in Ellen and Zachariah's old room. Ellen had given it to them and taken Gideon's bedroom for her own. Eugene lay quietly in his cradle next to the bed. Alma whispered, "Where have you been?"

"Alma," Gideon whispered back. "I have to tell you some things."

Alma looked worried, but she told Gideon to tell her whatever it was.

"Joe Beck came to tell me Henry hasn't kept his mouth shut since Reverend Leyden died."

Alma gasped, and Gideon put his hand on hers.

"No. Now no need to worry. It ain't got out far, and everyone knows Henry's a stinkin' drunk."

"What will we do, Gideon? We'll have to move away!"

Gideon thought for a moment and nearly kicked himself. That would have been far easier than killing a man. "Hell," he thought. "We coulda gone anywhere far enough from here, and we'd have no one to worry one whit about. No one would know us or Henry from Adam."

"No need to," he said. "I convinced Henry to go back to where he come from."

"Really? He'll leave?"

"It's going to cost me some money. I told him I'd stake him to go."

"But he agreed?"

"Probably why he took to talkin' about it in the first place. Wanted to get some money out of me, so he could go."

"I hate that man with all my heart."

"I hate him for you, but he's not going to be anywhere near us ever again," Gideon said. Then he told Alma that he was to meet Henry this night and ride with him out of the county, giving him his money once he was good and on his way.

"I won't give him the money without I'm sure he'll go. I'll be back in the morning, probably," he said. Then he kissed Alma and bent down to kiss Eugene on the forehead.

In the barn it struck Gideon that two men had been prepared to kill for Alma's sake. Her father had been ready to kill him, and he had killed Henry. He wondered how it was that love could drive a man's hate enough to kill for it.

Even as Gideon pondered this, the creature was collecting the battered soul of Henry Scott Douglas and laying down plans for Gideon's eternal misery.

He saddled Sadie and secured rope and a shovel to the saddle. Then he saddled one of the wagon horses. He tied a lantern to the wagon horse's saddle, and then secured the horse to Sadie's saddle with a long rope. Past midnight, he figured there wouldn't be anyone awake or around to see him. Even if someone did, Gideon doubted he'd be recognized in the dark.

He rode slowly along the road. He avoided the town, taking another road around, though it was farther to go. He got to the wood in a little over an hour. He hadn't seen a soul. He rode Sadie into the wood and tied her to a low tree branch. Then he took the wagon horse deeper into the wood, where Henry lay. He lighted the lantern but kept the flame low, burning just enough so Gideon could see what needed seeing in the dark wood.

Henry was easy enough for Gideon to lift, but rigor mortis made it hard to bend the body over the saddle. Gideon pushed down on Henry's neck, bending him. The act reminded him how Henry had pushed down on Alma's neck, bending her forward in his offices. Gideon wrenched Henry's body hard as he recalled Alma's tears when she described what had happened.

Finally, Gideon was able to tie Henry securely to the saddle. He extinguished the lantern and led the horse back to Sadie. He tied the two horses together again and rode east, taking the same route he would have to take if he intended to travel all the way to Pennsylvania. He rode for two hours. Then he found what he decided was a suitable bit of ground. No crops grew or looked as though they had ever grown. He rode Sadie off the road about fifty yards.

The ground was hard, and Gideon did not dig very deep. In his mind, he thought of stories that would account for Henry's burial and injury. Henry rode, drunk as always, and fell from his horse, hitting his head on a rock.

"Fell and bounced a few times," Gideon grimaced at the implausibility. "I should have smothered him to death. No way to tell he was murdered then."

Still, Gideon worked the idea of the fall over in his head. Henry falls. Dies. A passerby sees the corpse. No way to know who it is, so the passerby gives the body a quick Christian burial. Says a few words and goes about his business.

Gideon wondered if he should make a cross out of tree branches and place it over the grave, to make the story more likely to whoever might find the grave. Then he could let the horse that carried Henry ride free. When the horse was found, and if someone figured out it was his, he could always say he gave Henry the horse and money to leave, which had been his intention all along. He'd be absolved.

He pondered it a while and decided against it. He'd just be asking for someone to find Henry and count the number of times he would have had to bounce to account for all the places Gideon had struck him with the stone.

Gideon had a hard time getting the body flat again after he took it off the horse. Henry's legs stuck up in the air after Gideon lay him on his back in the grave. Gideon stood on the body, with one foot on the chest and the other on the legs. He bounced up and down until he heard a cracking sound. The legs straightened and lay flat. Then Gideon filled the grave in and covered it with dead brush.

He thought of the reverend then. He would not approve. To make up for it, Gideon decided to say a few words, but the only thing he could muster was, "Fuck you, Henry Scott Douglas. Rot in hell."

Gideon decided it was fitting enough for the wise man from the east.

It was dawn when Gideon rode home. He rode as fast as he could, hoping to avoid the people who would surely be up by now. He stuck to less traveled roads and counted himself lucky that he saw no one, other than men working at a distance in the fields. If anyone saw him, no one would recognize who he was.

Alma greeted him at the barn.

"Why do you have two horses, Gideon," she asked, holding Eugene in her arms.

"Was giving one to Henry, to make sure he would leave," Gideon said, dismounting Sadie. "He had his own horse though."

Gideon unsaddled the horses, quietly thinking what more he would say to Alma. She stood silently by, breastfeeding Eugene while Gideon fed and watered the animals. Finally, he said, "I rode with him for a few miles until I was sure he would keep going. Then I come home."

Alma looked doubtful.

"He's gone for good then?"

"Ain't never coming back."

"Good," Alma said, and she kissed Gideon on the cheek.

"Best we just don't talk about this no more," Gideon said. "Not to anyone. He's gone, and that's that."

"I understand," Alma told him, and he was certain she knew he had murdered Henry.

Gideon waited a long time for someone to question him about Henry, but no one ever did. Henry Scott Douglas disappeared from the face of the earth, and no one cared, except for Gideon, in whom the seed of guilt had begun to grow.

Apart from his guilt, which Gideon transformed, whenever he was able, to anger for all that Henry Scott Douglas had been and done, the years slipped by, happy and free. Gideon loved Alma, and Alma loved Gideon, and their son, the method of his inception forgotten in the souls of his parents, was dearly loved by both.

In time, Sam Smith turned his eye to the widow, Ellen Teague, and found a love he dared not speak. Ellen, strong, proud, brilliant Ellen Teague was beyond his reach, so he contented himself with being near her, hearing her words, admiring her thought and resolve. Then, to his surprise, Ellen Teague turned her eye to Sam Smith, daring to speak exactly what she felt.

Sam and Ellen married three years after Zachariah Teague was laid – not to rest, but to spiritual battle – in the earth. Sam built for Ellen the finest house he could, and he and Ellen made their happy home with Gideon, Alma, and Eugene just a stretch up the road, in the house Zachariah Teague had built.

Then came the fateful, freezing night when the spirit of Eugene "Hap" Teague's true father murdered his child to serve his master's will.

CHAPTER 26
ELLEN'S RETURN

"Gramma had to go away," Ellen Smith whispered to her grandson Gabriel, namesake to her own sweet child, wandering now somewhere in that unseen world in search of his father's threatened soul.

As she spoke to the younger Gabriel, a soft breeze gently rustled the high leaves of the old oak beside her. It might be only the wind, she considered, but her Gabriel had put it on her that the tree was more than ancient growth – it possessed its own sacred power. She thought perhaps the leaves' rustling was more than the wind, but expressions of her own lost loves – her son, her husband – whispering to her as she whispered to her grandson.

"I was on a long journey," Ellen told little Gabriel, "and I couldn't come back to you until just this very moment."

Ellen took stock of herself, here, now, fully back in the living world. The boy, her grandchild, was maybe six. So for more than six years she had been outside herself, brought to some plane of existence beyond the tactile world by a spirit who claimed to be the mother of Zachariah Teague.

The last she knew in that other world, Zachariah's mother and the spirit of her own son, Gabriel, were to find the lost Zachariah and free him from the designs of the creature that had once bargained with Abraham Teague. She had hoped herself to find Zachariah in that place and bring his strength to bear on the problem of their youngest, living son, Gideon. Yet she was given to understand Gideon would be her task alone. Bessie's spirit meant to free Zachariah from that place, not send him to help Ellen. Yet Bessie's spirit had shown Ellen the true workings behind Gideon's sorrow. It was for Ellen alone to use what she had learned to save Gideon.

"But why, Gramma?" Gabriel whispered conspiratorially, in keeping with Ellen's admonition to quiet. "Why were you on a journey?"

Ellen pointed to Alma, sleeping still above Hap's grave.

"You see your dear mother there?"

"Yes, Gramma."

"You know she loves you."

"Yes, she's my mom."

"And you know she would do anything to save you, don't you?"

"Yes, she always would."

"There, dear child, it is true," Ellen said. "And your father is my son."

"You're *his* mom."

"I am. And like your mother would for you, I will do anything to save my son."

Gabriel looked frightened by Ellen's words and asked, "Is something bad happening to my father?"

"Yes," Ellen said. "But do not be afraid for him. I have come home to save him."

Gabriel was not reassured. He began looking nervously about, suddenly feeling a deep fear for his father.

Ellen regarded her grandson, knowing he was Gideon's only true tether to this world, the only love left strong enough to save him. She felt sorrow and regret, but resolved her course. Gabriel's fear as it stood could not break through the spirit's hold over Gideon, and it was upon her to put more fear into the boy's heart than he had ever known.

But not yet. Not now. She calmed the boy instead, and set him to the task ahead, hiding from him her true purpose.

"Let your mother sleep," she said. "Stay with her, and when she wakes up, you go home and remember to do as I said."

"I will."

"And don't tell her we talked," Ellen added. "I want to surprise her all on my own."

"But I want to tell her! She'll be so happy!"

"Please?" Ellen implored. "For me?"

Gabe shuffled his feet at the ground a bit and finally agreed.

"That's a good child."

And Ellen began to walk away then, toward home and back to her husband, Sam Smith.

* * *

Alma slept upon Hap's grave, dreaming of the Gideon of old. Loving, happy. From her vantage point, sitting on the porch of the house she and Gideon shared, she watched as he worked around the barn, happily whistling a tune. Beside him another man worked, a man who seemed familiar to her, yet she could not decide who he was.

She squinted in her dream, to bring the man in clearer focus, and finally saw that it was her own father, Everett Ray Malone! But he was younger, younger than Gideon even. Still, seeing him warmed her heart. It had been a mistake to think him dead these years. He was young and alive.

As she watched, her father turned to look at her. He smiled. She smiled back and waved. Everett put his hand on Gideon's shoulder then, but Gideon had become the sullen Gideon once more, his head bowed, his shoulders slumped, defeated. Gideon did not notice the hand of Everett Ray upon him, but shuffled off into the barn, alone and in despair. Alma's heart sank.

Everett Ray watched Gideon go inside the barn, until he was out of sight. Then Everett began walking toward Alma.

She noticed something then that unsettled her more than seeing Gideon return to his sullen ways. The man looked like her father, but she saw some other aspect in the man's visage. Something dark and cruel, despite the happy grin the man wore on his face. She thought then that she saw Henry Scott Douglas coming to her.

Alma froze with fear, but Henry/Everett kept his pace, coming closer.

289

"Don't fear me," the man said then, soothing. "Never fear me, for I would never harm you."

Alma was about to scream when the man stopped in his tracks.

"I'll come no closer," Henry said. Only it wasn't exactly Henry either. The man for all the world looked like her father as much as he looked like the hated enemy that had brought ruin to her life.

Alma's scream faded, her emotions conflicted between the love she felt for Everett Ray Malone and the dread brought to her by thoughts of Douglas, the man and the spirit, both of which had tormented her, in life and in death.

"I cannot help the way I look," the man said. "It is in my lineage. But I have done you no harm. I am not the one you think you see."

Alma found her courage and shouted defiantly, demanding, "Who then?"

The man kicked the dirt and sighed.

"There's no easy way to tell it," he said. "A spirit put a hate upon you that still rests over your truest heart."

"Who!?!" Alma shouted again, demanding to know the man's identity.

The man did not answer the question, but instead told her, "I have a power to come to you now because you rest near the tree. You rest where I was buried."

"Buried?" Alma was confused. Was it her father telling her he was dead after all?

"Buried by my father's hand, so I could join *his* father and brother in the spirit of the tree."

Alma's fear faded then, and she felt a dark anger rising in her heart.

"Hap!" she screamed, recognizing her lost child hiding in the image of the man. "Hateful, hated Hap!"

"I *am* your son, dear Mother," the man admitted, a sad resolve coming over him at his mother's words. "I am your son, and you do not hate me."

"I hate the man that brought you," Alma accused. "And I hate you for it!"

The words felt good to Alma. Finally, she was free to fully rebuke the hated Hap.

"No," the man said. "The man's spirit put the hate in your heart. You always loved me, Mother."

"I hate you!" Alma resolved again. "You took my poor husband from me!"

"No," the man said once more. "The spirit of my true father has a hold over Gideon, my chosen father."

Alma was silent, confused. Suddenly, she could not remember hating her son the way she hated him now.

"I am your son, and your father is my grandfather, and I loved him as I love you, dear Mother."

Alma's mind settled into a confusion from which she seemed unable to think, to know what she felt. The hate seemed to weaken slightly in its hold over her, but she could not be sure.

The man continued speaking, "Other spirits have been here with me, bound within the power of this tree you sleep under. One is a mother, like you, with great power. She has collected her own child, Zachariah, and his child, too. They are free now and gone. The evil that sought to subdue them has lost them forever. But she felt your pain, Mother. She knew your sorrow. So she has left for you a bit of her strength. It rises from the earth even now and fights against the hold the spirit has placed on you."

Alma felt weakness driving into her bones, as if all of her will had been taken from her. She did not feel strength, if that was what had been given, but something near death settling over her.

"I cannot stay for it to take hold, Mother," the man said. "I am not so free as they have become. But I have enough resolve to be with you this moment, to tell you I love you, I always loved you, and I have always known your hate was not yours, but a lie given by a spirit of darkness. The same spirit that made your hate took my life from me, and I have been ever sorry to have left you so foolishly. But I was just a boy. I did not know. Forgive me, dear Mother, and know I have forgiven you, for never was it your true heart that hated me."

With that, the man turned to walk away, along the same road Gideon wandered through his long, sorrowful nights. As the man walked, his stature shrank, and he became a young man of twelve – Hap. Suddenly, Alma felt panic rising, replacing the sensation of death with frantic energy.

"Hap!" she called after her son. "Hap!"

Alma darted from the porch and ran desperately after her child, the hate lifted from her, and her full love for the fallen Eugene pouring back in, as powerfully as a river held back and then set free upon the breaking of a dam. The emotion flooded through her, overwhelmed her.

"Hap!"

But Hap had faded away, leaving Alma to cry out, desperate to be heard, "I love you!"

Alma opened her eyes, startled back to wakefulness with the revived revelation of her love for Hap. And she saw, directly, but upside down, inches from her nose, the smiling face of a playful Gabriel.

"I love you, too, Mommy," laughing Gabe said to her.

Alma rolled over and sat up, reaching for Gabe and dragging him into a hard embrace. Gabriel squirmed, and Alma held him tighter, needing more than ever to feel the touch of a beloved child.

"Oh, Gabe," she cried. "I love you! Nothing will ever stop me from loving you."

Gabe gave in and fell into Alma's hug, hugging her back.

"I love you, too, Mom!"

But Gabe sensed the anguish in Alma's touch and asked, worriedly, "Are you all right?"

Alma began to feel the first, fresh torments of the grief the spirit had never allowed her to feel for the loss of Hap. Helplessly, she rocked with Gabe in her arms, feeling the full measure of her grief, as if Hap had just died. In her mind, she imagined the anguish and suffering of her child, alone on that wickedly cold night, dying within steps of warmth and safety.

"Oh, Hap!" she said, grief pouring from her heart.

Gabe was confused, not knowing who Hap was, who his mother spoke to, though she held Gabe in her arms.

"Mom?"

Alma was shaken at Gabe's simple question, and realized she was scaring her living child.

Gently, she let go of Gabe and said, "I'm sorry, Gabe. I was thinking about your brother, Hap."

"My brother?"

Alma gasped. What secrets they had! Her heart filled with hate, she had never found it in her to tell Gabe about Hap, never wanted to say his name out loud. Hadn't Gideon told him of his brother? No, she decided. Gideon's sorrow lived in everlasting grief for his son, but he, too, could not say his name aloud where it would be heard by others.

"You brother," Alma finally said, trying to calm herself against a rising hysteria, so she could calm Gabriel in turn. "He was my dear sweet boy, but he died before you came into the world to bring us joy."

"Was he...?" Gabe started to ask, but Alma interrupted.

"Let's not speak of him right now," she said, fighting hard to bring her emotions to bay. "I will tell you everything about him soon, but I need some time, Gabe. I find myself missing him just now, and I don't have it in me to talk about it for a bit."

"Okay," Gabe reluctantly agreed. "But you'll tell me all about him?"

"Oh, I will, Gabe. I will."

Alma looked for Ellen then, her final charge before she could leave and begin her mourning in earnest.

"Your grandma, Gabe," she asked. "Where is she?"

Guilty with his secret, Gabe looked away and simply said, "I think she walked home."

Alma remembered how, before she had fallen asleep, she'd seen something akin to wakefulness in Ellen, with living emotion on her face as she held her hand against the tree. Part of her wanted to go to find her, to see if what she had witnessed in her mother-in-law had taken hold.

But Alma was wrecked. Her love for the lost Hap was wrecking her, and she wanted to go home, to look in Gabe's room and remember the boy who had once lived there, her beloved Hap.

She steeled her courage as best she could and reached down for Gabe's hand.

"Let's go home," she said, and began walking back to the house where Hap was born.

CHAPTER 27
REUNION AND DECEPTION

"How old am I?" Ellen wondered as she walked through the fields, finding her way back home. "How slowly does time pass in that place?"

She noticed pains in her body as she walked that she had never felt before, or, if so, certainly not so keen. Her step had slowed, too, and her confidence with each step was no longer as sure as she remembered its being.

Hap had been buried on the night she had gone over into that other place, and Gabriel was likely about six years old from what she had seen. Certainly, at the very least, a year would have passed between the time Hap had been lost and Gabriel had been born.

"I'm a woman in her sixties now, at least," she thought, not liking the idea of seven or more years having aged her without her living those years. What of Sam? She seemed to know he had been loyal, but wasn't sure how she knew it, other than she knew and loved Sam Smith and felt to the core of her being he would stay with her and tend to her no matter what, things she knew for certain she would do for him, had there been need.

So a homecoming was about to occur. Suddenly, she grew nervous, all thoughts of Zachariah fading with thoughts of Sam rushing in. Then just as suddenly, her nervousness was replaced with dread. She had a plan for Sam, and to make it work, she would have to deceive him. She might be about to lose the man who had waited for her down the years and whom she had desperately missed.

"But I will not let that happen first," she decided. "I cannot be so eager for Gideon's sake that I lose every bit of Sam getting there."

It was early afternoon when she reached the house. She gathered her courage, and went inside, but Sam was nowhere to be seen. She knew then where to go.

Upstairs, in their bedroom, she found her wardrobe, and began to dress more appropriately for riding. The pants she put on fit her loosely now. So she had lost weight, though not so much as to be a hindrance – the pants still fit for the most part.

She found her old boots, too, stiffened and cracked with age and neglect. But they slipped onto her feet nevertheless, hard and course, but serviceable.

She took the stairs slowly, entered the parlor, and took a look once more at the sofa Zachariah had purchased for her so many years before, with all its cracks and imperfections. For a moment, she let herself think about Zachariah again, feeling her love still there, alive, even if overshadowed now by her love for Sam.

In the barn, she found her horse, Nel, in her stable. "Well," she thought, "Not gone so many years to turn Nel into a nag."

She approached Nel slowly and raised her hand gently to the horse's nose. Nel sniffed cautiously, then snorted and stomped in recognition.

"Hello, Old Girl," Ellen smiled. "I missed you."

She found her saddle resting on its stand. Unlike her boots, the saddle had been carefully kept and oiled. Sam. It was the first sign that Sam had done more than wait; he'd kept hope along the way.

Ellen opened the gate and led Nel from the stable. She grabbed a blanket and threw it over Nel, then threw the saddle up and over, cinching it tight. Then she placed Nel's bit in her mouth, the whole time taking pleasure in the movements, surprised she wasn't so decrepit as she had feared.

Ellen put her boot in the stirrup and lifted herself onto the saddle. All-in-all, she thought, not too bad.

She kicked gently, and Nel began to walk from the barn. Once clear, Ellen urged the horse to a gallop, riding eagerly to the old place, the cabin built by Abraham and Bessie Teague.

* * *

Sam Smith sat with his men outside the old place at a long table. Two such tables were stretched out in the yard, making room for twenty men to sit with Sam for dinner. The cook, Old Pete, set a pot of stew and a basket of bread beside Sam.

"Got some for me to take home, Pete?" Sam asked.

"Keepin' it warm for you, Sam. It'll be ready for when you go."

"Thank you, Pete," Sam said. "The missus likes your stew."

Pete was silent. Everyone knew Sam's missus was an oddball, but none would ever say it to the man. Rumor had it one poor fellow had once dared to say within earshot of Sam, "I hear the old woman eats and shits, but just drools and farts otherwise."

Sam wasn't a young man anymore, but the rumor went he'd beaten the man within an inch of his life and sent him packing for good. Sam's good humor, all knew, ended the moment the subject of his wife came up. They all loved Sam anyway, so wouldn't say such a thing, but if the notion had ever struck, it was remembered that Sam was to be feared as much as loved, and only misery lay ahead for the man that forgot.

"Hey, Sam," one of the men said, pointing off down the road. "You expectin' lady company coming this way?"

"No," Sam answered, turning to look where the man had pointed.

Riding sure up the road, at a full gallop now, Sam saw the woman riding hard toward them, and from what he saw, he thought she was laughing.

"Never saw a woman out here before," another man joked. "You hiring women now, Sam?"

"I should," Sam said, joking back. "They'd probably work harder than you fellas."

Curious, Sam squinted to see who it might be riding their way, and then he felt his heart leap from his chest. He stood fast, spilling the pot of stew over the table, and he nearly knocked the long bench over with all the men sitting on it.

"Shit," he said. "Sorry, fellas, but that's no woman! That's my wife!"

Sam could not believe what he was seeing, but he felt a great joy rising despite his disbelief, and he ran as fast as he could to meet Ellen on the road.

"Sam!" Ellen hollered. "Sam Smith!"

Ellen brought Nel to stop and impossibly leapt from the saddle, landing sure-footed on the ground, her old boots still worthy of her trust. There she stopped, put her hands on her hips and laughed.

Sam did not say a word. He reached for Ellen and lifted her from the ground, tears streaming from his eyes.

"It's you," he shouted, laughing and crying at once. "You've come back to me!"

"Oh, now," Ellen cried. "Put me down, you old fool. You're making a spectacle."

Sam set her down then and kissed her hard.

"Easy," Ellen said. "I'm more fragile that I used to be."

"You was never fragile, Ellen Smith, and I don't believe it for a second."

* * *

Sam and Ellen rode back home. Sam brought the stew Old Pete had set aside, and the two of them sat at the kitchen table, slowly eating their first real dinner together in many years. Ellen felt like a blushing bride with the attention Sam was lavishing on her, and she allowed herself to enjoy every minute of it. There were hard things to come, she knew, but she pushed all thoughts other than her love of Sam aside. She would enjoy these moments with the man she loved for now, and everything and everyone else be damned.

She knew, too, that Sam was likewise setting things aside. You can't come back from the beyond without there being some concern over where you'd been. But Sam was all happiness and joy – for the moment.

But when they were through eating, Sam looked at her expectantly and asked, "Can you tell me what's been going on these years? I ain't asking with any rebuke, mind you, I just got to know the why and how of it, if you've a mind to tell it."

"I'll tell you everything, Sam," Ellen said, standing. "But we've got other catching up to do first."

Ellen grabbed Sam's hand then and led him upstairs.

* * *

The morning sun shone brightly through the kitchen curtains and windowpanes, laying two warped rectangles of morning light down over the breakfast table as Ellen finished her story. Sam had made his ritual breakfast for Ellen and himself, as he did every morning before dawn, only at this eating his wife was animate and alive to the moment, once again the woman he'd fallen in love with.

As the sun's hue changed from the first dim glow of sunrise to the bright golden shafts and shapes of the morning sun through the glass, she'd recounted everything she had experienced and seen since she began her traverse into that other world. She told him of the bargain of Abraham Teague, of the spirit set loose to destroy her son, and of Bessie, the tree, and her search for Zachariah. She told him all of it.

It was a tale, Sam reckoned, that the pragmatic, no-nonsense Ellen of old would not herself have countenanced. He smiled a bit thinking how she might once have scolded anyone so bold as to tell such a story.

When she was finished, Sam leaned back in his chair and said, "I'm not given much to religion, and I never gave much credence to talk of spirits or the beyond, but there's no way to talk about what's happened but to say it's been goddamned strange from the start."

"I know it's strange, Sam," she said. "But I'm needing you to believe it."

Sam held his coffee cup between his hands and looked Ellen in the eye.

"I do believe you," he said. "I know you, Ellen, and I got no reason to doubt you about anything. Never did. I don't think Gideon's even seen you since the night Hap was buried, the night you went away. So how could you know what's become of him? I suppose you might have heard Alma and me talk about it, but I don't think you were yourself enough to have understood.

And whether I've given credence to spirit talk or not, I believe I've experienced something of what you're talking about myself."

Sam looked down for a moment, dragging up from the depths of his shame memories of what had happened the night he and Gideon had gone to bury Hap.

"That night when I lost you, something happened with Gideon and me out on the hill," he said, reluctantly falling into a confession. "Something was there with us, Ellen. Whatever the hell it was, it had form enough to lay hands on me. I think I saw it, too. Call it a ghost, call it what you will, but it had its sights set on Gideon. I understood that, I think, but, Jesus, this is hard to admit – but I think it did something to my mind when we were there, and to Gideon's, too."

Sam sighed.

"I didn't come home when I did because we was finished burying Hap. I come home because I was scared. I was running away, Ellen. Whatever that thing was, it put a fear into me so strong I couldn't stand and do my duty by Hap or Gideon."

Ellen saw a tear fall from her husband's eye and knew how hard it was for him to confess such a thing. Sam Smith, next to Zachariah Teague, was the strongest man she had ever known. He was fearless, so far as she knew, at least outside of his shyness when it had come to professing his love for her for the first time, so many years ago. In all other things, Sam stood tall and would do so against all the world if need be.

"I ran, Ellen," he said. "I ran and I told myself I didn't, but I did. I don't know what I saw, but I knew it was after Gideon, whatever it was. And I let it be. I let it be because I was scared, and I left Gideon to it."

Ellen was silent, but she reached her hand across the table and grabbed onto Sam's. He looked at her and asked, "Can you forgive me?"

Ellen smiled. She thought of his great devotion to her and to her family all these years. He had been Gideon's guidepost into manhood, after Zachariah had died. She knew he loved Gideon as he would his own child.

"There's nothing to be forgiven, Sam," she told him. "It's said there are more things in heaven and earth than we know. I've seen it, and what's befallen us all isn't from heaven or earth, but it is powerful, and it's evil. It took a swipe at you, Sam, with more than any man could stand against. That you stood beside us even after that is because you are stronger than most can ever be. No, my love, there is nothing to forgive, for you have done so much for us all. Don't you set it on your own head that you failed us. You never have. It's just sometimes the enemy can be too strong."

Sam sighed.

"Thank you," he said. Then he thought and chuckled and said, "I hope you'll be as forgiving when you see the books. I lack your facility with figures, my dear."

Ellen smiled. "No promises there."

Sam settled back in his chair and asked, "But what now? What's to be done?"

"I came back with thoughts on that, Sam," Ellen told him, knowing she would have to keep the better part of her plan secret from Sam, or he would never agree. She did not doubt he must have taken to Gabriel as his true grandson over the years, and the Sam she knew would fight to protect the child, even from her. Yet Sam had a part to play, and if a lie was what it took for him to play his part, a lie it would have to be.

She hoped he would be able to forgive her.

"I've tried to sift through my experiences, Sam," she said. "And I know one thing is sure; such wonders demand something beyond who and what we are to happen in the first place. What I mean is that there has to be a purpose to it. Has to be. The only purpose I can make out is that it has come to me to set things right with Gideon, to free him from that spirit that's tormented him all this time."

"I can't say I find fault in your conclusion," Sam said, his tone making it clear he was ready to do whatever it took to help. "Do you have any idea how it's to be done?"

Ellen hesitated. She was ready to tell him most of it now.

"We walk in the mortal world now, Sam. Both of us. I don't see how we can reach into that spirit realm and fight the devil or his minion. Even if we could, we've both felt its power. We'd lose. So we're left to this world, and what we can do in it.

"So we have to pull on that part of Gideon that's still here and separate him from the spirit's influence. For some reason I figure we have to get Gideon back to where it started with Abraham, out to the meadow."

Ellen didn't truly know any such thing, but the place would do as well as any other, and getting Gideon there would distract Sam from the awful plan she had actually come to.

"That'll take some doing," Sam said. "I haven't been able to get him to go beyond the road outside their place. It's like he's got a lead tied to his neck that snaps him back whenever I've tried. Alma goes to town when it's needed, 'cause he won't."

Ellen looked at Sam and tried very hard to hide the pain she felt.

"I know how it can be done," she said. "Gabriel is the key."

The key, yes, Ellen thought. But it was going to take more than Gabriel's innocence to turn the lock and set Gideon free. She would have to take on the aspect of Abraham himself – not the foolish Abraham who'd bargained with the devil, but the Abraham who showed himself willing to do the terrible will of God.

CHAPTER 28
THE SACRIFICE

Sam had doubts, but he couldn't see a way around it. If Ellen was right, Gideon had to be led away from the path set out for him. Reason wouldn't do it, but there was some of the old Gideon left in his love for Gabriel. Maybe, just maybe, that *would* break him loose.

It was midnight when Sam crept into Gideon and Alma's house. A sliver moon let down its meager light into the sky, giving Sam just enough to see by. Barely he'd been able to make out the boundaries of the road and see the corn growing in the fields, the stalks rising eerily blacker than the night itself. Because in his heart he had fully accepted that he and Ellen were standing in the shadow of evil incarnate, he imagined each of the reaching stalks as an oppressive spirit, ready to strike him down and away from his purpose.

Absently, he understood that he was afraid. But it was not the fear driven into him by the spirit that had forced him away the night Hap was buried. It was the simple living fear all men might feel in the face of danger. To such fears, Sam Smith would never bend.

He spied ahead the dark shape of a man walking toward him on the road. It could only be Gideon, he thought. He doubted Gideon would notice him, even if the moon's light had been full. Wandering Gideon was forever bound within the world of his own sorrow, from which he seldom looked beyond, lost in whatever ruminations had taken hold of him. Still, Sam looked harder, past Gideon, to see if he might sight the spirit itself. But he saw no more than Gideon and the dark road.

Once he placed Gideon and assured himself the spirit was not there, at least where it could be seen, Sam had moved quietly as he could, taking cover in the fields, alert for whatever might lurk within. He felt somewhat the fool sneaking about, but it was the way it had to be played.

When he was sure Gideon had wandered far enough down the road, Sam stepped out of the field and onto the porch, slowly opening the screen and then the door. There was some squeaking, and Sam was startled.

"Damned Gideon," he thought, angrily. "The boy couldn't even take time to oil the hinges, the simplest of tasks."

He gently let the screen door shut and left the door open. He stood in the kitchen and listened for Alma. He thought he heard weeping, quietly coming from up the stairs.

"Poor girl," he thought. "Gideon's given her more than enough to weep over. Or maybe not Gideon, but that damnable spirit that's taken hold of him."

He took his boots off and set them aside. Quietly as he could, he worked his way to the stairs and began taking them cautiously. There were a few quiet creaks, but not so loud, he hoped as to rouse Alma.

Once he was on the landing above, he paused and listened. The weeping had subsided. Maybe Alma had fallen asleep.

He worked his way toward Gabe's room, stopping at the door and listening again. No sound came from Alma's room. He twisted the handle and slowly opened Gabriel's door. The hinges creaked madly, like the rusty hinges on the doors of an abandoned house rotting in a field. He cursed Gideon again.

A bell rang slightly as the door opened, and Sam stopped, listening again. Nothing.

The door was opened just wide enough for Sam to slip through.

He made his way to Gabe sleeping soundly in his bed. Gently, he shook the boy.

Gabe opened his eyes sleepily.

"Daddy," he said.

"Shhhh," Sam whispered. "It's me. Grandpa."

Gabe rubbed his eyes.

"Gramma said I was to go with you when you came."

"That's right. We need to sneak about it though. We don't want your mom or dad to know you're going to see Grandma just yet."

"Okay," Gabe agreed, sleepily compliant.

Sam helped Gabe get dressed. Then he picked the boy up.

"I can walk, Grandpa," Gabe whispered. "I'm not a baby."

"I know," Sam told him. "You're a big boy, and I'll let you walk as soon as we're outside, okay?"

"Okay."

Sam retraced his steps, slowly and listening for Alma to stir. But nothing stirred. Inside her room, her grieving turned now to sleep, Alma lay wrecked and cold in her misery over Hap's death.

Sam set Gabe down on the kitchen floor and put his boots on, reminding Gabe to keep quiet. Dutifully, Gabe did as he was told.

Then Sam held Gabe's hand and led him out of the house.

* * *

Ellen met him on the porch of her and Sam's house. Gabe had given into sleep along the way, and Sam had carried him the mile home.

"Sam," Ellen said. "You did it."

"Felt like a damned fool," Sam answered, "but I managed. Poor Gabe's tired though. You sure you want to do this tonight?"

"Can't see a way to back out now," she said. "You know the next part?"

"Too well," Sam said. "Can't say I have the stomach for it, but I guess it's got to be done."

"It does, Sam."

"I'll try, but Gideon's stubborn as hell. Leastwise, that spirit makes him so."

"That's why we need Gabriel, to lure him out from the spirit's grasp."

"All right. If it goes well then, I'll lead him out to the meadow."

304

"Help me get Gabriel on the horse with me first, if you could," Ellen forced a smile. "I'm not so spry as I used to be."

Ellen went to the barn for Nel, and Sam followed, carrying Gabe.

"Here now," Ellen reached down, and Sam handed Gabe up into her arms. Ellen settled him on the saddle in front of her and held him tight with one arm while she held the reins in the other. Two lanterns and rope hung from her saddle. Sam did not see the knife.

"I'm good now, Sam," she said. "Give it half an hour, then you go raise hell."

* * *

Ellen rode to the meadow with Gabe, jostling in the saddle, mostly asleep. When she reached the place by the stream, she held Gabe steady in the saddle by his arm and dismounted. Then she lifted Gabe to the ground.

"Gramma," Gabe asked, rubbing his eyes. "Why are we outside?"

"Just going to sleep out of doors tonight and see if we can bring your father here."

"Okay," Gabe answered, agreeing groggily. Ellen took a blanket from Nel's saddle and settled it down on the ground.

"You lie down here and rest some," Ellen told Gabe. The boy did as he was told and was instantly asleep.

Ellen took the lanterns then and lighted them, one near Gabe's feet and the other near his head. She needed Gideon to see clearly what was taking place.

She pulled the knife from the saddle then and looked at it, whispering, "I'm sorry, dear boy, but this has to be done."

She took the rope then and tied it gently around Gabe's feet, then bound his hands. He made no noise, gave no struggle.

When she was through, she patted Nel on her rump.

"Go home now, girl."

Nel knew the way and wandered off.

CHAPTER 29
RAISING GIDEON'S LOVE

Sam rode his horse to Gideon's place and halted on the road, watching for Gideon. Sam saw him soon enough, standing by the outhouse, muttering.

"Well," Sam sighed. "Time to be about it, I guess."

He rode slowly up to Gideon, staying on his horse.

"Gideon," he called.

Gideon looked up.

"Hey, Sam."

Gideon did not ask why Sam was there after midnight when he should be asleep. Curiosity escaped the man.

"Say, Gideon," Sam said. "Woke up seeing a small boy wandering near our place. Lost sight of him, so came here to see if Gabe's in bed where he should be."

"He is, Sam."

"You sure? Maybe you'd better look. I'm worried after seeing that boy wandering all alone."

Something resembling panic came over Gideon then. Beside him, the spirit felt its charge loosen from its control. It had been taken by surprise, but now it looked out and saw the old man who had once stood by Gideon's side.

"I'll look, Sam."

Gideon hurried off to the house and went in, shaking his head. Sam waited, feeling now a wave of fear trying to rise up inside him. The spirit had directed its energy to Sam, understanding the man was somehow trying to release Gideon from its hold.

Sam shuddered. Suddenly he wanted to turn and ride away as fast as he could. But he remembered the feeling, knew its source. He looked around him, trying to see the spirit's form, but he saw nothing.

"I know you, spirit," he said, fighting his urge to flee. "I know you, and you'll have no hold over me."

Unseen, the spirit floated above the ground and settled itself beside Sam, working harder to drive terror into Sam's heart. Sam felt the spirit's tendrils trying to work their way into his mind. He stood firm, fought the spirit with all his will.

The spirit became furious and tried to tap into its hate to grow stronger against the man. But something was happening with Gideon now, the spirit's charge and source of power. It felt the world beginning to fade, and it released Sam, directing its diminishing strength to holding its form in the night.

Sam felt the fear sliding away.

"Damn you to hell," he cursed. "Your time is over, spirit."

Then Sam heard Gideon shout, "Gabe! Gabe, come out! Where are you, boy?"

He heard tearing through the house then. Alma's voice came through, also, shouting, "Gabe!"

Fading, the spirit was desperate now. It flew to Alma's voice, to take what little it could from her, enough to keep it substantial in the night. But it found its way to her blocked, some unseen force pushing it away from her. Lost, the spirit returned to its master, in terror of the suffering that awaited it.

Gideon ran out of the house. It was the first time Sam had seen Gideon move with any vigor in a long, long while. He was encouraged. Maybe the spirit had lost!

"Well," Sam thought, triumphantly. "Ellen's instincts are right this far. Let's take it the rest of the way and put this damnable spirit out of our misery."

"Gabe," Gideon yelled at Sam. "Where'd you see him, Sam?"

Sam willed himself to forget his fear and his encounter with the spirit. He had to play the part, hold back whatever might try to distract him.

"Headed for the meadow," he answered. "Not sure it was him, but if he ain't here, it probably is."

Alma came running from the house after Gideon.

"Sam, what's going on?"

"Looks like Gabe wandered off," Sam said, back in control of himself. "Don't worry, Alma. Go back inside. Gideon and me will find him."

Gideon had run to the barn and came storming out on one of the horses. He didn't regard Sam or Alma in the least, but stormed past his friend and wife, riding hard toward the meadow.

Sam turned his horse around to follow.

"Don't worry, Alma," he shouted back. "We'll bring him home."

Then Sam rode after Gideon.

Alma did not take comfort in Sam's assurance. Her grief for Hap was still fresh and overwhelming, but her knowledge of the spirit had risen, too. She feared the evil had come now for Gabriel, and she would not let Gabe be taken from her like Hap had been without raising her own fierceness against it.

She ran into the house and retrieved her gun, not having any idea what such a thing could do against a spirit, but determined to take whatever she could to protect Gabe from the fate that had taken Hap.

She ran into the barn and mounted her horse, without its saddle, and followed Sam and Gideon into the night.

* * *

Back in the fiery cavern where its master lived, the spirit waited fearfully for the torments to begin. But its master sat, appearing thoughtful on a boulder settled into the river of fire. The spirit regarded its master with hate, loathing, and terror. In these times, it had some sense of itself, knew that its work above, in the world of night, was not its own doing, but the will of its master. But in that world of night, the spirit forgot its master and knew only its hate for Gideon Teague and the sweetness of his suffering.

The spirit waited for the torments, but they did not come.

Instead, its master regarded the spirit and spoke.

"You are too weak for the task at hand," its master said. "Forces have set themselves against me. This was unexpected. You are not fashioned to stand against them."

The spirit's master rose then, walking atop the river of fire to the shore where the spirit lay, prostrate, prepared for the unimaginable horrors that awaited it.

"Yet I will not lose in this," the master said. "I will not lose more than what is lost."

The master reached down to the spirit then, touching its hand. Suddenly, the spirit felt more power than had ever come to it since Gideon Teague murdered its living body. The power flowed inward, intoxicating. Instead of pain, the spirit felt itself becoming like a god.

"Take what is given," the spirit's master smiled. "Return to your charge, and do my will!"

* * *

Gideon was far ahead of Sam and began to see the lighted lanterns in the meadow. He slowed, stopped, and looked ahead.

"Mother?" he shouted, seeing Ellen for the first time since the night he'd buried Hap.

"I'm here, Gideon," Ellen shouted back.

Gideon seemed to be unaware of how long it had been since he had spoken to his mother and asked, "What are you doing out here? Where's Gabe?"

Sam rode up in time to see Ellen lift a long knife over her head. She kicked Gabe. The boy woke, then became terrified to find himself tied up.

"Gramma!" he screamed. "What are you doing?"

Sam felt a sudden rush of adrenaline fly to his limbs. His wife had lost her mind after all, and he believed she was about to kill his grandson.

"Ellen," he screamed. "Drop that knife, dammit! Let Gabe go!"

Gideon saw, too, and jumped from his horse, running toward his mother, frantic and furious, things that had never been upon him under the spirit's hold.

"Stop, Gideon!" Ellen yelled. "Stop, or I'll do it now!"

Ellen knelt beside Gabe, brandishing the blade up high to reflect in the lantern light.

Gideon stopped, watching as Gabe screamed bloody murder into the night.

His mind flew to possibilities. Reason with his mother, rush headlong at her and try to take the knife away. For the first time since the night he'd buried Hap, Gideon was Gideon, his full purpose set to the world before him, though the world he saw terrified him. His mother was about to murder his child, sweet Gabriel, and Gideon seemed powerless to stop it.

Nevertheless, Gideon's whole being was directed now to saving his son.

While Gideon did not know it, nor Sam, Ellen was overjoyed, almost weak with relief. She saw Gideon was Gideon again. Her plan had worked, and never, never would she have harmed Gabe in body, though he and Gideon both had had to believe in the danger, so Gideon could overcome the oppression that lay over him.

Had the spirit's master not entered the game, Ellen would have won. The spirit would never have been strong enough to return. But imbued with its master's own power, the spirit rushed into Gideon at that moment and drove into Gideon's mind great waves of despair and certainty that Gabe was already lost to his mother's blade.

Gideon struggled, put up a terrible fight, determined to save Gabriel's life. To the spirit's surprise, Gideon nearly withstood its power over him, his love for Gabriel so great as to rival the master's strength. But the master's power won out. The battle had taken place in an instant, but in the end, Gideon's love and will were pushed aside.

"It's to be," he thought, as the spirit's power took hold once more. "Can't do anything to stop it. Shouldn't have come to this. I took steps."

To Ellen's horror, Gideon turned and walked away, leaving Gabe's screams behind him.

He passed Alma as she rode toward the screams and to Gabe. He didn't notice she was there, that she'd passed him, or her fury.

Gideon walked. He heard a shot ring out and kept walking. He heard Sam scream "Ellen!" but kept walking. He heard Alma scream "Gabe!" but kept walking. He heard Sam scream "No!" farther away now, but Gideon kept walking.

CHAPTER 30
THE LAST GRAVE

No one followed Gideon. Eventually, he found himself on the long pathway of his nightly wanderings, the road laid down by his father, Zachariah Teague. It seemed to Gideon that the history of his life had played out one way or another on that road, his earliest childhood spent riding on the wagon at Zachariah's side, dutiful and amazed at his father's defiance, wisdom, and strength. Along the same road, his love for his father had transformed into the deep, unthinking resentment that had put enmity between them, and the same road pointed the way to the place of his father's funeral.

It was the same road, also, that had taken the life of his son Hap, and upon which the spirit had set him to his endless, mournful vigil for the dead.

Now the spirit pressed it into his mind that the vigil would be held for Gabe, as well, another loved one lost because of Gideon's failures.

The spirit was angry that Gideon had almost slipped away, roused from his malaise to protect his cherished child. But the spirit's anger was assuaged, the affront set right by the gift of its master's power, given to it to bring Gideon back to heel, back to sorrow and suffering.

Though Gabe stood unharmed in the meadow, safe in his mother's embrace, the spirit pressed into Gideon's mind the certainty that Gabe was dead. Such was the spirit's hold over him, were Gabe to appear before him this instant, Gideon would not have believed the child lived.

In the darkness, Gideon thought of Hap and the night he had buried him, so near his father – and his brother, Gabriel, too. He remembered how his father had expressed his belief that the tree under which they were buried had taken sustenance from Zachariah's son, Gabriel, but that Gabriel had in the process become a living part of the tree. He wondered if such a thing might be true, and whether Hap had likewise become so, and whether Gabe would, too.

Yet in such musings lay a kernel of hope, so the spirit stamped the possibility from Gideon's mind as quickly as it had risen.

Gideon came near the house and walked into the barn. There, he retrieved a shovel. "Another grave to be dug," he thought. "Dig another grave, for Gabe this time. All of my sons lost to me."

Gideon began walking up the road again, a deep hatred for his mother growing and festering in his mind. Why had she done it? Why had she murdered Gabe? What had taken place this night that such a thing could be?

Gideon looked ahead to where the road bent and began to turn. There, he would veer off, crossing the fields to the hill where the old oak stood, where Gabe would soon be buried.

"Gabe will follow Hap," he thought, numb with sorrow. "It's not right. I took steps."

Morosely, he remembered the nights he had wandered the road with a blanket and a mustard seed, seeking in faith the resurrection of his son, Hap. How he had thought, clenching that seed, that it would bring Hap forth on the road, alive and new to the world once more.

He walked and remembered the slow failing of faith, the helplessness in hope.

As he reached the bend in the road, Gideon saw a child standing in the dark. Gideon thought the child looked like Hap.

"God's tormenting me now," he thought, "making me believe I see Hap like I always longed to. I'll see Gabe next, to complete my torment."

Gideon shook his head and tried not to see Hap standing as he was in the road, dismayed at the vision sent to torture him.

As Gideon walked with the shovel in his hand, straying from the road and into the field for the trip to the old oak, the imagined Hap began walking alongside him. Silently then, Hap moved to Gideon's side and took his free hand in his. Together, they began walking into the field, journeying toward the tree.

"I came to save you many times, Father," Hap said sadly. "But he was always too strong."

"Who's too strong?" Gideon asked, absently accepting the image of Hap's presence, while disbelieving such a thing could be.

"My true father," Hap said. "Turn and regard him."

Hap pulled on Gideon's hand then, turning him to look in the field behind them.

Gideon looked.

"I don't see nothing there."

"He's there. It's Henry. You knew Henry was my father."

"I knew it," Gideon admitted. "Wasn't going to tell you though. You were my boy. I fought to keep it so. I took steps."

"I am your son, Father. Doesn't matter how I got into the world. I love you."

"Love you, too, Hap. But I couldn't save you. I couldn't save Gabe, neither."

The spirit stood regarding Gideon and the spirit child beside him. It was the boy whose life the spirit had taken long ago, to bind Gideon's sorrow, so the spirit could live in the night and do its master's will. The spirit remembered once feeling something like remorse for what it had done. Now, hearing the child call Gideon "Father" filled it with rage.

"You were not worthy of me!" the spirit cried out to the boy. "You are not worthy of me now."

The boy looked at the spirit and said, "You have not been worthy of you."

With great fury rising with the boy's words, the spirit sought then to bring some power against the child, to bring harm and drive the child's spirit away, to leave Gideon to his suffering. But the spirit's power found no hold against the boy.

To Gideon, Hap said, "Something has changed, Father."

"What's changed, Hap?" Gideon asked, believing himself in a dream, for only in a dream could Hap be with him now.

"My true father has the power now to free himself."

The words fell off of Gideon without meaning. But to the spirit of Henry Scott Douglas, they set a thought in motion. The spirit tried to grasp it, to follow the thought, but its master still held sway, and Henry felt the thought slipping away.

Angry in his confusion, Henry shouted out to Hap, "Power? What power? Tell me the secret of it!"

Hap looked to Henry and said, "I know you were once Henry Scott Douglas, and you wanted to bring light into the world."

The words struck a chord, a memory in the spirit. It remembered once living in hope, wishing to bring what it had learned as a gift to others, a new philosophy for living.

"Yet you went astray, Father," Hap continued. "You lost your way."

The child's words had an effect on the spirit. Its anger drained away, and it began to remember something of who it had been. The spirit said, "I lost my way, but I tried to make it right." Then memory brought anger to the spirit once more. It pointed its cane at Gideon and set forth the accusation: "But this one would not allow it! He took my life from me even as I sought to redeem it!"

Something of the old Henry awoke further and delved into the once wise man's earthly repertoire, and he screeched, "He killed me even as I was still gripped by sin, and because I did not get to repent, I was sent to death with all my sins still on my head!"

Gideon stood mutely by, not understanding what was happening, not seeing who Hap was speaking to.

"Yet it was your master who made you what you are, Father," Hap said to the spirit. "It has fashioned you from your sins, making you a creature for the taking of light, instead of the giver you sought to be."

The spirit of Henry Scott Douglas remembered its torments then, the horrors of its master's cave and the respite given, only to make Gideon Teague suffer in the night.

"Your master set you to the task of killing me, Father," Hap said.

"I..."

"You murdered me."

The spirit remembered taking the boy's life, but he could not remember knowing he was the child's father.

"Yet I forgive you, Father. It wasn't you really, was it?" Hap asked. "You murdered me, but it was your master's bidding."

The spirit was confused. It had no hold over this child, but the child seemed to have a hold over him. Hap had seen him, spoken to him for mere moments, yet his words brought back to Henry pieces of himself. He remembered being Henry Scott Douglas, and he felt sorrow for his sins. And instead of fear of its master, he began to feel the first sliver of defiance.

"I could not fight it," the spirit said. "It is forever strong, stronger than a man can be."

"Do you wish to free yourself, Father?"

Henry stood, knowing he had long wished to be free, even to go into death and whatever that might bring.

"I want to be free," he said. "But he is strong."

Hap looked at Henry, "I'm not strong enough to send you away."

"You are not," Henry answered. It was in him to answer pridefully, full now of his master's power, yet he was enough of Henry Scott Douglas, pulled to the surface by Hap, that he felt shame and regret. He felt no pride in the power given him.

"Father," Hap said then, looking at Henry. "Do you remember what your master gave you?"

"Yes," Henry said. "He gave me power, a demon's fury to take up from his den and wield against Gideon, which I did."

"Do you think your master made a mistake?" Hap asked.

"Mistake?"

"You feel that power, don't you?"

"It is in me."

"Do you want to be his slave forever?"

"I don't want to be his slave at all."

"He gave you power, and you have used it. Maybe you could use it on him, set yourself free."

Henry stood, afraid but seeing some hope in what Hap had said.

"Oh," Henry said, wistfully, "to be free!"

"You can leave Gideon to Gideon," Hap told Henry. "He will torment himself over your death, until his own comes to him. But your master will never leave you to you. Henry Scott Douglas's true spirit will never be so long as his master holds sway."

Henry's spirit considered, feeling his master's power still unbounded, unlimited within him. And Henry decided.

"You've saved me or damned me, child," he said. "I don't know which, but please accept my humble gratitude. I will fight to free myself. Fare well, my son."

Henry's spirit faded then, gone to battle at last for his own redemption.

Hap squeezed Gideon's hand.

"You are free now, too, Father. Remember who you are. Remember who you love."

Gideon blinked and regarded Hap, his consciousness slowing bringing forth the Gideon of old.

"You ain't Hap," Gideon finally said. "Hap was the happy boy. You have no mirth, little fellow. You talk to the wind and frown after death itself."

Hap smiled and let out a small laugh after all.

CHAPTER 31
A FATHER'S BLESSING

Gideon awoke with his back resting at the base of the old oak. It was dark. Gideon shook his head, trying to drive the sleep away. He remembered seeing Hap in his dream. For some reason, the dream's effect seemed to be with him still. He felt as if a burden had been lifted from him, though he wasn't certain why. Then he suddenly remembered Gabe and the danger he had been in. Gunshots, too? Hadn't he heard a gun go off?

He tried to stand, to move and to rush to the meadow where he had last seen his mother threatening Gabe. But he could not move.

"Oh, I'll say it, Gids," Gideon thought he heard a ghost. He thought he heard the voice of Zachariah Teague. "I'll say it, that boy of yours is a smart one."

Familiar laughter brayed into the night.

Gideon sat in wonder, looking about. He heard but he did not see his father, Zachariah Teague.

Despite the wonder of it, Gideon fought against the paralysis that held him to the tree. Gabe was in danger, and he was trying with every bit of his will to rise to save him.

"Now, don't worry about my grandson," Zachariah's voice said. "He ain't hurt a bit. Your mother was trying to scare the hell outta you, and she had to scare the hell outta Gabe to do it. She tripped up the devil himself in the

318

doing, too. Clever, clever woman. I done well by you making her your mother, Gids."

"I don't understand."

"Then don't understand," Zachariah said. "Think on it later, and you'll get the meaning thinking on it. Hap has moved on now, Gids. He loves you, Gids, but he's gone now. Let him go. But thanks to him, I got a second here with you. Like your mother, he plain outsmarted that devil below. Set your enemies upon each other to fight it out. Gave me a chance to come back for my brothers, to free their souls and bring them home. I done it, too, Gabriel and I did, thanks to your Hap. I'm glad to think on him as my own."

Gideon still didn't understand.

"Oh, you'll sort it all out soon enough, put the pieces together," Zachariah said. "But right now, you need to take hold. You got a mess, boy. Out there in that meadow, my sweet Ellen is shot. Hate is festering in your wife, and Sam doesn't understand any of it."

"Father?" Gideon finally grasped that somehow it was his father's true voice that he heard. "How can you be here?"

"Well, you're dreaming, that's how," Zachariah said. "That and my mother is a powerful lady. She's a loving mother, too. She's given me a moment with you now that the danger to me has passed."

"Father, I..."

"Shut up. You're my boy. I love you. But you got to take hold. Your sorrow's left a mess. Take to it, boy. Make it right."

Gideon opened his eyes, thinking how he didn't like being called "boy." He was sitting against the tree, like in his dream, but now he was awake, able to move, believing but not believing. Yet it didn't matter. There was Alma, Gabe, Sam, and his mother.

And Gideon had it in his heart to go to them all.

EPILOGUE

The creature sat, angry, brooding. Its defeat in this matter was unnerving, giving it doubt. Never before had it failed in its desires. Yet now it had lost everything, even its servant, the murdered soul that had served it so well for so long. Foolishly, its jealousy had driven it to impart some measure of its power to the spirit, so determined had it been not to lose its last hold over even one Teague, or the Teague souls already bargained for but now lost, all lost.

After a while, its brooding faded. In all of time, perhaps, a failure was to be expected. It would learn from it and go forth. There was a whole world opening, expanding, with humans full of desire and disappointment.

It turned its eye and knew it could look out in any direction to find what it wanted. Everything it desired lay before it.

"I'll forget this place and these people," it thought, finally. "Let them go. They mean nothing."

ABOUT THE AUTHOR

Michael Scott Hopkins is an attorney in Joliet, Illinois, where he lives with his wife of more than thirty years, Carla; his golden retriever, Charlie; and two black cats named Lolli and Pop. He earned an MA in English from Governors State University and graduated cum laude from The John Marshall Law School, where he was a member of The John Marshall Law Review. He and Carla have three sons, Tyler, Kyle, and Eric.

Michael's debut novel, *The Things in Heaven and Earth*, was published by Black Rose Writing in July of 2021.

NOTE FROM THE AUTHOR

Word-of-mouth is crucial for any author to succeed. If you enjoyed *Gideon's Sorrow*, please leave a review online—anywhere you are able. Even if it's just a sentence or two. It would make all the difference and would be very much appreciated.

Thanks!
Michael Scott Hopkins

We hope you enjoyed reading this title from:

BLACK ROSE
writing™

www.blackrosewriting.com

Subscribe to our mailing list – *The Rosevine* – and receive **FREE** books, daily deals, and stay current with news about upcoming releases and our hottest authors.
Scan the QR code below to sign up.

Already a subscriber? Please accept a sincere thank you for being a fan of Black Rose Writing authors.

View other Black Rose Writing titles at
www.blackrosewriting.com/books and use promo code
PRINT to receive a **20% discount** when purchasing.